FOR GOOD OR EVIL

**THE COLLECTED
STORIES OF
CLIVE SINCLAIR**

D0233860

PENGUIN BOOKS

PENGUIN BOOKS

Published by the Penguin Group
Penguin Books Ltd, 27 Wrights Lane, London W8 5TZ, England
Viking Penguin, a division of Penguin Books USA Inc.
375 Hudson Street, New York, New York 10014, USA
Penguin Books Australia Ltd, Ringwood, Victoria, Australia
Penguin Books Canada Ltd, 2801 John Street, Markham, Ontario, Canada L3R 1B4
Penguin Books (NZ) Ltd, 182–190 Wairau Road, Auckland 10, New Zealand

Penguin Books Ltd, Registered Offices: Harmondsworth, Middlesex, England

'Uncle Vlad', 'The Promised Land', 'A Moment of Happiness', 'Wingate Football Club',
'The Luftmensh', 'The Evolution of the Jews', 'The Texas State Steak-Eating Contest', 'The Creature
on My Back', 'Among School Children', 'Titillatio', 'Le Docteur Enchaîné', 'Tante Rouge' and
'Hearts of Gold' previously published in *Hearts of Gold* by Allison and Busby Ltd
1979. Published in Penguin Books 1982
'Bedbugs', 'Genesis', 'The Incredible Case of the Stack o' Wheats Murders',
'Tzimtzum', 'Somewhere over the Rainbow', 'America', 'Svoboda', 'Tsatske', 'Kayn Aynhoreh',
and 'Ashkenazia' previously published in *Bedbugs* by Allison and Busby Ltd 1982.
Published in Penguin Books 1983
This collection, including *Hearts of Gold*, *Bedbugs* and 'The Last Jewish Joker',
'The Golem's Story', 'Scriptophobia' and 'For Good or Evil'
first published as *For Good or Evil* in Penguin Books 1991

1 3 5 7 9 10 8 6 4 2

Copyright © Clive Sinclair 1979, 1982, 1991
The Acknowledgements on p. ix constitute an extension of this copyright page
All rights reserved

Filmset in 10/12 pt Monophoto Ehrhardt
Printed in England by Clays Ltd, St Ives plc

PENGUIN BOOKS

FOR GOOD OR EVIL

Clive Sinclair was born in London in 1948 and educated at the universities of East Anglia and California at Santa Cruz. His first novel, *Bibliosexuality*, was published in 1973. In 1980 he was awarded a Bicentennial Arts Fellowship, which allowed him to spend a year writing and teaching in the USA. In 1982 he was one of twenty writers chosen as 'Best of Young British Novelists'. He was literary editor of the *Jewish Chronicle* from 1983 to 1987 and in 1989 was the British Council Writer in Residence at the University of Uppsala, Sweden. His first book of stories, *Hearts of Gold* (Penguin, 1982), won the Somerset Maugham Award, and this was followed by a second collection, *Bedbugs* (Penguin, 1983); all those stories are included in this collection. He is also the author of two further novels, *Blood Libels* and *Cosmetic Effects* (Penguin, 1991), *The Brothers Singer*, a literary biography, and *Diaspora Blues*, a personal view of Israel. His work has been translated into eight languages. He lives in St Albans with his wife and son.

For Fran and Seth

Contents

ACKNOWLEDGEMENTS	ix
AUTHOR'S PREFACE	xi
Uncle Vlad	1
The Promised Land	13
A Moment of Happiness	22
Wingate Football Club	30
The Luftmensh	40
The Evolution of the Jews	53
The Texas State Steak-Eating Contest	59
The Creature on My Back	73
Among School Children	85
Titillatio	93
Le Docteur Enchaîné	103
Tante Rouge	110
Hearts of Gold	122
Bedbugs	133
Genesis	146
The Incredible Case of the Stack o' Wheats Murders	160
Tzimtzum	167
Somewhere over the Rainbow	182
America	192
Svoboda	206
Tsatske	222

Kayn Aynhoreh   226

Ashkenazia   238

The Last Jewish Joker   249

The Golem's Story   252

Scriptophobia   257

For Good or Evil   272

Acknowledgements

Acknowledgements are due to the following publications where some of these stories first appeared:

Encounter ('A Moment of Happiness', 'The Luftmensh', 'Bedbugs', 'Genesis', 'Ashkenazia'), *Transatlantic Review* ('Uncle Vlad'), *Club International* ('A French Letter', now entitled 'Tante Rouge'), *Penthouse* ('Trial by Ordeal', now entitled 'Le Docteur Enchaîné'), *London Magazine* ('The Creature on My Back', 'Tzim-tzum'), *Quatro* ('The Incredible Case of the Stack o' Wheats Murders', 'Somewhere over the Rainbow', 'Svoboda'), *Jewish Chronicle Literary Supplement* ('Tsatske', 'The Last Jewish Joker', 'The Golem's Story'), *The Listener* 'For Good or Evil').

'America' was first published in the Penguin anthology *Firebird 1*. 'Scriptophobia' first appeared in *London Tales* and subsequently became the first chapter of a novel called *Blood Libels*.

The lines on pages 20–21 are from 'A Song About Rest' by Yehuda Amichai, and translated by Ted Hughes; the poem was published in *Amen*, Oxford University Press, 1978.

The lines on page 41 are from 'I Should Have Died With You' by Halper Leivick; the poem is included in *An Anthology of Modern Yiddish Literature*, ed. Joseph Leftwich, The Hague, 1974.

The lines on page 46 originally appeared in *Black Power*, June 1967.

The lines on pages 136 and 140 are taken from 'Louse Hunting' in *Poems* by Issac Rosenberg, Heinemann, London, 1922. Those on page 220 come from 'Letter to My Wife' in *Forced March: Selected Poems* by Miklós Radnóti, translated by Clive Wilmer and George Gomori, Carcanet, Manchester, 1979.

Author's Preface

Most of these stories are the veterans of two collections: *Hearts of Gold* (1979) and *Bedbugs* (1982). The remainder were written between 1982 and 1985. 'Scriptophobia', the longest of these, first appeared in *London Tales* (1983) and subsequently became the first chapter of a novel called *Blood Libels*. It has now been restored to its original form. Indeed all the stories appear in their original form, despite the temptation to rewrite, to make improvements – for fear that something may be lost in the transition. A reviewer once called my stories 'evil little fictions'. She may be right, but I think they deserve the benefit of the doubt, which is why I have called this selection *For Good or Evil*.

CLIVE SINCLAIR, January 1991

Uncle Vlad

A small puff of powder cleared and I saw my aunt touch my uncle on his white cheek with such exquisite precision that she left lip marks like the wings of a ruby butterfly. I watched her for nine times nine swings of the golden pendulum as she walked from guest to guest leaving behind trails of the silver dust that sparkled in the lamplight. It was as though the entire effort of her toilet was not so much designed to establish a character as to create an impression that would leave a colourful insignia on the memory. Her voice floated on her breath, a soft wind that bent and bared the necks of her listeners before her; I heard her whisper imaginary family secrets to an English aesthete who made notes behind her back:

'I believe that Lupus thinks that Vlad married me on purely scientific principles as the best specimen he could find of a modern butterfly.'

The aesthete laughed. 'Well, Countess,' he said, 'I hope he won't stick pins into you.'

Then they both swirled away in a creamy whirl of silk out into the milky way of moonlight and left behind the delicate blooms and rouged cheeks. Uncle Vlad smiled at my aunt's joke and followed her silhouette as it flitted among the lace curtains, but he remained where he was, still standing beneath the candclabra, wax dripping on to his white hair, holding several glass jars, some containing ether, others containing frantic beating moths, one containing champagne.

Our family is old and distinguished, descended from the ancient mountain lords down into a lowland mansion. Uncle Vlad, tall and grand, the head of the house, is himself called after our most famous ancestor Vled the Impaler, who finally drove the Turks from Europe, so named because of his sanguine habit of tossing Turkish captives into the air and catching them on the point of a spear. We have a portrait in the Great Hall of Vled standing in a full field of flowers amid the dying Turks who, pierced through the middle, and waving their arms and lcgs, look like a multitude of ecstatic butterflies.

Beneath this scene in now smoked grey this legend is painted in Roman print – *Vled I called the Impaler.* 'Vlad' is the modern corruption of the venerable Vled, the result of an obscure etymological whim. However, there is no disguising the physical similarities; it is all but impossible to detect a difference between the painting of Vled and the face of Uncle Vlad. Uncle Vlad is an honoured lepidopterist, but, as a rule, does not sail about honey fields in short trousers; instead he goes out at night and gathers moths by candlelight. He exchanges these easily, because of his skill and their unique paleness, for the more brightly coloured varieties, which he mounts, simply, by driving a needle through their bodies. Uncle Vlad's pursuit is looked upon with much interest by the distant Viennese branch of our family which maintains, to a doctor, that it is a genuine genetic manifestation of his more barbaric prototype; while another more *émigré* branch claims that Uncle Vlad is a veritable paragon of the pattern of behaviourism in that, having seen the painting of Vled at an early age, he has ever since sought to realize the contents within the limitations of his own civilized environment. Uncle Vlad believes greatly in tradition.

Every year, on a fixed day, the entire family gathers at our home to celebrate the generations with a gorgeous extravagance. My uncle and aunt occupy weeks in anticipation of the fantastic evening, working and reworking menus, always seeking a sublime gastronomic equilibrium, so that the discards look like nothing more than the drafts of meticulous lyric poems. And what poets they are! *Garbure Béarnaise, Truites au Bleu, Grives au Genièvre, Canard au Sang, Crêpes Flambés aux Papillons.* They strive to astonish the most sophisticated taste, the only applause they seek is the thick sound of the satisfied tongue clapping the palatine papillae. Once Uncle Vlad said to my aunt, at the supreme moment before the food is collected, 'Should we not share the secrets of our art with the swine that starve?' And she replied, 'Let them eat words.'

Our family is proud and jealous of its dark arboreal rebus.

This year, being the first congregation since my coming of age, I was permitted to help in the preparations. On the eve, I went out alone into the nocturnal wood, carrying my rods and nets, and followed the overgrown path to the gilt river. And there I sat in silence for many hours until my nets were full, very content, for there are few sights more beautiful than that of the silver fish struggling in the moonlight. I left the fish where they were, because it was vital to keep them alive, and commenced the journey back, proud that I had completed my task so well. But I had gone no more than a kilometre towards the residence when I heard a rustling of dead leaves and the final cry of a bird in pain. I pushed my way through the bushes in the direction of the sound and came into the perfect circle of a moonbright glade. The air was full of the melodious song of a score or more of thrushes. The birds were all on the ground, trapped in Uncle Vlad's subtle snares, and they did not look real but seemed to be some eccentric ornament of the night.

Uncle Vlad himself, dressed by the shadows as a harlequin, was stepping among the thrushes and killing them one by one by gently pressing their soft necks between his thumb and forefinger. Each death, save for the single scream and the frightened flap of the wings, was conducted in complete silence: until the survivors sang again. Uncle Vlad saw me and allowed me to help.

'My boy,' he whispered to me as we worked, 'how was the fishing?'

'It was good, Uncle,' I replied, 'I caught twenty trout.'

When we had finished Uncle Vlad collected all the tight bodies into a little bundle and opened a sack of the finest silk. But before he dropped the birds into it he bit off their heads. Fine tributaries of blood ran from his swelling lips.

'The thrushes always come to this spot,' he said, 'they cannot resist my special snails.'

The kitchen was already full with the shadowy figures of our servants when we returned, and my aunt was throwing resinous logs into the dancing flames. One of the anonymous cooks was apparent through a vaporous curtain of steam, stirring a dull copper soup-pot bubbling with boiling water and vegetables.

'There must be no garlic in the *Garbure Béarnaise*!' Uncle Vlad called out as we entered.

'Of course not, my dear,' replied my aunt. 'Did you do well?'

Uncle Vlad emptied his bag out on to the ancient wooden table, and at once long fingers fluttered out of the obscurity and plucked the feathers from the bodies. Then the birds were split open with sharp knives and stuffed till they were full with peppercorn and juniper. When this was done to the satisfaction of my uncle the breasts were sewn up, and the birds wrapped in slices of pork lard, and bound, ready to be cooked.

'We shall eat well tomorrow,' said my aunt to me.

Exactly one hour before we were due to dine, when all our guests were safely arrived, we killed the ducks. We took seven regal mallards from the lake and suffocated them by wringing their necks and pressing their breasts. The carcasses were given to the cooks, under the supervision of my aunt, to dress and draw, while Uncle Vlad and I went out with a large tank to collect the patient trout. And when we carried it back into the kitchen the oval tank seemed to have a shining lid, so full was it with fish. The remains of the ducks were ready in the great meat press waiting only for my uncle to add his libation of red wine. Then the press was turned and the blood and wine was caught as it ran, by Uncle Vlad, in goblets of gold and poured into a silver bowl. Pure vinegar was heated in large pans, over the oven, until it boiled.

'Throw in the fish while they still live,' ordered my aunt, 'and let them cook until they shrivel and turn steel blue.'

Thus everything was made complete, and we went into the incandescent dining-room to join our guests.

The English aesthete, protégé of my blonde cousin Adorian, and Madeleine, adored but adopted daughter of the childless union of the Count Adolphus and the Countess Ada, were the only visitors I did not recognize from an earlier year.

'My dear, you look absolutely *ravissant*,' said myopic Countess Ada, 'you simply must meet Madeleine.'

However, before that happened the implacable gong gave out with sonorous tidings of the approaching pabulum and, at the sound, we all took our places, according to the established decorum, at the ebony table. I sat in velvet, as always, between my aunt and the ageing mistress, so old as to have been long accepted as a second or rather parallel wife, of General X. The *Garbure Béarnaise* was served in ochre bowls of rough clay, the *Truites au Bleu* came on dishes of silver garlanded with circles of lemon and round potatoes, and the *Grives au Genièvre* were carried high on plates of the finest porcelain. The bones crunched deliciously beneath white teeth, knives and forks flashed like smiles as they moved, faces shone, and the wine glowed like a living thing in the crystal glasses. Then amid a fanfare of the oohs and aahs of aroused and admiring appetites the *Canard au Sang* was brought on and, as Uncle Vlad flamed the pieces of meat with the sauce of blood and wine and a bottle of cognac, I looked toward Madeleine for the first time.

Her face was the shape of a slightly more serious moon than our own, and her nocturnal hair was as black as the ravens that fly in the hills beyond our lands. She seemed to be searching some distant horizon, for her crescent eyebrows hovered like the wings of a gliding bird, and her mouth was slightly open as if she were holding the most delicate bird's egg between her lips. When she noticed that I was regarding her so curiously she smiled a little and she blushed.

As was the custom, after the main course, our smooth glasses were filled with champagne, and we left the decadent table, before the dessert was served. The wonders of our cuisine were praised, by a familiar chorus, to the heights of our moulded ceilings; but my aunt went outside with the English aesthete to discuss synaesthesia, and Uncle Vlad took the opportunity to catch some moths. I looked for Madeleine, but I could not find her.

'I say, young fellow,' mumbled ancient Count Adolphus through his moustaches, 'have you seen Madeleine yet?'

But I did not see Madeleine again until the butterflies burst into ardent applause when we all sat down for the *Crêpes aux Papillons*. There was something indescribably wonderful, that night, in watching those blazing palettes puff away in smoke; it was very much as if the colours evaporated into the air and were absorbed by our breath. The crêpes too seemed suffused with this vibrant energy; it must be said, Uncle Vlad had created the most brilliant dessert of his life. I wondered afterwards if the extraordinary vitality had communicated itself to Madeleine, if her cheeks had grown roses, but when I looked I saw that she was already walking away from the table.

'I do believe that that young lady has dropped her handkerchief,' observed the mistress of General X. 'If I were you, young man, I should return it to her.'

I nodded. I could hear the violins beginning to play discordant themes in the ballroom.

The dance opened with a grand flourish of wind instruments and took off around the room on the resonant wings of the flutes and strings, and joined, in counterpoint, the butterflies released simultaneously by Uncle Vlad. My uncle and aunt, as much concerned with the macula lutea as with the more alimentary organs, had carefully planned to fill in the musical space with the most unusual sights. A pellucid cube of the purest crystal was suspended from the centre of the ceiling and rotated on a fixed cycle by means of a concealed clockwork motor, creating an optical illusion, for in each of the faces a single eye was carved, and in each of the eyes a prism had been planted; so that, as it revolved above the dancing floor, it caught the occasional beam of light and projected visionary rainbows. Benevolent Uncle Vlad, having led the dancers with my aunt in an energetic *pas de deux*, stood resting against an ormolu commode, pouring out tall glasses of punch from a commodious bowl, happily recording the performance of his decorated insects.

'Ah, Nephew,' he remarked as I emerged from among a crowd of dancers, 'have you noticed that spinal quiver in the little beasts when a certain note is sounded, high C, I believe?'

'As a matter of fact I have not,' I replied. 'I am trying to find Madeleine to return a handkerchief.'

Countess Ada and Count Adolphus came capering by and called out, 'She is beside the flowers in the garden.'

Madeleine was standing all alone beneath the moon, in the centre of a crazy path, skirted by a row of yellow gaslights and ghostly trees. As I approached nearer to her, along that long lane, I fancied that she was looking, as if fascinated, at the illuminated cupolas, each of which was nightly adorned with the tingling jewellery of bats. And I was reminded what a newcomer Madeleine really was, for this singular display was almost a family phenomenon; indeed, by coincidence, all true members of our family have a small but distinctive brown birthmark on the cheek that is said to resemble two open wings. Poor General X, as a result of this, was forced to grow a bushy beard, not because of his military manner, nor because of his virile dignity, but because he developed an unfortunate twitch.

'Hello,' I spoke into the night, 'hello.' I do not think that I have seen anyone look so beautiful as Madeleine looked at that moment with the full curve of her throat outlined against the blackness as if by the inspired stroke of an artist's brush.

She jumped a little, like a sleeper awakened, and turned towards me. Her brown eyes were excited and shining like an Indian summer. 'The night is so wonderful,' she said, 'I feel enchanted.'

'Let us walk together,' I replied, 'and I will show you the garden.'

Madeleine took my arm and in the instant that I felt the warm flesh of her own bare arm brush carelessly against my cold hand I experienced a sensation I can only call an emotional tickle; as if some hitherto secret nerve end had been suddenly revealed and stimulated.

6

That arm of hers was a marvellous thing, it was no single colour but a multitude of hues and tints, and covered with the finest down, except inside the elbow, where the smooth skin was pale and shy and utterly desirable. The flowers were everywhere but the famous roses were all spaced out before the french windows, so that they encircled the building like some blooming necklace. Madeleine reached out to pick one of the blossoms but managed only to prick her finger. She gave a little cry, and stared at the finger which was rapidly dropping beads of blood.

'Let me see,' I said, 'I know how to make it better.' And I took the wounded finger between my thumb and forefinger and squeezed it, very carefully, until the last few drops of blood came like red flowers, then I carried it to my lips and sucked away any hurt. I bandaged the flushed tip with Madeleine's own handkerchief.

She smiled.

'Will you dance?' I asked.

The slight dizziness I had felt when I tended to Madeleine's hurt was heightened by our mazy movement around the dance floor to the sound of a jazzy waltz; though it was not, in fact, at all an unpleasant feeling, rather like being drunk on champagne bubbles.

'Look!' shouted Countess Ada to my aunt. 'Look who Madeleine is dancing with.'

Madeleine coloured slightly, which only made her the more radiant, then as she raised her face to me the spectrum burst all over her, and all else retreated into spectral shades. In the magic of that moment I completely forgot that the entire illusion was due to the clever artifice of my uncle and aunt and quite unconsciously pulled Madeleine closer to me, she responded with a shiver along her back, as if she were waving invisible wings, and I drifted over a dream-like sea holding on to Madeleine's warm body. I have no idea how long that moment lasted, but in those seconds or minutes I experienced an extraordinary sensation: my senses were literally magnified, I saw her skin as mixtures of pure colour, I felt her every movement: the beat of her heart, the air in her lungs, the blood in her veins. But Madeleine suddenly broke the spell.

'Oh, no!' she cried. 'We have danced over a butterfly.'

When, at last, a sliver of sun shone through the leadlight windows and exploded over the trumpet section, the dancers all leaned against one another and walked from the floor into the corridors and dimness of the receding night. I led Madeleine by the hand to her chamber.

'I must sleep now,' she said, 'but we will meet again in the afternoon?'

'Yes, you must sleep,' I replied as I touched her tired eyelids with my fingertips, 'but I will plan a picnic for when you awaken, and I will show you the ruined castle of Vled.' I returned to the ballroom to find my uncle and aunt, to congratulate them upon their success, and found them both upon their knees collecting up the bruised bodies of the fallen butterflies. I joined them, to complete the family group, crawling about as if we were posing for a portrait of a surreal autumn in a sparkling land of leaves without trees.

'Your designs were wonderful, the execution was superb,' I said to them both, 'even I ignored the methods for the sake of the effect.'

'Everything worked perfectly,' agreed my aunt, 'and what is more you and Madeleine liked each other.'

'Yes, I wanted to speak to you about that,' I began. 'I have asked Madeleine to come with me beyond the woods, and I would like to take some food and wine with us,' I paused, 'so will you be kind enough to show me the cellars?'

Uncle Vlad looked very pleased with himself and beamed at my aunt as if all the credit for my request was owed to him. 'Of course, with pleasure,' he replied, with that smile of his, and added: 'Tell me, Nephew, do you intend to kiss her?'

No light at all came into the cellars except, that is, from the illumined rectangle at the head of the stairs, where the old oaken door was left open. I had never been into the cellars before, so it was all strange to me, but Uncle Vlad walked among the rows upon rows of green bottles as if this weird underwater world were his natural habitat.

'We are standing directly beneath our small lake,' he informed me. 'The cellars were designed that way deliberately so as to control the air temperature in here.'

Soon I was moving about freely on my own, and the longer I remained in the cellars the more I felt that I too belonged to this profound environment, that I was in truth the nephew of my uncle. The air was rich with the smells of the earth, the cellars were like a distillation of night and the world, the essence of the veil, the antithesis of those bright tedious rooms where everything is visible at once, where you forget that you are breathing. There should be an art to capturing beauty; it becomes merely banal when it is not hunted. Uncle Vlad emerged from the depths of a particularly dusty rack of vintage carrying two bottles of red wine by their swans' necks, one in each hand.

'These should be just the thing,' he said as he rubbed a label, 'Château Margaux.'

Then we went much deeper, beyond where the wine was stored, until we came to a dank natural cave which smelt very strongly of pelardon. Uncle Vlad picked up a few small rounds of the aged goats' cheese, carefully wrapped and tied in dusky vine leaves, and weighed them in his hands. 'Perfect,' he adjudged, 'just ripe. Now all you require is some pâté de foie gras.'

'You must beware of the sun,' said Madeleine, regarding my pale complexion with some concern. 'I do not want you to burn because of showing me the castle.'

She gave me her straw bonnet to wear, and the blue ribbons flew in the breeze on the slope of the hill. Lupus, the great dog, ran on through the waving corn and the poppies and waited for us, barking, at the start of the woods. Several birds flew out in a straight line, squawking with alarm. The woods were much cooler and greener than the sandy daylight, a delightful diurnal anachronism, an Eden free from gardeners; what is more, I knew all the paths. Lupus darted ahead and chased rabbits through the undergrowth; usually he caught them. I carried the picnic on my back in a creamy satchel made from a pelt of the softest goatskin, and led Madeleine by the hand, watching all the tonal variations that the light and the shade of the sun and the different leaves made over her body. It seemed that the life in her had come to the surface and was showing itself in this ebb and flow of moving colours. I chose the spot very carefully and spread a chequered cloth over the ground, and I put out all the food on it in the crafty design of a rather ingenious checkmate. We sat beneath the tall trees in the long grass. The picnic was excellent; the pâté provided the expected largesse, the cheese had just the right temperament, and I continually filled the glasses with the flowing wine. Madeleine ate a yellow pear for her dessert, and the juice dripped from her fingers; her black hair was just touching emerald leaves, also pear-shaped, and the attracted flies flew round her head like a halo.

'That was a lovely picnic,' she said, smiling. 'What shall we do now?'

'I must tell you something, Madeleine,' I confessed, by way of a reply, after some assumed consideration. 'I dabble in paronomasia.'

Madeleine put down the core of the pear. 'I thought that the game would be chess,' she gave me a sly smile, 'but now I suppose that it will be a crossword puzzle, am I right?'

She was right, of course. Nevertheless, I took a black crayon from the satchel and wrote on the white squares of the cloth – *many alive devils enliven living even in novel evils.*

'Oh, well,' laughed Madeleine, 'we all have our acrostics to bear.'

I don't know why, it certainly was not because Madeleine had beaten me at my own game, but her response made me shiver. Madeleine must have noticed because she touched my cheek with her lips.

'You are cold,' she said.

'There,' I said after we pushed through the last of the overgrown bushes, 'is Vled's castle.'

The ruined keep stood erect and solitary on the motte in melancholy grandeur. Ravens flew about the grey merlons in great circles. As we watched, the setting sun shone red through holes in the broken walls giving the whole, for a brief while, the appearance of a cavernous skull with bloodshot sockets. Although I had seen the same sight many times it still exerted over me an irresistible and hypnotic fascination; as if there really were some powerful force behind those empty carmine eyes. Then the sun deepened to purple and streaks of fiery clouds opened labial wounds in the sky. The castle looked even blacker, and all the more compelling. Madeleine did not blink, she stood transfixed, staring into the approaching gloom; her eyes reflected what she saw. I felt her hand tighten in mine and grow colder all the time; her entire being seemed frozen on the threshold of an irreversible event like a reluctant swimmer poised on the edge of a diving board. I touched her left breast with my right hand, just enough to feel the flesh.

'Will you go in, Madeleine?' I asked. She came without a word.

The graves of my ancestors were all covered with historic weeds, and the moat was dry, but a wooden table and twelve wooden chairs remained within the hollow keep. We walked through the grounds with all the care and respect due to fallen stones and came into the dining hall. It was evening. I lit many candles and covered the table with the chequered cloth and spread out upon it the remains of the picnic; there were a few cheeses, a little pâté, much fruit, and most of a bottle of wine, so that I was able to compose a creditable still life. It glowed in the glimmering light. On the walls beside where Madeleine sat there was the famed mural which represented, in picturesque detail, the narrative of Vled's many military victories; also, by way of interludes, either for himself or the spectator, the artist had included the faded delights of Vled's more carnal conquests. Even as I looked a single moonbeam suddenly shot as swift as an arrow through a crack in the annals and flashed directly on to Madeleine's face and neck.

'This is the most extraordinary supper,' she murmured, very coyly, 'that I have ever eaten.' She smiled across at me and I saw at once, in the luminous night, that her upper lip was shaped exactly like the famous longbow old Vled had used to lick the Turks. It quivered a little beneath my gaze, and the more I studied that priceless object the more I was filled with an increasing need to make it mine. I wanted to taste that secret egg. Then the light changed, or she moved. I followed the graceful arch of her neck to where her ear disappeared among her rich hair and I felt again, though I knew not why, that I had to possess that mysterious lobe that hung so full like a liquid jewel. Madeleine became in that chance instant of illumination a collection of individual treasures and temptations; I had never done it before, but I knew then that I had to kiss her. My desire was inevitable, as inevitable as the flame that burned above the candle.

In the courtyard beyond the keep, in the centre of a thirsty fountain, a small statue of Cupid was slowly falling to pieces.

There is an old belief in our family to the effect that any passion, if held strongly enough, can so influence the prevailing atmosphere as to establish conditions favourable for the realization of that same passion. It happened in the gathering night that Madeleine got up from her place at a table of crumbling foods and walked towards me, slowly, languorously, through the undulant waves and splashes of candlelight and wax. I couldn't take my eyes from her mouth; the tongue was just visible through the open lips; the teeth looked sharp and white. I rose too, unawares, in a state of hard anticipation. We met, quickly, flesh against flesh; and I knew, by a kind of ecstatic instinct, exactly what I had to do.

I put my hands on Madeleine's hot cheeks, making a prize cup of my hands and her cervix, and tilted her head to one side. She looked at me with a sleepy look, and half closed her eyes. Her lips started to move. I placed my face on Madeleine's offered neck and began to kiss her, moving my tongue over her smooth skin, seeking, seeking, pressing, until I could feel the blood pumping through her jugular vein. Then I took a roll of the powdered flesh between my lips so that it was pressed against my teeth. I had to hold Madeleine tight, for her whole body was swept again and again with a series of short but violent tremors. I could feel her breathing right into my ear, her warm breath came in gasps and clung to me for a few seconds before vanishing. I sank my teeth into the skin and pushed, harder, harder – suddenly a great wave seized me and with a convulsive spasm of my cervical spine I bit deeper into Madeleine's vein. Then my mouth was filled with her blood and I think I heard her shriek of pleasure through my own blaze of delight.

It was a perfect kiss! I kissed Madeleine until I had to stop for breath; by then she was quite relaxed, and the arms which had clutched me so firmly hung limp by her sides. I carried her gently to the table and rolled her over the chequered cloth so that she finished on her back. Her arms got in a bit of a tangle, so I straightened them out for her. And I leaned back in a chair, well satisfied. As I did so a rather large *acherontia atropos* flew into a candle flame and fell burning on to Madeleine's cheek. She was too weak to brush it off; her hands fluttered as vainly as the moth's wings.

'Madeleine,' I whispered in her ear as I blew off the ashes, 'now you are really one of the family.'

The Promised Land

Call me Schlemiel. You will after you've read this.

First let me tell you about my affair with Hannah Ratskin, I should have been so lucky.

Well, Hannah lived in Tel Aviv. We're in Israel, you understand. I'm some miles away, in Jerusalem, on holiday. So one day I go to visit Hannah. I have a quick *mitz tapuzim* – orange juice – at the bus station, look longingly at the *avatiah*, red wet slices of mouth-watering watermelon, then shove my way aboard a number 5, hanging on to a strap all the way along Allenby and Dizengoff, finally getting off at Arlosoroff. Hannah's apartment is around the corner, on Weizman.

She is pleased to see me. 'You must stay the night,' she says. 'It'll have to be on the couch,' she adds, 'unfortunately my bed is already occupied.'

Enter Ami Ben Tur: handsome, Israeli; curly-haired scion of a wealthy family. The noise he causes when he *shtups* Hannah keeps me up half the night.

The phone wakes me. Hannah answers it. Word has reached her parents that I have spent the night in her flat. For some reason they detest me; the idea that I may have fucked their daughter fills them with horror. They are on their way to see for themselves. Since they live around the corner I have very little time to decamp. I rush downstairs and hide behind a tree in the back garden. The neighbours come to see what I'm doing there. I cannot tell them because the Hebrew I've learned from Rivka, my teacher, has not equipped me for such an eventuality. I give the Ratskins plenty of time to complete their interrogation, but even so my re-entrance coincides with their exit.

Mrs Ratskin looks me in the eye. 'Did you spend the night with my daughter?' she says.

Of course I cannot bring myself to say 'Yes', but it is equally impossible to say 'No' since I am standing there in my pyjamas.

Upstairs Hannah is looking sick. 'You can come out now,' she says to Ami Ben Tur, who emerges naked from a wardrobe.

What with all the tension I drink half a bottle of whisky, tell Hannah that I love her, and subside into some kind of coma on the sofa. Once again I am roused by the telephone. It is the Ratskins. They want to know if I have gone yet. They inform Hannah that if I sleep one more night in her flat they will stop paying her rent. Further, it is hinted that if he is not obeyed Mr Ratskin will have a heart attack.

'Do you want the death of your father?' cries Mrs Ratskin.

Hannah is distraught, she turns to me for help. 'Please phone my father while we are out for dinner,' she pleads, 'and apologize.'

I drink some more whisky. And while Hannah dines in luxury with her lover, probably while she's tucking into the avocado, I dial the number. Mr Ratskin tells me that he has nothing against me personally, he simply objects to the fact that my presence is corrupting his daughter, and doing nothing for her reputation. He repeats his ultimatum, and reminds me that he never goes back on a decision. I behave like a gentleman, and prepare to bow out. But I begin to feel more and more like a *nebbish*, a nothing. I phone back. This time Mrs Ratskin wants me to herself. She says that because of me Mr Ratskin is on the brink of apoplexy. I increase the danger straight away by saying that I have decided to stay. Let Hannah choose. In all seriousness I say I'll pay her rent. This is the last straw.

'What do you want from my daughter?' Mrs Ratskin demands. 'I've seen your letters. I know that you love her. But she won't marry you. Don't you know that she has a boyfriend already? Ami Ben Tur. What must he think when he says goodnight, knowing you are sleeping in the flat? Why are you trying to divide our family? You have upset Mr Ratskin and I am sure you will upset Hannah when she hears what you have said. Why don't you go away?'

I put down the receiver. I feel a *mensh*.

I tell Hannah what I have done. She does not believe me. More phone calls, but no mercy. Hannah goes to bed with Ami Ben Tur. He gives me a last look of contempt. I have violent diarrhoea. I sit on the toilet and hear Hannah have her orgasm in the next room. Some time afterwards she reappears in a diaphanous gown and while I stare at her breasts she phones her parents and informs them that she is going to marry Ami Ben Tur. I am now considered an irrelevance, indeed Mr Ratskin repeats that he never had anything against me personally. In the following days things happen fast; a ring is purchased, a banqueting room is booked at the Hilton, invitations are printed. I am not asked. Still Hannah takes time to confide in me.

'Do you know why I decided to marry Ami?' she asks.

'No,' I say.

'Because he is the only man who has ever given me a vaginal orgasm,' she says.

Right after the wedding Ami Ben Tur gets called up.

Hannah phones me. 'Hello, Lem,' she says, 'I'm bored. Ami's away in Sinai and I've got nothing to do.'

I plan my advance carefully. I go into the Old City to obtain some hashish (oysters for the contemporary Casanova); I buy two full fingers. I catch a *sherut* from the corner of Ben Yehuda that'll take me into the centre of Tel Aviv, and as we drive through the hills around Jerusalem, passing the rust-proof wrecks of armoured cars and lorries, relics of the '48 war, I am polishing up my strategy for the final seduction of Hannah. It is my intention to stimulate her senses to such a degree that she will be compelled, both by her own desires and the overwhelming demands of her female hormones, to capitulate to your foolish narrator.

I'll tell you the theory. If alcohol is administered under the right conditions it invariably begins the process by which the perception of the drinkers is so altered that they become the participants in a series of events in which the only possible combinations are between those characters present – in this instance just Hannah and myself. It's a warm night and there's no problem getting Hannah tipsy. Our context is as sharply defined as is the world by a window-frame. I use the hashish to draw the curtains. But follow me, I'll lead you to a spot where you can peep through the glass.

You will see that the two personages have been swimming (a midnight dip); that red-headed Hannah is still wearing a yellow bikini designed by a lascivious geometrician. Her breasts are yash-maked beneath two tiny isosceles triangles, each topped with the pluckable outline of a nipple near the pinnacle, from which points two yellow ribbons run, a pair of twin hypotenuses, to yoke the whole design with a bow behind her neck. Her private parts are concealed beneath another triangle, this one with much greater angles at the base, so that the sides point generously to her genitals. Please understand how impressed I am with this garment, which must have been as finely calculated as the Great Pyramid itself. Your narrator is not quite so contented with his own attire, since he has been compelled to borrow a pair of horrible scarlet briefs from Ami Ben Tur's wardrobe, so I must ask you to forgive me should my excitement become too apparent. I begin to unwrap warm giggling Hannah by tweaking her vital bow between thumb and forefinger, at which point all mathematical pretensions collapse to reveal a fine bosom, looking rather pale compared to the tanned surrounding skin, with just a hint of colour in the depressed mamillae. What I find beneath the mid-section is even more arresting, dozens of curls pressed flat into the white delta of her belly, the calm red waves of a naturally warm sea. Hannah is now riding the crest, of her own volition she slides a fidgety finger tip along her dampening sex and sniffs. She giggles and puts her finger under my nose. Hannah herself removes Ami's trunks from my midriff and drops them on to the floor where they settle like a deformed grin. Things are certainly going to plan, I think.

I put some jazz on the record player. We undulate across the room to the sofa, in a sort of embrace, my tongue taking advantage of an open-mouthed kiss to say how-do-you-do to her soft uvula as well as sweet-talking her dangling epiglottis. Hannah sinks on to the sofa and before descending I look down on the land promised me long ago by that smile of hers. I look over her sentient softness and kiss her constellar aureole, teasing her nipple till it is firm, then my tongue slips on slippery lips down the slope of her breast, beyond her knotty navel, through her salty pubic hairs into her fuzzy hive. I pause on the brink. By now Hannah is whimpering and rocking her body from side to side; it would be wicked to stop, so I close my eyes (I've always been a fussy eater) and whisper her name, and as my tongue curls up on the final *ah* I push it between her labia, and lap her up to the rhythms of Charlie Mingus. Even in my darkness I know that her thighs and calves are golden as though honey were overflowing. It's no time for speeches, you'll agree, but gradually I become aware that Hannah is saying something.

'Are we going to fuck?' she says.

This stops me in my tracks. 'Aren't we?' I say.

'In that case I must tell you that I have stopped taking the pill,' says Hannah, 'because we are going to start a baby. And I'd like to be sure that Ami is the father. Have you any rubbers with you?'

Of course I haven't!

'Why don't you just finish what you were doing,' says Hannah, making herself comfortable and opening her legs a bit wider.

So here I am on my knees with my tongue up Hannah and my bum in the air when all of a sudden there's a commotion at the window. Ami Ben Tur, on a surprise weekend pass, bursts in. As is only to be expected, he threatens to kill me. Hannah screams. I retreat in disarray from the occupied territories, with a cocked Walther PPK pointing at my non-negotiable areas.

Half a year later there's a war on.

I'm in England at the time, in shul, on my annual visit, atoning for my sins, hoping God accepts the English translation of his prayers, when someone comes running in shouting, 'Those bastards have invaded Israel!' What a *mishegoss*!

A couple of days after, when it's clear how bad the fighting is, I go to give a pint of blood at the same shul, now converted into a blood transfusion centre. Inside there are about thirty clean beds, each one supporting a passive pale individual joined by what looks like an external vein to a reddening bottle. Nurses dressed in white walk through dusty sunbeams smiling at the bleeding people, while doctors have the sterner task of separating the Os from the ABs. I'm just about to be dismissed on account of my hayfever when it's discovered that I'm AB Rhesus-negative, very rare. So they put me on some freshly laundered sheets, puff up my arm, and stick a needle into a surprised vein just inside my elbow. It is at about this time, I later learn, that Ami Ben Tur is hit in the stomach by a piece of shrapnel. He is rushed by helicopter to the nearest hospital where it is discovered that his blood-group is also AB Rhesus-negative. He is given many transfusions. I do not know if he is given my blood, but when I next see him he is sneezing.

For several years I have been going to Israel a month at a time, you understand, and I have yet to bed an Israeli girl. Hannah was by no means my only near-miss, there was also Rivka, my Hebrew teacher. Say her name to yourself; just listen to the smooth flow of the *riv* as it glides into the soft mound of the final *ka*. Ah, I can see myself now, the bright boy of the class, reciting for Rivka the conjugations of the verb *ohev*, to love. '*Ani ohev*,' I say: 'I love', as metaphysical a statement as I'm ever likely to make. Anyway, as soon as the war breaks out Rivka's off to Israel like a shot, and I don't see her again till the following spring.

It's a hard job to find her house at Ramat Aviv, I can tell you. '*Slicha, efor Rehov Gruniman?*' I say to the locals, but cannot understand the reply. I don't blame Rivka, she didn't write the textbook after all, but outside of supermarkets my vocabulary is useless. There's one version of the Bible in which Moses attempts to extricate himself from God's command by stammering that his tongue is not circumcised. Well, that's exactly how I feel in Israel: I am Jewish, but my tongue is not circumcised. '*Ani lo mdaber ivrit,*' I say. I do not speak Hebrew.

'Thanks God,' says Rivka, 'you have arrived. I thought maybe you had got lost.'

She brings me a slice of *avatiah*, and sits very close beside me, so that her thigh is pressed against my leg. This proximity imports an unfortunate element of insincerity into our conversation; for while I am speaking of one thing my mind is diverted by a different matter entirely. Rivka has become enamoured by Gush Emunim, the Greater Israel movement.

'We must not give back an inch,' she says, 'not of anywhere, especially Jerusalem.' She then goes on to explain the importance of the land in this way: 'Make a triangle with points at Ba'Am (North), Gaza (West) and Eilat (South), so that Jerusalem is located at the centre of the long base. Then make a second triangle around Sinai. Join the two and you have the Mogen David, the Star of David, symbol of Israel.'

The eternal triangle, of which I already had much experience. 'What about the Palestinians?' I say. I do not hear her reply because I am imagining myself infiltrating her panties (which I can see as clearly as the rights of the case I am arguing) and consuming her burning bush. Just look at me, the politician, the moralist with my spadix blooming in my spathes!

Rivka invites me to accompany her to Caesaria for a spot of sea-bathing. Surely I am going to make it now, consummate my love for the country for which I had so recently shed blood. Caesaria is the only beach I know along Israel's west coast where swimmers are not pestered by waves. For this pacific enclave in the Mediterranean specific thanks must be given to the Romans who enclosed the bay within stone breakers. The road down from the Tel Aviv–Haifa highway is littered with broken columns, pushed aside in places by orange trees from the new kibbutz. There is an agglomeration of ruins: Roman, Crusader, Moslem; a reminder, I say to Rivka, of the temporary nature of military conquests.

'Greeks, Romans, bah!' she says. 'There were Jews in the time of the ancient Greeks, of the Romans, of the Phoenicians. We are still here. Where are they? Our God is still God. Where is Zeus? I'll tell you, sneaking in the backdoor at Suez, like the Egyptians.'

I shut up, and anticipate her bathing costume instead. She comes out of the changing room in a marvel of textile engineering; a backless strapless thing, looking like the letter q side-on; revealing a pleasing curvature on the reverse, extending from the nape of the neck over the vertebral rapids of the downy coccyx which merges into the tautologous material. We don't get back to Tel Aviv that night, but don't raise your hopes; Rivka wasn't that sort of girl.

She insists upon separate rooms in the small hotel we find. But during the night I hear a knock on my door and Rivka's there wrapped in a sheet. I follow her to her room, and she drops prone on to her bed. She is stark naked.

'Please do something,' she says, 'my back is on fire.'

Sure enough her back is the colour of a spectacular sunset. Her bum, quivering a little, is as pale as a nocturnal creature; but I see her buttocks and her legs as the meeting of two question marks. Obeying instructions I dip my fingers into a tin of Nivea Cream and begin to massage the stuff into her back, moving in a circular fashion from the soft heights covering her clavicula, over the triangular deltoideus (a divine D, very relaxed), down through her central valley, then along her sides just touching on the periphery of her breasts, and down again over her ribs to the pelvic plateau, where I pause before going over her smooth hillocks (much cooler than the rest of her), feeling my breath come quickest where the going is easiest. The tempo diminishes during the descent of her legs, but speeds up again when I return to her thighs and make her gasp at last as my finger gets on to the sensitive flesh that remains (on this occasion) no man's land.

'Thanks God,' says Rivka, 'I feel better already.' Such is the role of the diaspora in Israeli life.

I hope I haven't given the wrong impression about myself. I'm not really sex-mad, not very frivolous; in fact I'm rather a serious person. I've got this theory I want to tell you about; how it's materialism that's screwing us up. I mean real materialism, the belief that nothing exists but matter itself. Our trouble goes right back to the time when the Israelites, following Moses, got lost in the Sinai Desert. They were on their way to the Promised Land, you'll recall, the land 'flowing with milk and honey', when they panicked and translated God's words into a Golden Calf – milk into a calf, honey into gold – needing to see before they could believe. I'm the same. I want to believe in miracles, in love-on-earth and life-after-death, but I turn all abstractions into flesh and stone. To tell you the truth, I want to fuck Israel. Okay, so Ahab was obsessed with Moby Dick; well, my Promised Land is only an Israeli cunt! Jesus, when I had my bar mitzvah they gave me a tree in Israel, I've got a certificate to prove it. Now I'm a big boy, a *mensh* even, so why won't they let me leave my own seed in a fertile belly?

Yes, I am serious. Look at me, I am interviewing A., the famous Israeli writer, for a magazine published by the Hebrew University. At first A. was reluctant to be interviewed without payment, until I told him that I was not being paid either. We are sitting opposite one another, in his living room, sipping tea. No milk, no sugar. Beyond us in the honeydew light the walls of Jerusalem glow. When Jews pray they always face Jerusalem. I bend over my cup and the steam infused with lemon rises like incense. A. has his back to the city. A. is small but not delicate, compact; you'd guess that he was either a poet or a boxer. In his fifties, I'd say. From a generation that has survived wars and worse. Somehow wedded to the land, those that died have become the land of course. He has the dignity of a man whose suffering has not been self-inflicted. Many writers espouse suffering, wear tragedy like a parrot on their shoulder. A.'s poems come straight from the front line. This is my opinion, not a critical judgement. I switch on the tape-recorder. Questions and answers are recorded. He prefers poetry to prose. He has also led a life of action. In 1948 he ran guns for the Hagganah. Sure, he has risked his life. Now he is secure and famous. He recites a poem for me.

> ' "Never again will I find rest for my soul"
> Let me sit in the revolving chair.
> of an AA gunner, of a pianist,

of a barber, and I shall turn round and round
restfully until my end.'

The spool of my tape-recorder freewheels, the end of my tape claps.
The interview concludes, the babysitter arrives.

'Writing a novel,' says A., 'is like starting a marriage – in the
beginning you have no idea what you are letting yourself in for.' A.
has recently begun a second marriage, the baby-sitter has come to
mind the evidence of his continuing creative powers.

'Shalom,' we all say.

A.'s place is in *Yemin Moshe* – the Right Hand of Moses – a
higgledy-piggledy grouping of buildings, steps and alleys, the remains
of the first modern Jewish settlement outside of the Old City, now
being lovingly restored. On a hillside, facing Mount Zion. Beyond it
is waste ground leading down to the valley of Gai Hinnom (formerly
Gehenna) where children were once sacrificed to Moloch. I plan to
walk across to the Jaffa Gate to catch an Arab bus to Talpiot, but
instead I just hang about in the shadows outside A.'s house. Above
me a crescent moon continues to give a weak grin.

A. returns. The baby-sitter leaves. I follow her through the alleys,
over the waste ground, down toward Gai Hinnom. At the last
moment she looks around and sees me, but before she can scream I
am on her. She struggles. The tape-recorder drops with a thud and
turns itself on. I hear A.'s voice: 'Never again will I find rest for my
soul.' I prevail. No messing around with arithmetical underwear this
time, or caressing claviculas. I rip her pants right off. No mistake, I
rape her.

'Nazi!' she cries as I come.

'No,' I say, shocked, 'I'm a schlemiel.'

A Moment of Happiness

I live in fear. That's a state of mind, not my address.

Years ago I sat my exams at the Charles University. I had learned my work well and I was not nervous, until I saw the booklet that I was required to fill with my answers. I knew that in three hours it would be full, but I also foresaw the impossibility of my ever doing it; I felt that I was an insufficient motor to fulfil the inevitable. I tried to start the first question, but my hand was unable to control the pen. I could not form a single letter. Sweat began to roll along the lines on my hand and flow on to the page. I ran out of the hall. My sweat looked like teardrops on the page. All my professors were sympathetic, but they still failed me. Now no one will believe that I am an educated man.

It is six in the morning. Through my window I can see that the Vltava is turning gold with the rising of the sun. A beautiful sight, but I am immune to it; it fails to excite a single response in me. All it means is that it is time to move my bowels and to dress. Some days I am constipated, other days I have diarrhoea, less often I am regular. Every morning I examine the lavatory bowl, like an ancient sage, to see if I can divine what sort of day I have in store. This is fundamentally much more important than either the weather or the view. Today my movements have been very loose, which means I must pass the hours between now and bedtime in constant anticipation of further activity, presaging who knows what stomach complaint.

Once I discussed this morbid hypochondria with a doctor acquaintance and he, priding himself on his psychological insight, said that I did not trust my own body, would not believe that all those millions of interdependent functions could go on performing in harmony day after day without supervision. He accused me of introspective paranoia. Perhaps he is right. To me to get through a day is an achievement. As for the future, I have no faith in that at all. At best it is a process of gradual decomposition. I think only in the terms of the present and the past. I try to make the future as similar to the present as I can by sticking rigidly to an established dogma: I always get out of bed on the same side, I eat the same breakfast, I buy the same food in the same shops. My only desire in this life is to be a character in a photograph: smiling with remembered pleasure, eternally fixed in the present.

In many ways today is not normal. I have to work. *Rude Pravo* has a bold red headline: 'PLNÝ ZDAR XV SJEZDU STRANY!' It is, of course, the start of the XVth Party Congress. And my beloved Prague is full of flags; equal numbers of Czech flags and Russian flags. To mark the occasion our local shop is unusually well-stocked with imported fruit: grapefruit, oranges, bananas and pineapples. This glut, which lured me into over-indulgence, must explain this morning's diarrhoea (I have been a second time). My job, which is going to last the whole of this week, requires me to stand beside a stall piled high with miniature Czech and Russian flags. This is situated outside (of all places!) the Pan American office. I sell a few flags, but mostly people ignore me and look at the posters in the window which say, 'Come to the USA and help us celebrate our Bicentennial'. On the opposite side of the street a peasant woman in headscarf and embroidered apron is hawking painted eggs for Easter. When someone buys one she nicks the top and bottom off the shell and pulls a ribbon through it. I do not have much appetite, but I eat a little lunch: garlic sausage, a pickled cucumber and some rye bread. Afterwards I have to go to the toilet again.

In the afternoon the sun goes behind a black cloud and I begin to feel chilly standing around in the street. I notice a couple walking towards me carrying the English edition of Ctibor Rybár's *Guide to Prague*. I approach them waving a Russian flag and ask, 'Do you wish to exchange money?' I can see that this has surprised them. They have been saying 'no' to money-changers all day, but I have got them off guard.

'I will give you forty crowns to the pound,' I say. This is twice the official rate.

There is a moment's hesitation, then they ask to change £10.

We complete the transaction in the Café Europa. I hate it there. It is supposed to look like a Parisian café but looks are nothing; nowadays it is full of riff-raff: gypsies and workmen from the new Metro. The waiters wear ill-fitting tuxedos and are rude to everyone.

I do not understand how the authorities tolerate them; probably because they never enter the Café Europa. Very sensible. I was once served pork there that was off, and I ended up in bed for a week with terrible cramps. I assure the couple that it is an excellent place to dine. They order a glass of mineral water and a bottle of Coca-Cola. The girl tells me that a friend of theirs came to Prague, met a Jewess in the Staronová Synagogue, stayed with her nine days, and married her six months later. She shows me a clipping from the *New York Times*. It is an article the fellow has written about his trip to romantic Prague.

'For years Czech *émigrés* in New York and London had regaled me with memories of the beauty of Prague,' I read. 'The city itself claims the affection of the 1968 generation of emigrants who, often in the same breath, described the charms of its women and the bankruptcy of its politics.' The piece makes me want to vomit. I do not recognize the city he is writing about. It may as well be Xanadu.

'Robert couldn't get to the shul quickly enough,' says the girl. 'I think he was hoping to meet an exotic Jewish girl for himself.'

I look at this Robert more carefully and wonder how I did not see before that he is Jewish. I can tell by the sharp way his eyes are examining me. I do not like the Jews. They trust nobody but themselves. I can see that he is growing suspicious of me; he has noticed that my fingers are short and stubby. I have been told this is a sign that I am not a pleasant person. I sit on my hands. I smile at the girl and begin to explain that I was not always this insignificant.

'I once worked for Cedok,' I say, 'and I used to take tours all over Eastern Europe. But in 1969 they gave me an important tour to Italy. And this, I must tell you, was my downfall. You know why? It is very simple. I went out with twenty persons and I came back with four. On the last day, at Trieste, I am sitting in the coach waiting for my party and only these four turn up. The rest want political asylum! And you know what? The coach driver also vanished. They had to send me out a new driver. When we returned at last I was fired. Just like that. Is it my fault that people want to leave this country? I tell you, it's so bad now that no one trusts anyone any more. Everything must be a big secret!'

The girl is sympathetic, but that Robert is weighing up in his mind whether he should believe me. Well, it is the truth! I happen to know that a Cedok guide was sacked for losing practically a whole group in the West.

The staring eyes of the Jew have made me afraid. I make an excuse and hastily leave the café. There's no real reason, I've told those stories many times before. But walking back to my rooms, without warning, my stomach turns to water. I feel dizzy. I know every stone in the street but I lose all confidence in my ability to get to the other end. I begin to run, to race my fears, imagining fearful phantoms lurking in the shadows, the secret policemen of my subconscious, trying to grab me. To arrest me for what? For being a fraud, a counterfeit man? A drunk full of Pilsner staggers towards me. He nods to me as if in recognition of a fellow sufferer. Madness! I do not suffer. But even as I turn the corner I know that the drunk has straightened up and is watching me.

Next day I meet the couple again. I would rather not talk to them, but they seem anxious to tell me how much they have seen of Prague.

'This morning we saw the tomb of Rabbi Loew,' says the girl, 'and we left a note with our names on it.'

'Have you heard all about Rabbi Loew and his famous Golem?' I ask. Surely they are not interested in that superstitious rubbish! Then I recall that Robert is a Jew. I consider telling him why the Nazis did not destroy the Prague ghetto. Because they wanted to preserve it as a museum of a vanished race. Now there are hardly any Jews left in Prague and the synagogues are maintained by the government as museums. And the chief sightseers are our wonderful East German comrades. Such ironies give me much pleasure.

The girl is still talking.

Ah, now what has Mr Robert got to say?

'One thing I miss, not being able to speak the language,' he says, 'is the fun of eavesdropping. When we get back we will be asked, "What were the people like? Happy?" And all I will be able to say is that they looked like people: some looked pleased, others looked miserable. How am I supposed to tell what they are thinking?'

I am thinking: what if I were to accuse this Jewboy of being a Zionist and then rape his girlfriend? I nod sympathetically.

The girl pulls something out of her handbag and says, 'Look what we bought with the money we changed yesterday.'

It is an ancient coin, tiny and silver. What would anyone want with that?

'It's supposed to be a dinar of Vratislav II,' says Robert.

Supposed! The suspicious kike. If he got it at Starozitnost's it *is* a dinar of Vratislav II.

'I'll tell you two something,' I say confidentially, 'on my mother's side my ancestors go right back to this Vratislav II. He was the first real king of the Czechs, you know. Founded that monastery right up there on top of the castle. Strahov. Yes. I was once a person of high rank. I had money. When I was seventeen I inherited our family estates. They were worth something in the order of half a million. In those days, you can imagine! Well, I made a fantastic success of it. Implemented so many reforms in forestry that I was awarded an honorary degree in agriculture from Charles University. Then came the war. And you can guess what happened after that. The communists have it all now.'

A person approaches me to buy a Russian flag. I think it's a fellow. I look more carefully and see he's got a huge chest, like a hunchback turned around. Daft! They're tits. I look at the person's face again and see that it is a very ugly girl. I think: what sort of life can she lead?

Robert wants to know about some book. He says he has been asked to get it for a friend. He reads me the title from a notebook. *Vabank* by Alexej Pludek. Why should anyone he knows outside of Czechoslovakia want such trash? Perhaps he mixes with dissidents. In his notebook I glimpse the address of someone in Prague. Perhaps if he is taking out something he also brought in something. Something like illegal manuscripts. I memorize the address; tonight I will telephone it to the police.

'Ah, you want to buy *Vabank*,' I say. 'You know it has just been awarded our National Book Prize? It's all about Zionism. About the plot, begun in 1967 with the Six-Day War, continued in Czechoslovakia in 1968, and so on, for Jews to seize the governments of all the major world powers. A novel way of looking at the events of 1968, don't you agree? Oh! I believe I have just made a pun.'

I am beginning to enjoy myself. But both of my friends are looking uncomfortable. They do not know if I am serious or not.

'I am not against the State of Israel, you understand,' I say, 'far from it. But I think it should only be a homeland for Hebrews. Not Khazars. You see, most people who call themselves Jews are really Khazars, descendants of a Black Sea tribe who converted to Judaism for political reasons and then dispersed through Europe. These are the people of the Diaspora, not the Hebrews.'

What can they reply to that?

'I'll tell you something else,' I say, 'about the Dead Sea. We're all led to believe that it's dead because it's full of salt. Yes! But no one says that there are ten different mineral salts in it. I'll tell you something. Those salts are worth more than America's entire annual gross national product. How do I know? Well, I spent years working on the Dead Sea. But I was forced to suppress my findings. Because what I knew would have started a Holy War! *Jihad*, the Arabs call it. On the strength of rumours of my work I was offered the directorship of Amman University. It is all documented. I have the letters at home somewhere.'

It is apparent that Robert does not believe a word I am saying. He is not attempting to argue or contradict, he just wants to get away from me as quickly as possible. But I am enjoying myself too much. Did I not sense it was going to be a good day when I laid that near-perfect shit this morning?

'My brother, you know, is looked on by the Arabs as a Prince,' I inform the pair, 'a fake one, of course, like Lawrence of Arabia. He entered Cairo as a sergeant in the Aussie army sometime in '44 – oh, yes, he got out of Czechoslovakia in late '38 – and right away met this little Arab boy, Hamil. And Hamil asks, "What's your name, sergeant? You look more like one of us than an Aussie." And my brother says, "Saladin." You see, it's the first Arab name that comes into his head. Hamil looks at him, and runs off. About an hour later there's two thousand Arabs knocking on his quarters crying, "Saladin!" and Hamil says to my brother, "I've brought all your relatives to see you." I have to tell you that on a certain day of each year all the members of the Saladin family meet in Cairo. The very day that my brother showed up. There had been rumours. Stories that the head of the family had escaped the great massacre and fled to Australia. And here he was, returned. The next day there were newspaper headlines this high saying, "Prince Saladin is Back!" After that my brother stayed on in Cairo. He became an agent. He got behind German lines. Smuggled hashish and secrets. When the war was over he became the leader of twenty thousand students. I'll tell you, if it wasn't for my brother the whole of Cairo would have burned down in '52. You've heard of the Fires of Cairo? But my brother held his men under control. Nevertheless, Nasser had him tortured and thrown out. He was afraid of him.'

All dictators fear men who are popular. They must watch over the State like I monitor my body. They must counter any abnormality with severe repression; anti-communists must be met with antibodies. Secret policemen are the penicillin of the nation. Like mould growing on the corpse of a loaf, there's a thought. When the body is purged the machine will run efficiently. I have heard that if ants cannot function properly they are taken away from the nest by three fellow workers and destroyed: one holds down its legs, another flattens its abdomen, and the third injects it with poison. I an no insect, but I am frightened. Not of Germans or renegades, but of invisible germs; of a revolution within. The State does its best to ensure control of the future, but there is no guarantee. The best it can do is rearrange the past to suit itself, and to stabilize the present in such a way that it becomes, simultaneously, a reflection of both past and future, thus liable to strict checks.

Six long black Russian limousines are edging down the road; the first flies the Hammer and Sickle. They are full of delegates to the Party Congress. Chubby men in grey Homburgs with beige scarves in Vs around their necks and black overcoats buttoned right up; chaperoned and chauffeured by secret-service men; immunized against the world. They give me reassurance, but what a joy it would be to assassinate one of them. Suddenly I understood how the germs that I destroy daily must feel.

The two English tourists are too intrigued by this procession of the powerful to bother much over my latest monologue.

'We must go now,' says the girl in response to a look from Robert.

'Wait!' I say, 'I have one last thing to tell you.'

That's got them! No confessions from me, though. I have something else in mind.

'My brother lives in London now,' I say. 'I hear from him very often. He tells me that there is an excellent Czech restaurant in London. You must visit it. They serve magnificent knedliky. And schnitzels like you've never tasted. Not made with veal, but with pork that's been beaten flat till it's as thin as a pancake. Oooh, my mouth is watering. It is situated in Hampstead, West Hampstead. The Czech National House. You know of it? Our airmen who flew with the RAF founded it after the war was over. There is a photograph of the Queen on the wall encrusted with diamonds. How do I know this? My brother tells me. He also writes that all the Jews in

Golders Green come and eat there every night, because they are smart, and they know when they are on to a good thing. You will go there? Undoubtedly you will see my brother. He looks just like me. Can you do me one favour? I see that you have a camera around your neck. Will you take a photograph of me for my brother?'

Robert opens his camera case. He fiddles with the exposure meter, sets the speed and the correct aperture. He places the camera to his eye and twists the lens until he has me in sharp focus. I smile. The shutter clicks. And so on a small piece of celluloid is a picture of me. Preserving me for that single 1/6oth of a second in my life when I am not afraid.

Wingate Football Club

There are some dilemmas it is better not even to think about. I'll give you a for-instance. Suppose England were to play Israel in the World Cup. Who should I support? Ah, you will say, such a thing is very unlikely. England's football is stale, Israel's half-baked. But I'll tell you, stranger things have happened, like when Wingate won the London League Cup.

When I was a boy I used to go with my father to watch Wingate play on Saturday afternoons. Wingate were the only Jewish team in the entire football league; named in honour of our version of Lawrence, crazy Orde, a *goyisher* Zionist. Wingate were never a great team, and though they always had a couple of good players they usually spent the season near the bottom. So imagine our astonishment when we won a hard tie away from home and found ourselves in the London League Cup Final.

Our opponents were a dockland team, notorious for their anti-semitic supporters. They came to our ground like a wolf on the fold. But that year we had a brilliant outside-right, in real life a ladies' hairdresser. To me his dizzy runs down the wing were a thing of infinite beauty; left-backs tumbled to the ground when he passed, felled as if by magic. Pursued by these humbled clods he sprinted for the corner flag and unleashed acute crosses that sent their goalkeeper flailing in the air. Our centre-forward leapt and dived fearlessly to meet the winger's passes, but each time he missed by a hair's breadth.

'Only connect!' we yelled in encouragement.

The supporters of our opponents were prepared to tolerate our precocious start; content in the knowledge that Jews lacked spunk they waited for the crunching tackles to crush the life out of our challenge. And then our centre-forward did connect; his head met the pass fifteen yards out. The ball had 'goal' written all over it as it shot like a bullet towards the net. The goalkeeper was frozen, as helpless as a rabbit, but – would you believe it? – even as we were celebrating the ball hit the post and rebounded back into the centre of the field. We cheered, nevertheless. But my father said sadly, 'A miss is as good as a mile.' And in my disappointment I felt the full force of the simile; all that marvellous approach-work had been for nothing because finally the ball had missed, the nearness of the miss didn't enter into it, a miss is as good as a mile.

A minute later I learnt another lesson. The rebound initiated an enemy attack which petered out harmlessly in the midfield mud, but then our centre-half made a disastrous error; although unchallenged he passed back to the goalkeeper, and to our horror the ball again stuck in the mud. It was a race for the ball between our goalie and their centre-forward, an ox. The goalie was first to the ball but before he could fully grasp it the centre-forward had crashed into him, not illegally, but carried by the momentum of his run. The ball spun from our goalkeeper's hands and bounced into the back of the net. We protested, hurled abuse at the referee, but the goal stood.

'Take note of that, young man,' said the Prince of Shmattes who sported a velvet-collared camel hair overcoat. 'It is an important lesson to learn: that the end justifies the means. We Jews have always been too fussy. When did pussyfooting around ever get us anywhere? Why can't our forwards barge into goalkeepers like that? Look at me. Did I make a success by tapping on doors? Not on your life. No, I barged straight in. Believe me, that's the only way to get on in this life.'

Now that we were losing, the other side's supporters even cheered our outside-right and mocked their own left-back for being made to look foolish by the quicksilver Jewboy.

The second half started with a sensation. Straight from the kick-off the ball went to our outside-right who rounded his man with arrogant ease and set off on one of his runs. At the last possible moment he crossed the ball and our centre-forward rose like there were springs in his heels to meet that perfect pass. He seemed to be floating while the ball rested on his instep before he smacked it into the back of the net. The equalizer! We went delirious with joy, we felt the exultation that perfection excites; make no mistake, that goal was a work of art!

We breathed the ultimate in praise, 'The goalie never stood a chance.'

But try as they might Wingate just could not get that second all-important goal. Then ten minutes from time our right-half, laughingly overweight but astute with it, split their defence with a through ball which left our centre-forward alone with only the goalkeeper to beat.

'Shoot!' we pleaded.

He ran on, seemed to stumble, but kept his footing.

'Shoot!' we screamed.

But he hesitated. What was in his mind? Was he planning to dribble round the goalkeeper? However, before he had a chance to do a thing the goalkeeper suddenly rushed from his line and knocked him flat. The referee pointed to the spot. A penalty! Grown men, including my father, hid their faces as the centre-forward prepared to take the kick. This time there was no hesitation, before the tension had time to sink in the ball was in the goal. We could hardly believe it; less than ten minutes to go and we were ahead; we began to scent victory.

'WIN-GATE! WIN-GATE!' we chanted.

'How much longer?' I kept asking my father as the final minutes ticked away and the tension became unbearable. The attacks of our opponents grew increasingly desperate; their centre-forward charged again and again into our defence like a battering-ram. But our defence held. What a relief when the referee looked at his watch and put the whistle to his lips!

As the whistle blew a woman in a fake leopard-skin coat said out loud, 'Hitler was right! Send the Jews to the showers!'

The boy standing next to her was one of our supporters (he looked big to me, but I don't suppose he was older than fourteen). 'Keep quiet, you bitch!' he said.

Whereupon she slapped him round the face. He hit her back.

'You dirty Jew!' she cried.

Her companion moved in on the boy, but he never hit him more than once before Al Pinsky interceded. Now Al wasn't tall, so that golem just laughed, which was daft, because Al Pinsky was once the lightweight champion of Great Britain. The golem dropped the boy and took a swing at Pinsky. His fists were the size of hams. Pinsky ducked, like he was taking a bow, then straightened up and calmly knocked the follow cold. When the police came and listened to the various versions of the incident we tingled with the pleasure of righteous indignation. That evening as I walked home with my father toward the awaiting glass of milk and toasted chola I felt elated; we had not only won the cup but also a great moral victory over the *yoks*. They had called us dirty Jews and we had stood up to them and got away scot free; on the contrary, it was they who left with bloody noses.

Now I realize that part of the fun of going to Wingate was the possibility of encountering just such anti-semitism. Among our supporters it was axiomatic that if you scratch a *goy* you'll find an antisemite; our world-weary version of Shylock's great lament. Perhaps we had the mentality of people who go to the zoo to tease a caged lion and complain when it tries to bite them; but I think we welcomed the anti-semitism because it proved that we were morally superior; it may have confirmed our status as outcasts but it also reaffirmed our role as the chosen people. Although our daily existence gave us no evidence to support the fact there obviously was *something* different about us. And on Saturday afternoons we could flaunt this difference with pride, knowing that it would be recognized; we were the Wingate Supporters Club; our badge was the Mogen David. On the field our boys gave as good as they got, and on the sidelines if the *yoks* wanted trouble they could have it from us wholesale.

A couple of weeks after we won the cup, as if to rub in our moral superiority, the *Daily Mirror* ran an exposé on the horse-doping racket, and it turned out that most of the opposing team and many of their supporters were involved, including their centre-forward and the *shiksa* in the leopard-skin coat. That Saturday we were full of the news; it was too good to be true, not only were they anti-semites, they were criminals as well!

'What else can you expect from *yoks* like that?' said the Prince of Shmattes.

My father, a wittier man, said, '*Goys* will be *goys*.'

Of course my ambition was to play for Wingate. Every evening after school I would go into our backgarden and chase a football around. I divided myself into two imaginary teams: the first mounted dazzling attacks down the flank which were finished off by a deadly striker, and if a goal was not perfect they would not count it; the other was made up of plodders, grateful for any rebound or accidental goal, they were without grace and had no time for the brilliant individual. The first team did not necessarily win, but they were always a pleasure to watch. As I ran I daydreamed of being the prince of outside-rights; the outsider who hovers on the periphery of the match but whose brilliant interventions win the day. What better ambition for a Jewish boy?

Our games master at school had flaming red hair and a beak of a nose, though he wasn't Jewish. Since my natural expression was one of discomfort I was his constant butt.

'Stop looking like you are suffering,' he would say. 'Boys are supposed to enjoy games.'

My passion for football came as a surprise to him; in fact I was fleet-footed enough to be a good outside-right.

'Not bad,' he said, 'I didn't think your people liked physical activity.' He took a look at my expensive football boots and said, 'I bet your father earns a lot of money, eh?'

'I don't know,' I said. I hadn't been going to watch Wingate for nothing; I knew an anti-semite when I saw one. Because I enjoyed football I was spared actual physical torment. However, my friend Solomon was a different kettle of fish. Solomon hated all games, especially football.

Poor Solomon was a coward, and Beaky sensed this at once. He picked out the six biggest louts in our class and told them to stand in a line. Then he threw the ball to Solomon and ordered him to run at them. Solomon didn't move. He was too scared even to argue.

'Get going you milksop, or else,' said Beaky. Still no action from Solomon. So Beaky hit him, hard round the head. 'You have no choice, you greasy tub of chopped liver,' said Beaky.

Milchik or *flayshig*, it made no difference to him. Solomon ran at the boys in the line, kicking the ball far ahead of him, but not one of the boys bothered to go for the ball, taking their cue from their master they took Solomon instead. While Beaky watched they beat him up; not badly, but enough to make him cry. I make no excuses for my inactivity, I was only glad it wasn't happening to me; besides it was a part of our games lesson.

About the time I went away to university things began to go wrong for Wingate; lacking enough Jewish boys to make a *minyan* they had to co-opt non-Jewish players. It was true that Wingate was supposed to foster good-fellowship between Jewish and non-Jewish footballers, but most of our supporters felt this was going too far; this was – bite your tongue – assimilation. Gradually they stopped coming to watch Wingate and sure enough, as they had prophesied, the club lost its identity. The last time I saw them play the team was made up of strangers, men with names like Smith and Williams. The old atmosphere was gone. Wingate had become just another football team. At university I would continue to listen to the football results on the radio, but I could never feel for any other team what I had felt for Wingate; that sense of personal involvement was gone for ever. But by then I knew that there was more to life than football.

My parents assumed I had gone to university to get a degree, but I really went to lose my virginity. I became educated as a by-product. I discovered that the seminars were the great showplaces. So I made myself shine. Society functions were another good place to meet girls. I picked up Linda at the Jewish and Israel Society. Linda called herself the most experienced virgin in the western hemisphere; she would allow any physical intimacy short of intercourse. We slept together frequently, and sometimes I would get such a belly-ache from frustration that I could hardly stand up straight. In public we acted like lovers, but we were just going through the motions, like footballers without a ball. Still, thanks to Linda, I learned all about the role of the kibbutz in Israeli life. Not to mention the role of the Arab, the artist, the woman, the socialist and the *frum* Jew. One night a real Israeli came to speak. I had never seen a sabra before. He was swarthier than I expected. His subject was the role of peace in Israeli life. He was optimistic. He pointed out that it was now over a decade since Suez, and while there was no *de jure* peace there was clearly a *de facto modus vivendi*. A policy of live and let live. He believed that the Arabs had come to accept the presence of Israel, and that given time a normal relationship would develop between the former enemies. Had he got the wrong number!

When the Six Day War began we didn't know that it was only going to last six days, of course. What trauma there was in the Diaspora! No one gave Israel a chance. Every night we saw a different Arab army on the news. Their leaders promised to drive the Jews into the sea. Then Abba Eban would appear, sounding like a Cambridge don. The words of the Prince of Shmattes came back to me. 'We Jews have always been too fussy. When did pussyfooting around ever get us anywhere?' Even Solomon's mother knew better than Abba Eban what was what.

'The Israelis should give the Arabs a bomb already,' she said, 'they should only suffer one hundredth of what we Jews have been through.' She looked about ready to *plotz*.

No wonder, her son was in the Israeli army. After school, instead of going to university, Solomon had emigrated. We still kept in touch. He had a room in Jerusalem. Till the war-fever got me this had been my only real contact with Israel. But now it was time to separate the Jews from the *goys*. Of course I couldn't enlist in the Israeli army but I volunteered to go out as a driver of tractors or – God forbid – ambulances. I was warned that I might come under fire, but I brushed aside the possibility. However, my services were never required. The war ended too quickly.

It made for excellent television. Don't forget, it was my first war; I was too young to remember Suez. Every night I went to the television room next to the library to watch the late news. It was marvellous, our side were winning victory after victory. Films showed tanks scooting over the Sinai desert; the enemy was nowhere in sight. Soldiers hugged and kissed beneath the Western Wall of liberated Jerusalem, looking like they had just scored the winning goal. Experts explained with the aid of mobile diagrams the brilliance of the Israeli strategy; the daring raids, the lightning strikes. I had not felt such exultation since Wingate took the London League Cup; but I was older and I savoured my triumph in silence. Linda, beside me, was less circumspect. She screamed, she cried. I told her to shush, because we were not alone. Sitting by himself, the only other person in the room, was an Arab. Night by night his expression became progressively gloomier. When, on the seventh day, news came in of the Syrian atrocities, the captured Israeli pilot decapitated in front of the cameras and worse, he got up and walked out. 'What do you expect from Arabs?' said Linda.

Solomon's mother telephoned, *shepping naches*; her song was my son the hero. His next letter was modest enough, but it made me envious. Of all people, Solomon had become glamorous! An outside-right, as it were. Such madness, to feel deprived because I had missed a war! But both Linda and I were engulfed in the exuberant aftermath. We discussed the possibility of marriage. We planned to become Israeli citizens. My Jewish destiny was about to be fulfilled.

Or so I thought. But chance took control; I was offered a post at the university, too good an opportunity to be missed. My destiny was postponed. Many other things also happened; governments fell, El Fatah became fashionable, Germany were revenged upon England in the Mexico World Cup, my parents celebrated their silver wedding, Linda and I were married. We went to Israel for our honey-moon. Naturally we visited Solomon in Jerusalem. He was no longer the weedy Yid of our school-days; instead he moved through the city with self-confident ease. A man among men, a real Yiddisher *mensh*. One night after a street-corner supper of felafel we all went to the cinema in Zion Square. The first feature was a film about the Six Day War, made up cheaply from bits of old newsreel. It was received with wild enthusiasm. Though it is difficult to credit today the audience cheered every time Moshe Dayan or Itzak Rabin appeared on the screen. Unfortunately the main feature was less to their liking; the story of a man destroyed by Stalinism, fiction based on fact. The audience quickly lost interest, and only perked up when the unlucky victim was accused of being a Zionist. Finally, as the man looked through his prison bars towards the sky, someone shouted.

'He's expecting the Israeli airforce to come and rescue him!'

Everybody laughed. As we were leaving Linda, unable to restrain herself, started yelling at a bunch of the yahoos.

'What is the matter with you,' she cried, 'don't you have any respect for suffering?'

'*Ma zeh?*' they said, tapping their foreheads. Then Linda, out of control, spat in their faces. This caused them to forget their good humour; they swore at Linda, they called her a whore. They gathered their empty Coca-Cola bottles and flung them at us; and as the glass shattered on the concrete floor they began to close in. Four Esaus, looking for a fight. What sort of joke is this, I thought, to be beaten up in Israel by fellow Jews? With a single movement Solomon grabbed the leader, clutched him and positioned him; then with a graceful gesture cast him over his shoulder. The unsuspecting partner of this *pas de deux* performed a somersault in the air and crashed on to the floor. His hairy brethren rushed Solomon, but it was a half-hearted attack, and Solomon danced amongst them till they all fell dizzily to the ground, like the walls of Jericho.

'Where did you learn to fight like that?' I asked.

'In the army,' said Solomon, 'I was the lightweight wrestling champion.'

He invited us to feel his biceps. 'You know what,' he said, 'whenever I fight someone I still imagine I'm hitting Beaky, that anti-semitic bastard.'

'But they were Jews you beat up tonight, Solomon,' I said.

'Only Yemenite Jews,' he said, 'it's all they understand.'

So even in a nation of Jews there were still *yoks*.

Next thing we heard about Solomon was that he'd been chosen to represent Israel at the Munich Olympics. Quite an achievement for Solomon, the boy who hated games. We watched the opening ceremony on Solomon's mother's coloured television; you should have seen her *kvell* as her only son marched past behind the Israeli flag. I'll swear her chest swelled out a good six inches. Poor woman, it was her last bit of pleasure.

Solomon did moderately well in his competition, though he did not win a medal; but he had his day of fame, none the less. He was probably sleeping when the Black September terrorists burst into the Israeli athletes' quarters. All through that day we sat in front of the television set seeing nothing but those white walls and the gunmen on the balcony in the balaclava helmets, hearing nothing but banalities from sports commentators unaccustomed to dealing with such events. We knew that Solomon was inside. What could he be thinking? Deeper than the politics of the Middle East was he tormented by a single thought? That Beaky was having the last laugh. Solomon could not wrestle with men holding machine-guns; his skills were trumped, he was as helpless as a schoolboy again. When darkness fell we saw the coaches fill, ready to take the terrorists and their hostages to the airfield outside Munich. Linda swore that she could make out the features of Solomon, but all their faces looked the same to me. Written on them all was the awful realization that whatever they did the Jews were doomed to lose out; you learn to fight to defend yourself against the *yoks* and – what happens? – they get guns and shoot you instead. One of the athletes looked back on the steps of the coach – perhaps that was Solomon – and held out his hands as if to say, what more can we do? Then at midnight came the surprise news. There had been a shoot-out at the airfield. All the hostages were safe. The terrorists were dead.

'Thank God for that,' said Linda.

The *Daily Mirror* was sticking through our letter-box next morning, like a dagger in a corpse. The headline screamed: THE TRAGIC BLUNDER. It seemed that the German police had made a 'tragic blunder' in announcing the results of the shoot-out; they got it the wrong way round; it was the athletes who were wiped out, not the terrorists.

I began to shiver as the information sank in. Solomon was dead! I recalled with what pride he showed us his biceps that night in Jerusalem; but all the training was gone for nothing now. Solomon was dead. Linda cried all day, she cursed the Palestinians. But I could not see it like that, to me the Palestinians were instruments of fate. Solomon's inevitable nemesis; it was merely a cruel irony that this particular death struggle should be between two semitic peoples. Out of habit I turned to the sports section of the newspaper. But what I saw turned me cold. 'Queens Park Rangers went hurtling out of the League Cup,' I read, 'following two tragic blunders by Rangers defender Ian Evans.' It had been quite a night for tragic blunders! The carelessness of some sub-editor had equated the two events, the terrible with the trivial; or perhaps it did really reflect how others saw the Munich Massacre. As a good away win for the Palestinians. It was, indeed, confirmation of Beaky's final triumph.

All this happened a few years ago, already. Since then the news has not been too good; nothing seems to have gone right since the Yom Kippur War. They have even built a mosque in Regent's Park. Last week I met the Prince of Shmattes in the street. Only he isn't so clever any more, these days he has to wear his own *shmattes*. People stopped buying his suits and the economic crisis finished him off. He was on his way to the post office to collect his pension. Solomon's mother never recovered from the shock, and was senile before she was sixty. Now every young man who visits she thinks is her son, me included. And I go along with the pretence. What harm in that? My parents keep nagging me to give them a grandchild. But I want any child of mine to be born in Israel. *L'shanah haba-ah birushalayim*. Next year in Jerusalem.

The Luftmensh

What is Joshua Smolinsky, private eye, doing in Philip Roth's former room at a colony for writers? In New England, no less.

The answer begins, as do most things in my life, with a knock on my office door. He held the door open so long that the room filled with the stale air that passes for atmosphere in Los Angeles.

'Do you recognize me?' said my visitor.

'No,' I said, 'should I?'

'Such short memories,' he whispered. 'Once I was famous.'

'Sorry,' I said.

'It doesn't matter,' he said, 'I'm nothing but a hack now.'

'Sit down,' I said, 'you look like a ghost.'

His face turned from white to green. 'That's just what I am,' he said, 'not a ghost, but a ghost-writer.'

'Smolinsky,' I cried, 'that's who!' A string of scandalous best-sellers, much praised by critics, then silence, only noted by me because of the coincidence in names.

'Tell me,' he said, 'what is the worst thing that can happen to a writer?'

'Run out of ideas?' I said.

'No, no, no,' he said, 'it's far worse to lose your voice. To know that your ideas are not your own. That's what has happened to me. Every thought in my head belongs to Victor.'

'Who?'

'Victor Stenzil, the Yiddish writer,' he said. 'I have been chosen to ghost his life story.'

'Never heard of him,' I said. 'Is he still alive?'

'I don't know,' he said, 'that's what I want you to discover.'

'Need an ending for your book?' I said.

He didn't laugh. 'If he is still alive there is hope,' he said, 'perhaps he will release me from the contract. But if he is dead I am doomed to be his ghost for as long as I live. Please find him!'

'Where do I start?' I said.

'The colony,' he said.

'In the beginning,' said my client, 'it was wonderful at the colony. Each day a whole day of uninterrupted writing. No distractions: no visitors, no newspapers, no television. There were eight of us in residence. We lived as a community, and naturally we had rules. We took breakfast and dinner together in a communal dining-room, but between times we were expected to stay in our rooms and write. Of course conversation at table was lively; work-in-progress we read out to loud cheers and jeers; sometimes we got drunk. Once or twice women were obtained. Yes, everything was going swimmingly until the ninth guest arrived. Victor! What a sight! His hair looked like a hundred invisible hands were trying to tug it from his scalp. Meanwhile, other hands shoved tufts into his ears and up his nose. And what a nose! It hung between his eyes like a giant tear-drop. He introduced himself by reading a poem. Not even one of his own.

> "I should have died with you,
> But I found dying too hard.
> Now I do everything to hide with colour
> The convulsions of my body and word.
>
> Neither grief nor anger can drown
> The guilt of my living on,
> My guilt because the flames of Treblinka
> Didn't consume me flesh and bone."

We received it in silence. It was not the sort of poem you could cheer. "That's by Halper Leivick," he said, "I don't suppose you boys have ever heard of him. Am I right?" Night after night Victor went on, dominating our conversation, till we began to dread the evening meal. Eventually, rather than listen to him every evening, we began to sneak into town for supper.'

'So what happened?' I said.

'Victor broke the rules,' he said, 'he knocked on my door in writing-time. From that moment I have not written a word of my own. "I have chosen you," he said. "For what?" I said. "I want you to tell the story of my life," he said. "You are a writer," I said, "tell it yourself." "I cannot, I am cursed," he said, "I am a wanderer, always a wanderer." As we spoke in my doorway streamers of breath floated from our mouths, mingled, and became a single cloud. "Listen to me," said Victor, "it is my tragedy that the Nazis never reached New York. You think I am crazy? Perhaps. But look at me. What am I? A *luftmensh*. A man of air. Without substance. Possessed by history. Full of dreams and nightmares. All the war I was safe. Until the first survivors arrived from Europe. Oy, the guilt I felt then! I was ashamed. Come summer I wouldn't roll up my shirt-sleeves in case someone saw that I had no number on my arm. The mark of Abel! Because I was not a victim I felt like a murderer. I wanted to explain my guilt to you all. But no, what did you do? You ran away to your tootsies in town. Now you will not escape so easily." "Why me?" I said. "Choose someone else." But the next day a contract arrived from my agent. Which I signed. Don't ask me why. The fact is that Victor grew, in the space of a single day, from an object of irritation into a living obsession. He became my subject, and I his.'

'But where do you get all the facts from?' I said.

'That's the point,' he said, 'I am inventing his life. And I cannot stop. That's what's driving me mad!'

'So where was Victor last seen?'

'At the colony,' he said. 'He vanished that night. Without trace. Leaving all his things in his room.'

A beautiful fall day. Just cold enough to see the breath float from your body and drift through the still air like ectoplasm. A single hermit thrush sat singing on the picket fence; flute-like notes of joy, chucks of lamentation and a scolding *tuk-tuk-tuk*. All in the same song. The leaves blazed on the trees like fragments from an exploded patchwork quilt. New England! I checked into the colony as 'Smolinsky'. The girl at reception didn't know one Smolinsky from another. Nor did my fellow writers. There is only one difference between writers and detectives; writers invent plots whereas detectives discover them. And pretty soon my comrades were plotting against me. They wanted to know why I never contributed anything to the work-in-progress soirées. So they bribed a call-girl to rob me. I watched as she crept from the bed to the desk and began to search in vain for the booty. My anger mingled with desire as her body grew luminous in the moonlight; but it was business before pleasure, and in a moment I had her spreadeagled on the floor, a collection of movable parts, which soon confessed its crime. After that incident my colleagues lost patience and began abusing me behind my back.

'You know how he made it, don't you?' said one. 'Thanks to the Jewish literary mafia. They look after their own.' He wasn't really talking about me, he meant the other Smolinsky, but I became enraged anyway. I challenged him to a boxing match and gave him a bloody nose. This conduct was not considered becoming from a writer. A Jewish one to boot! Therefore I was expelled from the colony. But I had got what I had come for. I knew what had happened to Victor's belongings.

The red barn stood amid fields of fresh snow, like a bloodstain on a sheet. It was crowded with objects for the auction. Victor's property was Lot 100. In the meantime I nosed around a bit. Maybe it's because I'm a detective, but the place depressed me. In every bundle I could see finished lives. A chest full of precision tools, minute screwdrivers, pointed pincers, and tins, each containing a selection of watch parts; one tin for faces, another for hands, others for glasses, cases, mainsprings and all the paraphernalia from which we assemble time. So the local watchmaker had shuffled off the mortal coil, that was obvious. But I also knew what tobacco he smoked, what chocolates he liked, what pastilles he favoured for coughs, colds, sore throats, that he suffered indigestion for many years. No magic, I just read the labels on the tins. Lot 100 cost me five dollars. It consisted of a shaving-brush, a pair of old pants and two paperback books. One was a phrase book entitled *Say It in Yiddish*, the other was *A Streetcar Named Desire* by Tennessee Williams. The first amused me with its sections on how to deal with Customs and Passport Control; the new arrival was advised to say, '*Awt iz min pahs. Voo iz dehr tsawl-uhmt?*' meaning: 'This is my passport. Where is the customs?' I ask you, what country is this where Yiddish is the spoken language? A country of displaced persons and ghosts, not marked on any map. Victor's Utopia. An insight into his aspirations, but no use in pin-pointing his whereabouts. However, the second book provided a clue. Victor had marked the first line of the epigraph, 'And so it was I entered the broken world.' And had written alongside Stanley Kowalski's name in the cast list, 'A real anti-semitic Polak, that's what I need.'

*

'He wants to be a martyr,' said Smolinsky.

'So does our driver,' I said. He drove the Greyhound like the devil was on his tail under the influence of the rhythms of the redneck music that he played on his radio. And the further south we went the more reckless he became, jostling with the beat-up cars that criss-crossed our path like headless chickens. As we approached Nashville his mood changed. He calmed down, kept to his lane, and turned off the radio right in the middle of 'D-I-V-O-R-C-E'. Instead his voice issued from the speakers.

'Ladies and gentlemen,' he said, 'Nashville has one of the densest concentrations of millionaires in the nation. It is the Athens of the South, location of numerous colleges and universities, and site of the Parthenon, considered the finest example of classic Greek architecture and generally conceded to be the most beautiful building ever constructed. It is on your right now.'

And it was! The whole thing reconstructed on a green hill in Nashville, Tennessee. Representing the South's self-image, as a reflection of that former perfect society, also founded upon slavery. Our bus gathered speed again along the backroads where billboards posted by John Birchers demanded, 'Get the US out of the UN'. Where signs riddled with bullet holes read, 'It is Illegal to Shoot on Highways'. Dogs strayed beside the road, and every few miles we passed the body of another mashed into the dust by a careless car; sometimes huge black birds stooped over the corpse like mourners. One lifted its face to reveal the curved beak and naked head of a vulture. A pick-up truck flashed by at a crazy speed leaving the impression of the contents of its open back; two blond boys in dungarees sitting beside a stiffening deer. The land was flat and full of swollen rivers. Wide areas were flooded and deserted save for dead trees that protruded from the water like dislocated limbs.

'The land, like my life,' said Smolinsky, 'is out of joint.'

We cut across the narrow neck where Lake Pontchartrain filters into the Gulf of Mexico and entered New Orleans. We left the Greyhound near Canal Street and strolled into the Vieux Carré, sensing that tropical hint of violence in the quotidian. A black man dressed in top hat and midnight-blue suit rattled past in the cab of a horse and carriage. His white passengers in the rear craned their necks to catch his commentary. His melancholy face, with its statuesque features, was impassive. But I could read his mind. It was filled with terrible dreams of revenge, of revolution, of white necks bared for the guillotine.

Her elbows resting on the bar of the Bourbon Street club, the whore said to her client: 'Sometimes, sometimes I look at myself and wonder where my life has gone.' A talking blues, dependent not upon inner feeling but on the quality of performance; and this girl with her sfumato cadences and innocent eyes was a performer and a half.

In the background a naked girl swung back and forth beneath a giant clock. A living pendulum. At about nine-thirty the jazz band arrived. Old black men who carefully placed their jackets on hangers and patted out the creases. There were no long solos because their lungs were too worn out to sustain the effort; unlike the whore the feeling was there but the performers were weary. As each musician took a few choruses on his own the rest watched and smiled; some stomped their feet, others just sat as though hypnotized by the sound. An elegy for a messiah who never showed. And who is no longer expected. The music expressed those hopes, and its dying revealed their disillusion. I looked around. Only one black in the audience. And an out-of-towner, judging by the Kodak instamatic hanging from her wrist. Thus will the message be carried to the people, as a silent photograph! Old-time jazz does not appeal to young blacks, it reeks of bondage; they shun it like Israelis ignore their Yiddish heritage. At which point, as if in response to my cue, Victor walked out from the wings and joined the band on stage.

'So the old *meshuggener* is still alive,' said Smolinsky, 'how did you find him?'

'No problem,' I said, 'I bought *This Week in New Orleans*.'

The pianist played a twelve-bar blues and Victor began his monologue.

'Which would you rather be,' he began, 'a warder in a concentration camp or a prisoner? A Cain or an Abel? Let me tell you people something. I used to thank God for the holocaust. You want to know why? I'll tell you for nothing. Because it gave us Jews the right to sit in judgement on this stinking world. But now I am not sure. Why? On account of Israel, that's why. In our own country we Jews are also not perfect. Now answer my question! Cain or Abel? One or the other!'

But before anyone could open their mouths the club was suddenly invaded by a group of black dudes in white zoot suits and young

whites in denim duds. They shooed the old musicians from the
rostrum and set up their own instruments. 'The revolution has
come,' they announced, 'the old order giveth way to the new.'

Then a member of the combo began to play the bongos while
another in an Afro fright-wig chanted,

> 'Jew-Land, On a summer afternoon
> Really, Couldn't kill the Jews too soon
> Now dig. The Jews have stolen our bread
> Their filthy women tricked our men into bed
> So I won't rest until the Jews are dead.'

'Over here, you black Nazi!' yelled Victor. 'Make a start with me.'
And he ran up to the singer and spat in his face. Was Victor going to
become a martyr at last, in this seedy bar in New Orleans? 'Come
on, you *shvartzer*, show us what a *mensh* you are,' he shouted, 'stick
a knife in my old heart.'

The naked girl swung to and fro below the clock, Victor's spittle
rolled down the black man's cheek, and we all stood in silence. But it
isn't always that easy to get killed, even in New Orleans.

'Shit, I don't want to hurt you, old man,' said the singer, 'I didn't
mean the words literally. Personally, I like the Jews. I'm just sick and
tired of hearing how the Jews suffered. Man, you're hogs for punishment. Let someone else get a word in. Shit, we've suffered as much.'

'In that case, young man,' said Victor, 'you'd better improve your
script. Find yourself a writer!'

'Why aren't you back at your desk?' said Victor.

'I want to break the contract,' said Smolinsky, 'I've had enough.'

'A contract is a contract,' said Victor, 'you gave your word.'

'Well, at least stay in one place,' said Smolinsky, 'so we can get it
over with as quick as possible.'

'I told you,' said Victor, 'I'm a wanderer.'

'Then I'll wander with you,' said Smolinsky, 'till the book is
finished.'

'This trip could be dangerous,' said Victor, 'I've heard rumours of
a plantation near the Mississippi state line that still keeps slaves. I
intend to find it.'

The old bullshitter!

'Pardon me, gentlemen,' said a city slicker who had been listening in, 'but I've got a little tale that might interest you. About how I nearly shot a man. Well, this guy pulls up his truck just beside where me and Curtis are loading our guns for a duck-shoot and reaches for his glove compartment – you know, it's kinda sad that nowadays you're so suspicious of everyone – but I can see that Curtis is thinking the same thing, and in a second we've both levelled our guns at the guy. If he'd had a gun in there we'd have shot him in half before he could have twitched. Want to know what was in there? A dead duck. "Is this yours?" says he. Gentlemen, the moral is plain. It ain't safe to poke your nose into other folks' affairs. Even if your intentions are honourable.'

'What was all that about?' said Smolinsky.

I said I would stick with them for a while. My conduct was unprofessional, but I wanted to keep an eye on my namesake.

North of New Orleans Victor got caught by a cop pissing in the Mississippi. 'What the hell do you think you're doing?' the cop called out of his car window.

'Forgive me, officer,' said Victor, 'but these days my bladder has no resistance.'

'Come over here,' said the cop. Victor hesitated. 'Don't worry,' said the cop, 'I'm not going to bite you.' So Victor approached the battered black and white car. 'You're not from round here, are you?' said the cop.

'Correct,' said Victor, 'I'm from a village near Warsaw, in Poland.'

'No kidding,' said the cop, 'I was there during the war. Tell you what I remember most about the place. The goats' milk. Used to have it delivered to the camp every morning by an old woman. Till the Russians took control and we were sent packing. I often wonder what became of that old peasant and her goats. I can tell you, I was real sorry when Poland went communist. Believe me, I thank God I'm an American. Though not quite so often since Nixon's fucking caper. And then that Ford. Who did he give us for Vice-President? A billionaire who didn't know shit about us poor folks. Listen, if you say you've got a weak bladder I can understand that, because my bladder's weak too, but what can a man who was born rich know about poverty, tell me that? What we need in the White House is a farmer from around here who was raised in dirt. Now off you go, and try not to pee in your pants.'

'A man after my own heart,' said Victor as we tramped northwards over the rolling lands that seemed to take their rhythm from the river.

'Have you boys ever tasted goats' milk?' asked Victor. 'That's real milk. Milk that don't taste like water. Chock full of fatty globules and flocculent curds. My aunt used to sell the stuff. In the old country.'

We were sitting drinking beer in the warm winter sun by the banks of the Mississippi.

'My father was a rabbi in a *shtetl* outside Warsaw,' said Victor, 'and my mother was also descended from rabbis. Much good that did either of them when the defeated Russian army passed through the town. After the pogrom I was taken in by my Aunt Zelda. She was a spinster. Made her living from goats. Sold milk and cheese from a little stall in the market square. My job was to milk the goats every morning before *cheder*. I've never been happier. Sitting on the three-legged stool squeezing the milk into my bucket. As a rule Aunt Zelda left me alone with the goats except on those mornings when the nannies were especially fidgety, then she would come down with me and lock away all the billies. This was in accordance with an injunction she had found in the *Shulchan Aruch*, the Code of Jewish Law; namely, "One should not look when either animals, beasts, or fowl have intercourse." In response to my inquiries concerning this behaviour she quoted, "The thought of fornication only comes into a mind devoid of wisdom. So stop asking questions, go to *cheder* and learn." Being a spinster Aunt Zelda had peculiar ideas about sex, which she revealed to me soon after my *bar-mitzvah*. She informed me that my private parts had been given me by God so that I might know when the devil was filling my mind with evil thoughts. At which point my penis would grow hard. "One is forbidden to willingly harden himself or to bring to himself the thought about women," she quoted. If this should occur, God forbid, I must open the *Torah* and save myself with holy thoughts. One morning, to illustrate what would happen to me if I gave into temptation, she let the billy-goats loose and made me watch their junketings astride the nannies. Afterwards she showed me their eyes. "Look at those pupils," she said, "slanted like the devil's." Despite the warnings I could not control my dreams. At night the devil appeared in the guise of voluptuous females until I succumbed and stained my sheets. Naturally Zelda was horrified at the sight. So many lamentations you would have thought Jerusalem had fallen. Fortunately the *Shulchan Aruch* had an appropriate passage. "A man should be very careful to avoid hardening himself," she read, "therefore it is forbidden to sleep on one's back with his face upward, or to sleep with his face downward, but to sleep on his side, in order not to come to hardening himself." Thereafter I suffered dreadfully from insomnia, fearing to drop off in a proscribed position.'

'Carry on,' said Smolinsky. He was joyfully copying down every word.

'Despite my aunt I got a bit of an education,' continued Victor, 'thanks to the *mocher seforim*, the book pedlars, who passed through from time to time and always stopped for a glass of milk and a gossip. They told me stories of the world outside the *shtetl*. For instance, I learned how students in Germany were burning all books written by Jews. And I didn't even know that Jews were allowed to write books! I became the best customer of the *mocher seforim*. I swallowed every word I read, just as I had swallowed Aunt Zelda's teachings. And when I discovered how she had misled me I hated her. Instead of fasting on *Yom Kippur* I went to dances and ate pork. Then one day, without a word, I left for America. The Nazis were in power in Germany and I knew what they had planned for the Jews. I took what Hitler said literally. You see what I am saying? I left Zelda behind on purpose. I didn't try to persuade her to come with me. I condemned her to Treblinka! Now do you understand my guilt? Enough!'

Near St Francisville we happened upon a plantation house shining out from within a grove of live oak and crape myrtle bearded with Spanish moss, its jalousied galleries and colonnaded balconies back-lit by the cascading light. The place appeared to be haunted by a Southern belle who beckoned us inside.

'Would you care for the tour?' she said.

'Why not?' said Victor.

'The house has been restored,' she said, 'by the combined forces of the Daughters of the American Revolution and the National Society of the Colonial Dames of America. This lady here was our inspiration.' She pointed to a pen-and-ink portrait framed on the wall. 'Miss Eliza Pirrie. The young lady of the house when it was at the height of its glory. She was a pretty thing, don't you think? Many people see a resemblance to Julie Nixon.'

On the road again. 'History never repeats itself,' said Victor, 'but I wouldn't be surprised to see another Nixon in the White House. Julie, this time. Swept to power by the Nixons, the Eisenhowers and the followers of a resurrected Eliza Pirrie. Mark my words.'

'That's my job,' said Smolinsky.

There was an isolated plantation six miles below the Louisiana–Mississippi state line. Across a railway track, rusty with lack of use, down a bumpy unpaved road, over a wooden bridge and there was the rambling plantation house. A fading notice read, 'Accommodation'. We knocked. There was shouting within, then a boy emerged, his teeth in braces.

'What do you want?' he said.

'A room,' we said.

'Follow me,' he said. He led us through a gate at the side of the house, to where a second gallery ran off at right angles. He opened one of the doors in this gallery. Inside was a grand room with oak panels, old prints on the walls and lead-light windows with wooden shutters.

'Look through the windows,' said Victor, 'see how their panes distort everything. That's because the slaves who had to make them couldn't produce perfect glass.'

'You like the room?' said the kid.

'Magnificent,' said Victor, 'just what we were looking for. You'll be able to work here all right, eh, Smolinsky?'

So the kid left us. Because he was not suspicious of us I became suspicious of him. Why no registration? No payment in advance? No number on the door? And no key? But Victor was more interested in a ledger laid open on the desk. It contained an inventory of the slaves. All neatly displayed. Column one, name; column two, age, weight, and brief description; column three, price; column four, present value.

'Look at the date,' cried Victor, 'this book is still being used!'

The sky was stained red where it touched the land. The winter silhouettes of the trees lurked like moving creatures. We sat on our porch watching the darkness fall. There was no denying the edgy fascination of the place. Indeed, it was this vaguely dangerous charm that made it so sensational. Everything seemed magnified: the house, our isolation, the moon as it rose. Pale nocturnal creatures snuffed the ground, owls hooted. Slowly the sky sucked up the moon. Until it shone so brightly that all the buildings on the plantation began to glow; and even the distant slave quarters glimmered.

'It was one family per hut,' said Victor, 'didn't matter if there were two or twenty in the family.'

Suddenly screams filled the air. Real blood-curdling screams! My perception went into overdrive. I began to imagine impossible things. The trees seemed to be creeping closer. New sounds. Not imagination. The chink of metal on metal. Through the night I saw the shimmer of chains in motion. Moving towards us. And then as if being formed out of the darkness itself there emerged a huge Negro. Naked except for the chains around his ankles. It was as though the past had come to life.

'It can't be a ghost!' hissed Smolinsky.

'No way,' I said. 'Ghosts don't bleed.'

'What is your name?' said Victor.

'Abel,' replied the slave.

Then two more faces floated out of the darkness like white balloons. It could almost have been a party for there were orange flashes and bangs. Except they were guns going off. And the game, as the man in the club had warned us, was kill the intruders. So we ran like rabbits. But Abel slowed us down, with his chains and his wounds. And they caught us by the deserted road.

'Thank your friends, nigger,' they said, 'on account of them we're going to kill you.'

They would have, too, if Victor hadn't stepped in the way and got shot instead.

'Don't die!' begged Smolinsky.

Victor was groaning in the dirt, bleeding to death. Abel was gasping for breath. Me and Smolinsky were petrified. Awaiting our turn in front of the firing squad. When in the distance we all saw the blue lights of the Highway Patrol. As a rule I don't expect much from cops. But our saviour just happened to be Victor's fellow capriphile. So Victor lived. What's more he persuaded those southern cops that a plantation worked by slaves was operating under their noses. The slaves were freed. Smolinsky's contract was cancelled. And Victor was a hero. He played all the clubs with a bandage wrapped around his head. With his new partner. They called themselves 'Cain and Abel'.

'Once we were slaves,' they said, 'but now we are free. As free as air!'

Smolinsky, on the other hand, is learning Yiddish.

The Evolution of the Jews

'Remember you are a Jew,' my father said when I was old enough to stand on my own four feet. As if the anti-semites would let me forget! They have been killing Jews in the miombo ever since the drought began. Before that there were pogroms in the nyika to the east. Now they have my scent. And I am in danger. They came upon us during our old-fashioned mating rituals. You'd think the rabbis would relax some of the rules at a time like this. But no. 'We must obey God's commandments,' they say. So we males have got to knock ourselves silly with the head-slamming competition. And after that, if we're still capable, we're expected to nibble the rear end of a female so that she wees into our mouth. The odours are supposed to suffuse our olfactory membranes to let us know whether the lady's on heat or not, but between you and me I spit the stuff out as quick as I can. Personally, I'd much rather just give the girl a nudge in the backside, and if she's not interested she can walk off. But there's no arguing against tradition. Just my luck this afternoon I got a real athlete. A dozen times in four hours she made me perform. Then the lookouts spotted the lions. Two of the brutes. Moving in our direction. 'Run!' they signalled. Fat chance!

You're probably wondering what a community of Jews is doing living in the African savanna. Well, we're the lost tribe. How do I know? My father told me. What proof can I give? For starters, there's the statue of Moses wearing horns. Just like mine. Put the rest down to evolution. If every other creature in the world wanted to do you in you'd also head for the lowlands and grow a long neck. And four legs are faster than two. I know a long neck is a life-saver, but sometimes I think of it as a curse. Because all animals are our enemies and because we can see them coming with our long necks we spend all day watching for them. We don't relax for a minute. What sort of life is that? We stand still for hours grazing on the tree-tops. Then we ruminate. Chewing over our food again and again, chewing over our worries also, belching all the while. The only problem we Jews have been spared is indigestion. All in all we are pessimistic creatures. With a tendency to melancholia. To raise our spirits we say that while our feet stand in shit our heads are in the clouds. Believe it or not, that daft saying got us into our present difficulties.

When the rains did not come, we knew we would be blamed. We were blamed for the floods. Why not the drought? During the floods the stupider animals begged us to eat the clouds. We laughed. So they killed us. The floods subsided. Now we are accused of stealing the clouds. Let me quote a typical anti-semitic libel. 'They say their heads are in the clouds,' it goes, 'so they must know where they have gone. Friends, the Jews have stolen our clouds!' We are accused of being alien, aloof, stiff-necked. And worse. 'If it were not for the Jews,' runs the libel, 'there would be no problems. Neither floods. Nor droughts.' To be rid of such problems forever they decide to wipe out the Jews. Which explains my predicament. Hunted by lions.

They have found me. I can hear the snuffing of their snouts. Their excited gurgles and growls. I can smell the stale blood on their disgusting breath. It will be an ignominious death, to be ripped apart by such obnoxious beasts. I retreat slowly, backing away. My hoofs carefully testing the ground. Suddenly one of my back legs slips, for I have reached an escarpment, and in a panic I all but tumble over. For an instant I am more frightened of falling than of the lions. I remember the unfortunate fate of one of my uncles who stepped backwards while browsing at a tree by the edge of a drop and found no ground beneath his feet. His neck caught in a fork between branches and he hung choking, twenty inches of tongue hanging out of his mouth buzzing with flies. When we discovered him lions were already feeding from his hind legs. Ugh! Since that day I have been terrified of falling. It has become a phobia. Indeed when I see my reflection in a water-hole it seems a miracle that such a creature can stand at all. Trapped. There can be no escape on account of the escarpment. Lions leap. I turn and kick out with my heels. I catch the first lion in the belly and it rolls over grunting. But the second lands on my back. I try to shake the brute off but its claws are in my flanks. Forgetting that I stand on the brink of an escarpment, I gallop forward, the lion still riding on my back. The slope is so steep that we reach a dizzying speed and the lion is now hanging on, not to kill me, but to save its own skin. I am safe. So long as I do not stop. But then above the thunder of my hoofs I hear a deeper rumble from the heavens. And I feel rain upon my muzzle. What *mazel*! The lion springs off my back leaving long raking scars – the butcher – and runs around catching raindrops on its tongue. The drought is over. God be praised. The Jews will live a few more days.

What else can I tell you about us? That we are big-hearted is well known. We need big hearts to pump the blood all the way up to our heads. Which are not so big. Our diet is strictly controlled. We are permitted to eat only fruit that grows on trees; all food from the ground is forbidden as unclean. 'If God had wanted us to eat dirt,' the rabbis say, 'He would have given us short necks like pigs.' So day after day we chew mimosa and prickly acacia, though my papillae cry out for variety. We sleep very little, no more than a few minutes at a time. Which is just as well, as far as I am concerned, for no sooner do I shut my eyes than I am visited with the most terrifying nightmares. I dream of death in all its varieties: by tooth, by claw, by drought, by flood, by disease, by fire. I dream of pogroms, of massacres, of trials, of tortures. I hear the cruel laughter of anti-semites. But the nightmare that frightens me the most is the shortest. I dream that I fall. And cannot get up. At which point, of course, I awaken and climb to my feet. Neck. Backwards. Forwards. On to knees. Neck. Hind legs. Neck again. Stretch. A shake of the tail.

All is quiet in the miombo. There is neither flood nor drought. Everything is growing according to its season. Except for the odd outbreak of anti-semitism we are left alone. We know that it cannot last. The peace. But we try to make the most of it. Our neck muscles begin to feel like elastic rather than rods of iron. In short, we relax. One day in search of a more arcane variety of acacia I wander off alone, far away from my fellow Jews. Following an unfamiliar path my eye is attracted by a glimmer in the grass. I look down upon a row of brightly coloured fruits stretching as far as I can see. Which is a long way. I am tempted. And against my better judgement I begin to follow this trail of fruit. The aroma that wafts up as some squash beneath my hoofs convinces me that they will taste better than anything I have eaten before. Until at last I can resist the temptation no longer. I bend my neck and take a step forward, my tongue tingling in anticipation of the forbidden fruit, and walk straight into the pit. The ground gives way beneath my feet and I fall among a shower of branches and brightly coloured fruit into a deep hole. I am buried alive. Only my head is above ground. A nightmare come true! It is a miracle that I do not have a heart attack.

I curse myself for my greed. For my carelessness. Why did I forget that Jews are never safe? That behind every gift lurks danger? That for every pleasure comes a punishment? I would cry out. But for screams you need vocal chords, which we Jews have not got. And you cannot *whisper* for help! So I must await my fate. At least I am not dead.

I wait all day. Then as the sun sinks strange creatures approach. My instinct is to run, but I cannot move. So I try to scare them. I stretch out my neck until my head is horizontal, my ears spread stiffly, my nostrils flaring, my eyes blazing. But my captors do not run away. Instead they continue their entry out of the sun. And when I finally recognize them I really do have a heart attack, anyway the blood rushes from my head and I almost faint. For these creatures walk upon two legs and have short necks just as we Jews once had. I have fallen into the clutches of the worst anti-semites of them all. Men! And they are going to lynch me. One of the murderers has a pole with a noose attached. They toss the loop over my head and as it tightens I feel the rope bite into my neck. Knowing the end is near I begin to recite, '*Shema yisroel* . . .' Then everything goes black.

It goes black because they have thrown a blanket over my head. Thus blinded and trussed, I am dragged from my trap like Samson among the Philistines. Again my heart stops pumping. I swoon. And one of my tormentors cries out, '*Ma zeh?*' I recognize the language. *Ma.* What. *Zeh.* Is this? Hebrew! So Hebrew is still spoken in the world. Oh, irony of ironies. I have been kidnapped by Jews. Unevolved, original Jews. I try to communicate with them the lost tribe has been found, but it is no use; my neck too long, my voice too low. Or else they do not know Yiddish. However, there is nothing wrong with my hearing. I learn that I am to be transported to the Promised Land. Their country. My country! Which explains why they have not developed like us. What need for a long neck when all men are your brothers? What need for four legs when there is no assassin to flee? I want to explain to my co-religionists that I will gladly go wherever they lead. But I cannot. And so I return to Israel in chains.

But the bondage does not last. I am taken to Jerusalem and released in a park fragrant with mimosa. At first I ask myself, 'Why do they not invite me into their homes?' But then I remember my neck and smile. They would have to build tall houses to accommodate me.

How popular I am! Every day scores of parents bring their kids to visit me. They laugh and clap their hands to see such a Jew. I bend my neck to whisper to them. But they do not hear or do not understand. Never mind. We are brothers. What happiness! What security! I am a king in Israel. And all around me, snarling behind bars, are the anti-semites that once lorded it over the miombo. God is in his heaven. But even now in this lovely land – my own country – I cannot stop worrying. What is there to worry about? I'll tell you. The evolution of the Jews. Make no mistake, evolution happens every day. I tremble for the kids. I am frightened by the way the hair forms thick and mane-like upon their heads. By the way their teeth grow sharp, their nails claw-like. And each time I see a Jew carrying a gun I shiver. Because I am reminded of the accursed Sir Samuel Butler – may his memory be blotted out – a Haman who shot Jews for sport. And once tasted our flesh! 'When roasted,' he gloated, 'it is delicious.' Even in this park I hear things. Stories of battles. Roars of triumph. Strange words. Uranium. Plutonium. If only I could warn them. Tell them that evolution is the secret weapon of the anti-semites. That evolution is not inevitable. And must be fought. I want to cry, 'Do you not see how you are changing?' But in Israel I am dumb.

Jews may change but the laws are eternal. Here also I am only permitted to eat acacia and mimosa. However, I have noticed a tree in the next enclosure which bears orange fruit. When the wind blows right the scent from them prickles my papillae. 'Shlomo,' I say to myself, 'remember what happened last time you were tempted. You almost died.' 'Ah, but God works in strange ways,' I reply, 'if I had not fallen into the pit I would not be in Israel now.' I decide to see if I can reach the fruit. That will be the test. If God doesn't want me to eat it He will have put it out of reach. So I lean my chest against the fence and stretch out my neck. The orange fruit dangles in between my eyes. Just a few more inches. And then my tongue curls around its tangy skin. But before I can pluck the fruit from the tree the fence collapses beneath my weight and my legs splay outwards. I wave my neck backwards and forwards. But it is hopeless. I cannot get up!

'Shlomo,' I say to myself, 'you're done for.' With such a conclusion you need a bit of consolation. Who likes to die in vain? So I ask myself, 'Why has God done this to you?' And I answer, 'I have been sent as a warning to Israel. I am dumb, but my fate speaks.' I am a prophet!

The Texas State Steak-Eating Contest

The kid was dressed all in black. He looked like he was in mourning for life. Actually it was just for his father, Hammond Hammerhead I, Texas cattle baron, recently deceased.

'I don't think my father's death was an accident,' he said, 'I think he was murdered.'

That was the gist of his opening statement. It was full of flights of fancy but I excused him on account of the fact he'd just returned from a European university. Meanwhile, back at the Hammerhead Ranch things had been happening fast; his Uncle Claude had declared himself boss and likewise taken possession of his widowed sister-in-law, so that poor Hammond Hammerhead II, arriving too late for his father's funeral was just in time for his mother's wedding. Now the kid's mind was full of mayhem; he was convinced that his uncle had bumped off his father and robbed him of his inheritance. But he seemed a bit short on evidence. So I offered a Freudian interpretation of his obsession, mentioning Oedipus by name.

The kid was not impressed. 'Listen, shamus, if I want my motives analysed I'll pay a shrink,' he snapped back, his European refinement gone west. 'You're an investigator, an empiricist, so go and investigate.'

'Why come all the way from Amarillo to hire me?' I said. 'Aren't there any good detectives in Texas?'

'First, I'm too well-known in Texas; if I was seen within half a mile of a private eye people would know,' said the kid. 'Second, my uncle owns most of the detectives in Texas, not to mention half the police force. So I came out to Los Angeles and picked the unlikeliest sounding investigator in the book. Who ever heard of a private eye called Joshua Smolinsky?'

I defended my good name, but the kid wasn't interested.

'I'll tell you what, Joshua,' he said, 'come down to the ranch with me. I'll introduce you as my Professor of Literature. Do you know anything about literature, Joshua?'

*

The cowboy stood larger-than-life outside the Big Texan Steak Ranch, on a billboard welcoming me to the 'Home of the Free 72oz Steak'. Obviously an irresistible invitation to freedom-loving Texans, for the place was full of aborigines behaving like no one ever would outside of Texas. The décor was nineteenth-century Texan, with scant respect to verisimilitude, and the staff were 'six-gun-toting waitresses', dressed according to anatomy rather than historical accuracy, for each had a skirt up to her *tochis*. We joined a crowd round one of the tables where a gent was actually trying to devour seventy-two ounces of steak: it was only free, of course, if you finished the lot. His progress was watched over by big men in stetsons who shook their heads pessimistically. The head waiter, identified by his sheriff's star, came over to see how he was doing. By now he was in trouble. 'Hey, Sheriff,' he said, 'do I have to eat baked potato too?'

'You surely do,' came the reply. Beside the baked potato four thick steaks sat growing cold. Unkindly, as if to rub in the guy's failure, the head-waiter announced that a fellow in a yellow shirt had just licked up the last of his 72oz dinner. The cowboys trooped off to observe this phenomenon, to memorize his face, for he could be a good bet in the restaurant's upcoming Texas State Championship Steak-Eating Contest. The head-waiter spied Hammond.

'Good to see you again, Mr Hammerhead,' he said, 'we're hoping for great things from you in this year's contest.'

'Not much to beat,' said Hammond, 'the last winner only managed sixteen pounds in two hours.'

A fiddler and a girl country singer emerged caterwauling from the restaurant's obscurity. They cavorted before a pair of quivering carnivores. The fiddler cocked his head to one side and jerked his hand like he was giving himself an upper-cut; at once notes leaped from the screeching catgut. The girl stood her ground, shook her curly brown hair, leaned back and yelled out 'D-I-V-O-R-C-E!' Out came the words, in went the meat. The man at the table fished in his pocket for some dollar bills, and with a flashing smile pushed them under the lace garters that both musicians wore on their arms. A 'six-gun-toting waitress' brought more food and as she put the plates down her bum pointed skywards revealing red satin and cheap frills. The fiddler produced a cascade of notes and the couple at the table whooped and stomped. Their plump legs looked like oil-pumps from the Texas fields as they pounded up and down.

'That's my Uncle Claude,' said Hammond, 'the lady with him's my mother.'

'Mother . . . um . . . Uncle, I want you to meet Professor Joshua Smolinsky,' said Hammond. 'A Professor of Literature. Just arrived from Europe.' Uncle Claude stared at me. 'Harold Robbins says he is the finest writer in the world,' he said, 'and I agree.'

Hammond's mother, Gertie, blushed. Her parents had been Jewish and it showed in her voluptuous lips, her full bosom and her admiration for professors.

'Professor Smolinsky, please excuse my husband,' she said. 'I'm afraid he doesn't have much respect for learning.'

'I've nothing against learning 'cept the time it takes,' said Claude. 'The world doesn't stand still waiting for you to finish your education.'

I looked at Hammond. But he didn't say a word.

'There's more to university than book-learning,' I said just to fill the silence.

'Why, Professor Smolinsky!' exclaimed Gertie, 'you have a Los Angeles accent.'

'I was raised there,' I said, 'my parents were refugees.' Refugees from New York.

'I was born in Malibu,' said Gertie.

'You see what a great country America is?' said Claude. 'What other country turns its refugees into professors? I hope you are grateful, Professor Smolinsky. You're not a commie, are you?'

'Mother,' said Hammond, 'I've asked Professor Smolinsky to spend a few days at the ranch.'

The Hammerhead Ranch covered an area about the size of Denmark. Hanging from the bar over the gate, just below the horns and skull of a bull, was a hammer and sickle burned into a piece of wood.

'We had it first,' growled Claude, 'and I'll be damned if I'd change our brand on account of some commie bastards.'

The ranch-house itself was as big as an average castle. Instead of a moat it was surrounded by a swimming pool. On the night before Gertie's second marriage Claude had employed a score of Navajo craftsmen to inlay the walls of the pool with polished turquoise. As the drawbridge was lowered floodlights blazed into life and we were dazzled by scintillas of blue that came shooting from below the water. Except for Claude who was wearing his gold-rimmed shades.

'Oh, Claude,' said Gertie, 'why didn't you remind me to put on my sunglasses?'

Hammond took me to my room, which was twice the size of my entire Los Angeles apartment. There was a telephone in every corner, and one beside the bed with a tiny screen which showed the face of the caller.

'Tell me again how your father died,' I said to Hammond.

'My father was a king among men,' said Hammond, 'and like a king he loved to entertain. Often he would perform stunts for his guests. His favourite was the Hopi Snake Dance. In which he was partnered by a rattlesnake. Fangless, of course. Naturally his audience was horrified. They assumed the snake was dangerous. Well, on that last occasion they were right. The snake turned on my father and sank its fangs into his tongue. His tongue swelled to the size of a shoe. And he choked to death. The police concluded that my father had been careless. Picked up the wrong snake. An accident. But I know that my father was too sure-footed to do anything so stupid. So someone must have switched the snakes.'

'Your Uncle Claude?'

'Who else?'

My room was filled with bells. The telephone. I picked up the receiver beside my bed and Gertie's face appeared on the screen.

'Hello, Professor,' she said, 'have you everything you need?'

'Thank you, yes,' I said.

From the expression on her face I knew that she wanted to tell me something. 'Professor Smolinsky, you are Hammond's friend?'

'Yes.'

'Did he ever tell you why we sent him to a European university?' she said.

'He hinted.'

'So he told you about Olivia?'

'He led me to believe,' I said, treading carefully, 'that he was sent away because of a girl.'

'Nothing more?'

'You must understand, Mrs Hammerhead, that we spoke of such things in terms of literary analogies,' I said. 'I had to deduce for myself how they related to his life.'

Gertie liked that. 'Professor Smolinsky,' she said, 'my husband – that's my late husband – sent Hammond to Europe to get him away

62

from our foreman's daughter.' A second figure appeared on the screen. It was Hammond. He was wearing a T-shirt and jockey shorts. Then Gertie put down the receiver and the screen went blank.

I awoke in the middle of the night to find someone in my room. My eyes focused on a grey object that emerged from the shrouds of sleep and took on the features of Claude Hammerhead. 'Professor, you look startled,' he said, 'were you expecting a ghost?'

'What ghost?'

'You tell me.' He laughed. 'Let's cut out the crap,' he said, 'are you going to say why you've come to the ranch?'

'Your nephew invited me.'

'But why?' He sat down on the end of the bed. 'If you want to know, Smolinsky, I don't believe you're a professor,' he said, 'I figure you're a detective. Hired by my punk of a nephew to find his father's murderer. Am I right?'

'You have a point, Mr Hammerhead,' I said, 'we Professors of Literature are like detectives in that we must comb texts for clues as to their real meanings.'

'Bullshit!' Claude walked to the door. 'Ask Hammond what happened to the last private eye who came snooping round here.'

Next morning I came face to face with Hammond in the pool.

'Hi, Joshua,' he said, 'sleep well?'

'Fine,' I said, 'but you seem to be a family of somnambulists.'

'Did someone bother you?'

'I had a visit from your Uncle Claude.'

'What did he want?'

'He made an educated guess as to why I'm here.'

'You didn't tell him anything?'

I shook my head.

'Hammond, what happened to the first detective you hired?'

'He had an accident.'

'What sort of accident?'

'He pulled a gun on a cop.'

'But the cop was quicker?'

'That's about it,' said Hammond.

'One more thing,' I said, 'who's Olivia?'

'If you're asking you must know.'

'Where is she now?'

'No idea,' said Hammond, 'after I left she went to join some hippie commune in New Mexico.'

'So who might know? Her father?'

'No. Her father's gone. Only Larry.'

'Larry?'

'Her brother. He runs a restaurant for freaks in Santa Fe.'

'Will you lend me your car?' I said. 'I'm thinking of taking a trip to Sante Fe.'

Thunder rumbled round the mountains of New Mexico. Torrential rain filled Santa Fe's valley bowl. Lightning flashed till past midnight, lighting up the ghostly peaks. Next morning Santa Fe was as bright as a new pin. Old men sat arguing and nodding on benches in the plaza. A colourful poster pinned to an adobe wall advertised a rodeo with crude pictures of bronco-busters. Indians spread their blankets and displayed their trinkets and fakes on the porch of the ancient Palace of the Governors. Santa Fe was a cosmopolitan mix of Indian architecture, European town-planning and American money.

I stepped off Cerrillos Road into the Golden Temple Natural Foods Center. It was full of plants and very airy. The waiters and waitresses were soft-spoken, they wore spotless white robes and turbans. I ate gratefully, relieved to know that nothing artificial was descending the oesophagus. A purgatorial meal of avocado, sour cream, cheese and hot peppers; afterwards I cooled off with Golden Ice Cream, also made with natural products.

'Is Larry around?' I asked a waitress. A couple of minutes later a mountain of a man appeared in regulation robes and turban; they suited him like a wedding dress becomes a boxer.

'I'm Larry.'

'I'm looking for your sister,' I said.

'And who are you?'

'Joshua Smolinsky. *Professor* Joshua Smolinsky.'

'Don't mean a thing.'

'A friend of Hammond,' I said. 'He's back in Amarillo.'

'That worm,' said Larry, 'she's better off without him.'

'Isn't that for Olivia to decide?'

'A professor, huh?'

'Of literature.'

'OK, Professor,' he said suddenly, 'I'll take you to her.'

We left Santa Fe going northwards over the red Sangre de Cristo mountains, then eastwards through the Rio Grande Gorge towards Taos.

'Does Olivia live in Taos?' I said.

'Not any more,' said Larry. 'She came up here with her hippie friends after Hammond left her. She was going to join the Indian Pueblo. But the Indians didn't want to know. They had no time for hippies.'

We drove through Taos on Kit Carson Road, passing the great scout's house. I'd a soft spot for Kit ever since I'd read the story of his meeting with General Sherman. 'I cannot express my surprise,' Sherman wrote in a letter, 'at beholding a small stoop-shouldered man, with reddish hair, freckled face, soft blue eyes, and nothing to indicate extraordinary courage or daring.' That's Joshua Smolinsky, to the life!

Soon we were far into the Carson Forest, climbing high up pine-covered mountains, then turning deeper into the woods at a sign marked 'San Cristobel'. Larry forced his old Ford Falcon up a steep unpaved road, muddy from the rains, full of boulders and puddles, and as narrow as a bookmark. We continued slowly for seven miles until we reached a small ranch-house built of wood and mud. On the grass within the dooryard were some cones, a broom, several logs, a rusty seat from a tractor, the pelvis of an ox and a wooden box marked 'US Mail'.

'Olivia's place?' I said. Larry didn't answer. He got out the car and began to walk up a winding path that led eventually to a white building surrounded by trees. It looked like a shrine. There was no sound except for the water dripping from the trees.

'Inside,' said Larry.

Olivia wasn't there. Instead there was a big stone which read: 'D. H. Lawrence 1885–1930.'

'Alrightee, Professor,' said Larry, 'how's about giving me a lecture on Lawrence in America?'

I gabbed on for a few minutes. But Larry didn't take any notes.

'Thought so,' he said, 'you're a professor like I'm an Indian guru.' I lifted my hands. 'Now are you going to tell me what you're really after?'

'I'm a private investigator,' I confessed, 'Hammond hired me to prove that Claude murdered his father.'

'What's that got to do with Olivia?'

'She lived at Hammerhead Ranch,' I said, 'she may know something.'

'And why should she tell you anything?'

'If Claude is guilty,' I said, 'Hammond will get the ranch.'

'So?'

'Olivia will be his wife.' In arranging this *shiddach* I was going beyond my brief, but I could see no other way of getting Larry to talk.

'She works in the Visitors Center at the Navajo Tribal Park,' he said.

I sped over the great Colorado Plateau aiming to reach Monument Valley before sundown. By late afternoon I was in Utah. Already puffy white mushrooms were growing in the sky, and cloud-bursts criss-crossed the highway as I rushed toward the atomic storms in Hammond's car, feeling as insecure as an insect in the gigantic landscape. Finally I crossed into Navajoland, a separate country in the heart of the continent. Olivia was sitting in the Visitors Center, the only blonde in miles. She was reading a back number of *True Confessions*.

'Hello, Olivia,' I said.

She looked up. Her eyes were as bright as the stones in Gertie's swimming pool. 'Who are you?'

'Joshua Smolinsky,' I said, 'I've come from Hammond. He wants to marry you.'

She examined me with those blue eyes. 'Mr Smolinsky, do you know why Hammond was sent to Europe?'

'I was told it was because of you.'

'No, Mr Smolinsky, that wasn't the reason,' she said, 'he was sent away because he shot my daddy.'

Outside the low sun flickered through a layer of boiling, swirling cloud. The earth was like a red sea from which rose the monoliths of Monument Valley, grey going brown beneath a sky as purple as a hot-house grape. The air was full of electric tension, fat drops of rain fell, pitting the sand with as many pinpricks as there were in Olivia's arms.

'It was hushed up,' she said, 'no one was told. Not even Larry. I knew and the Hammerheads knew. No one else. Except the cops of course.'

'But why?'

'Why was he shot? Easy. He saw Hammond fucking his mother.'

'Come on.' But I remembered what I had seen on that little screen before Gertie had cut us off.

'If you don't believe me,' said Olivia, 'there's nothing more to say.'

There was a tremendous crack of thunder right over us. Then the vision. The final shaft of sunlight struck the furthest monolith and while that flamed against the mauve sky the others began to glow, stronger and stronger, like red-hot coals. The scene flared like a firework, then faded as the sun sank, leaving only the tip of a rainbow as an afterglow between the colourless stones. It was like that tab of truth that sticks to every crime, the tab which I had just begun to feel.

'I believe you.'

'You understand why I could never marry Hammond?'

'Yes.' Olivia smiled.

'But you still love him?' I said.

'Right first time, Mr S,' she said.

'Will you come back with me,' I said, 'for your father's sake?'

'I'm confused,' she said, 'I will ask Chief Silena what to do.'

'Who?'

Olivia rolled herself another joint. She had been smoking marijuana since early morning when we left the motel in Mexican Hat for the Hopi Reservation. The Hopi had been there undisturbed since the thirteenth century. Their land was so barren no one else wanted it. On the slopes of the mesas were a few artificial fields, irrigated by the midsummer rains, in which grew corn, squash and beans. The mesas jutted out over the plain like the prows of three giant ships; far below the plain looked like a shimmering silver sea. In the distance were the San Francisco Mountains, home of the Hopi gods.

'I really love maps,' said Olivia as she navigated, 'they are so full of possibilities.'

'Like blueprints for a life.'

'Hey, Mr Smolinsky, that's good!'

We drove some miles down route 264, then turned off on to a dirt track. In front was an expanse of brown dust, piles of grey rock, clumps of spiky grass; a feverish wind, the slope to the edge of the mesa, the houses of undressed brown stone; beyond a glimpse of the valley below and the dark encircling mountains.

'This is it,' said Olivia, 'Shongopovi.'

It must have been some kind of holiday because Shongopovi was chock-a-block with Hopi.

'Come on,' said Olivia.

'If you're sure it's all right.'

We trailed down the dusty street towards the houses, all built pueblo-style, each level connected by a wooden ladder. On the topmost roofs golden eagles were chained. They spread their wings to rise on the wind, trying to break free, only to be jerked back again and again by their leg-irons. So what chance would there be for a down-at-heel private eye? We reached the plaza where the crowds were thickest. In the centre a dozen men were standing in a diagonal line, larger-than-life in that confined space. They wore square masks over their faces, kaolin-covered, decorated with a variety of features, feathered head-dresses, capes hanging from their shoulders and brightly-coloured kilts.

'Kachinas,' whispered Olivia, 'today must be a *niman*.'

I didn't understand a word. Brown paper bags were passed along the line. Cobs of corn, melons and oranges were plucked from within and thrown at us, much to the delight of the kids. Suddenly there was silence as the elders of the tribe entered the plaza. The most venerable walked to the head of the fancy-dress parade and began a chant.

'That's Silena, Chief of the Sun Clan,' whispered Olivia. 'He's thanking the gods for a good harvest.' Well, at least no one was starving.

When the ceremony was over Olivia pushed through the crowds to get to her guru.

She was back in a minute. 'I'm coming with you,' she said.

'What did he say to convince you?' I said.

'To thine own self be true.'

'You know, Chief Silena has a theory about Hammerhead's death?' said Olivia as we were approaching Amarillo. 'He says the gods killed him. They were angry because he mocked their dance. So they turned the snake upon him and made it potent again.'

'It's a theory.' Then we passed beneath the Hammer and Sickle.

The swimming pool looked fine. Except that two of the turquoise stones seemed to be floating towards the surface. Then I saw that they were not stones but eyes, eyes wide open in a white face. Olivia's face. Then there was a shoulder and a breast and a thigh and soon her whole body had broken through the film of water and was floating lifelessly on the surface. She was naked, offering herself to the sky, like a bride on her bed. I pulled her out of the water. She was cold, very cold. Poor Olivia. I covered her.

'Look at her arm,' said Claude, 'a heroin addict!'

'Suicide,' agreed the cops.

'Poor girl,' said Claude, 'let's call it an accident.'

'Another accident,' I said.

'What do you mean by that?' said Claude.

I was the only one who attended Olivia's funeral. Larry wasn't told. Hammond was too depressed, he said. But he let me have his car. It was a lonely affair. Returning to the ranch two cars swerved in front, their blue lights flashing, forcing me to stop. Luckily I had emptied the ashtrays. Formerly full of Olivia's roaches. The cops wouldn't have needed another thing.

'Your car?' they said.

They knew it was Hammond's. They knew I was driving. They knew everything.

'Get out.'

The only thing they didn't know was that the ashtrays were empty. They pulled them out. Nothing. They were not pleased. They let the air out of the tyres, dragged out the seats, peered into the gas tank and searched under the chassis with flashlights. It was as if they were not human beings at all. In place of heads they wore shiny helmets, in place of eyes they had reflecting shades with black lenses, no hands, just leather gloves; each sported a blue nylon jacket, short and padded, that stopped just above the gun butt. The Hopi saw the Kachinas as messengers from their gods; I wondered what manner of gods these creatures represented.

'OK, smartass,' said one, 'where have you hidden it?'

'Hidden what?' I had to be careful. We were beside a busy road, but they could always take me to a quiet spot.

'We had a tip-off,' said another, 'we know you're carrying dope.'

'Why? Need some? Run out at the station?'

'A joker!' said the third as he searched in my stomach for my lunch. I doubled up, retching.

'That's enough,' said number four, 'he's had his warning.' If they'd hung around they'd have seen that I'd eaten hamburger, french fries and salad with thousand island dressing.

I didn't get undressed. I was expecting visitors. Claude arrived first.

'What do you know?' he said.

'That Hammond murdered Olivia's father,' I said.

'Know why?'

'Because he was blackmailing Gertie.'

Claude laughed.

'Listen,' he said, 'Hammond got Olivia's father to switch the snakes. Then he shot him. And went to Europe to wait for the bad news. Unfortunately he didn't reckon on my intervention.'

'What about Olivia?'

'Hammond too. She must have found out the real reason for her father's death.'

'Very convincing,' I said.

'It certainly convinced Larry,' said Claude, 'in fact he's coming here to have a chat with Hammond.' Exit Claude.

Gertie came next.

'Since you arrived here there's been nothing but trouble,' she said, 'why don't you leave us alone. Go away!'

'And miss the Texas State Steak-Eating Contest? Sorry.'

'What do you want of us? Money?'

'I want to know who killed Olivia.'

'All right, I did,' said Gertie, 'she wasn't good enough for my boy. Satisfied?'

'You're joking.'

'Professor Smolinsky – or whoever you are,' she said, 'I would do anything to protect my family.' She walked to the door. 'You have been warned.'

Finally Hammond showed up. My client. 'You're not doing very well, are you, Joshua?' he said. 'Uncle Claude is still going round murdering people.'

'But why should Claude kill Olivia?'

'Because she found out that he paid her father to switch the snakes.'

'How?'

'She found a letter.'

'A letter?'

'More like a confession.'

'So Claude shot her father?'

'Who else?'

Then I told him that Larry was coming down for the Texas State Steak-Eating Contest. Hammond just laughed. The fool.

The Big Texan Steak Ranch was jam-packed for the big night. The night of the Texas State Championship Steak-Eating Contest. Convoys of 'six-gun-toting waitresses' were conveying piles of raw meat to a long trestle table where they dropped them sizzling on to electric hot-plates. There was a great deal of whooping and stomping and hollering. Men wearing sashes marked 'Judge' were checking their stop-watches. Another man in a striped shirt was writing a list of names on a blackboard with spaces left blank in the 'Pounds of Steak Consumed' and 'Time Taken' columns. Hammond was the favourite to win, but Larry – a last-minute entrant – was the dark horse. There was a gasp and some giggles as Larry took his place at the table next to Hammond, for he was still wearing his outfit from the Golden Temple Natural Foods Center, the turban and the robes.

'Ready, gentlemen?' said a judge.

'Go!' screamed Miss Texas.

Immediately the men at the table bent forward and stuck into their steaks, slobbering meat and juices all over the place. At the end of the first hour Hammond and Larry had each consumed nine pounds of meat. After ninety minutes they were the only two survivors. By the beginning of the third hour Hammond was ready to concede. But Larry persuaded him to continue. He had no subtle arguments, just a gun.

'Keep eating,' he said. Gertie tried to grab Larry, but Claude held her back.

'Our pride is at stake,' he said. So we all watched as Hammond ate himself to death. His face took on a purplish hue, like a varicose vein. He could no longer speak, his tongue was too swollen. Then he was gasping for breath, vomiting, bringing up pounds of meat. Finally he sat bolt upright as a spasm passed through his body, and fell forward face down in his plate. Larry lifted his limp arm.

'The champion,' he said.

'Murderer!' screamed Gertie.

'An accident,' said Claude.

'Hammond didn't kill your sister,' Gertie shouted, 'I did!'

Very slowly Larry turned towards the Hammerheads. There were shots and poppies seemed to be growing all over Larry's robes. Then there were more shots.

By the time the cops arrived there was more dead meat on the floor than on the table. I quit. Let the cops work it out for themselves. And without a Hammerhead left to tell them what to think it would take them a long time. They were all dead, and I was glad. One of them had murdered Olivia, now it no longer mattered which. They were all guilty.

I had had a belly-full of Texas. Now I was in a hurry to go home. I took Hammond's car. I figured he owed me at least that. The hammer and sickle was swinging aimlessly in the wind as I passed through the gates for the last time. The ranch was ownerless, and there was no one left to inherit it. I turned on the car radio.

'Ladies and gentlemen,' said a voice, 'now it is midnight let us pause and give thanks that we live in the greatest country in the world. Our national anthem.'

Tell it to the Indians. I drove on through the night. There was a lot of rain. In the morning there were rainbows. I kept my foot down. I was dreaming of Los Angeles where you get Hippo Hamburgers dressed with pickles and ice-cream all in one bun.

The Creature on My Back

I have a creature on my back. It is invisible. No one knows it is there but me. It clings to my shoulders like an imp and tries to pull me to the ground. Paul Klee has written the line: 'To stand despite all possibilities to fall.' That about sums up my life. A constant struggle not to fall. In moments of despair I joke about the gravity of my situation. Naturally I can tell no one about the creature, what could I say? I envy hunchbacks, at least everyone can see the burden they carry.

I did not feel the creature climb on to my back. It was not there when I went to see the headhunter. I do not know why she is called a headhunter. She is not a hot-shot with a blow-pipe, a collector of shrunken heads, but just an agent who finds work for creative types in advertising agencies. She had landed me a two-week job writing the new campaign for Aphrodite – you know, the soap that put Aphro into Aphrodisiac. She was feeding chocolate drops to the Pekinese that was curled like a caddie above her crotch. Her scarlet lips smiled. She flattered me, but I too was insincere. Once when her dog was ill I telephoned to inquire after its health.

Aphrodite is manufactured by a multi-national giant, Player & Gamble. Player & Gamble is run like a holy order; equally concerned with converting the masses and preserving its own mysteries. Before I was allowed to work on their product I was compelled to take certain oaths. I was also handed a document entitled 'Player & Gamble Security Requirements'. It contained a brief prolegomenon on the necessity of security, followed by a series of commandments. 1. Thou shalt treat all documents from the originator as secret. 2. Thou shalt speak in a mutually understandable code when discussing P&G business over the telephone. 3. Thou shalt not talk of P&G in public places. Etcetera. Then there were the parables, telling of men led astray by 'strangers', 'reporters', 'intruders', 'men in dark glasses', 'seductresses' and other agents of the Great Competitor. But I was not troubled. The new campaign became a great success.

However, the success did nothing for Sarah. Sarah is my wife. Poor Sarah was having a bad time. Late one night she came into my study.

'Well,' she said, 'it seems that I have been going through a very real emotional crisis.'

I didn't take her seriously, which was a mistake.

'There is no such state as "very real",' I said, 'something is either real or it isn't.'

'Jesus,' she said.

'Further,' I said, 'to whom does "it seem"? I bet you wouldn't have known a thing about it if good Dr Eggplant hadn't winkled out this "emotional crisis".'

'His name is Dr Eckhardt,' she said. She was grim-faced, white, breathing hard. None of them good signs.

'Well,' I said, 'it seems to me that these visits to Dr Eckhardt are doing you no good at all.'

I had gone too far.

'JESUS CHRIST!' Sarah screamed. 'I walk in and tell you I've practically had a nervous breakdown and all you do is give me literary criticism. All right, my use of language may not satisfy your precious New Critics, but I'm not talking about some book, I'm talking about me. I mean real life. I MEAN, DO I HAVE TO EXPRESS MY FEELINGS IN POETIC FORM BEFORE YOU'LL TAKE ANY NOTICE? Right! I'll tell you exactly what I'm feeling now, as precisely as possible. FUCK YOU!'

She slammed the door. The front door also slammed.

An hour later, when I was becoming frantic with worry, she returned. I apologized. We discussed Dr Eckhardt's findings seriously.

'Dr Eckhardt says,' she said, 'that my mind is stalling on a one-way track. It seems that this is messing up everything; it means that I am only functioning at one-third effectiveness.'

Of course I knew what the real problem was. Sarah's shoulder was not wept upon. Too much of my life was hidden, even from Sarah. This was my fault, but I could not correct it. We had talked it over many times, my self-sufficiency.

'So what remedy does the doctor recommend?' I asked.

'He doesn't know yet,' she said. 'He wants me to see him more often.'

Without warning my heart swelled like a balloon. In truth, I was terrified of losing Sarah. Then the words came into my mind. I forced myself to voice them.

'Sarah,' I said, 'let's have a baby.'

Sarah said she must ask Dr Eckhardt first.

He advised her to wait, explained that what she required was an egocentric not a concentric solution. He suggested that rather than have a baby she should experiment with infidelity. He said that it would do her more good than having a baby. Why? Because if she slept around she could choose her role, examine her options dispassionately, and control her emotions, letting them flow outward only when she decided. Thus growing emotionally self-sufficient.

'That's what you want, isn't it?' he said.

'I think so,' said Sarah.

He told her that she must decide.

Sarah sat in his office, looking glum. She wasn't sure if she was ready to have a baby, but Dr Eckhardt's alternative was unattractive.

'I'll tell you what,' said the doctor, 'as a compromise try acting.'

By coincidence they were planning the Christmas show at Sarah's school (Sarah being a teacher of history at Edgebrook High, a progressive establishment). After weeks of impassioned discussion, hours of self-analysis, careful examination of how the play would affect the teacher–kid relationship they threw out the classics and plumped instead for Picasso's *Four Girls*. They were thrilled with the interdisciplinary nature of this, an opportunity to draw together the art and drama departments. The only serious objection came from some of the more conservative members of staff.

'Do you realize,' they said, 'that the characters are naked most of the play?'

This was hotly debated, but on a democratic vote the radicals prevailed. A motion by some militant women teachers that two of the girls should be played by boys was also carried.

'To force the kids to re-evaluate their respective roles in society.'

Casting did not take long. Sarah got her part by default. No one else wanted it.

'I have to slaughter a goat and drink its blood while I'm starkers,' explained Sarah. 'Dr Eckhardt is delighted.'

Body-stockings were *de rigueur* during rehearsals. 'To make sure you feel really naked on the night,' said the director.

Unlike Dr Eckhardt I had misgivings. 'Do you think this is the sort of thing the Head of History should be doing?' I asked. But I needn't have worried.

The press got hold of the story. WOMEN TEACHERS TO APPEAR NAKED WITH BOYS IN PICASSO SEX SHOW. There was a scandal. The production was killed.

'That's a relief,' confessed Sarah.

She gets pregnant instead.

Lisa is the first person we tell. We are spending the evening with Lisa and Robin. Cross-legged on their floor watching television. Robin wrote the score for the Aphrodite commercial, a moody moog background to our lathered lady in the shower. So the pair of us sit; he a musician of some standing, having written for the Canadian National Ballet, but wanting to be a rock 'n' roll star; me a novelist with sales below 1000, wanting to be as famous as Leonard Cohen; getting kudos from a soap commercial. Lisa accuses us both of exploiting women. She shakes her shapely head; her silver earrings shiver. A long man with an erect penis hangs from her left lobe, from her right dangles a woman with a swollen belly. Woman's fate. Lisa's fate.

Then Sarah announces, 'I'm pregnant.'

There is a knock at the door. Enter Helga and Ron. Helga is Robin's former wife, Ron is his best friend, best-man at their wedding. Ron is carrying a young boy, asleep in his arms; the son of Robin and Helga. He is put quietly into the bedroom which already contain's Eve and Mai, Lisa's daughters by Robin and her former husband. A couple of joints are lit up and passed around. Wine is poured. A wind blowing off Lake Ontario rattles the bamboo blinds and rustles the leaves of the avocado plants that stand on the window sills. We get very stoned.

'Do you know,' said Lisa to Sarah, 'when you said you were pregnant I didn't know whether to congratulate you or tell you the name of a good abortionist.'

'Oh,' says Sarah, 'we definitely want it.'

'Abortion is such an ugly word,' says Helga, 'though termination of pregnancy isn't any better.'

'I know a terrible story about an abortionist,' says Ron, 'do you want to hear it?'

'Oh, yes!'

'Well, up in Catholic Quebec,' begins Ron, 'where a lot of people are still uptight about women – you know the French – abortions are not so readily available. I had this friend, a real nice lady, who got herself with child. The father didn't want to know about it. She can't turn to her family. Very upright. So she asks me for help. I find out the name of a woman who does douches, an old French woman who lives on a farm in the middle of nowhere. Batiscan, that's the place. We go there, one beautiful mid-winter day. It doesn't take long. Walking away I notice drops of blood on the snow. Very dark blood. The miscarriage was beginning. Twenty hours too early. Why am I telling you this? It's a horrible story. The girl died. Had a haemorrhage and bled to death. Shit! I wish I'd kept my mouth shut!'

Then the soap commercial reappears on the television. It makes us giggle. Even Ron who is crying and giggling at the same time.

Next morning something odd occurs while I am leafing through the newspaper. I become convinced that someone else is looking at it over my shoulder. I even know what article is being read. A report concerning the burial in Israel of two bars of soap. Made by the Nazis out of human fats. Sarah is being sick in the bathroom, I taste vomit in my mouth too, and feel a sudden spasm of pain between my shoulder blades, an embryonic kick in the back. What a grotesque spectacle that funeral must have been! What a metaphor for the human condition! I thank God I didn't know about this last night. Or I might have blurted it out like Ron's story of the dead girl. We would have invented a commercial for the soap. We would have giggled. In the bathroom I hear Sarah rinsing her mouth and washing her hands. If the Nazis had had their way she could be washing her hands with the mortal remains of Sigmund Freud.

When my pay from Player & Gamble arrives we decide to take a trip. To spend Easter in Quebec. We take the Turbo to Montreal. The woman in the seat behind starts to smoke a cigarette just as the train pulls out of the station. I turn around and tell her she's in a no-smoking section. The woman looks amazed. Without a word she gets up and walks away. Only the smoke remains, hovering like a ghost over her empty seat. We pick up speed as we skim through the townships of Oshawa and Nepanee. We flit through forests of pine and silver birch. Everywhere the snow is melting, so that the land-scape looks like a half-finished painting. After Kingstown we follow the St Lawrence north-east on its course to Montreal.

Vieux Montreal is deserted in the icy drizzle of early Saturday morning. There are many antique shops full of objects from the back-country; especially expertly carved duck decoys. The fashion stores fill their windows with lady decoys. Sarah is finally attracted by one displaying a bright red dress. Inside the couturière has lifeless blonde hair and a lop-sided face. She is enormously tall. Sarah asks the price of the dress and when she exclaims it's way too much the lady drops the price by twenty dollars. Still too expensive, but Sarah decides to try it on. I watch her legs grow naked beneath the wooden door of the cubicle; and I am reminded of the shower scene in the soap commercial. Unexpectedly I feel a sudden fear of separation from Sarah.

I am beckoned. I see that Sarah has on a clinging dress made of some velvety material. Its main feature is the way it is cut in the front to show off the greater part of her tits. If she leaned forward you could see her nipples. The neckline is not a traditional V but open-ended so that the whole of her belly is also on show as though prepared for surgery. The woman is smiling horribly at me.

'It's a bit revealing, isn't it?' asks Sarah.

'There's a modesty flap you can sew on the front,' says the lady, 'most people do.'

'I don't think so,' says Sarah, 'it's not for me.'

'It fits you like a glove,' says the woman. 'I'll let you have it for thirty-five dollars.'

I am no longer rational. I will be upset if Sarah buys the dress.

'No,' she says.

'You are making a mistake,' says the lady. She is annoyed. 'I don't know why she won't buy it,' the woman says to me. 'I made her a perfectly good offer.'

I sense hostility between the shop-owner and myself, as though she blamed me for Sarah's refusal to buy.

'You didn't like that dress, did you?' says Sarah, when we are outside again.

'I hated it.'

'I can't explain, but there was something creepy about that shop,' says Sarah, 'that woman, she reminded me of a witch from Grimms' fairy-tales.'

Or a wardress from a concentration camp.

We rent a car and drive out into the country for dinner. A note outside the restaurant reads: 'After 6.00 pm we appreciate gentlemen wearing jackets and ties.' That sort of place. We are seated beside a picture window. Beyond Lake Massawippi is frozen and floodlit, a sea of glass. It is a big dining room, but there are no other diners. Loudspeakers hang from the wooden beams.

'What is the music?' I ask the waitress

'Strauss waltzes,' she says, 'my favourite composer.'

We order escargots to start; they come fat and juicy; they drip butter and taste of garlic. A man enters the dining-room; distinguished, wearing a jacket and tie; white-haired, ruddy-faced, blind drunk. He lurches across the room to the strains of 'The Blue Danube', bumping into tables, attempting to stay on course with the aid of chair backs. The waitress sees him, rushes over, helps him to a seat. It is clear that the waitress is fond of him.

'Would you like something to eat, doctor?' she asks.

'I'm not hungry,' he says, 'just bring me a drink.'

'Come on, Doc, you've got to eat something,' the waitress says.

'Just bring me a drink!'

She goes to the bar.

'Terrible, terrible,' mutters the doctor. 'I've had a terrible day.' He begins to moan.

We continue eating, but in the deserted dining room the doctor is impossible to ignore. 'Dr Eckhardt's ghost,' jokes Sarah.

'Terrible, terrible,' he repeats, again and again. Suddenly he pushes himself to his feet. His chair topples backwards but does not fall. 'I don't want to live any more!' he cries. He weaves a way around the wooden tables and walks sobbing out of the room. Before he vanishes I glimpse, fleetingly, the form of a homunculus clinging to his back.

We look like Lisa's earrings. Sarah's naked, belly swelling. I'm erect. Our bodies have silver linings, outlined by light from the frozen lake. Sarah gasps as I enter her, feeling an expansion of flesh in flesh. Her breath comes in pants. HHH, HHH. Like a train. Our rhythms gather speed. Up and down. Like a train. My body concentrates, my thoughts freewheel. No smoking on this train. Verboten. You must have a shower. The doctor will give you a bar of soap. It's the woman from the dress shop. Aphrodite, the soap that put Aphro into Aphrodisiac. The doctor will turn you into a bar of soap. Herr Doktor. What if he is a Nazi doctor tormented by his past? GO AWAY!

'I'm coming! I'm coming!' screams Sarah.

She jerks, shudders to a halt. Then all thoughts are mercifully sucked from my mind. Swelling. Swelling. Swell ... They say that the blood-soaked ground in Germany and Poland still cries out *in memoriam*. Here in Canada our only echoes from the past are visual, immediate, reflections. My favourite building in Toronto stands on the corner of York Street, a skyscraper that's like a giant mirror; looking as though a lake had been taken, poured into a rectangular receptacle, squared off, then placed in a vertical plane. Usually it is full of blue sky and puffs of cloud. Canada seems to have absorbed nothing; all thoughts, all feelings bounce off frozen surfaces and vanish in the unpolluted air.

On a back-country road heading north to Quebec. Driving through a peaceful valley. The dark pines on the hilltops give the sky a ragged edge. The air is luminous, the snow tinted rose-red by the sun, all dramatized by the fathomless cobalt sky. The bellies of the drifting clouds shine as their shadows cross the fields of snow. We are looking forward to our dinner in Quebec. Sarah says something, but I have no chance to reply. My head is suddenly jerked back, my fingers loosen their grip on the steering-wheel, and the car runs out of control. It swerves left across the road. I react instinctively; I pull the car back towards the right. For an instant I think I've got it under control. But the car hits black ice and I can't hold it.

'We're going!' I yell. I'm not thinking any more. I put my arm around Sarah, shielding her. The other hand's still on the wheel but I can't do anything now. We shoot off the road at some crazy angle and for a second we're in the air. We tilt towards Sarah's side, but I've got her tight. Then there's a thump and we hit the ground and stop.

Dead silence.

'Sarah?' No reply. 'SARAH?'

'I'm okay,' she whispers. I put my hand on her belly. 'That's all right, too,' she says.

We blame the ice. The hook from the tow-truck bites into the car and heaves us back on to the road. No damage, not even a scratch. I do not tell Sarah that the creature on my back has tried to kill us. We dine in Quebec.

We breakfast at a café called Le Gaulois, among intellectual Quebecois. The man at the next table eats his fried egg in an ostentatious manner; he balances the unbroken yolk on his fork and takes it in one mouthful. Tiny yellow bubbles appear on his lips. We must hurry. The fast-flowing St Lawrence is filled with ice floes. It has been snowing all morning. Already there have been many accidents; cars colliding, unable to stop at crossroads. On the outskirts of Quebec I must make a decision: whether to stay north and go down to Montreal on Route 138, or to take the Trans-Canada Highway, south of the river.

'We'll start off on 138,' I say, 'but if the snow gets worse we'll cross to the Trans-Canada at Trois Rivières.'

It gets much worse. The snow is no longer coming down in flakes, but rather in thin pencil lines, drawn horizontal by the wind, as though it were trying to fill in all the space around us with white. We are travelling in convoy now, a line of cars trying to follow the curve of the road (which, in turn, must be following the indentations of the river, lost in white) going slower and slower with each mile. We tick off the miles we do this way; the signposts to Trois Rivières are regular; they appear every two miles: 30 to go, 28, 26, 24. We're passing them every ten minutes or so. All we have to do is keep this up.

But the weather isn't getting any better. 'The blizzard, which came in last night from the Great Lakes states has already dumped a foot of snow on Montreal, and as yet shows no sign of abating,' says the man on the car radio. So we've been driving into the blizzard all day! 'Watch out for "white-outs",' warns the man. What? On an exposed flank of a curve in the road, with the wind blowing directly at us from across the river a 'white-out' is defined; the car is suddenly immersed in snow, swept over by a wave of white nothingness which hits the windshield with a splat. At about four in the afternoon we pass the 22-mile marker. The weather continues to worsen; even without 'white-outs' the visibility is practically nil. Sarah is very tense. We cross the Petite Rivière Batiscan. There are huge drifts on either side of the road. Snow is blowing wildly off the tops. Not only must I keep the car going down this narrow alley between the banks of snow, avoiding abandoned trucks, without thinking about oncoming traffic, but now I've got to do it blindfold. It is as if the creature on my back has expanded to fill the whole world, and it is this shrieking banshee of a world that I am fighting as I wrestle with the steering-wheel. Finally, blinded, I drive straight into a drift. We're stuck.

'What shall we do?' says Sarah.

I haven't a clue.

Between gusts of wind I can make out a house about one hundred yards to our right, and I think I can see someone moving about in there. We remain where we are until it begins to get dark, expecting rescue; but no one comes, nor any snow ploughs. The car is almost buried; we must leave. We can just open my door wide enough for us to squeeze out. We have decided to make for the house. Beyond the door is bedlam. The wind is so loud we cannot speak; it rushes at us like an animal, clawing us with snow. Given the chance it would rip our clothes and our bodies too. We clamber to the top of the drift so that we are on a level with the car roof, and we begin to walk in the direction of the house. We see it as a flickering light. In seconds we're soaked. Already we're panting. Snow is hurled non-stop against us, icy air flies up our nostrils. It is difficult to breathe.

The light has almost gone from the day. More, the known world has been obliterated as utterly as at Pompeii. Through the gloom we can see the house glimmering, the only certain fixture in the landscape. I hold Sarah tight. Twice the creature tries to take her from me as she is sucked into the soft snow; twice I pull her back. The snow is deepest here, the high drifts around the house, but now we're past them too, slipping down towards the back door of the place. Sanctuary.

We can smell wood smoke, a wonderful smell.

An old man opens the door. Dressed in a faded blue French peasant smock. He fusses around us, concerned to see that we don't drip on the linoleum. A fat woman (about the right age to be his daughter) takes our coats and hats and hangs them near the stove. She has a few words of English.

'Welcome,' she says. 'Please sit down with the others.' She beckons us through the cheerful kitchen with its great wood-burning stove into the L-shaped living-room.

The ancient has already returned, sitting in his rocking-chair, listening to the radio. We are introduced to the woman's husband, a Gallic type; his shoulders poised permanently on the point of a shrug. At the table half a dozen other refugees from the storm sit drinking gin. I tick off the characters: the smooth travelling salesman, the joker with the goatee beard, his silent resentful wife, a pretty girl with a diamond engagement ring, an unrelated moody youth who clenches his fists in response to some inner tension, the old lady with the lap dog. Eight strangers trapped by the raging blizzard. A favourite movie plot.

Actually there is an old movie on the television in the other part of the room which no one is watching, a Randolph Scott yarn dubbed into French. Above the set, pinned to the wall, is Christ crucified. A bookcase is filled with religious texts, mainly on Catholicism. At the end of the L stands a piano upon which rests a coloured photograph of a young girl in nurse's uniform; I assume it is of the woman's daughter, but upon closer inspection it seems altogether too old-fashioned. We find the bathroom, a doorless cubicle in the couple's bedroom, containing both toilet and sink. The bedroom is gloomy; there is another cross on the wall and plastic flowers in vases on the dressing-table, alongside many pills for the symptoms of old age. Conversation continues at the table. Only the boy has departed, gone around the corner to watch the cowboy film.

'We did not expect the snow,' says the farmer in French, 'we were planning to tap our maple trees today. But now the sap has frozen again.'

I wander back to the television. The commercials are on; would you believe it, it's Aphrodite again! The kid seems to fancy the girl in the shower. I do not like the look of him, those clenched fists; I fear that later, in the night, he will try to rape Sarah.

We sleep fully clothed on the sofa. We are not disturbed. But at dawn Sarah rises and rushes to the cubicle in the bedroom where she is sick several times. Later the farmer's wife looks carefully into her pale face and says, 'Are you sure you came here by accident, my dear, you weren't looking for me, were you?' She stares at me and says, 'Are you the father?'

I am speechless. Where are we? Then I remember. BATISCAN. Is it possible? Have we landed up with the abortionist who killed Ron's friend? I calm down, no need to be over-dramatic. This woman is not evil; most probably she thinks she is doing us a kindness, thinks we need coaxing before we'll admit why we have come. But how can she be an abortionist? She is Catholic.

'It is very clean here,' says the woman, opening the bedroom door for our inspection, showing us the cubicle with its spotless sink and the two bars of soap. 'There is no danger, I used to be a nurse.'

I am helpless, the creature on my back has its hands firmly clasped over my mouth.

'Come into the cubicle, my dear,' she says to Sarah, 'and let me examine you.'

I cry out, 'Don't go!' but the words are soundless. I cannot help Sarah.

'You're mistaken,' says Sarah, 'I want the baby.'

As Sarah's belly grows so do my struggles with the creature on my back. I wrestle with it constantly. In the mornings it attempts to hold me to the bed. During the day it tries to throw me to the ground. Even at nights I am not free. I dream that I am pinned to the floor and must watch helpless while a bloody embryo is torn from Sarah's open belly. The thing is made of soap. At last I confide in Sarah. But the confession does not lift the weight from my shoulders. So Sarah suggests that I see her shrink. Next I tell Dr Eckhardt about the creature on my back. He walks around me.

'I can see nothing,' he says.

'It is there, none the less,' I say.

'Well, you are a *mensh*, you know life is a struggle,' says Dr Eckhardt, 'there is a Yiddish saying: "Shoulders are from God, and burdens too".'

'Why my shoulders?' I ask.

'Listen,' says Dr Eckhardt, 'you are lucky. You have a creature on your back. Such things are not common in Canada. It may yet go away. As for myself, I have a number on my arm. A souvenir of Europe.'

Among School Children

Since our flat lacks a phone I have to do the inviting from the booth near Wardour Street. As I wait to make the calls a girl approaches me and says, 'Piss off, mister, this is my patch.' Inside the booth I spread out the two-penny pieces on the spines of the directories and I begin.

'Hello,' I say, 'Sophie and I are getting married next Wednesday. There's a party afterwards at our place. Can you come?' I notice as I talk that the windows are covered with obscene graffiti, so that Soho is overlaid with CUNTS scribbled crudely, and the dialling codes are obscured by the calling cards of prostitutes, one of whom is also named Sophie. I consider phoning this vulgar variant, but I would not desert Sophie for such an ape of love. I get plenty of opportunities in my job, and take none of them.

I am a photographer by trade, and even now I am shocked by what girls will do in front of my camera, those faceless girls who touch themselves on my say-so. More than once as I focus down on the pressed curls of pubic hair that cling to the brownish folds of flesh held apart for my benefit I am reminded of a reptilian eye, and the musky smell that fills my nostrils and my mouth seems entirely appropriate.

Our wedding goes off without a hitch, but the party turns out to be a disaster. Someone asks me if Sophie has any faults.

'Only one,' I say, 'she will leave the bath full of her pubic hair. And when she shaves her legs . . .'

Hearing that Sophie blows up. 'You fastidious little worm!' she cries. And so we have the first row of our married life. However, that is but the prelude to the real disaster.

Around midnight our clapped out lavatory backfires. And a guest emerges, somewhat flushed, pursued by a torrent of waterborne shit. My closest friends stay to help with the cleaning up, everyone else goes home. Sophie locks herself in the bedroom.

'Best to take things like this philosophically,' I am advised. Exactly.

Plato thought this world but a shadow of some better substance, but that is only half the truth. For this world of ours rests on a bed of shit. And every so often it breaks through.

Sophie continues to refuse to speak to me. So I retire to my darkroom. I am no artist, no creator, merely limited by my camera to mimesis, to producing shadows of shadows; even so I still feel a thrill when the image first appears on the Kodak paper suspended in the developer. Somehow the finished prints never quite live up to this promise. Thus I spend my wedding night; reviving images of naked girls; first grains, then ghosts, then full-bodied women, a host of succubae.

Nevertheless, the first year of our marriage is happy. We even dine in civilized fashion with my parents. Indeed, every time we visit their house my mother insists upon giving Sophie a dress or a skirt or a jumper that she claims no longer fits. By our second anniversary Sophie seems to be dressing exclusively in my mother's clothes. One night, as we embrace and I begin to unbutton Sophie's blouse, it occurs to me that, in close-up, the floral-pattern blouse could as well be on my mother to whom it once belonged. Immediately my erection goes spineless. From that moment fucking Sophie becomes a problem; in fact I can only function at all if the conditions are exactly right. To convince me that she is not my mother Sophie has to act the whore; I demand utter wantonness. Sophie, fortunately, is very patient; the result of years as a teacher. Which reminds me of one of my more curious assignments; shooting the illustrations for a limited edition of the Yeats poem, 'Among School Children'. On the quiet, without parental permission, young girls are brought to my studio and photographed in the nude; dreadful creatures who make dirty jokes about the Vaseline I rub on my lens and pout like they're posing for David Hamilton. 'Jailbait', my assistant calls them, and lays them one after another. What they need is a good wallop or a harsh reproof. 'Solider Aristotle played the taws,' says Yeats, 'upon the bottom of a king of kings.' So Sophie kneels naked before our bed, at my insistence, arms outstretched legs splayed so that her bottom is open and defenceless. As I hit her with lochgelly taws I chant from 'Among School Children' until I gob helplessly over her bent back at the lines, 'Plato thought nature but a spume that plays upon a ghostly paradigm of things.'

Come to think of it, there is another habit of Sophie's that drives me mad, which must come from all the teaching she does; we have some friends who have two daughters, whom Sophie will never call by name but always 'girls'. One of them is called Cathy.

It is high summer, the third summer of our marriage. We are in the northern town of Y—, looking after Cathy and her sister while the parents holiday in Venice. The sunshine is brilliant, Devochka, white-walled and Georgian, stands illuminated amid lawns of shimmering green; Cathy and sister, both in white, romp with Podger, offspring of an Old English Sheepdog and an unknown tramp who led the silly bitch up the garden path. The scent of flowers hangs heavy, bees fill the foxgloves. Sophie and I sit on wicker chairs, sipping gin-and-tonics, watching the girls play. Cathy's hair is dark and short, strands clinging to her damp forehead, her eyes are brown and wide. She is ten years and eleven months; of an age but a world apart from the girls in my studio; not a little but a 'liddell' girl. When she smiles her lips reveal her secret; they bud like those of Alice Liddell, photographed ages ago by the perspiring Reverend Charles Lutwidge Dodgson. As Cathy flickers across the lawn she continually brings to mind fading images from old albums; Dymphna Ellis, dreamy Amy Hughes and the incredible Irene Macdonald who (at the age of eight or nine) has the eyes and mouth of an Eastern courtesan, all of whom wrung groans from poor tormented Dodgson. Then the summer light grows umbral, and Cathy's bare arms and legs glow sepia from woody reflections. Evocative new images develop; for example, Rejlander's astonishing photographs of little girls in the most provocative poses, bare tantalizing things, artfully lit to give a heart-rending illusion of vitality. Of course such things are not real. However, sometimes, looking at Cathy, the image and the reality appear to coincide; her knife-edge innocence seems immortal, tangible; she exists without implication of a future life. She is the promise that all women break when they assume roles as lovers, virgins, wives and mothers; she is the blueprint which her growth will betray. But her present quality cannot be possessed; that is the paradox that frustrates, for any act of possession will be the act of destruction. To follow the desires that Cathy excites will render her immaculate no longer, for she will be made self-conscious. My passion for Cathy must remain platonic. Instead I shadow her through the garden, round the house, with my loaded camera; trying to capture her spirit.

Each morning I wake full of hope and lie supine staring at the ceiling to watch the chandelier fill with rainbows as the sun rises. Sophie sleeps on for an hour or so longer and sometimes I examine her face and those parts of her body exposed by the eiderdown. My love for Sophie has changed, I no longer want to possess her; recently our love-making has become an elaborate disguise for masturbation. Actually we have not touched one another since our arrival at Devochka, and I feel much refreshed. After getting up we take turns to visit the water closet, a special feature of this remarkable house; it consists of a bowl of white porcelain decorated with blue laurels, encased in a frame and seat of ruddy mahogany; soon such visits are known as 'resting on your laurels'. At breakfast as usual Cathy says, 'What shall we do today?'

Today we plan to take the girls to Haworth. In our different ways both Sophie and I have connections with Emily Brontë, erstwhile inhabitant of Haworth Parsonage; Sophie, because she teaches *Wuthering Heights* for the English Literature 'A' Level; myself, because I once had to shoot a lurid photograph of a dark man whipping a naked girl for a paperback edition billed as 'the strangest love story ever told'. Cathy and her sister loll in the back of the car with Podger between them, giggling at some secret joke, while Sophie sits beside me with the map. The way through the northern moorland is desolate and exciting, mist floats over the greyish-green ground and above the patches of purple heather that look like bruises, such a change from the dazzling clarity of the preceding days. Shadows solidify into boulders; shapes become grazing ponies. Sophie and Cathy's sister play at guessing what other shapes will become, but Cathy sits silently and her eyes stay fixed gazing out over the wilderness.

The Parsonage stands at the end of a steep and cobbled main street. Half-way up this street is a sweet shop, which boasts of its home-made produce. The owner, a fat man with a black moustache and greasy hair, wears a transparent plastic glove to dip his sinister hand into the fruit fudge and the rum truffles, the same perfumed hand with which, to my disgust, he pats the cheek of Cathy, who smiles like a little flirt. Most of the visitors to the Parsonage seem to be old ladies satisfied to see a slipper 'said to have fitted Emily Brontë's foot', unconscious of the tragic paradoxes with which she struggled, not hearing an echo of Heathcliff's dreadful cry, 'I could almost see her, and yet I could not!' Poor Heathcliff, tortured by the cternal absence of Catherine, who yet remained close enough to haunt him. Standing alone, dreaming in the play-room with its quietened toys and pencil drawings on the cream walls, Cathy's sudden appearance makes me jump.

'Those toys look fun,' says Cathy, 'whose were they?'

'Emily Brontë's,' I say. 'Have you heard of her?'

'Oh, yes,' says Cathy, 'she wrote *Wuthering Heights*.'

'Have you read it?' I ask.

'Oh, no,' says Cathy, 'it's much too grown-up for me.'

In Plato's *Symposium* Aristophanes proposes that love is 'the desire and pursuit of the whole'. Hence Heathcliff's mania to be reunited, literally, with his Catherine. Hence also my obsession with Cathy. I am convinced that I can be made whole by Cathy, but I have no idea how to go about this reunification.

We eat by candlelight in the middle of the huge dining room, our intimacy emphasized by the space and the gathering darkness beyond our illuminated circle. We all drink white wine which sparkles in tall crystal glasses. Cathy insists upon finishing off a whole glass.

And so we sit until Sophie says, 'Come on, girls, you must be dog-tired, it's time for bed.'

Podger yawns under the table. Cathy rises, claims to be drunk, giggles and falls flat on her back; whereupon her frock of corn-flowers, purchased at a jumble sale, obeys its own gravity and falls up her legs, showing off her creamy panties which are caught tight between the cheeks of her bum. Her older sister blushes. Later Sophie returns and says, 'They want you to say goodnight to them.' So I visit their bedroom and kiss Cathy and her sister and Cathy's teddy-bear. In the lounge Sophie is already reclining on the settee, right hand limp among the tassels, so I take my place in the armchair opposite, and we begin to talk. I don't know if it is because of the wine but gradually my mind withdraws from the conversation and soon Sophie is talking to herself. I watch her alter and realter her position, as if she were a model posing for one of my photographic sessions; first she rests her arm above her head, her hand in her hair, revealing that smooth, sweeping con-cavity between the soft uppers of her arm and the bare skin of her side; then she bends towards me so that her jumper falls free of her body and her breasts are exposed. She is saying something which I do not catch. Suddenly Sophie jumps up.

'I saw the way you looked at Cathy's crotch,' she says. I deny it. 'Wouldn't you prefer mine?' she says, pulling down her skirt and pants. 'Look,' she says, pointing a moist finger at my face, 'it wants you.'

'What are you, a tart?' I shout.

'No, I'm your wife,' cries Sophie, 'and I want you to fuck me!'

'I'm taking Podger for a walk,' I say. I breathe in the night air. I know that Sophie is trapped in a role of my making, one which I now realize fills me with disgust.

Next morning Cathy says, 'Why is Sophie in such a bad mood?'

'I'm not,' says Sophie. And she insists upon preparing breakfast for us all.

I can tell by the way her shoulder blades pull together as she slices the bread that she is fighting her anger and the humiliating knowledge that she is jealous of Cathy. Once again the sun blazes in a vacant blue sky as we tour the abbey ruins of Rievaulx and Fountains, trying to recreate the original vision from the standing foundations, for these foundations have become our blue prints. At Fountains Abbey Cathy sinks into the river up to the hem of her dress which subsequently clings to her knees as she runs up and down the wooded inclines. The sun is setting now and beams of light pour through the gaping holes in the ruined walls, like a projector ray through film, so that I am tempted to search the eastern sky for images from the Abbey's past, as if we were at a drive-in movie. The light also shines through Cathy's dress, outlining her body, filling me with such a longing I almost groan. But a longing for what? Aristophanes adds in the *Symposium*, 'It is clear that the soul of each (lover) has some other longing which it cannot express, but can only surmise and obscurely hint at.' A fat lot of good that does me, my craving is such that if I get no relief I fear what might happen.

'Look what I can do!' yells Cathy, pointing to a stone that goes skimming over the surface of the water, as flighty as her affection for me.

The ruins of Bolton Abbey are on a long sweep of parkland, which unrolls down towards a broad river, at which black and white cows with lengthening shadows are drinking. I wander off to explore the remains by myself, and feel slightly uneasy to be alone in that spiritual place at twilight. Much of the chapel is still intact, and as I approach the impressive portico, quietly over the stone pavement, I am startled to hear the sound of an organ rising from the darkness within; the notes, made of wind and air, are discordant and melancholy. Inside I can just make out a small boy fiddling at the keyboard, and as I stare into the gloom I feel a small cold hand slip into mine.

'I don't like to be alone in the dark,' whispers Cathy, 'can I hold your hand?' Her fingers tickle my palm.

Outside the first stars are shining. Cathy's sister wants to know if it is true that some of the stars we can see are no longer there.

'Yes, dear,' says Sophie, 'because they are so far away their light takes a long time to reach us, longer than their lives.' To be nothing more than light, like Alice Liddell and those other Victorian girls, images left behind of a single moment of perfection.

I am dreading the night, sure that once more Sophie will try to force me into love-making. I do not see how I can face it, tormented as I am by Cathy. But I am wrong, Sophie simply announces that when we return to London she is going to leave me. She switches out the light. But I cannot sleep. Hours later I am roused from an unsatisfactory doze by the sound of Podger barking. I go downstairs and find the dog shivering from a nightmare. I stroke him till he relaxes once more. Then I listen to the silence of the sleeping house and I am filled with disquiet. Returning upstairs I notice that the bathroom light is on; inside stands Cathy, oblivious of my presence. Now I have seen all manner of naked women, but none of them has ever moved me as I am by the sight of Cathy standing there, slowly lifting her flannel nightgown over her head. Her body shines in the neon light; two Cathies; herself and her image in the looking-glass. The first begins to examine the second, and I do likewise and see in her body the embryo of all my desires; around her breasts there is a barely perceptible swelling, a slight pinkish flush, and below her belly are her labial palps, still uncovered, oh my palpitating heart. And watching I weep, because I know that I will never be able to fix that image in the mirror.

My desires at last take concrete form, I have an erection that cannot be denied. Of course I consider approaching Cathy, but apart from anything else I am not certain how to go about such things with a prepubescent girl. So I return reluctantly to the bedroom. Once behind the closed door I pull the quilt off Sophie and ponder her naked body.

At length I wake her and say, 'Sophie, if you shave off all your pubic hair I'll fuck you.'

'Piss off, mister,' she says, 'I'm not removing my patch for you.'
So I hit her until she is too weak to put up any resistance; then I
straddle her and with a pair of nail scissors snip off her pubic hair to
the roots. The stubble looks so unsightly that Sophie agrees to
remove it with the Veeto cream that she now uses on her legs. She
rubs it over the grey triangle, between her legs and even in her anus.

'So you've turned out to be a poofter like Ruskin,' says Sophie.

'I can't explain,' I say, 'just do it, please.'

'It burns like hell,' says Sophie.

'I'm sorry,' I say. But eventually the inflammation subsides and
Sophie's belly is completely smooth.

'Let me look at you,' I say.

Sophie, also curious, examines herself in the mirror. For a second
I see in her reflection the image of Cathy. 'And thereupon my heart
is driven wild: she stands before me as a living child.'

Titillatio

Bedded in her double divan wedded Bella, miles away, is suddenly robbed of her senses and instinctively buttock-shoves husband
Quentin deeper inside of her, responding at last to his pumping with
helpless spasms of her own until, with a final cry of 'I'm coming!'
she reaches her climax.

'How do you feel?' asks Quentin.

'Good,' says Bella, yawning, and promptly falling asleep. Quentin,
too, after wiping himself with a Kleenex, nods off.

Bella, next morning, hears the phone ring. She picks up the
receiver.

'What are you doing?' the other end asks.

'I am writing about ethics,' she replies.

'I don't know much about ethics,' the man says, 'but I know what
I like.' This remark is somewhat ingenuous, since the speaker (a
famous Professor of Philosophy) is in fact the supervisor of Bella's
thesis.

'And what do you like?' whispers Bella, assuming a familiar role.

'Bathing you,' he answers, 'feeling your soap-smooth skin, smelling
a mixture of you and the talc.'

Bella smiles. He isn't like that, really. And knowing him well, as
she does, she recognizes that he is excited and that he is, however
obscure the origin of his impulse, attempting to involve her in the
same experience. She knows exactly what he wants.

'Tonight,' she whispers.

'Tonight,' he agrees.

Do not be misled into thinking that Bella is whispering for the
sake of any extraneous erotic effect, on the contrary it is a necessary
precaution, because her eldest daughter (aged twelve) is now standing
in the doorway behind her, requiring maternal attention.

The husband, as is often the case, knows nothing about the true
nature of his wife's relationship with her academic mentor. There is,
moreover, an especial irony in his situation; for it was he who finally

persuaded Bella to take her Masters degree, and who felt the greatest pride in her achievement when she was invited to complete her doctorate. Such is the bad luck of a husband who encourages his wife to be, simultaneously, a Master of Arts and the mistress of an ageing Professor of Philosophy. But if we say that Quentin is a builder of bridges we are not making fun of the cuckold, we are talking about his occupation. Quentin's achievements at linking opposite banks of a river filled his doting, spoiling mother with a perverse joy; for had her own husband (Quentin's father) not died beside the River Kwai? This suggestion of son-succeeding-where-father-failed gives Quentin a sense of security (expressed outwardly in the ancient sturdy home that houses his family), and in reflective moments he is wont to view his happy predicament with genial satisfaction. Nor does the smile leave his fond face when his younger daughter (aged eleven) comes in with the news that he has to prepare dinner tonight because Mummy has to go to an important meeting at the university.

Needless to say, the important meeting (if that is what we choose to call it) does not take place at the university, but rather in a flat rented by the prophetic Professor of Philosophy for just such occasions. The apartment is bare; a single large room containing nothing but a double bed. A key is inserted into a lock, a door opens, our illicit couple enters. Perhaps we may pause to wonder just what there is about this fifty-five-year-old professor that has so captivated his thirty-year-old student. Hair: grey, thick at sides, thin on top. Eyes: also grey, surrounded by laughter lines, underlined by bags.

'Just as a hotel receptionist is suspicious of a guest who arrives without luggage,' says the Professor, 'so you should be wary of a man without bags. He will not stay with you longer than a night.' His mouth, then, is witty and wise. His voice is generally gentle, thought it can be stern, whereupon it reveals a continental accent. He has a nose to match; large, slightly curved. His chief vanity is his assumed resemblance to Saul Bellow. We could go on, but will it make Bella's infatuation any easier to understand? Indeed, the whole affair will appear even more improbable when we reveal that, for the past few years, the Professor of Philosophy has been, more or less, impotent.

They have never made love properly. This is what generally happens: Bella undresses and lies supine on the bed, while the

Professor touches, strokes her compliant responsive flesh, slowly but clearly exciting her, until she directs his hand herself, moving her pelvis up and down, rubbing herself against his firm fingertip, stimulating her clitoris, ticklish at first, then tenser, till her orgasm comes. While Bella concentrates all of herself to this one end the Professor is, as it were, left alone with his thoughts. He remembers, with a certain degree of embarrassment, Spinoza's 'active emotions' of which joy or *hilaritas* is the chief and most vital expression of the whole personality, whereas sensuous pleasure or *titillatio* is but the automatic reaction to the local stimulation of an organ. Sometimes Bella's transports convince him that she is indeed expressing a joy that comes from her whole being, and then he allows her to deal in a like manner with his own out-of-tune organ so that, by dint of prolonged fondling, and perhaps some further oral persuasion, he too has an orgasm.

Tonight, in the flat, the Professor introduces a variation. As he makes his way, in his familiar meticulous fashion, over Bella's naked body, he gives her a running commentary.

'Here's Bella's flat belly, and down this slope, down here, between her thighs, there's a slit, covered with curly hair; you can open it up, and inside are damp, shiny folds of pinkish flesh, and now there's her smell and this little knob – shall I go on?'

'Please.'

'What will happen if I touch just here?'

'Yes, yes, yes, touch.' Bella closes her eyes and awaits the moving finger.

Afterwards, laughing with pleasure and relief, she curls up on the bed, cuddles up against her man, and begins to hum an old song, 'My Heart Belongs to Daddy'.

Bella's own father was the head waiter in a large hotel on the South Coast of England in the austere but tranquil post-war years. Her late mother, unfortunately, had artistic aspirations, which led her to desert her husband for the fading intellectual blossoms of Bloomsbury, leaving everything behind, including her daughter. But poor little Bella was not destined to spend happy hours with Papa either; after just a few months alone together he packed Bella off to London, packed his own belongings and vanished for ever, leaving his daughter with half-remembered memories of seaside walks and talks on sandy windswept beaches. Very different to serving tea to homosexual authors, wine to artists who sported velvet hats and fucked heiresses for their livelihood, and cigarettes to poets who dedicated their lives to finding a rhyme for Eliot. Quentin's mother appeared at one such soirée, as these gatherings were known, and in time Bella and Quentin were introduced. Quentin was handsome and Bella was young, well-developed, eager to learn the mysterious ways of a man with a maid. She got pregnant at the age of seventeen, and married soon after; but that is just as they wanted it because, have no doubts, they were in love. From the very beginning, Quentin was anxious that his new wife should be happy, so he initiated his dangerous policy of allowing her to make most decisions for them both. From a mere indulgence this grew into a way of life that characterized their whole relationship, until Bella became the dominant partner in the marriage, and more and more impatient with Quentin's inability to make up his mind on any subject without first consulting her.

Such is the explanation (for which Quentin searched in vain) of Bella's otherwise inexplicable behaviour on the night of their thirteenth wedding anniversary.

Quentin suggested that they dine out, Bella agreed, a baby-sitter was obtained to look after the girls. There remained only the decision about the restaurant. Although Bella kept maintaining that she couldn't care less where they ate, she took considerable trouble over her appearance, and finally emerged from the bathroom with false eyelashes, lashings of mascara, rosy cheeks and brand-new lipstick; dressed also in the long gown reserved exclusively for special events. But Quentin had no table booked, and by the time he had decided where to try it was too late to get a table anywhere; so they ended up on their thirteenth anniversary dining in the local pizza parlour. It was there, when Quentin was dallying over the wine list, that Bella had hysterics. Quentin was amazed, he couldn't understand why Bella was so upset. It never occurred to him that sometimes Bella simply wanted to have a fuss made of her, wanted to be taken out for treats; in effect, she wanted all the delights due to a favourite daughter. But this role Bella fancied for herself was constantly undermined by the presence of her own children; frequently she wondered where these two human beings could have come from, it seemed inconceivable that they could have emerged from her womb. When they were born she had refused to breast-feed either one. She was frightened by their dependence upon her; later she came to feel that the whole security of their home was founded upon a lie, for she was too weak to carry the burden of all their lives; secretly Bella longed to be dependent upon someone else. She chose the Professor of Philosophy.

Therefore, one night (soon after that disastrous thirteenth wedding anniversary) the Professor was astonished to have his flirtatious banter returned with a passion that, in a single moment, threw into question thirty-five years of self-doubt. The Professor was even more astonished when he later learned that Quentin was a most competent lover (unlike himself). But it was Quentin's very competence that worked against him; for in his love-making with Bella he neither asked for anything, nor ever needed help, so that the whole became a process of giving, for the benefit of Bella; on the other hand, with the Professor, it was Bella who gave the pleasure, Bella who sometimes made him come. You will observe, then, how unfair are the ways of the heart, for when Bella wanted to be dominated Quentin was passive, but when Quentin was active, under the sheets, between her thighs, was the very time that Bella required a sign of weakness. This is what Bella wanted: she wanted a man who was strong in the eyes of the world, but whose very strength concealed secret fallibilities, which she alone knew, which she alone could overcome.

After a final chorus of 'My Heart Belongs to Daddy' Bella looks up into the face of the Professor and, seeing acquiescence there, begins to kiss his balls and lick his penis, until she can feel upward jerks and the thing beginning to grow beneath her mouth. The Professor gazes with gratitude at this girl who will do anything for him, but he is still wise enough to know that self-gratification is, by itself, a form of bondage.

'When I am driven to an act by external stimuli or by desire, such as I now have, I am not truly free,' he reasons, 'for neither Bella's action nor my desire is rational, and so long as it remains irrational I am a slave to my passions.'

By this time his penis is very big.

'We say that we love one another, yet if love ceases to be an agent of goodness it is surely a false love, and our love threatens the happiness of five other people; no, I am certainly not free,' concludes the Professor. Simultaneously his penis stabs the air and his glans opens releasing little spurts of semen.

'Was it good?' asks Bella.

'I think so,' answers the Professor.

Bella laughs and wipes her mouth with a Kleenex.

'Why am I doing this?' wonders the Professor. 'Why am I allowing it to happen to me?'

Once, when the Professor had actually voiced these doubts to Bella she had said, 'Fuck Spinoza. Listen to Kant.'

The Professor had listened.

'Freedom is the choice you make in deciding whether or not you submit to your passion or submit to your duty,' Bella had said, 'so make up your mind, mister, passion or duty?'

But even as the Professor surrendered to his instincts he tried to discern if his affair with Bella was the result of a unique coincidence of personalities or merely a coincidence of events. Destiny or opportunity? However, none of these worries prevented him from continuing. Despite his wisdom he had no answer to his student's tongue.

'Titillatio.'

'Fellatio.'

'Spinoza.'

'Spermatozoa.'

'Kant.'

'Cunt.' She got him every time. Thus unadulterated pleasure can make a hypocrite and an adulterer of the most ethical of men.

Quentin, as we have noted, considers that he is happy, blessed with a trouble-free life; which just goes to show that men who are accustomed to scrutinizing every detail to ensure that the bridges they build will not topple are not necessarily the best judges when it comes to an assessment of the grounds upon which they base their own existence. He assumes, in his complacency, that he has constructed a secure family unit for himself, supported by foundations that are sunk deep into the love that he and Bella share. And he could have been right, had he not forgotten the simple fact that marriage is a dynamic state, and that fundamentals which were true ten years ago need no longer be in operation a decade later. Both he and Bella have developed as personalities in the time they have lived together, but their relationship has not grown, indeed it has become repressed, smothered by Quentin's feather-brained pillow of easy acquiescence.

We've already made a flippant reference to the beginnings of Quentin's career as a builder of bridges so, in fairness, we should add a few more details. For the truth of the matter is that Quentin had wanted to be an engineer from the moment he received his first Meccano set; and all the troubled years between puberty and manhood were spanned by balsa-wood replicas of the world's greatest bridges. Indeed, so good were some of the models that Quentin still displays them in his private study. He is relaxing in a leather armchair in that very room when Bella returns (so he thinks) from her university meeting.

'Hello,' she says, 'are the children in bed?'

'Hours ago,' replies Quentin, without a trace of sarcasm; although Bella is back late it does not occur to him to be annoyed.

'Did you have a good meeting?' he asks.

'I enjoyed myself,' Bella replies, truthfully.

Although, as we've disclosed, the Professor (*pace* conscience) is content in the progress of his affair with Bella, it would be a mistake to assume that he will be satisfied to let things continue the way they are. He feels, in some odd way, that it would be somehow selfish of him, egocentric, as it were, and that he ought to give pleasure as well as receive it. He is a man after all, and he considers that fifty-five is too early an age to bid farewell to his potency forever. However, as he does not understand the cause of his own impotence, indeed had been amazed to discover that he was impotent, he is quite powerless to reassert his previous prowess. Is it, he asks himself, some ill-defined punishment on his wife's behalf for all those times he had made loveless love to her, regular as clockwork, with his cock hooded like some thief in the night? Having decided that one unknowable daughter was sufficient. Is it something to do with Kant? If Bella's analysis was correct, and freedom is the choice between passion and duty, and if he had clearly decided to go along with passion, why then was his penis not acting in accordance with his will? Does it mean that he is not a free man after all, that he is, in effect, the captive of a duty he does not comprehend? Is Kant's unanswerable criterion that one should act 'as if the maxim of your actions were to become by your will law universal' putting a block on his animal instincts? The Professor of Philosophy, a rational man, is perplexed. It does not occur to him that there is something darker, less flattering, in his passion; and at the root of his impotence. So we leave him, still in two minds, once more dialling the number of his mistress.

'According to Kinsey,' says Bella to Quentin as the telephone starts to ring, 'some psychoanalysts contend that they have never had a patient who has not had incestuous relationships. Sort of kith and Kinsey. Don't worry, I'll get it.'

'What is the significance of that?' asks Quentin. But Bella is already whispering into the receiver.

'Bet you didn't know,' says Bella, returning to the conversation, 'that if unofficial American estimates are anything to go by seventy-eight per cent of all incestuous relationships are between father and daughter, while only one per cent occur between mother and son. So I'll be keeping an eye on you, Daddy.'

'Don't be daft,' says Quentin.

Over the telephone the Professor of Philosophy had invited Bella to the farewell party of one of his more eccentric graduate students; an American, shortly to be deported for possession of a small amount of cocaine. Bella, who rather liked the American, accepted at once, and now informs her husband that she will have to go out two nights hence.

The party begins quietly, and though that soon changes it does not have much effect upon the Professor and Bella who stand chatting over chalices of Spanish Burgundy, that is, until the curly American asks Bella to dance. Actually, Bella's American host was rather glad to see her arrive, gladder still to see her without her husband. Innocent, he assumes that an estrangement has occurred, and that Bella has come round to him for comfort. Needless to say, he is quite ignorant of her affair with the Professor, as his actions will testify; however anarchic, all American graduates have a highly developed sense of academic hierarchy. The music's rocking, Rolling Stones stuff, but still he holds her tight. The Professor, who has never before had any reason to doubt Bella's devotion, is suddenly seized by jealousy, a juvenile luxury, and piqued accepts a stranger's offer of a sniff of cocaine.

'They say it's an aphrodisiac, Prof,' the tempter whispers, 'but I wouldn't know about that.'

However, all that happens to the Professor is that his nose goes numb. Just as well, as it turns out.

Fifteen minutes pass and Bella remains in the American's arms, revolving like a lamb on a spit. The Professor of Philosophy, despite himself, is increasingly tormented; not only by the actual image of Bella in revolution, but also by the fearful illusion that what is being re-enacted in front of him is nothing less than the deflowering of his own daughter, long imagined. Gradually Bella and his daughter become hopelessly confused in his fogged mind and his resentment towards the American grows from simple jealousy into an insane conviction that he is deliberately mocking his quality as a lover and, worse, as a father. In other words, he feels himself provoked, and already driven thus far it only takes a trick of the light (or is he really kissing Bella?) to make him leap upon the astounded American!

'What are you doing? Vot are you doing, you bloody Yank?' screams the Professor, aiming several blows at the American.

The American, not really grasping what is going on, lashes out in self-defence and connects with the Professor's curved beak. The Professor, still in an uncontrollable fury, grabs Bella, too shocked to move of her own accord, and drags her out of the flat.

Nor do they stop until they reach the Professor's private address. Once inside, with the light on, Bella screams. Not because she is scared, but because the Professor's face is covered with blood.

'What's the matter?' asks the Professor. Thanks to the cocaine, which is acting as a sort of anaesthetic, he does not know that the American's punch has broken his nose.

Bella cleans the Professor's face with a sponge and warm water. She asks for no explanation, for she has no doubts that the Professor will give one in his own time. Instead, she smooths down his hair. She kisses him on the forehead. Then, humming, she undresses. Face-up on the bed she suddenly realizes that the events of the evening have excited her. And the Professor, also carried along by the momentum of the night, finds an erect member in his pants, a single drop glittering at the tip; overwhelmed, seized with joy, he kneels and pushes his penis between Bella's warm and palpy walls.

With a yelp of amazed pleasure Bella clasps the Professor of Philosophy, and wildly out of control thrashes her hips crying, 'Fuck me, fuck me, daddy-o!'

His last restraint vanishing with that cry the Professor gives himself over utterly to his grotesque jerks, and with great shudders comes inside Bella at last. He rolls over gasping, his cock glistening, his eyes shining and his cheeks wet from crying.

When Bella returns home, long after everyone is in bed, she creeps straight into Quentin's darkened study and, carefully lighting a safety match, sets fire to all his bridges.

However, at his own house, the Professor of Philosophy is in an entirely different mood; part remorseful, over his behaviour at the party; part terrified by his spectacular return to potency. Bella had misinterpreted his tears as tears of joy, and he hadn't the heart to disabuse her; how could he tell her that he was weeping for shame? For he had suddenly seen, quite clearly, what had caused his impotence. But at least this awareness now gives him the opportunity to regain his freedom, to re-establish the primacy of rationality over desire, to obey his all-powerful sense of duty. So he sits at his desk and writes two letters. The first is a letter of apology to the American. The second is what is called an 'anonymous letter'. It is addressed to Quentin. It informs him that, for the past year, his wife has been unfaithful. Having completed the task the Professor stands up, a free man.

He feels good.

Le Docteur Enchaîné

Ladies and gentlemen, believe me, among a certain type of girl insanity is a status symbol. You know that all men are supposed to be latent homos; well, let me tell you that all women are latent schizophrenics, but don't ask me why. There is the classic case, I could tell you, of the Nordic lass who informed me (I quote): 'I am a woman with a beautiful skin like Greta Garbo' – a real walnut if ever I saw one. Incidentally, between you and me, just as girls who have problems about dancing are called 'wallflowers', so I call girls who have problems about sex 'walnuts' (sex being the only true cause of madness as old father Freud tells us) – but I suppose you guessed that. Anyway, this poor girl honestly believed that because she articulated the sentence it was true. It is my sad duty to inform you, ladies and gentlemen, that she was a bad judge of female form; any resemblance to Greta Garbo was entirely fictional. She had her wish, she was left alone.

However, more frightening are those misguided girls who know who they are but who think that you are someone else. There was once this female loon who grabbed me in a crowded place and called me by an unfamiliar name, as if the name had something intimate to do with me and she had something intimate to do with the same. Both these examples are members of the species *prole* (viz., the dowdies) in the social grouping of the female mad; it is among the *aristos*, of course, that a touch of the moon is a greatly to be desired public grace. When a beautiful lady says 'I'm mad' it means (forgive me, ladies) 'get in my pants if you can'; and you want to, there's the rub. You see, the combination of madness and beauty is not only a status symbol, it's a damned aphrodisiac – yes, it's all about sex.

And I say, without fear of contradiction, that psychiatrists are prostitutes of the mind. As in days of old when all the rich young men took their French letters of introduction to the family madam, so now the priceless girlies pay their mind doctors for all the experience and the relief they lack; it is a form of self-assurance. Indeed,

103

there is a kind of january flavour to the distinction between self-knowledge and vanity; as if the whole sea of troubles were but the signal for our prosperous magician to calm the waters and thus be able to give the answer to the real question – 'Mirror, mirror on the wall, who is the fairest of them all?' – until the brittle ladies become reflections of themselves, and a breed of succubae is let loose upon the world. I predict, if it isn't so already (a dire warning, ladies and gentlemen), that in time to come all the husbands will run mistresses as they now run second cars, and all the wives will keep their medicine men in houses full of cupboard love – oh, it will be a fine time when all the happy families dance around the totem pole. Have I made myself clear? If mad ladies get laid because they are mad and cool walnuts get married too, then the role of our classy call-boy has nothing to do with the recovery of the senses; on the contrary, he teaches girls how to act mad. I ought to know, I'm a sort of lay psychiatrist myself. Just think of the phrases minted for the purpose of amorous description: 'madly in love', 'wildly in love', 'crazy about you', 'potty about you', 'head-over-heels in love'. I am convinced, beyond doubt, that the function of the psychiatrist is to rationalize the unreasonable.

There's madness and madness, ladies and gentlemen, and if my meaning has been taken aright you'll know what kind of insanity I'm talking about. In ascending social order I'm concerned with the slippery slope between delusion and illusion – but you knew that already. Anyhow, just as there's madness and madness, so there are orgasms and orgasms; for the purposes of this history I've divided them into Socratic Orgasms and Biblical Orgasms (SOS and BOS), a division, one might say, contingent upon different meanings of the verb 'to know' (viz., in the first instance 'man, know thyself', and in the second 'Adam knew Eve'). Obviously (referring to my future image of marital bliss) the first O is the domain of the psychiatrist, and the second Ohhhhh is the prerogative of the husband (lucky chap). We psychiatrists are the true heirs of Descartes; not only are we prostitutes of the mind, but we are also the dedicated pimps and panders who convince our clients of their being by having them repeat (and act out) the phrase, *amo ergo sum*. Ladies and gentlemen, you're probably asking yourselves, 'OK, but what's in it for the psychiatrist, does he do it just for the money?' I'll tell you quick enough: psychiatrists ain't normal, we do not choose but are the chosen; we're the eunuchs in the harem, the fools who speak the truth (whatever that is). We play Plato to the lady's Socks. We are the foot that kicks the ball. We deliver the goodies for the boss. Up up and we're away. SOS. Save our souls.

That's right, ladies and gentlemen, this is the history of my castration. Nothing of mine has been chopped off, of course; but I have been cut to the quick just the same. My tender parts have suited me only to tenor parts in the great operatic joke of our *modus vivendi*. Help me! I beg of you, let the mirror crack from side to side, tell the ego to gogo to hell; ladies and gentlemen, join me in libido lib. Liberate my id! By the way, ladies on your couches, have you ever noticed how the word 'ego' resembles the male articles: that round e and that round o on either side of the dangling g all coiled up and ready to go? What do you make of that, eh? Your ego is really my id in disguise! Do the both of us a favour, liberate my id! Please! That was an outburst of passion, whether it was genuine or not I cannot tell, though its spontaneity seems suspect to me. Good God! I can't even trust myself, my hands are tied, and that ain't all.

So when did it start? I don't know, I don't know, but perhaps the last entry in my journal (not diary) is relevant: 'Sunshine sunny day sunday. A cookoo flew. I met a madman, "How are your troubles?" he asked. "They had me certified insane," he said, "because I wanted to do something to benefit mankind." I did not find out what. He wore brown tweeds. As the sun went down Y was miserable, and she asked me to her room. There I was paid the ambivalent compliment of becoming a shoulder to cry on.' That's how it ends. Oh, I intended to write up all she confided in me, but I could never face the task. If you like, I'll confess that this manifestation of apparent laziness was but a cover for the appalling fact that I had ceased to be the main character in my own autobiography; I had become a step-brother to the narrators of *The Great Gatsby*, *Le Grand Meaulnes*, and significantly, *The Sun Also Rises* – well, the sun might also rise, but I know what damn well didn't – we were all inoperative voyeurs. Jesus Christ! I know myself inside out – fuck you, Socrates. I just want to stick my dick through the crack in the looking glass. But no! the word has gone round that psychiatrists have taken the vow of celibacy – fuck that hypocritical oath – as if we were the priests of a new religion; which is what we are, of course. What a combination – a pimp, a priest, and a prostitute – all in one. I think if the whole world were suddenly struck dumb I might begin to enjoy myself. And that, ladies and gentlemen of the jury, is how I came to be found with a bloody knife in my hand.

I don't know what your friends are like, but every so often one of mine goes mad; not stark-staring bonkers of course, but enough to make it noticeable. You know, I am beginning to think that my friends only keep me on as a guide to lead them back into the real world (wherever that is), sometimes I wish that I had given them all a push in the opposite direction. One such friend, on the rebound from one brick wall or another, managed by judicious dropping of her pants (upon my advice, naturally) to persuade the management of a theatre club to produce her latest pornographic play, *The Sabre-Toothed Cunt*, all about a prick eater – some wit that girl had! I had to go and see the play – this is a statement of fact, not an intimation of reluctance; I assure you, my gentlemen friends, that had you but seen the leading lady you too would have been buzzing around that queen bee's box-office like greedy wasps – so I took with me as a companion a friend even more lately insane than the lamented authoress. How can I best describe the auditorium? If you can imagine those ancient Greek monuments as giant fruit-bowls, then this basement left-over was an up-turned orange crate; we the audience sat on the four sides facing the centre. The play itself (in case you don't read newspapers) consisted of a naked girl (absolutely ravishing, as I said) challenging any member (ha ha) or members in the audience to give her an orgasm. The movements of my companion made me feel uncomfortable; I did not know what was in her mind. I knew that I could arrange a SOS job for the lady now humping on the stage, but I feared that the big BOS coup was beyond my powers – I had been for too long that dispensable part of the double act when three becomes a crowd (now that I think about it, there is an honourable literary tradition of the second fiddler playing to the bass drum, from Holly and Vincey in *She* to Lumière and Garth in the *Daily Mirror*) – yes, folks, I fiddled while my id burned. And the semen fell all around us like tropical rain.

After the performance, during which our heroine accommodated six gentlemen and two ladies without loss of composure, I rose to go and spied another friend escorting a girl whom I recognized. This girl had blue eyes and blonde hair; she carried her head like a rose upon a stalk. I said, 'Hello.' She said, 'Haven't I seen you somewhere before?' I reminded her. She said, 'I remember you, you have a nice face, I used to stare at you for hours and think that we would never meet.' I said, 'We must meet.' She said, 'Give me your telephone number; I'll call you because I like your face.' I was in ecstasies, sat by the telephone for days on end; you see, it doesn't take much to make me happy. Yes, ladies, flattery will get you anywhere. In the meantime I had lunch with our mutual acquaintance; I told him that I was waiting for Z to phone. He laughed, told me that in his opinion she was certifiably insane, offered me some evidence, then went to buy his round of drinks. We were joined by a stranger, a foreign poetess, who informed me that she was divorced, childless, and abandoned by umpteen lovers. My companion wrote down her address. When we were alone he winked at me. 'She's mad, you know,' he said.

Z telephoned me one week after our unexpected reunion, at eight-thirty in the morning. She was crying. She said that she didn't remember who I was (lose five points), but she thought I must be someone important, for she had my number underlined (score five points). 'I'm in trouble,' she said, 'my lover has kicked me out.' 'Do you need any help?' I said for the nth time. She said, 'Yes,' and put down the receiver. She phoned me back in the afternoon. 'I've moved,' she said. 'Are you better?' I asked. She said, 'Yes, I saw my doctor this afternoon, he told me that I do not have VD.' I said 'Good.' She said, 'The doctor gave me some sedatives.' I said, 'Oh.' She said, 'Would you like to come to a party tonight?' I said, 'Yes.' She said, 'I'll call you when I'm ready to go,' and put down the receiver again. She phoned back at midnight, 'I decided not to go,' she said, 'because my friend is too unbalanced to meet anyone new.' I said, 'Really?' She said, 'Would you like to come to a party tomorrow?' I said, 'Yes.' She said, 'I'll meet you at the Angel at eight,' and put down the receiver once more. I waited at the Angel station until nine, but she didn't turn up. When I got home the phone was ringing. It was Z. 'I'm sorry,' she said, 'but the friend I was visiting had a nervous breakdown while I was there and when I wanted to leave to meet you he held me to the floor.' I could hear music in the background. I did not expect to see Z again. But I did, nine weeks later, in a bookshop; I thought that this meeting was fate (you see what a fool I am, ladies and gentlemen) and asked her out to dinner. 'Pick me up at my flat,' she said.

And now, ladies and gentlemen, we come to the climax of my sorry tale. On the night in question one of her neighbours let me into the flat. Z was sitting on her bed; she was wearing a black hat and a nightdress. Her room was dirty. 'My grandfather has gone mad,' she said, 'what shall I write to him?' She showed me the postcard she intended to use; it was a painting of a clown. Then she got up and said, 'I can't eat dinner tonight.' She walked around me and stood in front of the window; the light shone through and through her nightdress. I could see that she was naked beneath the transparent gown, and that she had a beautiful body. She sat down on the edge of the bed, 'I've had two men this week,' she said, 'do you want to make it the hat trick?' She pulled her nightdress up to her navel and opened her legs; oh, indeed, up flew the web and floated wide, the thighs cracked from side to side. 'Do you like this pose?' she asked. 'Charming,' I said. She said, 'I went to Soho last week and had some pornographic photographs taken.' I was sitting on a hard chair. We sat in silence. Z went out of the room and made a telephone call. Suddenly I had a revelation. The girl was clearly sick, a real walnut, a mind in sore need of the faithful SOS treatment; but her body was so beautiful, it was a terrible waste, if only I could be her BOS and benefactor too. But how, ladies and gentlemen? How was I going to rid myself of the responsibility for her mind, that terrible thing? How was I to resolve my Cartesian dilemma? I looked into her small kitchen, a cupboard. 'Coffee?' she inquired. But before I could answer the doorbell rang. A man came in. He paid Z some money and began to undress. He nodded at me. Z took off her nightdress and was naked. I did not sit still. As the man moved on into Z I slashed him from shoulder to shoulder with a carving knife from the filthy kitchen; it must have been painful for him, but it was not dangerous. I held the knife to his throat and ordered him to tie Z to the bed, then I told him to go. I knelt on Z's chest so that she had to gasp for breath, and while her mouth was wide open I cut out her tongue. It wasn't easy, ladies and gentlemen, believe me; Z thrashed about so much that I thought she must be having an orgasm. Then she began to gurgle, so I cut her loose and sat her up. I was ready to take her, or so I thought, but when I came to check the famous equipment I saw, to my astonishment, that I had already come, and realized that I must have shot my bolt while slicing her tongue. I knelt at her feet, at this discovery, and began to stroke her belly. She was shivering. I pressed my face against her body, and took one of her nipples between my lips. And I sucked and sucked while she sat silent and still with blood pouring out of her mouth and on to my hair.

And that, ladies and gentlemen of the jury, is how the police found us when they burst in. The judge has called my crime the most horrible he has come across in all his years on the bench. And I readily admit that I have done wrong in his eyes, but who among you can blame me? In fact, ladies and gentlemen, I believe that my unorthodox treatment has at least enabled Z to come to terms with herself, certainly she is now more beautiful than ever. The questions you must decide, ladies and gentlemen, are whether I was more sinned against than sinning, and whether, in the final analysis, I did more good than harm. If you don't believe me, ask Z.

Tante Rouge

My toothbrush has four blue scores behind its head that look as if they had been made by a cat's paw dipped in ink, they are only explicable if their presence is gratuitous. My toothbrush is a long white bone and I keep it in a perspex box, at present it is in the bathroom of Sylvie's aunt. *Quelle chambre!* (as they say in France): ultramarine bath the size of an aquarium, tiles as rosy as an ear's conch, recorded sea sounds, water as limitless as the unconscious, which place is where I was when Sylvie woke me with a scream. Unusual, because I do not usually sleep later than my ladies, perhaps because I wish to preserve my ubiquity, like the Cheshire Cat. Well, there is not much going through the looking-glass when you are awake, so even though our vast bed was as comfortable as a pacific ocean, I opened a blue eye and observed that Sylvie was peeping through the winter window. Her unclothed pale skin was slightly flushed from the cold, the shade of a blushing carnation, though I must say what I first thought of when I saw her standing in her goose pimples was my old pinkish ping-pong bat. Incompatible images? However, I had a more important question to answer, namely, why was Sylvie screaming? I noticed in addition, as I considered the possible causes, an antiphony that came from beyond the window, something like *skyow skyou*, a feathered echo of her plaintive cry. Such was the dawn chorus that morning.

'*Regarde*,' exclaimed Sylvie as soon as I was close, '*le lac!*'

I should explain. Sylvie and I were temporary residents at the mansion of her aunt, the famed Tante Rouge. Commie and divorcée as may be, the aunt was still an aristocrat, therefore in her gardens there was a lake. The lake was a gem, a sparkling jewel in the over-dressed park, ruby red, full of nourishing dye to keep the flamingoes in fiery plumage. The aunt, you see, collected flamingoes, an exotic hobby, far more difficult and dignified than breeding peacocks. Anyway, it being a cold winter morning following a frosty night, the priceless water had turned icy, and a prize flamingo, sleeping late, had been trapped by its feet in the frozen pond. It struggled to get free, wings as red as my Sylvie's cheeks, but its flames didn't cut any ice with Jack Frost. Furthermore, to make matters worse for the poor bird, Sylvie's aunt's handsome Persian puss (Le Chat de Perse, Pliny thought its whiteness came from eating snow), was creeping carefully over the glazed lake towards its frightened and frantic breakfast. The bird screeched in terror, *skyow skyou skyooooooooooow*!

'Oh, *mon Dieu!*' wailed Sylvie. 'Save it!' *Skyow skyou!*

I am ready to admit that there are many people in this world with a more cheerful disposition than me the first thing in the morning, however, Le Chat de Perse was not one of them. Natural history experts and cat lovers both are perhaps aware of this fact already, that autocratic cats do not take kindly to being prevented from enjoying their chosen meal. Consequently, as I pushed the furry beast away from its all but extinguished prey, Persius lashed out a white paw in fury and with claws as sinister as its national scimitar left four red lines on the back of my right hand. I jumped away in surprise and pain, a natural mistake, as a result of which I lost my delicate footing on the thin ice; for a few seconds I juggled with my feet to keep my balance, but it wasn't any use, and I tumbled backwards. If the same thing has happened to you, or if you are perchance an Eskimo, you will know that the sound of cracking ice is quite unmistakable; I broke up the lake all right; splits raced outwards from my gaping hole like ripples of frozen laughter. I spluttered, splashed, and shivered, my body contracted as if to prevent the appalling water from entering my pores, I squirmed, and swam, and all the while in the background to this bubbling cacophony I imagined I could hear icicles of glacial giggling. There is nothing at all dignified in drowning. As for the flamingo, the *sine qua non* of my unenviable plight, it hopped away without so much as a *skyou*, let alone a thank you. I hope it gets chilblains.

'Is it permanent, do you think?' I asked, examining my hands, which had turned scarlet.

My face was scarlet too, and there were stains of a lighter red on various portions of my anatomy where the dye had seeped through my discarded clothing, all in all, I looked like a man caught in a state of peculiar embarrassment. Sylvia rubbed my numb body with a prickly towel, the texture and size of a schooner's mainsail; I gather that only the very rich can afford such Spartan luxuries.

'You must not worry,' began Sylvie with relish, 'it stays only on fla-mingoes, *jusqu'à ce que tu sois comme d'habitude* (laughter) you should keep away from the lady flamingoes, it would not be fair to them.'

I was not amused. For years flamingoes did not breed in captivity, until some bright spark realized that the mature birds required their alluring pigmentation, somehow lost by the waters of Babylon, to remind them to perform coitus, up to then a faded figment of the collective instinct. So the word went around among the cognoscenti; turn 'em red, and watch 'em go. I was a victim of this advance in scientific knowledge.

Sylvie threw the towel to the winds and hugged me, the next stage in my rehabilitation, she whispered in my ear, '*Je comprends le goût de madame le flamant*,' meaning red hands and a red face drive a girl wild, a further scientific advance it seems.

So we kissed, and I got a little warmer, until sensations began to reappear over my body like coordinates on an ordnance survey map.

'*Attends!*' hissed Sylvie as she attempted to attract the attention of my frigid cock (but as I said, my whole body had contracted in the drink), and my south pole appeared to want to remain *pays inconnu*. '*Attends!*'

Patience is a virtue. Sylvie returned from the mediterranean bath-room decked out like some quattrocento goddess of love in rouges and perfumes. She was of course as naked as a sea nymph. In her hand she held, not a magic wand, but a tube of toothpaste. She unscrewed the top, as though she were some artist preparing for a day's work, and squeezed a white wriggling worm on to my ice cap. Then she rubbed some more of the paste into that place where I believe my foreskin would have been had I not been a member of the chosen race.

'I cannot resist the peppermint flavour,' said Sylvie as she came down on me on that soft eiderdown for the third time, some artist!

'Well, well, well,' I thought as the warm winds blew, 'fellatio!'

'In the summer I make pedalo on that lake,' reminisced Sylvie when we were back in her flat, away from the mansion of La Tante Rouge (fellow traveller, first class), back to the potato-seller downstairs, the wine merchant across the street, back to the ghetto in the fourth arrondissement, where corks bob all winter in the rainwater that runs along the gutters. Sylvie told me that.

I first met her in the autumn by design. 'Would you mind delivering a letter?' I had been asked by a fellow Francophile who was crossing La Manche in the opposite direction. 'It is to a girl who lives in Paris.' And that is how Sylvie became this theme played on a name and an address. There is no postmark on the letter, so the exact date of my entry into Sylvie's life is not a recorded fact, nothing was registered, I simply inquired of the potato-seller and part-time concierge *pour l'étage juste.*

'*Petites patates,*' replied the dirty old man with a chip on his shoulder, '*petites patates.*'

'*Pourquoi?*' asked a customer who got the dusty joke.

'Because I have a French letter for someone,' I answered.

The stairs inside were wooden and worn, wedded to a shiny banister that twisted upward into the centre of the ancient building like a corkscrew into a bottle of wine. Sylvie dwelt by the more untrodden ways, the sixth floor, where the sky touched the roof, so high that I was dizzy by the time that I tapped on her door. This is the only excuse I can give to explain how it was that I walked into her bathroom by mistake and saw Sylvie sitting in the tub soaping herself.

'*Qui êtes-vous?*' demanded Sylvie as suds slipped all over her shiny body and drips dripped from her nipples.

'*Le facteur,*' I said, holding out the letter as if it were a laissez-passer or a passport into personal chambers, which is what it turned out to be in effect.

Sylvie took the letter from my hand in a way which made my presence seem to be nothing out of the ordinary, presumably convinced by the evidence of my blushing visage that I was no malefactor, and proceeded to study the handwriting on the envelope.

'Is it true,' she asked, 'that all English men are very shy?'

I had no answer to that. She dropped the letter into the water where it floated undisturbed until she got out of the bath, at which point the envelope stuck to her wet back. I could still read her name and address very clearly, just above her private mail box. As a result of this encounter we spent the autumn, as the French say, looking at leaves upside-down. I have my memories too. Writers do not meet many girls like Sylvie.

And who is Sylvie? I have looked at her and have seen the way cheeky dimples sneak into her face when she smiles, the way pimples rise on the coral aureola of her breast when she is aroused, have felt the way she scratches my back with ferocious fingernails like diamonds from a pack of cards. Right now, in this kitchen, her hair is pulled back in a bun, after the fashion of the peasants of northern France, showing off the roundness of her face. Her eyes are as dark as chocolate. Her skin is as fine as sifted flour. She has been baking a cake.

'What are you thinking?' she asks. 'Why do you smile?'

There in a couple of questions you have the difference between us; Sylvie wonders what goes on in my head, while I watch for the idiosyncrasies that will characterize her. Oscar Wilde proclaimed somewhere or other that it is a shallow man who does not judge by appearances, and I hope he is right, yet I cannot help but sometimes feel like an ornithologist who knows he has seen a golden oriole by its bright yellow plumage, its black wings, and the dark bar on its tail. Is Sylvie simply a common girl (*femina femina vulgaris*) with regulation mammary glands, a black bush beneath her belly button, and labia between her legs, or is it just my imagination that makes her a unique specimen who opens her thighs for me not merely because I tend to have red hands and a red face, but also because she feels an ulterior motive which we shall not embarrass by naming? And what do I feel? Ah, now we are on the horns of my paradox; I should like to know Sylvie, in the same way as I want Sylvie to desire and know me, yet I can only respond to her decorations (natural and unnatural). When she embroiders herself for me, it is the image that I (as the French put it) *baiser*.

'*Imbécile!*' yells Sylvie. '*Imbécile!* have you lost your sense of smell?' The abuse was well deserved, the great writer had burnt the cake.

Though the gâteau was a chocolate affair the top was too tanned to contemplate with any appetite, even after I had swept it with such cutting strokes that cinders flew like sand in a desert storm. We had a cake but we couldn't eat it.

'*Bouffon!*' mocked Sylvie. 'See what you have done!'

'Wait,' I commanded, 'and watch what I will do, just wait!'

With purposeful strides towards the table I began the transformation scene, spread out all the ingredients I would require, washed my hands, wiped them on a white towel, and set to work. I broke a three-ounce block of plain chocolate into small pieces, placed them in a copper pan where water already waited, and allowed the thickening combination to mingle over a gentle heat. As soon as the contents began to boil I turned off the gas, let the mixture cool till all the brown bubbles stopped breathing, and beat in fine icing-sugar (a spoonful at a time), salad oil, and three drops of vanilla essence. While this concoction warmed on the stove I searched Sylvie's cupboards for what I wanted; a forcing bag and a set of icing pipes. And so the moment arrived when I turned the bitter ashes into sweetness itself, as I slowly spread the rich icing over the cake.

'*Voilà!*' I cried in triumph. I waved sticky fingers, dipped in the gluey chocolate, beneath Sylvie's sensitive nostrils, they flared (*narines flambées*), and a hot tongue slipped through moist lips to languorously lick my fingers clean.

'*O monsieur,*' she gasped, '*tu es un génie.*'

However, I was not finished yet; as a preface to the climax of my act I fitted a writing pipe to the tip of the forcing bag and poured in the remainder of the chocolate glacé. I squeezed the fat bag with tender care, so that I was almost caressing it, and Sylvie watched open-mouthed as I manoeuvred the flowing line into the alphabetical shape of an ornamental dedication. It was a masterpiece. And, what is more, I had discovered a new aphrodisiac. We made a lot of chocolate icing that winter, enough to coat a body many times over, those sweetmeat sessions. Oh, you with the liquorice lips, say you will be mine.

Is it true what they sing, those songs about Paris, so romantic, rhapsodic, is it the capital city of Wonderland, where real feelings burst into imaginary blossom at the drop of an awakening note? I'll never know, because I woke too soon, but what a musical winter we had, Sylvie and I. We hibernated. Grew together in Sylvie's fertile flat, her gracious gynaeceum entertained my stamen in all manner of arrangements, hypogynous, perigynous, and epigynous, and my rapacious stamen entered her gynaeceum through the anterior lobes and the posterior lobes, the upper lips and the lower lips, we made love like the crocus and the lotus, until we had been through every flower in the perfumed garden. We played all the tunes known to Pan's pipes. We sought to improve upon nature's schemes, borrowed colour techniques from great painters, and rhythms from famous composers, but after my polychrome can had watered her lavender labia for the umpteenth time I knew that our culture was at an impasse. I had grown impatient with impasto, my fingers itched to touch what my eye could see, and soft sfumato no longer sufficed to excite me, I wanted to taste the voluptuous veal that hid behind the veil. So temperate Sylvie has turned to the ways of bright tempera. She sits silent, cross-legged on sofa cushions, breaking eggs. The music comes from the one-eyed box where Sam plays a tune, while old lovers meet, and bare trees bloom in Memory Forest, then there is a flashback to those former times beneath Paris's pleasure dome. What do you say, Sam?

'You must remember this, a kiss is still a kiss, a sigh is just a sigh; The fundamental things apply, as time goes by.'

With my other eye I watch Sylvie skilfully separate the yolks from the whites, and roll the viscous balls across the palms of her hands. One such ball, more adventurous than most, escapes and slides down her belly to explode over her curly roots, making them clammy and glutinous and quite irresistible, oh how those thick drips between the thighs made my umbrella rise! The rest of the sacs are punctured, not by my hydrophobic desires, but by Sylvie with a silver pin. Pigments made with hues from natural earth are mixed in with mother hen's yellows and the paints are ready for use.

'*Quelles couleurs, aujourd'hui?*' asks Sylvie, an impossible question.

'A hint of rose madder on the bosom drives me to distraction, and raw sienna under the arms is a blow below the belt,' I explain. 'Perhaps you could try a little burnt umber on the buttocks for the monkey glands, and violet anywhere, oh, it isn't fair.' And I give up.

Sylvie wets the sable brush, browses over the eyes, and descends to the body, adding layers of translucent tones until the semi-opaque colour shines on her skin with a luminous light, and I adore my apricot mademoiselle; but oh my illuminated Sylvie, why did we go out?

'She likes to meet writers,' Sylvie said, 'how do you say? because it puts another feather in her cap?'

'That's right.' I had asked why it was that her aunt had invited me to the château for dinner. It was an unusually warm day, a rare day, and there was a distinctly Parisian pleasure in sitting at an open table in one of the local pavement cafés sipping coffee and eating croissants. Sylvie was wearing a low-cut black dress that made her breasts seem like a pair of crescent moons shining in the night. A necklace of expensive diamond, tourmaline, amethyst and aquamarine sparkled at her throat like the aurora borealis; she looked very glamorous. Her long fingers, so well known to me for a variety of services, were concealed beneath silky evening gloves. The waiter who served us was a chic fellow, he didn't so much as bat a mascara eyelid at Sylvie's outfit, but to me it seemed that Sylvie was sporting the uniform of an exclusive society to which I did not belong. My own suit and tie made me feel earthbound, I could not match Sylvie's astronomical elegance.

'*Vingt francs*,' demanded the effeminate *garçon*, who affected a look of surprise when I paid the bill.

Sylvie took my arm as we strolled down the Rue de Rivoli and through the Jardin des Tuileries in the afternoon sunshine of that false spring day, followed all the while by the intimate ghosts of our shadows. (There is no élitism among shadows, all shadows are equal.) We walked a little way along the banks of the Seine, where contented fishermen sat among their straw hampers and bottles of *vin ordinaire* waiting for the *goujons*, following the curve of the river until we stood opposite the Tour Eiffel. As we watched the sun caught the spray from the fountains and created a momentary rainbow, as if the day were not already vainglorious enough. It was splendid.

'Paris can be very beautiful,' murmured Sylvie, catching the tune of my familiar continental mermaid, catching an echo of my own thoughts. But at our backs, on the Avenue de Versailles, the traffic honked and hooted like a ravenous pack of diurnal predators. 'Come, let us go,' said Sylvie, 'we must not be late.' A taxi took us to our destination, *la maison de sa tante*, midway between Paris and Versailles. I noticed as we pushed our way through the thick ivy to reach the dangling bell that there were sleepy hedgehogs crawling over lawns as unnaturally green as emeralds. It seems that mother nature has got as many tricks up her sleeve as any artist, the old cheat.

As befits an aristocrat of her political colour, Sylvie's aunt did not keep servants, instead our meal was served by male and female mannequins liberated from the house of the most exalted haut couturier in Paris. The girl who poured me extravagant glasses of wine was a beauty of flawless perfection, so much so that when she stood still it was difficult to believe that she was real, an illusion emphasized by the facts that she neither spoke nor even smiled. Not so Sylvie's aunt.

'My niece,' she confided to me midway through the second course, 'has a heart like an artichoke.' And so saying she took another petal of that vegetable and scooped out the flavoured flesh with a pair of dazzling incisors.

'That is not polite, Auntie!' interrupted Sylvie. '*Tu n'es pas gentille.*'

'*Oui, monsieur,*' continued the aunt polishing off another petal, 'guard your emotions, Sylvie is not a constant lover, she likes variety.'

'You talk so much, *ma tante,*' chided Sylvie wagging an extraneous silver fork, 'that you have neglected to ask our guest if he is enjoying his food.'

'*Pardon, tu as raison.* Are you?' she asked.

'Very much, thank you,' I replied, though in truth the first course, called *Potage d'Hérisson,* a heavily spiced soup which could not quite conceal the taste of privet hedges, was not entirely successful.

The plates were cleared by our silent helpers, and the star of the banquet was carried in on an oval platter that shone with the reflected light of the congregation of candles; not to be outdone, the main course itself burned with a blue flame as very special cognac evaporated into the air. A roasted breast was placed daintily on my plate by hands that were as graceful and quick as a bird. I cut a slice and tasted the dish, it was more delicate by far than any wild duck, I could almost hear the applause and cries of encore in my stomach for this gastronomic hit.

'It is magnificent,' I complimented my hostess. 'Now tell me what I am eating.'

'I thought that you would like it,' the proud lady said, 'we call it *Filet de Flamant Flambé.*'

'You eat your flamingoes?' I was astonished.

'In France we have a saying, monsieur,' Sylvie's aunt began grandly, '*s'il mouvait on le mange;* if it moves, eat it. Why else should one keep flamingoes, may I ask?'

I now understood the ingratitude of the flamingo I had saved; to it I was just another flamingo-eater. I felt guilty for my kind.

'*Et maintenant, mes amis,*' announced our elegant M C, our mistress of ceremonies, '*nous allons à la chambre des pieuvres.*'

So Sylvie and I quit the scene of our feast and followed La Tante Rouge down a flight of filigree steps, in and out of a labyrinth of passages, and through an oaken door into a dark room suffused with the saline smell of the sea. We both still held in our hands, as though I were Atlas and she my helpmate, two hemispheres stuffed full of ice-cream, hot morello cherries, and cake.

'You must be very flattered, my aunt has honoured you,' whispered Sylvie as she fed me spoonfuls of the bitter-sweet desert. 'Not many persons have been here before you.'

Slowly waves of blue-green light filtered into the chamber and I saw simultaneously that one of the walls was constructed of glass and that the world beyond was not made of air but of water.

'Ah, *c'est merveilleux, mon vieux*,' said Sylvie's aunt, 'they are coming, monsieur, and now you are going to witness something very special.'

I certainly did. From out of a sandy nook or cranny at the base of that very private aquarium an octopus emerged, its movements surprisingly delicate, like the disembodied hands of a famous artist, with no hint of the strangler of the sailors' shanties. At the entrance of a second octopus from the shadowy wings the first turned as white as a tutu and stood upon tiptoe moving towards the newcomer like a ballet dancer on points.

'Once I watched him execute an exquisite *entrechat*,' said Sylvie's aunt.

'A duet of lovers is a beautiful thing,' added Sylvie, still feeding me ice-cream and cake.

However, the female of the species was not nearly as impressed as the audience, probably because she had seen better performances in the proper ocean, and paid no attention to her partner even as he approached her with the third tentacle on his right side fully erect, and aiming in her direction. But the male was no mere sucker either, he too must have had better times and still had a trick or two up his sleeve; he covered his body with stripes of black and white, managed an energetic pirouette, and swung back like a compass pointing at his lady friend, who must have found this display of foreplay quite irresistible because she joined her mate in the famous *pas de deux* which ended in his stiff limb sticking into an orifice in her rear *tout de suite*. Very soon a seam beneath the straight arm began to undulate from him to her, but before the grand finale could be reached Sylvie's aunt (who should have known better) burst into spontaneous raptures and put the male lead right off his stroke. Indeed, so alarmed was the poor fellow that he squirted ink all over the place instead, so that the water became full of black clouds and nothing more was visible.

'Never mind, *n'importe*,' said Sylvie's aunt, 'it is time for the entertainments, anyway.'

The cabaret was another surprise. The five male and the five female mannequins, each pair apparently a replica of a prototype concealed deep in the vaults of a Paris bank, returned from the kitchens and removed their identical costumes with a series of gestures that must have been copied from an obscure choreography. The rest of their performance was more ordinary; the men fucked the women. However, I soon found that I was not enjoying myself, any more than I would have gained pleasure from seeing the couple in Jan Van Eyck's famous canvas strip down and get on with the job of sharing out their conjugal rights. Not only was the spectacle unerotic at heart, it also devalued the worth of my own antics between the sheets with Sylvie, like any miser with his money I have always believed that things are more valuable when examined in the privacy of the bedroom (or whichever room is handy). It is a great problem, for this artist at any rate, to come to terms with the realization that he is not unique, not the first nor the last. I had just begun to consider my own role in the proceedings when Sylvie stood up.

'Would you please unclasp my necklace?' she asked. Her gloves, dress, shoes, and lingerie followed her jewellery to the floor, in that order; it turned out that my Sylvie was an experienced stripper.

I did what was expected of me up to the sticking point, but could do no more, when it came to the moment of truth I was as limp as a drowning man amid that sea of humping bums. Alone with Sylvie I had always managed to counterfeit the impression that what we were doing was somehow an original breakthrough in the intimate relations between man and woman, now I was confronted with five separate sets of proof that my coin was not so special; result, no ink in the pen.

'It is useless, Sylvie,' I confessed, 'I would never be able to write in front of an audience, so how can you expect me to make love in public?'

'Do not be alarmed; it happens to everyone the first time,' called Sylvie's aunt across the room. 'Put on your clothes and come here, I have a souvenir for you.' My old enemy, Le Chat de Perse, sat on her lap lace; it may only have been my mood, but it seemed to me that there was an unmistakable look of triumph in its inscrutable eyes. The present was a long pink feather, with grateful thanks from the late flamingo.

There is a lot that a man and a woman alone together can do with a feather; for example, I know the exact location of every spot on Sylvie's body where she is most ticklish, a tempting invitation to the fandango if ever there was one. Sylvie hadn't bothered to remove her clothes from the dining-room, and at this moment she is prone upon the bed in a classic pose, *in puris naturalibus*, her Pandora's box open wide, letting the world know all the little secrets of *femina femina vulgaris*. And myself? Despite the pulsating ache situated in the region of my groin that represents the time-honoured desire to fill her carnal knowledge with my own store of wisdom, I am seated at a table dipping my quill into a black inkwell. It is my conclusion that literature must transcend the stale pleasures of the flesh if it is to become a useful guide into the country of fresh excess, or else the writer will finish his career as a mere mime-artist grinding out an infinite procession of bumps in the night. That's right, I want to be the Natty Bumppo of sexual experience, diviner of dark delights, not just another gigolo.

'Come to me,' Sylvie calls, 'come with me, *j'ai faim, j'ai soif, j'ai besoin de toi.*'

Au revoir, Sylvie, I've been there before, so long, Sylvie, your paint is fading fast. The four scars on the back of my hand throb as I write, but I've got to set out for the territory ahead of the rest. In the end it comes to this, the pen is mightier than the penis! What do you say, Sam?

Hearts of Gold

There are not many happy families. Not among the rich. You soon learn that in my line of business. So why was I down? I wasn't rich and I had no family. It was one of those oppressive days when you feel like you've been trapped in a kitchen by a homicidal cook who's frying burgers and onions in gasoline. A regular Los Angeles summer day. But there was something more nagging me. The knock on the door reminded me what it was. Mrs Virginia Lyle walked in. My client. Her perfume was the sort you smell in wet dreams. She looked like a second-rate opera singer, but then I was a second-rate private eye, so we suited each other just fine.

'Have you brought the letter?' I said.

'Right here,' she said, patting her purse.

'I still don't know why you don't mail it,' I said, 'this'll cost more than a thirteen cent stamp.'

'Listen, Mr Smolinsky, I've mailed a dozen letters and they've all come back marked "return to sender",' said Mrs Lyle, 'this one I want to be sure Laura gets.'

'How will I find your daughter?' I said.

'I don't know her address,' said Mrs Lyle, 'but she dances every night with the Jackettes at Mikel Ratskin's joint on the Strip at Vegas.'

'OK,' I said.

'One more thing, Mr Smolinsky,' said Mrs Lyle, 'wait while Laura reads the letter, I want to know her reaction.'

When she was gone I opened my window to be rid of her fragrance, it kept reminding me of my status as a messenger boy for retired whores. No use. It clung to my clothes for hours.

I drove non-stop to Las Vegas in my old Volkswagen. The desert sky was turning emerald green as I arrived, a beauty unremarked by the inhabitants. I toured around a bit before I finally checked into a cheap motel built on the outskirts of the city beside a road-sign which read: 'Leave Paradise, enter Winchester.' The motel, forming a rebus from Paradise, called itself the Pair of Dice. The air-conditioning in my room didn't work, making it hotter than hell inside. It was too early to look up Laura. So I put on a jacket and tie and went to dine at Howard Johnsons, which also served breakfast twenty-four hours a day. The doorman was a former cop. He was still wearing a gun. I ordered a steak, other people were eating eggs, for them the day was just beginning. You could see the man at the next table had just got up. He was combing his grey hair and patting down the sides with his hands. His pink shirt was open to the *pupik* and he wore a gold medallion around his neck. Life had given him a thirty-year head start on his latest wife who had yellow hair that was whipped up like a piece of confectionery. When the waiter brought their breakfast the man squeezed his wife's breasts like they were oranges.

'Hey, Franco, what is a fifty-five-year-old guy doing with a wife with such firm tits?' he said. 'Franco, Franco, you should have seen her last night in her red dress – what a number! – I swear she drove twenty men bananas – at least!' The golden charm palpitated on his hairy chest.

In the corner by the pay-phone a drunk in a mohair suit was blubbering down the receiver, 'You're my favourite granddaughter, sweetheart, you know how the song goes, "My one and only".'

I paid my check. On the streets things were no better. A giggling group of greaseballs tumbled out of the Lady Luck Wedding Chapel, which also offered wedding suites bookable by the hour, yelling, 'Give it to her, Billy-boy!' Then on the Strip itself where low-life habits were transformed by electricity into glamorous pursuits, as the neon lights burned the sky, eclipsing the stars and turning night to noon. And the biggest lights shone for Ratskin's 'Palace of the Princess'.

I stood by the bar and ordered a whisky sour. The place was crowded with smart folk, for the Jackettes were the hottest thing in town. Wild rumours circulated about their origins; some said that Ratskin had trained them with lumber jacks in the days when he controlled the wood and paper rackets. Certainly the girls were all giantesses. They seemed so much larger than life as they strutted out on to the tiny stage in their jackboots and their birthday suits. Laura Lyle was at their head, the only blonde in the troupe. Their bodies were oiled and the sweat rolled down and splashed while they undulated to the sound of bongos, flickering through the spotlights like vamps from a 3-D nightmare. The audience hushed as they began to dance round a male mannequin, faster and faster, till they were the puppets of the drumbeats; then spinning, sweating, these naked savages picked up axes and as the silver heads flashed hacked the wax model to pieces. When it was quiet the audience went wild. I tried to get backstage. The doorman blocked my way.

'Take it easy, mister,' he said, 'ain't no one allowed back there.'

I took out my cheque book. 'How much will it cost?' I said.

'Cheques are bad news,' he said, 'can't bank 'em 'cos bribes are non-deductable. Bring me one hundred dollars cash tomorrow night and I'll see what I can do.'

Which meant another night in Las Vegas.

The Bank of Nevada still had Nixon's official inauguration patch hanging on its wall. Underneath ran this legend, 'January 20 1973, Richard M. Nixon, President of the United States, resigned August 9 1974. Spiro T. Agnew, Vice-President of the United States, resigned October 10 1973.' Not the sort of pair you'd want to be reminded of, especially in a bank. But this was Las Vegas. The air might be cleaner than Los Angeles, but that just made the smell of corruption more sickly-sweet; it stuck to you like the lacquer the women used to protect their permanent waves from the desert wind. I got my money and spent the rest of the day beside the cool blue pool, watching couples move silently from their autos to their motel rooms as if their thoughts were too dirty for the open air. I decided to catch Laura before the show, so when the sky began to turn lemon I buttoned my shirt and walked up the Strip towards the Palace of the Princess. The wind had blown up during the afternoon displacing many letters from the sign that spelt out JACKETTES so men now ran up and down ladders carrying them on their backs. The doorman remembered me. I gave him his hundred dollars. Laura Lyle was alone in the dressing-room, naked from the waist down. Her legs were long and brown, like life-size swizzle sticks. She was dusting her pubic hair with silver powder so as to match her dyed head.

She looked at me and said, 'Whatever you offer won't be enough, I don't screw with shmucks.'

I smiled. 'I'm a private detective,' I said, 'I've come to deliver a letter.'

'All right, mister mailman,' she said, 'let's see it.'

I handed her Virginia's letter. She opened it and snorted.

'Any message?' I said.

'Yes,' said Laura, 'tell the old bitch to go fuck herself with a zucchini.'

That seemed to be the end of that. Beyond the dressing-room I could hear the sound of axes hitting wood; the Jackettes were practising for the night's performance.

Outside the doorman was waiting for me. 'The boss wants to see you,' he said. He was holding a gun.

Mikel Ratskin was once a famous man. In the days when he controlled the paper supply every newspaper syndicate depended upon his goodwill to keep going. Sycophants wrote biographies. Nightclub comedians invented jokes about him. Politicians were photographed in his company. What finally blew Mikel's empire apart was a glut of cheap paper from Eastern Europe followed immediately by a clutch of accusations in the press. So Mikel gathered his family and his possessions and retired to Las Vegas. His business activities might have been gangsterish but his private life was blameless; he remained faithful to his wife and he doted on his little daughter. Ratskin was smaller than I expected. I wondered what he could want with me.

'Listen, son,' he said, 'are you going to tell me why you wanted to see Laura so much?'

There was no harm in him knowing, so I told him about Virginia's letter.

At which he grunted with laughter. 'My boy,' he said, 'do you have any idea what was in that letter? Well, I'll tell you. Virginia Lyle has run a couple of cat houses on Sunset Boulevard for years, these days they've got fancy names like the "Institute of Oral Love" and the "Participating Center of Sexual Experience". But the service is still the same. Now get this. Laura, her one daughter, turned out to be the best hooker she ever had and the customers keep asking for her, so Virginia – that's Laura's *mother* – keeps begging her to come home. To fuck strangers for money!'

'I don't think Laura will be going,' I said.

'Of course not,' said Ratskin. 'Laura's a sweet kid. In fact Mr –'
'Smolinsky.'

'– Mr Smolinsky, she's my daughter's companion. That's really why I asked for you to come to my office. We get all kinds of kooks trying to get to Princess through Laura. You can't be too careful.'

He looked at me sharply, as if he were trying to judge my character with a single glance.

'Sit down, Mr Smolinsky,' he said at last, 'I've decided to take you into my confidence. You are a Jewish private detective. *Nu?* So you understand how important is a family. Well, Mr Smolinsky, until recently I thought I had a happy home. Now I'm not so sure. To tell you the truth, Mr Smolinsky, I think someone is *shtupping* my wife.' He rose from his desk, upon which stood an antique telephone and an enlargement of his family, and walked to where I sat. He put his arm around my shoulder. 'Everything I have done has been for my family,' he said, 'my wife, my daughter and my future son-in-law. I don't want to see it all go to nothing. Help me, Mr Smolinsky.' His arms tightened. 'Find the son-of-a-bitch who's *shtupping* my wife!'

'Mr Ratskin,' I said, 'have you any proof that this lover exists?'

'Proof!' he shouted, 'proof! It's your job to find proof. I just need suspicions.'

I took the job.

'Wonderful,' said Ratskin, 'now come back and meet the family. Have dinner with us.'

Mikel Ratskin's house was modest for someone with more money than the average European treasury. As he opened the front door a girl flung herself into his arms.

'Poppa!' she cried.

Mikel laughed and patted her head. Around her neck the word PRINCESS dangled like a charm from a golden chain. Above the letter 'I' was a tiny Mogen David.

'Princess,' said Ratskin, 'I want you to meet Mr Smolinsky.'

'Hi,' she said.

She was a beauty. Her hair was chestnut red. Her eyes were brown. I was not in her class. I belonged in the B-movie with the Las Vegas background along with the likes of Virginia and Laura Lyle. Ratskin, too, despite his wealth and the patina of refinement that went with it was still a B-movie mobster. But he had achieved one of his ambitions at least, his daughter was of better quality than he or his wife could ever be. And didn't Anna Ratskin know it. The looks she gave Princess were full of envy.

We dined on artichokes and fresh salmon. Princess had a voluptuous way with artichokes; she pulled off each leaf as if she were undressing the vegetable, then she dipped it in the hot butter sauce and slid it in and out of her mouth like she had learned to eat the thing at the Institute of Oral Love. Rivulets of butter overflowed her lower lip and filled the dimple in her chin. When she reached the centre of the artichoke she pushed her finger between the silver hairs and pulled apart the purple lips to reveal the soft green heart within. The salmon came fresh and pink as though blushing with its nakedness. Its flesh was soft and sweet. When the meal was over, Anna rose.

'Please excuse me, Mr Smolinsky,' she said, 'I have to pack a few things. Mikel, I've decided to spend a few days at the house in Furnace Creek.'

'Stay as long as you like, my dear,' he said, 'Princess and I can manage on our own. 'Ratskin looked at me. I knew what the look meant. His eyes were full of tears.

I drove back to Los Angeles that night. On the seat beside me was a gift from Mikel Ratskin, a globe artichoke of some size and weight. I promised it to myself for a late supper. But first I had to make a stop at the Institute of Oral Love. I had a message for Virginia Lyle. I left the Volkswagen in a parking lot and strolled along Sunset Boulevard looking for the place. A black kid in a tuxedo several sizes too large danced alongside me holding a pumpkin pie.

'Friend,' he said, 'you don't hate Negroes, do you? I'm selling pumpkin pies for the Muhammad Ali Muslim Project. To help the black kids in Watts. See that man over there, he don't hate Negroes, he just gave fifty dollars.'

I said, 'I'll give you a dollar if you can tell me where I'll find the Institute of Oral Love.'

Outside the Institute the cops had nothing better to do than tow away a car parked in front of a fire hydrant; its registration plate said, I NEED U. Inside a dusky girl said, 'Hi, I'm Laila Tov, from Israel.'

I said, 'I'm Joshua Smolinksy from Smolensk. I want to see Virginia.'

Virginia Lyle sat at a pink desk in a room with pink walls and a deep pink carpet on the floor that looked like a tongue. 'Did you give her the letter?' she said.

'Yes,' I said.

'Any message?' she said.

I said, 'Laura said you should go fuck yourself with a zucchini.'

Back in my own apartment I plopped the artichoke into boiling water. Later, when I peeled off the leaves I imagined I was undressing Princess, more and more came off until there was a pile of her clothes around the plate and she was naked; then I began to probe the heart and I knew that something was wrong for the heart was as hard as a rock. I parted the fur and petals and saw in place of the green heart a nugget of gold.

Fairfax Avenue could as well be a street in Tel Aviv with its Hebrew signs swinging in the morning breeze. But the shop in Farmers Market selling yamulkas for dogs could only be in Los Angeles. The stalls in Farmers Market were full of wonderful fruits and vegetables: peaches, plums, grapes, nectarines, cherries, apples, tomatoes, all glowing red, oranges and grapefruit shining like suns and moons, cucumbers, squashes, even zucchinis but not an artichoke to be seen. I asked one of the stallholders why there were no artichokes.

'Don't ask me,' he said, 'ask the people in Castroville – the so-called Artichoke Capital of the World – they say they haven't got any for us. According to them the entire crop is earmarked for export.' I guessed that I was uncovering the beginning of one of Mikel Ratskin's grand designs. But where did I fit in? I didn't know the answer so I ordered some cheeze blintzes.

You know you've arrived when you see the sign which reads, 'How to survive in Death Valley'. Furnace Creek is an oasis a few miles into the valley; though it is kept smart for the tourists it retains the uneasy atmosphere of a frontier town. I checked in at the only motel, then walked over to the saloon for a beer. A few horses were grazing in the shadows of the palm trees. It was evening but the temperature was still over one hundred. Inside the bar the juke-box was playing at full volume, above the racket the barmaid was shouting at a hunchbacked dwarf who was wearing a hearing-aid. He stared at me as I sat down. He looked hostile, as though he wanted to pick a fight.

'Don't take any notice of him,' said the barmaid, 'he's a mean bastard but he's too small to do anything about it.'

In fact the dwarf seemed to hold the place together; everyone talked about him, pushed him, laughed at him and bought him drinks. Without him there would have been nothing to do except watch television. By nightfall all the men were drunk. A woman came in singing the words to 'D-I-V-O-R-C-E'. She was holding a raw steak to a black eye.

A man called out, 'Hello, wife!' She took no notice but went to the juke-box where she played every Country and Western hit over and over.

Later Anna Ratskin entered. She was alone. She saw me.

'Why, Mr Smolinsky,' she said, 'this is a coincidence.'

I got her a beer.

'I suppose Mikel sent you to keep an eye on me,' she said.

'He thinks you're having an affair,' I said.

Anna Ratskin laughed. 'No, Mr Smolinsky,' she said, 'I'm not having an affair. I'm leaving him because he sleeps with our daughter.'

That took me by surprise.

'I see you don't believe me,' she said, 'but mark my words, Mikel is planning something big. Then he and Princess will disappear.'

'Something to do with artichokes?' I said.

'Maybe,' she said, 'there have been trips to Castroville.'

I didn't know who to believe any more.

'Listen, Mr Smolinsky,' said Anna Ratskin, 'I have lived with Mikel for twenty-eight years always doing what he wanted. I have gone along with all his schemes. But now he has gone too far. How can I remain his wife while he is fucking our daughter? I have had enough of compromises. I think I will be happier alone. I no longer need anyone with whom to share my feelings.' She stood up.

We left the bar together. It was a beautiful night. The moon was full and the desert filled with reflections. I decided to take the short drive up to Zabriskie Point. At the sharp bend just below the Point I came across an old Mustang that had skidded off the road, a drunk from the bar was slumped over the wheel, the one who had called, 'Hello, wife!' A Chevrolet pulled up alongside and the woman with the black eye got out.

'Thanks a million,' she said to me, 'but Momma can handle this.'

'That's right,' said the man, 'Momma'll take care of me.'

'I told you to come home with me,' she said, 'now look what you've gone and done.'

'Sorry, Momma,' said the man.

Such is family life in Death Valley.

I reckoned that Anna Ratskin was telling the truth but even so I decided to hang around Furnace Creek a while longer just to see if she met up with anyone. A couple of nights later I tailed her out to Zabriskie Point. I kept a long way behind, driving with my lights off. Someone was already there, waiting for her. They embraced. Had Mikel Ratskin been on the level after all? I left the car and crept toward where the couple was standing. The white rocks of Zabriskie Point glowed in the moonlight, making a scene so unearthly that it seemed as if a giant looking-glass were being held toward the moon. The moonlight also shone on the platinum hair of Anna's companion. This near the hair and the figure were unmistakable. What was Laura Lyle doing here? I crawled closer so that I could catch what they were saying.

'Mikel's been exploiting us both for years,' Anna said. 'I was his slave, you were his pimp. I raised Princess for him, now you've trained her to be good in bed. We can't let it go on.'

'Mikel's always been kind to me,' said Laura, 'but you're right, what he's doing with Princess is disgusting.'

'He'll pay for it,' said Anna. 'I intend to break his heart.'

'How?' said Laura.

'By robbing him of the only thing he values,' said Anna. 'With your help I'm going to remove Princess from the scene.'

'When?' said Laura. 'Tomorrow night,' said Anna, 'bring her to the Palace. I'll arrange the rest.'

I'd heard enough. Now I was in a hurry. But right on the bend at the bottom of the hill a Death Valley fox was loping across the road. I braked but nothing happened, my foot went down to the floor, and the car swerved into the dunes. I was lucky, but the car was stuck like a beetle in a bathtub. So I hiked the rest of the way back to Furnace Creek.

I told the barmaid what had happened. 'It's that frigging hunchback,' she said, 'if he doesn't like your face he'll fix your brakes.'

It was dark when I finally got to Las Vegas. Ratskin was at the house.

'Where's Princess?' I called.

'With Laura,' he said, 'at the Palace.'

Too late! 'Listen carefully,' I said, 'there was no man. Anna was plotting with Laura to kidnap Princess.'

Ratskin's look confirmed that Anna had been telling the truth.

'I suppose she told you about me and Princess,' he said. 'Well, you know what she looks like, Mr Smolinsky, can you blame me? Look, my shrink kept saying to me, "If you're functioning okay with your repressions it's not worth the pain of getting rid of them." But day by day Princess was getting more beautiful. And older. I began to dread the day when she would want to leave home. Finally I could stand it no longer. I told Laura. She arranged it all. Princess became my mistress. But now Laura is blackmailing me. So I decided on one final coup. I persuaded the farmers of Castroville to sell me their entire artichoke crop. I arranged for the hearts to be removed and replaced with nuggets of gold. Then I planned to export the whole lot to Israel. I intended to start a new life there. Just me and Princess.' By the time he finished he was crying.

'Come on,' I said, 'we had better get to the Palace of the Princess.'

Anna was already there. 'Why, it's Mr Smolinsky,' she said, 'fancy seeing you again.'

'Where's Princess?' hissed Ratskin.

'Won't you join me at my table,' said Anna, 'and we'll discuss the matter.'

Ratskin had no choice. I stayed at the bar. The lights dimmed. Out came the Jackettes led by Laura Lyle; tonight they seemed even more manic, as if they were high before they began. There was something different about the mannequin too; tonight the female body looked all but animate as it lay crumpled in the corner waiting to be hacked to pieces. Then came a frenzy of movement as the Jackettes dragged the thing toward the centre of the stage. As the spotlight fell upon it I saw something that knocked me sideways, for around the mannequin's neck was a gold chain from which hung the word PRINCESS. I cried out but the noise of the bongos drowned my voice. Ratskin too had recognized the limp body on the stage. He was on his feet in an instant, but just as quick Anna pulled a gun and dared him to move. He was forced to watch helplessly as the Jackettes raved around the body of his daughter. So this was her revenge! I began to spring toward the stage but I didn't get half-way there before a couple of Ratskin's gorillas grabbed me and thinking that I was a freak began twisting my arms. Meanwhile the Jackettes were approaching their climax, already several axes had bitten into the stage only inches from where Princess lay.

Suddenly there was a rush of air as every door was flung open and cops streamed in through the entrances.

'Don't anybody move!' they yelled.

Seeing her prize about to be snatched from her grasp Anna cracked. 'Kill! Kill!' she screamed as she began to shoot wildly at the stage with her Saturday night special.

Immediately the cops opened fire on her, knocking her backwards over her own table. Panic-stricken the Jackettes fled in all directions. Only Princess remained on stage as the house lights went up, unconscious and naked. She was wrapped in a film of plastic that gave her skin an unnatural shiny look.

'Thank God you've come!' cried Ratskin as he ran towards his daughter.

'Hold your horses, Ratskin!' yelled the police chief, 'I don't know what we interrupted here but we came for you. A matter of artichokes.'

And Ratskin, already broken by his wife's plot, went quietly.

Virginia Lyle, getting wind of the circumstances, wrote to Princess offering her a job at the Institute of Oral Love. Laura tried to persuade her to accept. I argued against.

'But, Mr Smolinsky,' said Princess, 'who is going to look after me now Momma's dead and Poppa's in jail?'

'We'll find someone,' I said.

'You don't understand, Mr Smolinsky,' she said, 'I'm three months pregnant. That's why Poppa and I were going to run away. I need a husband.'

Being poor and having no family had not made me happy. Perhaps it was time to try being rich and married.

'Princess,' I said, 'will you be my wife?'

'Oh, Mr Smolinsky,' said Princess, 'you've got a heart of gold.'

Bedbugs

During the night I have a vision of bedbugs in congress. A concrescence of male and female. The polluted mass pulsates, masculine organs pullulate, grow into dangerous spikes that, blinded by passion, miss the proffered orifices and stab deep into the soft bellies of their consorts. While I thus dream, my blood is sucked and the satiated bugs, too bloated to return to their hiding places, excrete their waste upon the sheets and make their getaway. When I awake I observe the tell-tale black stains and become conscious of new islands of itchiness erupting upon my body. Life has taken a turn for the better for the dispossessed bedbugs, homeless since the demolition of the ancient slums, with the construction of the concrete college. Here at last the flat-bodied bugs have found sanctuary in the snug crevices, and plenty of food in the beds, even during the long summer vacation when the abandoned beds are filled by foreign students and their teachers – the former having come to Cambridge to improve their English, the latter to improve their finances. I am among the latter.

Some weeks previously I had been telephoned by a director of Literature & Linguistics Ltd, hitherto unknown, and been offered a job as a tutor at their Cambridge Summer School, held annually in the vacated university. He was frank. He said that they had been let down at the last minute and that someone had given him my name; he apologized for the short notice and inquired if I knew anything about the poets of the Great War, the course set by the deserter, for which books had already been purchased and despatched to the students; he added that these students tended to be young, German, intelligent, fluent and – with a chuckle – female; he said by way of conclusion that Literature & Linguistics Ltd was a reputable company and that the salary was equally respectable. I promised to let him know the following day.

Here was irony! Teaching First World War poetry to Germans, who had cut short the careers of most of the poets. Being Jewish I also felt a more personal thin-skinned irony. But was such irony justified? Neither I nor the students were even born in the days of the Third Reich, so could I blame them for the fact that had their parents proved victorious I would never have been born at all? Easily. Then what made me take the position? Money? Of course. But even more persuasive was Isaac Rosenberg. On account of a little-known biographical detail: his affair with my grandmother. He was ten and she was seven. They kissed one fine afternoon outside the Rosenbergs' house in Stepney, a few doors down from my great-grandfather's greengrocery. Furthermore, when Rosenberg decided to enlist he ran away from home and joined a bantam battalion in Bury St Edmunds. You can see his barracks from our bedroom window. The grotesque red-brick pastiche of a castle looms over me as I call the director to announce my acceptance. I do not mention that I have renamed the course Rosenberg's Revenge.

However, the German girls completely disarm me. They are charming, receptive and funny. Above all they seem so innocent. Our first class began in a tentative way, polite, giggly, until one of the girls demanded to know why we were studying such poetry.

'The concerns of the poets are out of date, they do not mean anything to us,' she said, 'especially since we are mostly girls here and not interested in war one bit. So why do you make us read about these horrible things?'

Other girls snorted, to be interpreted as derisive. In that parallel course running in my head, Rosenberg's Revenge, I rubbed the cow's nose in Nazi atrocities, but in our Cambridge classroom I was patient, persuasive. I did not mention the pink stain on her neck which I took to be a love bite, sign of her preoccupations.

'Why? Because the poetry transcends its environment,' I said. 'War becomes the inspiration. A source of destruction, but also creation. A paradox to contemplate. The proximity of death added to the intensity of the poet. Their minds were concentrated wonderfully.'

My allies moved in to attack. Women not interested in war? What nonsense! War involves everybody. My enemy was routed, isolated, leaving the rest of us clear to commence the course. In that introductory meeting, relationships were established, and I was pleased to note that foremost among my supporters was the most attractive girl in the room. Vanity also is an inspiration.

There are two tutors for the twenty students: myself for literature, the other for linguistics, with composition shared. Although Bury St Edmunds is only thirty miles from Cambridge I am expected to sleep in the college, since my duties include evening entertainment. Tonight my colleague is giving a lecture on phonemes, freeing me to telephone my wife. As I listen to the ringing tone I consider the fact that while each peal is identical, subsequent conversation gives it a retrospective value; from phoney, wrong number, to euphony for a lover.

'Hello, love,' says my wife, 'miss me?'

'Lots,' I say.

So our catechism continues, a pleasant exchange of self-confidences, until I realize with alarm that my answers are counterfeit. I am not thinking about her. I do not miss her. I am a liar. Second sight suddenly reveals this peccadillo as prophetic and I foresee the wreck of our marriage. Doubtless this is a romantic fallacy to be dismissed as easily as the psychosomatic cramp that has gripped my stomach. What harm can there be in euphemism if it makes her happy?

'Sleep well,' says my wife, 'sweet dreams.'

But the belly-ache won't go away. Back in my room I stretch upon the bed. My room is modernistic, without extraneous matter; for example there are no handles on the drawers, just holes for fingers to pull them open. Being double the room is a duplex, and in the steps that connect the levels the style reaches its apotheosis. Granted that only fifty per cent of a regular staircase is used, since just one foot presses on each step, what does the architect do? Lop off the redundant half, of course. Leaving steps that alternate, right, left, right, left, etcetera. True, the residents have tried to impress their personalities upon this chamber by decorating the walls with posters, but in their absence, devoid of their possessions, these emphasize the emptiness. Nor are there any books on the shelves, save my war poems, and a book marked with a single yellow star. The ghetto journal of a Warsaw Jew. The diary was discovered after the war, his body never was. Actually, I did not bring the book along to read, rather as a reminder of an evil that cannot be exorcized. Nevertheless, flat out with colic I read it from cover to cover. What can I say? In class we talk of literature but this is not art. The writer chronicles everything as dispassionately as possible, a record for future historians, until in the end he can restrain himself no longer.

'Daughter of Germany!' he curses. 'Blessed is he who will seize your babes and smash them against the rock!'

Sweet dreams! I dream of flesh in torment and awaken to find my body in a rash. No stranger to hives, I blame my brain, never suspecting the true culprits. But instead of fading, the hives swell so that by mid-morning, my class in full swing, they are throbbing in sympathy with the soldiers in the trenches. Fighting the temptation to scratch I ask my enemy to read Rosenberg's 'Louse Hunting'. Blushing she begins.

> 'Nudes, stark and glistening,
> Yelling in lurid glee. Grinning faces
> And raging limbs
> Whirl over the floor on fire;
> For a shirt verminously busy
> Yon soldier tore from his throat
> With oaths
> Godhead might shrink at, but not the lice . . .'

And gets no further. Bursting into tears she cries. 'You mock me! You see the bites on my neck and you think I am dirty! But only here have I got them! There are bugs in my bed!'

'She means Franz,' says someone, referring to my only male student, likewise bitten.

'My dictionary tells me that a bug is a ghost, a bogeyman, a night prowler,' says another, 'so Franz could be defined as a bedbug.'

'But they are not the only ones who have been bitten,' I say, 'look at my arms.' Whereupon my enemy regards me with something like gratitude. 'You see,' I say, 'the poems are relevant to our condition after all.'

Tonight it is my turn to amuse the students. So I have arranged a visit to the Cambridge Arts Theatre. Since the play is Ionesco's *The Lesson*, which ends with the pedagogue stabbing his pupil and donning Nazi uniform, we have made attendance voluntary. In the event I am accompanied only by my erstwhile enemy, Franz, and my most attractive acolyte. Naturally I am curious to see how my charges will react to the drama. Franz and Monika fidget as the dead girl drops immodestly into a chair and her professor pulls on his swastika armband. On the other hand Inge is impressed.

'Such a play explains much about fascism,' she says, 'and about Germany.'

'Perhaps Germany as it was,' says Franz, 'but today things are different.'

'Nonsense,' says Inge, 'we remain a nation of *hausfrauen* who thrive on order. We didn't like the Jews so we make them disappear. Just like dust. We were frightened by the Baader-Meinhof gang so we killed them. Pouf! No more terrorism. We adore neatness. That is why Monika is horrified by her bedbugs. They leave marks. So she cannot forget them. She cannot sweep them under the carpet – is that what you say?'

'Suicide,' says Franz, 'they killed themselves.'

'That is what we are told,' says Inge, 'what you are pleased to believe.'

Monika looks at Franz.

'We must go,' he says, 'we are tired.'

'Not me,' says Inge, 'the play has given me an appetite.'

The Castle, an unexceptional pub on the road back to college. We request drinks and curries. The landlord motions us to a table. It is midweek and the pub is deserted save for a couple sitting in a darkened corner. The man is not in his right mind.

'Tell me, George,' he says to the landlord, 'now the season is a fortnight old what do you think of our esteemed football team?'

'My name is not George,' says the landlord.

'No spunk, that's their problem,' he says, 'not enough aggression.'

'They've only lost two games,' says the landlord.

'But how many more?' says the man. 'Listen, George, you know everyone in Cambridge. You tell the manager I've got some advice for him. A bastard I may be, pardon my French – father was killed in the war before he had time to do the honourable thing – but I'm related to lords, the highest in the land. Therefore the manager will listen to me. Did you hear about that Aussie coach who showed his team newsreels of Nazi war crimes before a big match? That got their blood up! Went straight out and thrashed the opposition. I've plenty of ideas as good as that. I'm counting on you, George. Tell the manager the bastard wants to see him.'

'Wash your mouth out,' shouts the landlord, 'I won't have bad language in this pub. Not when there's ladies present. If you won't behave you can clear off.'

But Inge is not embarrassed. 'That was a fine play we saw tonight,' she says, 'perhaps we could produce something like that in our composition class?'

'Good idea,' I say, 'but it will be difficult with so many people. You and Monika will never agree about anything. You'll argue over every word and nothing will get written.'

'You are right, of course,' says Inge.

'Maybe we could do something with a smaller group,' I say, 'you, me and one or two others.'

'But then those who are left out might become envious,' says Inge. 'They will accuse us of élitism.'

'Then we must arrange a cabaret for the last night,' I say. 'Everyone will be invited to help. I'll advertise for poets, singers, even stripteasers. Our contribution will be the play.'

Inge laughs. Her shoulders tremble. Not for the first time I observe the body beneath the shirt.

Two plates of curry stand in the serving-hatch growing cold. We watch them while the landlord sulks. Finally I deliver them myself. But before we can begin our meal the loony snatches Inge's plate and scurries to his table.

'You've taken our dinner,' he yells, 'we were here before you!' His companion looks miserable, but remains silent.

As if awaiting this opportunity the landlord reappears. 'You have gone too far,' he bellows, 'apologize to these people at once!'

The man is outraged. He puckers his lips as if about to blow a kiss. 'Sir,' he says, 'it is they who should apologize to us for stealing our food.'

The landlord's wrath descends upon the lunatic who flees for his life.

'I might be illegitimate,' he cries into the night, 'but I do not copulate with Germans.'

Now I am angry. But I am a hypocrite, the half-wit is a prophet.

Brushing my teeth in preparation for bed there is a knock on the door. Foaming at the mouth I admit Inge.

'This afternoon I purchased equipment to purge your bedbugs,' she says. 'I planned to tell you after the theatre but the events in the pub drove it from my mind.'

I rinse out the toothpaste. Inge meanwhile is crumbling a firelighter into a large metal fruit-bowl and mixing the fragments with charcoal chips. The result is ignited. Flames leap from the bowl like tongues ravenous for bedbugs.

'Now we must wait,' says Inge, 'until the charcoal becomes red hot.'

We sit looking at one another.

'You are married?' says Inge.

'Yes,' I say.

'I am not married, though I have a man in Germany,' she says. 'Here I am free, there I am a prisoner. You understand? Always we must do what he wants. Do you know the word "eudemonism"? It means you act for another's happiness. It is your moral duty. That is always the role of women, don't you think? Your wife, does she work?'

'No,' I say.

'Why not?' says Inge.

'She was pregnant,' I say, 'but she lost the baby. She is going back to work soon.'

'Is she – how do you say? – in a depression?' asks Inge.

'She is over it now,' I say, 'we don't talk about it any more.'

We feel the heat from the glowing coals.

'Let us hope the bowl does not crack,' says Inge, 'it isn't mine, it comes from my room.'

As if casting a spell she pours yellow powder on to the embers. Asphyxiating fumes immediately fill the room.

'Sulphur,' she says. 'The gas it makes will kill all the bugs.' Coughing I lead her upstairs.

We stare into the underworld.

'Look,' says Inge, 'as I said.'

Sure enough, bugs are dropping lifelessly from crannies in the ceiling. Suddenly an unexpected twang! The bowl has split.

'Oh, no,' cries Inge.

Brilliant as the steps are in conception it is dangerous to descend them at speed, as Inge learns. She tumbles, hits the floor with a thump, and remains utterly inert. Spreadeagled, supine. There is no blood, but I do not know if this is a good or a bad sign. Her hand is limp. I feel for the pulse, but it is either stopped or I have my thumb in the wrong spot. Her heart. Situated, of all places, beneath her left breast. I place my hand upon the breast. It is warm certainly. But I can feel no heartbeat, though the nipple tantalizingly hardens. However, for all I know this may be a posthumous reflex action or even the beginnings of rigor mortis. I am no doctor. At a loss I rock forward upon my knees and part her lips with my tongue, intending to administer the kiss of life. But as I begin to blow into her mouth I feel Inge's right arm curl around my neck. And as she presses me closer I realize that my hand is still upon her breast.

Bugs continue to fall as Inge glides out of her pants. Possessed now, I turn out the lights so that Inge's naked body is illuminated only by the smouldering charcoal, a serpentine shape, splashed with red, an undulant stream of lava into which I fling myself.

'Take me,' hisses Inge, 'here, as I am, on the floor.'

While the madness lasts I pump my body into her, aware only of our sweat and the uncontrollable pleasure, dimly conscious of the mocking parody the dying embers cast upon the wall. Spent, prone upon Inge's salty body, I gasp for breath in the sulphurous air.

'Please,' whispers Inge, 'I am not finished.' She directs my hand down her belly to a damper place. Slowly my senses settle as I watch Inge's spectre writhe, and listen to her ecstatic groans, which dissolve as a deeper voice fills my ear:

> 'Soon like a demons' pantomime
> This plunge was raging.
> See the silhouettes agape,
> See the gibbering shadows
> Mix with the baffled arms on the wall.'

A man emerges from the shadows. He is dressed in khaki and puttees, but looks too delicate to be a soldier. 'Do you like my poem?' he says.

'Yes,' I say, 'you were a genius.'

'Tell that to the Germans,' he says.

I nod. I am. 'Do you hate them?' I ask.

'You cannot hate the dead,' he says, 'and you lose touch with the living.'

Inge, oblivious, cavorts on the end of my finger.

'I'm doing this for you,' I say.

He shrugs. 'Why bother with humbug when you've got bedbugs?' he says. 'Jews, Germans, we're all the same to them. They have cosmopolitan sympathies. We destroy one another and the bedbugs take revenge.'

'Not here,' I say, 'they're all dead.'

'So am I,' he says.

'Do you remember my grandmother?' I ask. 'Eva Zelinsky, she lived near you in Oxford Street.'

'What does she look like?' he asks.

'An old lady, white hair, in her eighties,' I say.

He smiles. 'Everything changes,' he says, 'except the dead.'

'Aaaaaaah!' cries Inge. She comes, he goes. There is quiet in the room. Inge is drowsy with delight. The charcoal has burned itself out.

'Come,' I say, 'let's go to bed.' During the night I have a vision of bedbugs in congress.

Throughout the day Inge wears a silk scarf to conceal the bites upon her neck. Likewise, when I telephone my wife, I hide the truth from her. Better keep quiet and skip the consequences. In two weeks Inge will be back in Germany with her jailer. At the moment, however, she is in my room again. We are awaiting another girl, selected to complete our playwriting team.

'When you took off your clothes,' says Inge, 'I saw something. That you are a Jew. Please, you must tell me. When you fucked me, was it for revenge?'

I shake my head. 'No,' I say, 'I did it because I wanted you. I forgot you were a German.'

'I am glad,' says Inge. 'You know, I have always admired the Jewish people. You have read Martin Buber?'

'Buber? Sure,' I say. 'I know my melancholy fate is to turn every *thou* into an *it*, every person into a thing. Last night you were a *thou*, this afternoon already you are an *it*, last night we had intercourse, a real spiritual dialogue, this afternoon we must write dialogue.'

Inge grins, 'And do you have any ideas?' she says.

'No,' I say, 'I am the producer. Ideas are not my responsibility. Do you?'

'Only simple ones,' she says 'like a husband and wife, eating dinner, watching television, talking but not communicating. Just one twist, a girl will be the husband and you must play the wife.'

The other girl arrives and accepts the idea with enthusiasm. We work on the play through the evening and into the night The other girl goes. Inge stays. Martin Buber? *A boobe-myseh!*

On the last Saturday I escort all the students to Bury St Edmunds. A coach has been hired and I sit up beside the driver holding a microphone. As we approach the town along the Newmarket Road I indicate, to the left, the barracks where Rosenberg trained, on the right, my house. The coach halts in the large square at the top of Angel Hill.

'Okay,' I say, 'I'll tell you what there is to see in Bury St Edmunds. Opposite are the walls of the abbey, behind are the ruins and a park. There is a cathedral. Go up Abbeygate Street and you'll come to the market. Fruit. Vegetables. Junk. Beyond the market is Moyses Hall. Built by a Jew in 1180. Unfortunately for him all the Jews were expelled from Bury in 1190. Now off you go. Back here at three o'clock.'

Gradually the others slip away until I am left with only Inge for company. It is a hot day, dusty with heat. The locals look white and sweaty, like creatures unused to the light. The women wear drab moth-proofed frocks that show off the freckles on their breasts; the men roll up their shirt-sleeves to reveal the tattoos upon their arms. It is a mystery, this abundance of sample-book tattooing, all of course applied by choice. By contrast Inge's spectacular sexuality stops people in their tracks: her black scarf, her red tee-shirt, clinging like a second skin, her denim shorts and – this I know – no underwear.

'I feel so good today,' says Inge, 'I should like a souvenir. Is there perhaps a booth where we can have our photograph taken together?'

'There's one in Woolworth's,' I say. A photograph! Thus far the affair has been vague, nothing to do with my real life, as insubstantial as a dream. It will be a simple trick to persuade myself that it never happened. But a photograph! Our faces fixed, cheek by cheek, our relationship projected into the foreseeable future. Proof snatched from the lethal fingers of time.

The booth is already occupied by three small boys. We can see their legs, and hear their excited giggling. Then as the first flash fades we hear, above their laughter, the screech of a creature in terror. Inge tears back the curtain and exposes the boys, including one who is dangling a kitten by its tail in front of the camera. The kitten flails about uselessly, tensing and squealing in horror at each flash, only to redouble its efforts in the lacuna.

'You monsters,' cries Inge, 'stop torturing that poor animal!'

The boys grin. The kitten swings. Faster and faster. Until the boy lets go. The kitten lands on Inge's shoulders. Seeking to steady itself it raises its paw and sinks its claw into her ear. Inge gently lifts the kitten so her ear is not torn although the lobe is pierced and bleeding profusely, staining her tee-shirt a deeper red. I give her my handkerchief to press against the wound.

'It looks worse than it is,' says Inge, 'it does not hurt.'

'Nevertheless, you must come back to our house,' I say, 'you must wash and change. You can't go around covered in blood.' Once again a curious accident has left me with no choice. Inge will meet my wife.

We surprise my wife sunbathing naked in the garden.

'Hello, love,' she says, 'I didn't know you were bringing somebody back with you.'

'Only one of my students,' I say, 'she's been wounded.'

My wife, wrapping a towel around herself, approaches Inge and leads her off to the bathroom. They reappear in identical cotton shirts, bargains from the market. A stranger might take them for sisters. I cook omelettes for lunch, with a few beans from my garden, and serve them on the lawn where my wife had been alone less than an hour before. I am astonished how relaxed we all are. Inge rattles off examples of her lover's male chauvinism. We all laugh. I feel no guilt, my wife feels no pain. She suspects nothing. She waves the flies from our food and throws breadcrumbs down for the sparrows.

'Are you enjoying the course?' she asks.

'Very much,' says Inge, 'especially our little playwriting group. Has Joshua told you about our play? Yes? Of course. You must come to our cabaret and see it performed.'

'I shall look forward to that,' says my wife. She removes the plates and returns with a bowl of peaches. They are sweet and juicy and attract many wasps. Our fingers become sticky.

'I am glad everything is going so well,' says my wife, 'without any problems.'

'Only the bedbugs,' I say, 'look what they've done to my arms.'

'Poor thing,' says my wife, 'can't you move into a different room?'

'No need,' I say, 'they've been exterminated.'

My wife smiles. What contentment! I realize now why I feel so untroubled; I do not really believe that I have made love to Inge. She is what she seems, just a visitor. My wife is my wife. We belong. Cambridge is a foreign city. To which I must return, however.

I kiss my wife. 'See you on Wednesday,' I say.

'What a nuisance,' says Inge as the coach passes our house, 'I have left my scarf behind.'

'Never mind,' I say, 'I'll pick it up on Wednesday. Besides, you can hardly see the bites now.'

On Tuesday we complete the play. In the evening the heatwave breaks with a tremendous storm. Knowing how much my wife dreads thunder I telephone her. She does not answer. Later, when the rain has stopped, Inge and I stroll to the Castle to toast our success. Afterwards we return to my room where Inge now sleeps as a matter of course. In the morning I telephone my wife again. No reply. Probably shopping. Lunch over, teaching being at an end, I drive home to collect her. There are three milk bottles on the doorstep, the first already sour. Its top is off, filling the stagnant air with a nauseous odour. Within is a different smell, naggingly familiar. I shout my wife's name. But there is no response. The house seems deserted. Bedrooms, bathroom, dining room, all empty. On the table is Inge's black scarf, neatly folded, and a note:

Don't forget this, Love Rachel.
PS. Hope the bedbugs have stopped biting Inge.

Then in the kitchen I realize what the smell reminds me of. A butcher's shop. Naked, legs splayed, my wife sits up on the kitchen floor with the wooden handle of our carving knife protruding from her belly. Her back rests against the wall, her arms hang stiffly down, her eyes are open wide. The blood is dry. It flowed down from her wound, between her thighs, and formed puddles on the floor. The only sound is the buzzing of flies. They walk upon her breasts, mass around her vagina where the hair is matted with blood. This horror is too shocking to be true! It is a phantasmagoria produced by my conscience. Art, not life.

'Your face is very white,' says Inge, 'is everything all right?'

'I'm just nervous about this evening,' I say.

We have gathered all the props we require: cutlery, crockery, sauce bottles, and a starting pistol loaded with blanks. And while Monika – of all people! – strips down to her underwear in front of the directors of Literature & Linguistics Ltd, Inge and I exchange clothes. A suit and tie for her, a dress for me. 'This is Cambridge,' I think, 'this is my life. There is nothing else.'

We hear Franz sing his folk songs. Then applause. We are joined by the third member of the cast. We walk out to cheers and laughter.

'Your wife is in the audience?' asks Inge.

'I hope so,' I say, 'she is coming by train.'

The play begins.

Inge – my husband – is a bank clerk. I am a housewife. The other girl is a television set. Inge orders me to switch her on. We hear the news. I serve dinner to my husband and our two children who are invisible. An argument develops between us over the boy's long curls.

'You'll turn your son into a pansy with your ways of bringing him up,' yells Inge.

'They're always my children when there is something the matter,' I shout. 'I don't think you really wanted them. I won't forget how you treated me when I was pregnant. You didn't even try to hide your disgust. But you're the one who's disgusting!'

What am I talking about? Why am I pretending to be my wife? Wife? I have no wife. How these silly words have confused me! What next? Oh, yes, I am supposed to take the gun from my handbag. I point the gun at Inge. Why? Because I hate her. But why? Because she seduced me? Because she murdered my wife? Wife? I can't even remember her name. With her shirt and tie and pencil moustache, Inge looks like a creature from pre-war Berlin. I hate her because she is German. A Nazi! I fire the gun. The blast fills my head.

'Daughter of Germany!' I scream. 'Daughter of Germany!'

I shoot at her until the gun is empty.

Genesis

How Los Angeles has changed since my last visit! Then the giant sloth and the mastodon roamed the length of Wilshire Boulevard, the great condor nested in skyscraper cliffs, and I sported with a hairy woman. Her desires were those of an ignorant animal, too carnivorous for your fastidious narrator. Still we rolled upon the slimy grass beside black pools of oil and tar, gross symbols of her cyclopic sexual organs. She was growing dangerously impatient with my pussy-footing when our liaison was permanently fractured by the interruption of a sabre-toothed tiger. My immediate response was to tear it apart with my bare hands, but then I remembered the rules: no trespassing into the jurisdiction of the Angel of Death. So I shed my ballast and floated to freedom, while my unfortunate mate sank slowly into the sticky tarpit as the tiger roared its disapproval. What did she matter? She was only a character in a primitive drama.

Now what do I find upon that sentimental spot? A museum. To be precise, the George C. Page Museum of the La Brea Discoveries. Imagine my surprise when, wandering curiously among the reconstructed remains of my former hosts, I see a glass tomb containing the skeleton of a woman. As I stare at those bones in their dark container, flesh suddenly begins to grow upon them and I am once again in the presence of my ancient seducer. Even after all this time her powerful body is unmistakable, as is her voracious face. See how her long black locks tumble over her breasts, teasingly parted to reveal her nipples. She sensed I was exceptional, and begged me to share my knowledge with her. But it was forbidden. Now, nine thousand years later, she has got me into trouble. My imagination has developed the ability to create, and I quake for my hubris. Lucifer was shot down in flames for less. Then the vision disappears, and I am left staring into the sockets of a skull. A label beside the exhibit calmly informs me that I have experienced the magic of a three-dimensional hologram. Poor La Brea! What a way to spend eternity: to be recreated every couple of minutes as a lifeless golem!

What a demonstration, also, of the limitations of human ingenuity. Forever the ape of God.

I have flown out of the shadows into the substance of your world. Where I dwell we are free from the contagion of language, our feelings float through the empyrean like balloons in a comic book. We lack appetites. We spin the Garden of Eden out of dreams, while you have transformed it into Safeways. In supermarkets the frozen lamb lies with the shark, the naked daughters of Eve smile knowingly from the magazine racks, and the fruits of the earth are gathered together. Pomegranates, persimmons, pears, plums, melons, peaches, potatoes, tomatoes, avocados, mangoes, gooseberries, strawberries, grapes, grapefruit, artichokes, asparagus, oranges, apricots, nectarines, figs; not forgetting apples. Nor is the tree of knowledge unshaken. Beside the varied versions of Eve other newspapers peddle forbidden fruit: the birth of a monster in Arkansas, the truth about the crack-up of a certain star's third marriage, a famous mother's heartbreak over her drug-addicted son. Only yesterday the thrifty shoppers of America were informed by the *Globe* or the *Star* that a recent spate of flying saucers were piloted by angels on a mission from God. A dunderhead preacher from the Deep South gave the *Globe*'s correspondent scientific proof that the angels were the Messiah's advance guard. Meanwhile, the *Star* reported that a Wyoming woman and her ailing child had been kidnapped by the angelic crew of a flying saucer. Within the craft they were forced to witness the horrible vivisection of a calf, which had inexplicably meritorious results. The child, the despair of doctors, was restored to health. Only I am qualified to judge the accuracy of these rumours, for I did land upon earth in a flying saucer, as my friend – the writer – observed. Driving down Laurel Canyon one evening last October he saw a yellow light flash across the smoggy sky. Without excitement he announced to his wife, 'I've just seen a UFO,' and thought no more about it. His sighting was confirmed on the eleven o'clock news. Now he sits at his desk, overlooking the Pacific, inventing his fictions. Awaiting inspiration he watches a whale swim breathtakingly past. Let me tell you a secret: his inspiration is actually telepathic communication. From an angel; to wit, me.

You will be curious about certain matters. Above all, you will want to know: does He exist? Certainly. In fact, He is your *sine qua non.* Be warned, your doubts are His despair; what *chutzpa* to question the existence of your creator! What is Heaven like? Like nothing on earth. Do angels have wings? No. We are not subject to the laws of gravity (we are equally exempt from the laws of space and time, not to mention fiction). Actually, gravity is one of God's stylistic flourishes; He invented it as a metaphor for the consequences of the original sin. A constant reminder of your condition. Just think! Adam and Eve eat an apple – Man falls. Years later Issac Newton is snoozing beneath an apple tree. Suddenly he is awakened by the falling fruit, and twigs gravity. Hey presto – a scientific explanation for your earthbound state. Grounded by the gravity of the grave. As a result I walk around Los Angeles (where else?) with heavy steps, for my shoes are filled with lead. Without those weighty soles I would float back to Heaven like a bubble of helium. To find such shoes was not as easy as you might imagine, for the feet of angels are minute. Eventually I tracked down a pair on First Street in Little Tokyo. 'Never stray far from the Oriental quarter if you want to find shoes that fit,' advised the sales assistant.

Shod in Chinese slippers I shuffle from the Museum into a trio of demons sent to chastise me. They look like death, their transparent black flesh revealing all their muscles and bones. Yet they pass unnoticed among the crowd in Hancock Park attending the annual Festival of Masks. They are disguised as musicians, playing melancholy folk tunes upon antique instruments. Their disquieting thoughts reach me upon harmonious waves.

Something for your information: the only difference between angels and devils is one of occupation; angels are the Almighty's sycophants, whereas devils are His secret service. Heaven is Utopia. Perfect because it is only theoretical; you know what your writers say, theories would be fine if only there weren't politicians to put them into practice. But Hell is material, sure enough; a place of exile, the exquisite conclusion of all your mass movements. In short, your political philosophies begin in Heaven and end in Hell. Among its tortured denizens are those who questioned the ethical foundations of Heaven; what right had it to tranquillity when its substantial counterpart, God's creation, was in agony? Several angels demanded that God do something about the suffering on earth, and were sent straight to Hell for their pains. My brother among them. Being one of God's favourites, I dared ask for clemency. WHY SUCH A SHEM-

OZZL OVER A FEW EARTHLINGS? AFTER ALL, THEY ARE
MERELY FIGMENTS OF MY IMAGINATION. SUBSTANCE WITH-
OUT SPIRIT. Like creators everywhere, God felt that His critics
misunderstood His intentions. He agreed that humanity's misfortunes
were upsetting, but insisted that this was a deliberate effect of His
art. PERHAPS MY TALENT FOR VERISIMILITUDE IS A LITTLE
DISTURBING, BUT YOU MUST REMEMBER THAT WHAT YOU
SEE IS NOT REAL. IT IS A FICTION. HEAVEN CAN BE DULL.
THAT'S WHY I CREATED THE WORLD. TO PROVIDE MY SUB-
JECTS WITH AN INFINITE SOURCE OF ENTERTAINMENT. AND
BELIEVE ME, WITHOUT TSURIS THERE WOULD BE NO
STORIES. Then God offered me a deal. (Forgive the capitals, but I
could hardly use an image like the burning bush; these days no one –
except the *Globe* – would believe it). Anyway – the deal. Freedom
for my brother if I could spend a year on earth without becoming
involved in one of God's plots. KEEP AWAY FROM WOMEN,
cautioned God, REMEMBER WHAT HAPPENED LAST TIME. He
wanted to test my objectivity.

It was all very well for God to warn me off women, but the
unearthly beauty of my shining face makes me irresistible to them.
Of course their carnal desires are of little interest to me, but I can't
just tell them to get lost; besides, without a woman I am dangerously
vulnerable to lecherous men. Therefore, the Festival of Masks is a
godsend. At last, among the masked, I can wander freely – unmasked,
unmolested. I am admired not for myself, but for what others take to
be my brilliant costume. Indeed, the Park is littered with abandoned
selves. Even innocent children are lining up to have their faces
painted by men with chalky visages, red noses, and black eyes. Oh,
yes, everyone is anxious to improve upon the appearance vouchsafed
them by their Maker. Obviously, deep in their minds is the idea of
masked revel, an anonymous inconsequential bacchanalia, but I'll
tell you what image comes to me: the toyshop in *Coppelia*. I love the
ballet. It is the only one of your art forms that gives an inkling of
what it is like to be divine. How I rejoice, from the obscurity of my
seat in the gods, to see the dancers defy gravity. What a ballet-
dancer I would make! My *entrechats* would be the talk of Los
Angeles.

As well as the decorated children there are men and women
merrymakers disguised by masks made of papier-mâché, feathers

and plaster of Paris, as gargoyles, birds, horses and demons. Alchemy
is at work. The sun, turning coppery as Copernicus had predicted, is
transmuting the smog into fool's gold. Gradually the grass ceases to
be green, as darkness imprisons the prism, and eyes no longer dazzle
the brain with impressions of the carnival. Instead, noses – excited
by hitherto unnoticed perfumes of hotdog, kebab, tortilla, coffee and
marijuana – contact the stomach via the nervous system. As if with
one mind the crowds begin to make for the portable dinettes that
enclose them in a square. Manikins, masks and marionettes watch
open-eyed as their former admirers are blinded to their charms by
aroused appetites. Somehow the twilight makes everything more
grotesque; the masks look like the disembodied faces that haunt a
guilty conscience, while the marionettes hang from the scaffolding
like a row of political prisoners.

Abandoned now, 'Masques du Ballet' is minded by a man whose
melancholy eyes belie the grinning mouthpiece he sports. His lips
resemble scarlet bananas. His teeth look like piano ivories. But his
eyes are real, and for a moment I am sure that he can see right
through me, that he knows what I am. He knows, all right – not that
I am an angel, but that I am his wife's destiny. For years husband
and wife have been trying to conceive; all medical remedies have
been sampled, wonder rabbis have been consulted; they have made
love dosed with pills, lubricated with ointments and ornamented
with amulets. But again and again they are defeated by the man's
helplessly low sperm count. Eventually, broken by his wife's frantic
desire for a child, he has agreed to artificial insemination. The next
problem – a donor. His wife refuses to countenance the unknown
medical student, and demands the right to choose the baby's father
for herself. She is a fussy woman and thus far no candidate has
sufficed. Until she sees me. Her unspoken desires bombard me;
better than Nijinsky, better than Nureyev, better even than Bar-
ishnikov!

'That's the man!'

But her cry is unnecessary. Her husband knows, hence those sad
eyes. I know. Her mask twitches, as though her real face were ready
to burst with excitement. Standing beside her husband she looks like
a swan on stilts. I flee as fast as my feet will carry me.

It is the mating season. The orchard that clings to the slopes of

my garden is in blossom. The air is thick with pollen. Branches are
heavy with birds obediently reproducing the species, for example,
this pair of hooded orioles. She lowers her back, her wings vibrate,
while he lightly lands upon her rump. From the western windows of
the house I rent high on Mystic Way I can see the golden crust of
Laguna Beach, and the unformed waters of the Pacific Ocean. Just
now the grey whales are returning from the warm lagoons of Baja
California, the pregnant females leading the new-born pups to their
home waters off Alaska. The path of their migration is exactly as it
was nine thousand years ago, foreshortened only by the infrequent
ice-age. They provide the one continuity with my previous visit;
everything else has changed, except perhaps the flight pattern of
pelicans. Being immortal, I have been spared these seasonal movements, for there are neither births nor deaths in Heaven. Nor are
there mansions. We live like whales in the water, in ecological harmony with the clouds. But here, on earth, I must copy my facsimiles
and acquire a roof for my head; thus my permanent status is disguised
by my temporary residence. And how do I finance my splendid
hacienda? Well, in the backyard is the aerodynamic masterpiece that
ferried me through the hellish heat of the earth's atmosphere, erroue-
ously identified by my neighbours as one of Buckminster Fuller's
geodesic domes. I have converted the interior into an ultra-modern
gymnasium, which I advertise as the Academy of Anti-Gravity. I
have assumed the credentials and credibility of an orthopaedist and
run weekly Gravity Guidance Workshops for which I charge outrageous fees.

At the commencement of each class my patients don their Gravity
Inversion Boots (patented by me, in partnership with my Oriental
shoe supplier) and climb the wooden bars, from which they hang
upside down for the best part of an hour, during which I demonstrate
an uncommon variety of postures designed to combat the com-
pressive force of gravity on the human spine.

'Is this what you call alignment awareness education?' asks one of
my gulls.

'I don't appease gravity, I piss upon it,' I thunder. 'You want
Rolfing? Go to a Rolfer!'

'How do you intend to release my body's natural energy flow,' he
whispers, 'without moving me towards verticality?'

I am merciless. I bend outward at the knees, I straighten, I bend,

I straighten . . . and continue upwards until my fingertips are almost at the apex of the A-frame which encloses the gym. Eyes filled with adoration, mouths agape, my batty pupils call me magus, though I joke that it is all done with magnets. Repenting my pride I explain that my spectacular abilities are based upon the springy strength of the syssarcosis in my legs, available to all with the proper exercise. Nevertheless, my leap is considered something of a phenomenon by aficionados of gossip. Soon my reputation spreads to balletomanes who arrive to see for themselves. And are astounded. After them come ballet-dancers anxious to acquire my secrets. Before long I am coaching several in private, while fending off the advances of both genders.

My most persistent suitor is Nancy, a statuesque woman some six feet tall. She towers above the other acolytes at my Wednesday night class, her flushed forehead glistening at the apogee of her hundredth *plié*. Proud and strong, she still joins the après-gymnastics line-up, patiently awaiting her turn for an attempt at seduction. Being well trained my students unconsciously form an even gradient from the shortest in the front to the tallest at the back. Thus Nancy is the lucky girl who gets me alone. She disguises self-loathing with aggression.

'I suppose you think I'm a freak,' she says. 'A giantess who wants to be a ballerina. Well, I'm sick of the conventional wisdom that says ballerinas have to be as fragile as fairies. For God's sake, dancers are tough, they've got the stamina of marathon runners. So why the pretence? Because of a few outmoded conventions dreamed up during some of the most autocratic regimes in history? You'll never see me tangled in the tulle of a tutu. My choreography is rugged, earthy, my feet are bare, my costume is a body stocking.' She hesitates. 'Sometimes I dance naked. Would you be interested in a *pas de deux?*'

I shake my head, which she bites off. 'So you're just like all the rest!' she yells. 'You want to screw sylphs. You've got no balls, you fucking Ariel!'

Her fit of vulgarity is followed by tears.

'Goddamn my sex!' she cries. 'All my adolescence I dreamed of being a ballerina. But my body had other ideas. It grew and grew. Who am I kidding with my kung fu? My fate is always to want what I cannot have: a career, children – you.' She laughs. 'The trouble with me is that I'm too big for my boots.' Self-pity signals defeat.

'Enough,' I say, 'it's time for zero gravity.'

Showered, powdered, my students stand at attention beside the Samadhi flotation tanks. The contraptions come from San Francisco. One of the company's sales representatives invited me for a 'be-with session' immediately after I had sampled the experience, hoping to catch me in an over-receptive frame of mind. When I ordered six, you could feel his faith in zero gravity suddenly ascend to the clouds. But it's true enough: a little while in one of these tanks and an average human is amenable to any suggestion.

Deprived of all senses, my pupils lie upon salt water with the tank lids closed upon them. Out they step hours later, blank pages ready to be rewritten for my angelic amusement. In my cramped laboratory I repeat God's universal experiment. Tod and Bob are lovers, so I persuade Bob to couple with Nancy while Tod watches in tears. I allow the charade to develop until Tod tries to strangle Bob with his leotard. With six students the permutations are endless. One week Nancy is involved in a lesbian relationship with Ilana, the next she is on her knees among the men. I invent lusts and gratifications, and wonder at the passions I unleash. Thanks to the hot water in the tanks the risk of unwanted pregnancies is close to nil, nor do the characters retain any recollections. They return home with but one memory: their love for me. Her senses still reeling, Nancy wants me to accompany her, 'to see how the other half lives'.

'Come and meet my husband, the failed writer,' she says.

Why on earth do I accept such an invitation? Am I experiencing previously unknown feelings such as guilt? Impossible! Guilt is as alien to angels as loneliness. Or is it curiosity, that damnable motive? Whatever the reason, I drive down to their place the following Friday.

Their apartment is a dilapidated beachfront duplex in the grubbiest section of Malibu. By the time I track it down, the sacrificed sun is already bleeding into the Pacific. A somewhat primitive image, you may think, but no sooner have I been admitted than Nancy lights two candles in honour of the Sabbath.

'*Shabbat shalom*,' she says. Then kisses me on the mouth. 'It makes a change not having to stoop,' she adds.

Her diminutive husband, Artie, approaches from the dismal shadows of his silent study. His melancholy eyes are unmistakable. 'Welcome,' he says.

Welcome! Only by imagining themselves in the prow of a schooner bound for the Orient could habitation in such a dump be tolerable. We slump into beanbags sipping Zinfandel. On the walls of the lounge are a variety of masks, the swan's head Nancy had worn on the day of the festival being perched menacingly above my seat.

'We have a proposition for you,' begins Artie. Is he really artful enough to persuade an angel into bed with his wife?

'Go on, you fool,' prompts Nancy, 'he's not a mind reader.'

'I want you to sleep with Nancy,' says Artie.

He explains about his sterility. The idiot, does he actually believe that he can snare me in his plot? But before I can dismiss the offer the earth shakes, as one of the local fault lines slips, dropping the swan's head upon my own.

'Me Leda,' laughs Nancy, 'you Zeus.'

My anger knows no bounds; it is greater than the weights in my shoes and I fly to the ceiling. Blinded by the mask I crash around the upper reaches of the room, while my hosts watch thunderstruck. But angels don't experience anger! The thought that I might be losing control returns me to terra firma.

'Now you know,' I say, 'I'm an angel.'

'Save that for the *National Enquirer*,' snaps Artie. Deep-set jealousy prevents him seeing anything but a pagan phallic performance; already he is attempting to divine the meaning of which my acrobatics are but a symbolic manifestation.

Nancy's interpretation is no less self-centred. 'Will I learn to levitate like that?' she asks.

'Certainly,' I reply. 'Next Wednesday we'll all hold hands and float through the roof.'

She goes through it soon enough, metaphorically speaking, when I reject Artie's request. She calls me a snob, says I think I'm too good for her; worse, she knows she is right. Sadly Artie invites me into his study for a man-to-man talk. His wife's passion has failed, as will his resignation. What do I know of compassion?

Believe it or not, Artie's study is papered with rejection slips. His bookshelves are filled with the volumes of his acclaimed contemporaries, only a small space in the bottom right-hand corner being reserved for the few magazines that have published his stories. Closer inspection of the walls reveals that strata are slowly being formed; printed rejections are the bedrock, above those are the personal rebuffs – like the one from *Esquire* which reads, 'Dear Mr Wiseman, A special story, but not special enough' – and finally, providing a very sparse top layer, are the acceptances.

'You shouldn't take it all so personally,' I say.

He looks at me as if I were mad. 'So who else are they rejecting,' he cries, 'Mahatma Gandhi?'

'Adopt the detachment of the voyeur,' I advise.

'There's only one thing I want to adopt at the moment,' he replies, 'and that's your child.'

'No,' I say, 'it's out of the question. I cannot risk attachments.'

For some reason this animates Artie. 'What are you, emotionally retarded?' he shouts. 'At the age of ten I was a regular little monster, pulling the pigtails of girls in the school-yard and making them cry. Then I had a dream. I don't remember what it was about, but it changed me. As a result I lost my freedom of action. I guess I grew a conscience, or something. Where's yours, mister?'

I have no answer, nor do I like the expression on his face, so I look towards the window instead. Not twenty feet away is another building, which consists of four apartments. One of the windows is illuminated, and within a girl is pacing back and forth. She is wearing a red dress. But not for long. Her brassière is one of those that unhook at the front. She opens it like a book to show me her breasts. They have a curious effect upon me; my breathing is no longer relaxed, nor is my heartbeat regular. Needless to say, the girl has no interest in the condition of my respiratory system. Seeing her standing there, stark naked, nearly takes my feet off the ground for a second time. I have to concentrate upon faking my gravity.

'I see you've spotted our night club,' says Artie. His grin is sly. I laugh but I accept his invitation to stay for dinner.

Soon I am a regular Friday night guest. Naturally, neither Artie nor Nancy has an inkling of the real reason for my frequent visits; they assume our growing friendship is gradually lowering my resistance. But they are as wrong as those who believed the earth was flat so that if you sailed far enough you would drop off the edge. Without fail I find some excuse to spend time alone in Artie's study, which enables me to watch the girl prepare herself for the weekend. It is a game I do not always win. Sometimes I am frustrated by her avocado plant, the leaves of which cover her nakedness. Or she turns her face towards me, so that I must go on all fours for fear of discovery. On those occasions I emerge in an evil temper, and take it out upon Nancy the following Wednesday. To compensate for such disappointments I begin to keep a log of my successes; jotting down such remarks as 'Fine sight of her breasts as she lifted her hands to curl her hair'; or: 'Excellent view of pudenda as she administered vaginal deodorant.' But there are glorious instances when I can feast my eyes upon her entire anatomy, newly minted by the setting sun. Like some Ptolemaic astronomer she thinks herself the centre of the universe, inspecting her reflection in the mirror, but of course she is merely a moon held in weekly orbit by the gravity of my desire. Then I re-enter the dining room in an elated state. Mistaking my motivation, Artie and Nancy exchange hopeful glances.

One Friday when I arrive at the apartment as usual only Nancy is home.

'Where's Artie?' I ask.

'Don't you read the newspapers?' Nancy replies. 'The Klan fire-bombed the Temple yesterday. He's on guard duty tonight.'

However, this selfless act does not prevent Nancy from trying to seduce me yet again. And to my horror I find that I am weakening, that I actually consider intercourse with no little pleasure. For in my imagination the woman squirming beneath is not Nancy but the girl whose body I have mapped in secret without ever seeing her face. She is the abstraction of sexual desire, of which Nancy is a material counterpart. I must have been lost in a daydream, for I am suddenly aware that Nancy has betrayed my jeans to gravity. Not only are they crumpled around my ankles, but my shirt is also unbuttoned to the waist. Nancy, likewise, is no longer dressed. She stares at me in wonder.

'You're not circumcised!' she exclaims. She is so taken aback to discover that I am not Jewish that she fails to notice an even more significant feature: a belly without a belly-button. Angels are immaculate, and knowing God we require no religion. A gnosticism Nancy is prepared to forgive when she spies my erection. But biblical knowing would be unforgivable. Briefly, if I copulated with Nancy she would be burned to a crisp. A price Nancy seems prepared to pay.

'Please, Nancy,' I say, 'I like Artie too much to do this to him, especially tonight. Besides, we're not in this for pleasure but to reproduce. Let me collect my sperm in a jar, and we'll impregnate you by hand.' Otherwise Artie would do better to run home with his fire-extinguisher. Nancy remains unconvinced until my penis decides the issue by ceasing its anti-gravitational antic. So I shuffle shackle-ankled into Artie's study to masturbate while Nancy curses my behind.

No sooner do I look at the window than the girl's image develops upon the glass. Off comes her dress, up goes my periscope. But instead of removing her underwear she executes a series of yoga exercises she didn't learn at the Academy of Anti-Gravity. My penis is in bud, but it will not open until she is fully exposed. Frustration causes me to groan out loud. At which Nancy bursts in, and seeing at last the true object of my appetites she cries out:

'That slut had an abortion less than three months ago!'

But I am too far gone to care, and groan even louder as she finally parts company with her brassière and steps out of her pants – to reveal yet another layer. But have no fear, she disposes of her sanitary towel as expertly as a stripper slips off her G-string. She is naked and I am lost. As my semen hits the bottom of an empty jar of artichoke hearts I know that I was mistaken about planetary motion. That girl is no moon. On the contrary, I am her satellite. I am subject to her comings and goings, not she to my desires. She pulls me towards her, at specific times, and now she has even drawn the semen from my body. Only one season has passed and already I am in danger. I turn to Nancy, frightened for my future. Incensed, she dips a poultry-baster in the pot labelled HEARTS OF GOLD and squeezes the liquid into her vagina.

'Ouch,' she hisses, 'it's hot!'

Nine months later my child is due, although Artie is naturally credited with its paternity. He actually wants me to attend the birth, but I refuse. What has it to do with me? Half-way through the proceedings, I get a telephone call. It is Artie.

'Come quick,' he begs, 'Nancy's in trouble.'

I find her flat-out on a table in the labour room, an intravenous drip affixed to her wrist through which she is being fed glucose. In addition a bevy of attachments is strapped to her belly. She smiles at me.

'It's so silly,' she says, 'everything was going so well, then the labour stopped.'

'They got worried about the baby,' Artie explains.

The baby's heart is displayed on a foetal monitor; the figure jumps between 140 and 90. Each time it drops to 90 I will it back up again. Always it responds. Until, without warning, it dives to zero. And there it remains.

Artie doesn't. He rushes into the corridor, yelling. I cannot believe my helplessness. The obstetrician, smiling, demonstrates that the baby's apparent death was caused by a microphone sliding off Nancy's undulant abdomen. Shortly thereafter Nancy's wrist is penetrated by a second tube, through which pitocin is administered. Thus stimulated by the hormonal equivalent of inspiration her womb heaves, completing its dilation and catapulting the baby's head into the vagina. Simultaneously the foetal monitor registers the severity of the contraction on a tongue of paper that unrolls from its intestines. Nancy, waving, is wheeled into the delivery room.

Eight days afterwards I am invited to my son's circumcision.

I have not been to the apartment for some time, thinking it tactful to keep my distance. Besides, I needed to prove to myself that I possessed the will-power to break away from the girl in the window – that I was still independent. Don't forget, the baby is Artie's dependant, not mine. And how happy it makes him! 'I've never seen Artie looking so pleased,' I tell Nancy.

'Yes,' she replies, 'he's beaten his creative block at last.'

'Because of the child?' I ask.

'Heavens no! she says. 'He's been to a workshop. A potent brew. Creative writing and Jin Shin Do.'

'It helped?'

'You bet,' says Nancy. 'You should hear him explain how acupressure has opened up new territories of the imagination. No more typing for Artie, he taps his acupoints instead, and waits for the energy to flow. What a workshop! He sang the body electric. Also fucked his instructor on her yoga mat.'

Artie approaches, laughing. 'Nancy's jealous that I had better luck with my teacher than she had with you,' he says.

'Sweetheart,' snaps Nancy, 'you may have learned the language of the body and how to embody yourself in language, but words are about the limit of your body-building abilities.'

Artie winks, turning Nancy against me.

'It wouldn't do you any harm to read Artie's latest story,' she continues. 'The act of love – narrated by a penis. You see, Artie's been taught to empathize with his liberated organs.'

The door-bell chimes. Artie hurries to admit the rabbi.

'It'll serve you right if you identify with your son's penis tonight!' shouts Nancy.

There are no circumcisions in Heaven, so I am caught unawares by the intensity of the occasion. The baby is strapped into an Olympus Circumstraint by the *mohel*, whereupon his jaw trembles, his tongue flutters in his open mouth, and his face turns bright red. He howls in anticipation of the awful sacrifice, notwithstanding Artie's attempts to calm him with a pinkie dipped in kosher wine. I begin to feel somewhat queasy, as if the walls of the room were closing in upon me. I want to push them away, but my hands are bound. I scream. Someone pushes a finger in my mouth. A large face hangs above me. Where are his hands? Pain! Pain! A plastic cap is forced over the head of my penis. Snap go the surgical scissors. The rabbi concludes the ceremony with the traditional blessings, but they fall on deaf ears – for I have fainted.

'Unfasten his tie,' commands the *mohel*, 'take off his shoes!'

When I recover my senses I am lying with a bag of ice upon my forehead. None the less, it is my feet that are cold, *sans* shoes, *sans* socks.

'Give me air,' I mumble. I stumble barefoot into the Los Angeles night, a fallen angel. I stare at the stars in the heavens, an infinite distance away, and see the former Academy of Anti-Gravity graduate into darkness. I shake as Copernicus must have done when he confirmed his terrible suspicions.

Somewhere God will be laughing, as His minions communicate their report. I have breathed life into a sterile womb, and now I will have to pay with my own death. I weep for my fate. I weep for my brother. I weep for my son. But if I am doomed to become the shade of a shadow I can still turn Artie into a man of substance. He publishes a book. It becomes a best-seller. What's more, the critics love it. 'Artie Wiseman,' reports the *New York Review of Books*, 'writes like an angel.'

The Incredible Case of
the Stack o' Wheats Murders

A TRUE STORY

It was a red-letter day for Joshua Smolinsky, private eye. No kooks, cretins or clients had come to call. On the contrary, he was entertaining Sir Isaiah Berlin. They were sipping VSOP brandy and discussing famous terrorists. Bakunin, among others. 'Morally careless,' Sir Isaiah called him, 'intellectually irresponsible, a man who, in his love for humanity in the abstract, was prepared, like Robespierre, to wade through seas of blood; and thereby constitute a link in the tradition of cynical terrorism and unconcern for individual human beings, the practice of which is the main contribution of our own century, thus far, to political thought.'

Joshua Smolinsky nodded in agreement. 'You've reminded me of an incident that took place at the University of California about a year ago – not here in Los Angeles but up the coast at Santa Cruz.' He paused. 'Would you be interested?' he inquired.

'Please,' said Sir Isaiah, 'go ahead.'

'Ever heard of Les Krims?' asked Smolinsky.

Sir Isaiah shook his head.

'He's a photographer,' said Smolinsky. 'Takes some pretty weird shots. But don't get me wrong. He's not some pornographer. Actually, he's a Professor of Photography over at Buffalo. His name was across all the papers a few years ago. On account of four photographs included in a big exhibit at the Memphis Academy of Art. You see, some psycho objected to them and kidnapped the thirteen-year-old son of the curator to make his point. He offered the boy's life in exchange for the removal of the offending prints. Here's the joke: he didn't want his own son corrupted by the images. Of course the authorities complied. In fact, so many good citizens agreed with the lunatic's action that the Mayor of Memphis was compelled to form a committee to decide if the photographs were obscene. As a matter of interest, they found them innocent.

'Anyway, back in 1972 an anonymous lecturer at Santa Cruz (the university won't name him for fear he'll be torn limb from limb) ordered a set of Les Krims's pictures for a course he was teaching on the aesthetics of photography. Ten prints, postcard size, arrived in a box. Each print depicted a naked woman sprawled in a provocative pose, in her bathroom, her bedroom, her kitchen, the front yard. All were bound, some were blindfolded, others gagged. All appeared to have been stabbed, for pools of blood spilled from their bodies. Suggestive imagery also implied that they had been raped. Beside each corpse was a pile of pancakes dripping with pats of melting butter, the Stack o' Wheats, the signature of the murderer. This gave the collection its title, *The Incredible Case of the Stack o' Wheats Murders*. On first viewing the photos were shocking, not least because they were extremely erotic. Did that make me a potential rapist or worse? Then my training took over, I began to seek clues. I soon surmised that the puddles were not blood but pints of chocolate syrup, and that the murderer was not me. Finally, I found the pictures amusing. As Les Krims no doubt intended. The complete portfolio of signed fourteen-by-seventeen-inch Kodalith prints on lightweight Strathmore paper (for which the box was a sampler) comes complete with eight ounces of Hershey's chocolate syrup and enough pancake mix to make one complete Stack o' Wheats.

'However, not everyone was amused. For years the box of photographs gathered dust uncatalogued in the Special Collections room of the library at Santa Cruz, until word was leaked by a sympathetic librarian to one of the many feminist organizations that had proliferated in the meantime. An angry article in the student newspaper accused the library of being soft on hard-core porn. Action was demanded. The photographs were stolen, then returned after lengthy negotiation.

'But this gesture was not sufficient for one woman. Her name was Deborah Spray. She hailed from Dallas, where she had been raped at knife-point aged fifteen. Her reaction was typical: not personal but universal. She seized moral superiority. Founded a group called Women Armed for Self-Protection. They taught themselves to use guns, with which they intended to execute rapists vigilante-style. Maybe she did, maybe she didn't. A bimbo like that could say or do anything. She even had another name. Nikki Craft. Well, she got wind of the Stack o' Wheats.

'She took a look. Next day Spray or Craft read in the *San Francisco Chronicle* about a young woman stabbed to death on Mount Tamalpais. The paper described her corpse as curled in the foetal position. Her blouse was drenched with blood. A dog licked her lifeless arm. Was there any connection between that crime and the box she had opened in Special Collections? Spray decided there was. Like a paranoid she dispensed with the distinction between art and life. Listen, Sir Isaiah. I'll confess that the pictures got me excited. But I'm not about to cut a girl to pieces. You've got to be crazy to start with. And if you're crazy enough you'll get all the stimulation you need from the news ... Spray decided that the girls weren't really sleeping, that the chocolate syrup was really blood. Moved by moral urgency she swore vengeance upon the photographs in the name of all women everywhere.

'For two weeks she concentrated upon winning the trust of the women who staffed Special Collections. So successfully that my friend Rita Bottoms, department head, bent the rules to allow her to copy the photographs. Spray explained that she needed the copies for a class she was taking on Violence Against Women. Rita even helped Spray with her camera (a new one) and allowed her own shawl to be used as a backdrop. A week later Spray returned with a professional photographer, claiming that her first effort had been a failure. It was a Monday. Rita was off-duty, as Spray was aware. A librarian named Carol was in charge. She assisted Spray with her set, which consisted of a cup, an orange plate, knife, fork, spoon, a vase of roses and a flag which read: This is Violence Against Women. Carol returned to her office. The next thing she heard was hysterical laughter. Spray's. The photographer was shooting at top speed while Spray tore the Stack o' Wheats to shreds and poured chocolate syrup upon the remains. Carol opened her door. But was stopped in her tracks when Spray moved aggressively towards her. She was scared. Meanwhile the photographer continued his work, even snapping Carol although she was in obvious distress. Those photographs were subsequently published without Carol's permission, upsetting her so much that her health was affected. Spray was arrested and charged with conspiracy to destroy Library property. She called the charges fascist. She left behind the roses. And a note:

Dearest Rita, Carol, etcetera, My hope is that what has

happened here today will not make your lives more complicated and that it will not be interpreted as anything personal to each of you. These roses are a symbol of my thanks for your helpfulness and understanding. With my love, Deborah Spray.

Concealed among the roses was a flask of chocolate syrup. Later Spray telephoned Rita Bottoms:

SPRAY: I just wanted to know if you had got my flowers and the note . . . the roses and the note?

BOTTOMS: Yes.

SPRAY: I just wanted to let you know that there was something that I left in the vase by accident . . . I wanted to let you know that it wasn't left there for any sort of symbolic meaning. It was a container of chocolate syrup that I brought in with the flowers . . . I just forgot about it . . . Listen, I known that Carol was pretty upset . . . She said that her job had been placed in jeopardy and that she had a whole lot of concerns that she would like to talk about . . . I wondered if there was anything specific that she had in mind . . .?

BOTTOMS: What you did was an act of violence against her, wasn't it?

SPRAY: I'm really sorry that you felt you were manipulated . . . I really don't like to manipulate people . . .

BOTTOMS: Yes, but what you did was an act of violence against her.

SPRAY: I really didn't enjoy manipulating you . . . It was just something I had to do.

'Give Spray credit, she'd planned the happening to the last detail. As she was destroying the Stack o' Wheats, her supporters were saturating the campus with fliers justifying her action. I quote:

Violent pornography is an expression of something profoundly real in male psychology. Violent pornography is the theory; rape is the practice. To expect women to tolerate the protection of this sadistic chic in their school library is unreasonable. Blacks would not tolerate the 'humorous' prints of Klan lynchings. Jews would not tolerate the satirical depiction of Jews in bakery ovens. To ask women to be good civil libertarians at a time when they are being mutilated, raped and murdered in

massive numbers is to ask us to passively accept our own victim-
ization. Today, 31 March 1980, I have destroyed the Stack o'
Wheat prints by tearing them into pieces and pouring chocolate
syrup over them. I destroy these women-hating prints in the
name of all women who must live moment by moment with the
awareness that they may become the next statistic on some
police file; for all women who must live their lives as if in a war
zone, constantly on guard ... I take sole responsibility for this
artistic expression.

Singular art in the name of plurality! Sir Isaiah, I don't have to
point out the logical flaws, exaggerations and misrepresentations to a
gentleman of your intelligence, but I will say as a Jew I don't like
the cheap image pilfered from the holocaust. Speak for yourself,
Spray – I'll decide for myself what I will or will not tolerate. What
egoism! What *chutzpa*!

'Lucky Spray. The university dropped the charges against her. In
return Spray offered to reimburse the library for the damage. The
bill amounted to $13. But that was not all she offered:

In addition, I offer to provide free of charge, a collection of
all materials from the controversy about the prints and about
my decision to destroy them in protest against violent pornography. This will help preserve what is now an essential part of
the history of the University of California at Santa Cruz.

The library took the money. Spray also suggested an exhibit in the
library foyer. No way: "The Library retains the authority to arrange
exhibitions and will not provide an additional forum for theatrical
events." In fact, Spray's collection is now in the Reserve Section of
the library where it is on a twenty-four-hour watch.

'But the fun didn't stop there. Faculty members (who should have
known better) sprang to her side, hundreds of students agitated on
her behalf. A public forum was called to discuss the implications of
the deed. During the course of that evening several professors stood
up to thank Spray for bringing the issues into the open. Unconscious
sexism was confessed. Braver souls spoke in favour of academic
freedom. None of them recommended rape, mutilation or murder of
women. Spray defended herself against charges of censorship. She
recalled that, as a student in Dallas, she had denounced her school

newspaper for refusing to print a poem with the word "uterus". I don't need to explain the association of "denounced" to you, Sir Isaiah. Spray's defence of disobedience was subsequently printed. A pretty piece. It looked like a redwood forest, so full was it with the letter "I"! "I confronted ... I denounced ... I ordered ... I felt ... I decided ... I voice ... I support ... I hope ... I have chosen." Thus were her moral approvals and disapprovals dealt out. Nor were her sacrifices forgotten.

I hope my commitment to this issue has been made clear. I have spent over $500 of my own money, and incurred significant debts, in making this action possible. One month of my life has been consumed in making the educational impact that was my intent from the beginning. My intent was not to repress or silence; quite the contrary. I have acted in the spirit of total creativity and have encouraged all to explore this realm within themselves.

'In recognition of such sacrifices Spray was nominated for the Chancellor's Undergraduate Award, given for "outstanding contribution to campus understanding of ethical principles", by David Cope, Provost of College V, Helene Moglen, Provost of Kresge, Gillian Greensite, Coordinator of Rape Prevention Education Program, Michael Rotkin, Lecturer in Community Studies, and Jack Churchill, her arresting officer. Good old Jack! He didn't want to arrest her in the first place. "I had no choice but to do my job and uphold the law. But I can still arrest people with love." Despite the fact that Spray's nomination contained over three hundred signatures, Chancellor Sinsheimer declined to give her the award. "I'm embarrassed that, as a student here, Deborah Spray hasn't learned more about the importance of intellectual and artistic freedom," he said. "And I'm disappointed that a number of our students and faculty haven't acquired a deeper appreciation of the meaning of freedom of expression."

'Rita Bottoms hit the roof. "I'm talking about some basic human issues, about the way human beings treat each other. So when I hear some of the faculty here refer to what she did as an act of civil disobedience, I want to puke. I am horrified she would be nominated for the Chancellor's prize." Spray was just as angry. She demanded an explanation from the Chancellor for his rejection. She threatened to disrupt the prize-giving with a demonstration. No idle threat.

'She graduated, of course. She's still in Santa Cruz, where you can be whatever you want, providing you have will enough. Actually, I saw her in Los Angeles last week. There she was on Century Park East holding up a placard which read, *HUSTLER* HAS BEEN TEARING UP WOMEN LONG ENOUGH, IT'S TIME FOR WOMEN TO START TEARING UP *HUSTLER*. Her group – the Preying Mantis Women's Brigade – was after Larry Flynt. They ripped up his magazine and poured chocolate syrup upon the pieces.'

Joshua Smolinsky fell silent. He awaited Sir Isaiah Berlin's response.

Tzimtzum

Sometimes people act out of character. Observe my wife standing at the head of a group of demonstrators shouting, 'Death to the fascists!' The police, for their part, advance upon us in rows, protected from brick-bats by their perspex shields, and knock her to the ground. Immediately one of their number steps out of the ranks and drags Ruth away by the hair. I give chase but she is already behind the transparent wall and beyond my reach. Most of all I want to straighten her dress which has ridden up her thighs and uncovered her pants. She is spotted by a few Nazi youths, whom the police are escorting, and they wave their Union Jacks and yell, 'Give her to us! We know how to look after commie whores!' But the police are too engrossed in their own activities to hear, they have become voyeurs excited by their own violence. Those shields have conned them into believing that their actions will have no consequences. But they are wrong, I have the bruises to prove it.

The postman reads the address on the envelope, then delivers a note from my agent. It informs me that he is unable to find an American publisher for my latest book. This is a big disappointment.

'Any mail?' calls my wife from the bedroom.

'No,' I reply, burning the evidence in the grate.

'There's a peculiar smell in here,' says Ruth over breakfast.

'I burnt the toast,' I say.

Ruth has the morning off, since she has to go to court. In the witness box a policeman convincingly describes how my wife attacked him, compelling him to subdue and detain her. Ruth tells a different story. Nevertheless, she is found guilty and fined. The magistrate — no judge of character — adds that he is shocked to hear of a teacher behaving in such a manner, and hopes that her antics will not have a detrimental effect upon the pupils.

'At least we've made sure that there'll never be another National Front meeting held in our school,' says my wife during the victory celebration in the local pub.

The school is a large comprehensive in South-East London, with a great many West Indian and Asian pupils. Hence the outrage over the presence of the National Front. The forebodings are justified. That meeting, not Ruth's behaviour, is to blame for what happens next: the formation of anti-immigrant gangs led by white bullies.

Ruth is prejudiced to see the best in everyone, but even she can find no extenuating circumstances; so when black girls begin to weep inexplicably in the middle of lessons she asserts her power to maintain order. During the following staff-meeting she makes several proposals to improve the situation, involving discussion groups, outside speakers on race relations, and inter-racial parent–pupil–teacher sessions. But her recommendations are greeted with indifference by her fellow teachers and courteously killed by the headmaster. She hears the whispered comment, 'Ruth's being idealistic again.' This apathy depresses her even more than the disruption in her classes.

'No one was supportive,' she says. 'They're all prepared to sit and watch the school being torn in half. Am I being foolish wanting to do something? I would have given anything to have had one teacher stand up and say, "Ruth's right." Just one!'

Then there is a scandal. A Pakistani girl in the fifth-year claims she has been molested by a group of white sixth-formers. Naturally the culprits deny the charge. So the girl names a witness. The witness disappears. And suddenly the outbreak of racial bickering is over. Only one problem remains unresolved.

'The mother of the boy who ran away was in school today,' says Ruth. 'He's joined a religious commune in Sussex. She wants me to talk to him.'

The community is situated in a lordly estate on top of a hill. The gates give no clue as to its identity, but they are open. The grounds seem to be full of young students, all of whom wander around with self-absorbed smiles on their faces. The first notices we see are in the car park where spaces have been reserved for 'The Guardian' and 'The Chief'. We find a board which displays a plan of the domain, picking out buildings such as 'Dianetics', 'Testing', 'Success' and 'Headquarters'. Beside it is a sign which informs us: 'All Visitors Must Register At Headquarters Immediately'. Which we endeavour to do. The front door of the Chief's mansion has two functions: it gives security, it asks questions. These are the questions: 'Do You Have A Good Personal Ethics Record?' and 'Are You Efficient And

Can You Produce?' If the answers are in the affirmative you are invited within. We enter anyway.

At once a smiling attendant asks our business, and we tell him we are looking for a boy named Robin.

'What does he look like?' he asks.

'He is very beautiful,' replies Ruth.

'We are all beautiful here,' says the attendant. So Ruth shows him a photograph.

We are directed to a vegetable patch where Robin is busy cultivating orchids. Ruth is right. He looks like an angel. Bees buzz among the orchids, some even appear to be copulating with blooms that bear an uncanny resemblance to the female of their species.

'Will you come home with us?' Ruth asks Robin.

'No,' he says.

'Why not?' asks Ruth.

'You believe that the true purpose of education is to make people happy, don't you?' he says.

'Yes,' replies Ruth, but slowly.

'Are people happy?' he asks.

'No,' says Ruth.

'Therefore education is a failure,' he says.

'You can't make generalizations like that,' she says.

'Look around you,' he says. 'What do you see? Smiling faces everywhere. And what do you see at school? Only scowls. Why should I give up my smile for a scowl?'

It is an unanswerable question, so I ask another: 'What are you smiling at?'

'The world,' says Robin. 'Because it's mine. Because I am exactly where I want to be. Thinking can't get you there. Nothing can get you there, because you're there already. All you need is someone to say, "Hey, slow down! Everything's beautiful. You're where it's at." Look at these flowers. They're beautiful too, and they know it. They're so cool they don't even have to move to reproduce themselves. The bees do all the work for them. We aim to match their serenity.' With a dazzling smile Robin returns to his orchids. We return to our house in Greenwich.

The next Ruth hears of Robin is when she is summoned to court to give evidence on his behalf. He has been charged with exposure and indecent assault. Apparently it had been his habit to run through

the park in the early evening and expose himself to women pedestrians taking the short cut from the railway station, no doubt in the
hope that they would fling themselves upon his member and carry
off his seed. This was tolerated until he grew bolder and began to
grab between their legs as he trotted past. Eventually the police
picked him up. No one could understand why he needed to pester
women at all; with his looks he could have had any girl he desired.
On the same day I travel to Cambridge to give a lecture to some
German students on the subject of Isaac Bashevis Singer. My friend,
who runs the summer school, greets me at the station. He ac-
companies me into the lecture theatre. I tell the students about
tzimtzum, the cabbalistic doctrine which explains creativity as a
synthesis of good and evil. I quote the example of Gimpel the Fool,
who becomes a storyteller only after learning of his wife's infidelities.
'His new role is the only legitimate offspring of a marriage which
produced six bastards,' I explain. When I have finished I ask if there
are any questions. But there is only silence.

'It was all very new to them,' whispers my friend. We both sit
looking at the downcast faces.

Suddenly a girl explodes. 'Will someone say something,' she cries,
'this silence is driving me mad!' Afterwards she approaches me to
apologize.

'There is no need,' I say.

Her eyes fill with tears. I offer to buy her a drink. 'I know just
how you felt,' I say. We are sitting on stools in front of the bar.

'No,' she says, 'you cannot understand. You are like the others, a
Westerner. I am from the East. Before I came to Stuttgart I was in
an East German prison for eighteen months. For seven weeks I was
kept in solitary confinement. When they took me out I told them
everything they wanted to know. They didn't even need to ask
questions. I talked because I couldn't bear the silence.' She is trem-
bling, and her eyes seek mine for reassurance.

'Why were you arrested?' I ask.

'Because of my boyfriend,' she says. 'He escaped to the West.
When he was over he sent word for another girl to follow him – not
me. Unfortunately she was a police informer. She gave them my
name. It is hard to forgive such things. Now I have a different
boyfriend. We live together. But my nightmares haven't left me. In
my dreams my interrogator and my betrayer become confused. And

it is true; fascism, communism – call them what you want – are matters of personality not politics. My faith in people has been destroyed. I have become a little paranoid. Some nights I am too frightened to sleep, so I stay awake and write poetry. My experiences have made me an artist. Now, thanks to you, I even have a name for my condition. I am suffering from *tzimtzum*.'

I also am no stranger to insomnia. Many nights I lie awake listening to the World Service of the BBC. At the moment my wife is sleeping through news of civil war, assassination and natural disaster. I recall the East German girl and imagine what dark productive hours we could share. Ruth's mouth opens slightly and her eyelids flicker as if something deep inside is rising to protest against my vision, but at the final moment it is smothered by sleep. She was home from the witness stand before me.

'Did the lecture go well?' she asks.

'Fine,' I say, 'how about your court appearance?'

'Guess who was on the bench?' she says. 'That swine who fined me. I could see he thought I was to blame for Robin's mis- demeanours. You could hear his mind ringing up the clichés: Sex Education, Permissive Society, Free Love.'

'So what happened?' I ask.

'He was bound over for psychiatric reports.'

In the morning I watch the postman walk by our house without pausing.

'Still nothing about America?' asks Ruth. She wants to show me sympathy, but doesn't dare. Success will bring us together, but failure is impossible to share. However, I do not want to blame our situation for what is really a flaw in my character. Let me give an example. During the Easter vacation Ruth invited a new teacher and his wife around for dinner; I'll call them Martin and Maria. We are introduced.

'Are you in the profession too?' asks Martin.

'No,' I say. Silence.

'What do you do?' asks Maria.

'I'm a writer,' I say.

Silence. Ruth, recognizing the symptoms, hurriedly offers drinks. Over dinner the conversation safely explores the subject of teaching. I do not say a word, because I have nothing to add. Nor do I join in when the discussion moves to the National Front.

'Believe me,' says Martin, 'they'll only be a force when they get a leader with real charisma.'

After they have gone Ruth turns on me. 'You might have made an effort,' she says. 'I want people to like you, not to think that you are a stuck-up bastard.'

'You know I'm shy,' I say.

'That's no excuse,' she says.

'Fascist,' I say. 'In a democracy all inhibitions must be respected.'

'You're the one with the fascist mentality,' she says. 'You guard your feelings as if they were state secrets.'

That night as usual my wife slept the sleep of the just.

We begin to see a lot of Martin and Maria. Martin is a music teacher. That is another problem; I am tone deaf.

'There's no such thing,' says Martin, 'you're just frightened to let go. Music is a great release mechanism. As far as I am concerned, a scream can be just as beautiful as Mozart. Come on, let's hear you scream.'

'Aargh,' I say.

'You do have a problem,' says Martin, 'but it's nothing to do with music.'

Martin's dream is to start his own school. He has already opened an account at Barclays in the school's name, which I won't mention.

'As I filled in those routine forms at the bank I could see my dream beginning to take shape,' he says. 'God knows, these aren't days for dreamers, but to me the whole concept has never seemed like a dream, more just the way it should be. Some pretty wonderful people are interested and want to be part of my scheme, including several professors. One day I plan to persuade Ruth to join us. She's wasted in the state system.'

Martin's ideas? He wants to build the school near Glastonbury, close to the source of England's collective unconscious. He believes, of course, that education should be directed at the heart not the head, that feeling is more important than thinking.

'In that case,' I say, 'how come you're so pleased to have the approval of the academics?'

'Why must you pick holes in everything?' asks Martin. 'If you're so suspicious why don't you sit in on one of my classes?'

At Ruth's insistence I attend Martin's elementary music class the following week, the first lesson of the new school year.

'I suppose you're all a bit nervous,' says Martin to the thirty-odd thirteen-year-olds. 'Well, that's okay. Just don't try to hide your feelings. Music is all about expressing feelings. I'm also NER-VOUS! Now let's hear from you. What are you all?'

'NER-VOUS!' they shout.

'Very good,' says Martin, 'I think we've got the basis of a fine group here. Listen carefully, I want to explain what's going to happen. In the next three months we are all going to develop as human beings, we are going to communicate with one another by expressing our feelings through music. In that way I want you to tell me things you wouldn't dream of telling your parents. It's going to be a lot of hard work, but by the end of term I want us to be a group – not just an ordinary group – but a loving group.'

There are a few giggles at that, but I can see that most of the class is spellbound. Clearly, they have never heard such sentiments from a teacher before.

Martin decides to end the lesson with a sing-song. 'Something you all know,' he says, 'the National Anthem. I want everyone singing at the top of their voice. Miming will be regarded as an act of treachery.'

As Martin thumps out the tune on the piano the class roars its way through to the final 'God save the Queen', with the exception of an ungainly boy who makes fish-like gestures in a desperate attempt to conceal his crime. But Martin observes.

'Didn't you hear what I said?' he demands. 'What is the point of being here if you aren't prepared to join in? Everyone else is ready to take the risk of singing. Why should you be different?'

'I can't sing,' says the boy.

Martin smiles at me, acknowledging my presence for the first time. 'Yes, you can,' he says. 'There's no such thing as a bad voice, only a repressed one. Repressions stunt your growth. You do want to grow up, don't you?'

The boy nods. The class howls.

'I'm going to give you another chance,' says Martin, 'you sing, I'll play.'

The boy flounders hopelessly, so lost that he does not even notice when Martin begins to play the Marseillaise. However, his classmates do. They laugh joyously at their comrade's humiliation.

'Did you tune into the feedback I was getting?' says Martin in the staff-room. 'Now perhaps you'll give some credit to my methods?'

'Don't you think you were a bit hard on that kid at the end?' I ask.

'I thought you'd single him out,' says Martin, 'a weedy mother's boy. Listen, when he's fucking girls at fifteen instead of blubbering into chicken soup he'll thank me for today.'

'But at the moment he hates you,' I say.

'Negative feelings are just as valid as positive ones,' he says. 'At least I've got him feeling.'

'Your school is going to be quite a place,' I say.

'You know, you could be a pretty good writer,' he says, 'if only you could free yourself of your obsession with structure. Loosen up a bit. Get a dialogue going with your unconscious. Then you'd be our ideal writer-in-residence.'

That evening, in bed, my wife asks me what I thought of Martin's class. 'The kids love him,' she adds. This statement makes me vindictive. I arouse Ruth, but refuse to have intercourse. She cries herself to sleep instead. Alone, I attempt to analyse Martin's 'dream', not according to standard symbols, but as an expression of his unconscious. If only I hadn't nodded off.

Glastonbury Tor can be interpreted in a variety of ways, with its single tower on top pointing directly to heaven. We are picnicking on its lower slopes, our food dispersed upon a blanket. Martin has artfully arranged a half-term trip for the sixth-form choir to Wells Cathedral, so he can look for a pocket of land on which to build his school. We have been invited along as fellow prospectors. I could not refuse, for some of Martin's enthusiasm has rubbed off on Ruth, and I sense that she has faith in him. This is disquieting. She talks about his 'presence', whereas I am described as 'remote'. It is a beautiful summer day. Martin, Maria and Ruth sit discussing the boundaries of education like three magicians, while I lackadaisically watch the swallows catch flies. Seeking greater stimulation I try to decipher a mirage that has formed where the ground begins to rise towards us. Gradually it resolves itself into a golden boy who is shimmering over the grass in our direction.

'We have raised the *genius loci*,' exclaims Martin. 'Welcome to where it's at.'

Robin smiles. 'Can't stop,' he says, 'I'm on the track of a rare orchid.' And returns to the heat haze whence he came.

'It's time we started moving,' says Martin. 'I want to go up the Tor and pick out a site for the school.'

'It's too hot,' complains Maria.

'And I get acrophobia,' I say.

'Can't sing, can't climb,' says Martin, 'you're a bit of a poor relation, aren't you?'

'Don't tease,' says Ruth, 'he really is terrified of hcights. Please come,' she adds, 'I'll help you.'

'Go without me,' I say.

'Phobias are fascinating,' says Martin. 'I'm assisting a friend with his desensitization technique. What we'd do in your case is stand you on a table and relax you with music, so that you'd begin to associate high places with pleasurable sensations. Pity you think it's all mumbo-jumbo.'

'Oh, leave him,' says Ruth.

With Martin and Ruth gone it occurs to me that I have never been alone with Maria before. I look at her with a smile and suddenly become conscious of an unexpected set of associations; she chain smokes, she wears silver chains on both wrists and carries her watch on a chain around her neck.

'I know you're staring at me,' she says. 'Am I so interesting?' She snorts. 'Would it surprise you to learn that I see a shrink every week?'

'Why?' I inquire. 'You seem fine to me.'

'Oh, I function pretty well at surface level,' says Maria, 'but I'm right out of touch with my true self. I just can't seem to express what I'm really feeling. And of course Martin being so deep makes me feel even more inadequate. He's so patient, I only wish I could respond more. To tell you the truth, I'm afraid I'm frigid. That I don't display my emotions because I haven't got any.'

'So why are you crying?' I ask. 'I don't see any onions around.'

When Martin and Ruth return Maria's eyes are no longer puffy.

'Did you find somewhere?' she asks.

'Just the spot,' replies Martin.

'Plus we discovered Robin's orchids,' says Ruth.

'I've decided to adopt the orchid as a symbol for my school,' continues Martin. 'An orchid in bloom, roots and all. You know its name comes from the Greek word for testicles, because of the shape of its tubers. What a potent combination – beauty and virility! Our motto will be: "Power grows from the shaft of a phallus". In Greek, of course.' He laughs. Maria hugs her husband. Life isn't simple, but it isn't that complicated either.

Soon, however, life hands me a real complication. In the shape of an anonymous letter.

> *Thought you'd like to know. Your wife is making it with the music master.*

'Anything in the post?' calls Ruth from the bathroom.

• 'Nothing interesting,' I answer. She no longer bothers to question me further.

'Why didn't you say there was something for me?' asks Ruth, having joined me at breakfast.

'Brown envelopes never contain anything important,' I reply.

'It's from Amnesty International,' says Ruth. 'Urgent action required in the case of Anatoly Shcharansky.'

The enclosure gives details of his trial, and quotes from his address to the court. 'I am happy that I have lived honestly and in peace with my conscience, and never lied even when I was threatened with death,' he said. 'I am happy to have helped people . . .' His words vivify a character dormant in my memory. And Gimpel the Fool – equally consistent – repeats in my ear, 'I believed them, and I hope at least that did them some good . . . What's the good of *not* believing? Today it's your wife you don't believe; tomorrow it's God Himself you won't take stock in.' This was Gimpel's foolishness; he believed what he was told. No sooner do I think of Shcharansky's trial in fictional terms than it becomes real. I see him in the courtroom talking to the wall. The audience remains silent until his sentence is pronounced. Then they break into spontaneous applause. 'It serves him right!' they yell. 'He should have got more!' He is called a weed that must be uprooted from Russia's sacred soil. And what was his crime? He told the truth. Most of us accept that the self must evolve to survive; we are chameleons, not leopards. When they tell us to sing, we sing. If it were possible I would weep. I did not help the boy in Martin's class, I cannot help Shcharansky. 'Anatoly,' I say, 'after the orchids have sickened and died they will ask you to make sense of the mess. Just hang on.'

Ruth is writing to President Brezhnev. But what can a letter do?

After school we play tennis with Martin and Maria. Mixed doubles. Martin is a superior player who demands the fullest concentration, but today my mind isn't on the match. I am watching Ruth for any signs that the letter might be true. Every time she serves I imagine that she is stretching to reach Martin, and rallies between them take on the air of an intimate conversation that excludes me. We are thrashed.

'What's the matter?' asks Ruth.

'Nothing,' I say. I no longer have it in my power to share my feelings with my wife. If I haven't already lost her, I soon will. I tell myself not to be so dramatic.

Unfortunately my subconscious refuses to accept the advice. My face turns green. So does Ruth's. We are walking through a coniferous forest, following the course of a fast-flowing river. Without warning, the motion of the water becomes perpendicular. The forest disappears. Our faces become white. We are on the edge of a precipice watching the river drop down the sheer side of a cliff. The effervescence makes the chasm seem bottomless. As it is winter the spray crystallizes on contact with the air, forming a great mound like a loaf of sugar. Ruth strolls towards the brink, nearer than I dare go. I have a sudden horror that she will vanish from my life. My heart freezes with fear.

'Ruth!' I cry. 'For God's sake come back here!' But she doesn't listen, and dissolves into the mist.

Then Robin appears. Since he has wings I ask him to hover above the waterfall and look for Ruth. Instead he pulls down his shorts, to reveal a bloody flower! Even insomniacs have nightmares.

Our decline continues.

'Did you have a good day?' asks my wife on her return from school.

'Not bad,' I say.

'What did you do?' she asks.

'Writing,' I reply. Whereupon she quits my study, and is usually not re-encountered until I find her in bed already asleep.

One day, however, I surprise her by responding in the affirmative.

'Yes?' she repeats.

'My agent phoned me an hour ago,' I say, 'he's sold the American rights for ten thousand dollars. We're rich!'

I make plans. I laugh. But Ruth is crying. Not for joy.

'We've got to part,' she says. I know some terrible revelation is on its way, and I feel my wife's pain in summoning up the courage to tell me.

'I'm in love with someone else,' she says at last.

'Martin?' I say. She nods. 'What do you mean by "in love"?' I ask. 'Have you slept with him?'

'As good as,' she says. 'We made love that afternoon at Glastonbury. It's funny, when I left you I had no intention of doing anything. I even said no when Martin first suggested it. I was very flattered, of course. A man like Martin saying he loved me. Then he said how much he needed me and I thought of you – how little you need me. That's when I said yes. Two words – "need" and "yes" – and it was done. Don't make any mistake, it was good. Martin told me not to feel any guilt, but he needn't have bothered. It was easy keeping up the pretence while you were being such a shit, but now you're suddenly nice again I can't pretend any longer.' She moans. It is extraordinary; her body is expressing my feelings.

'Do you want to leave me?' I ask.

'I don't know,' she says. 'I expected you to throw me out.'

'Do you still love me?' I ask.

'Of course,' she says.

'So what do you want to do?'

'I don't know.'

Silence. And in my solitude I dimly perceive the cruelty of the East German girl's tormentors. I also have been emptied of all sensations. Events have torn my stomach inside out. I also am ready to confess to anything. But confession will not alter the fact that my wife is in love with Martin. Slowly my tongue unrolls, until words pour from me in torrents. By mutual consent we make extreme efforts to save ourselves, ignoring any deeper damage for the sake of the moment. Indeed, it is impossible to do otherwise; future wretchedness cannot be put into words since it has no immediate expression. So our language is descriptive, our tense the present. We talk through the night and into the afternoon. School is abandoned. By evening we have reached a new *modus vivendi* that does not include Martin.

But such excommunication cannot be accomplished with a simple fiat. For one thing, Martin remains Ruth's colleague; for another, she still loves him. Consequently she insists upon telling him what has happened before he hears it on the nine o'clock news.

'Leave me alone,' she says. She dials his number. Secretly I pick up the extension. Martin answers simultaneously.

'Hello,' says Ruth, 'is Maria out?'

'Out cold, my amorous anima,' replies Martin. 'God, how I love you, Ruthie. I'd given up hoping to feel real love again. You've got grace, beauty, and such gut-level sensuality! You wanted me so much. Your body was like an instrument only I could play. Listen, I'm going to tell you a secret. When we climaxed together it was my first time in perfect harmony.' He pauses.

I can hear my wife breathing. Is she going to tell him? It is almost irrelevant now. I cannot burn Martin's words like an unwanted letter; on the contrary, they have been branded on my memory. Nor do I stop at words, images come unbidden. My enemy and my wife making love, in a hollow surrounded by trees, watched not by Robin but by me.

'I've told Jonathan everything,' says Ruth.

'Everything?'

'Yes.'

'Has he kicked you out?'

'No.'

'Are you leaving him?'

'No.'

'Do you love him?'

'Yes.'

'Do you love me?'

'Yes.'

'I see,' says Martin.

Is he holding back his tears? Ruth certainly isn't.

'If I can't be your lover, at least let me be your guide,' he says. 'Please don't think I'm being sceptical if I tell you a little story. It's about two friends who are going through an ugly experience. The root of their sickness is the one's insistence upon control of the other. Instead of two healthy people who appreciate each other for what they are, the man has tried to turn his wife into an appendage of himself. So that her psyche has become hopelessly entwined with him. I may not have taught you much, Ruthie, but I hope you'll always remember that a healthy selfness is a must for a sound love relationship.'

I feel nauseous. I replace the receiver as quietly as I can. But I cannot shut out the sight of their copulation. It reappears most frequently when we make love, and though I go through the motions I am not really participating. My wife is stimulating Martin, she is responding to his thrusts, she is wiping off his semen. I am merely watching from behind a tree.

Otherwise things are fine. Months pass. The government falls. Ruth sees Martin at school only when she has to. She goes off the pill in preparation for starting a baby. Then one day Martin walks up the garden path wearing an orchid in his buttonhole. It is the first time I have seen him since Glastonbury.

'Hello,' he says, 'I've come to ask for your votes.'

'Why?' I say.

'Didn't you know,' he says, 'I'm your National Front candidate for the general election?'

'You're joking,' says Ruth.

'Not at all,' says Martin. 'The National Front may be tainted with Nazi ideology but that's all old hat. It's today's radical movement. Labour is the party of reaction. Thirty years out of date. Why not open your minds to new ideas? No other party dares speak of the spiritual regeneration of the British people. Note the words, "spiritual regeneration". In the right hands the National Front could be the salvation of this country.'

'But it's fascist and racist,' protests Ruth.

'Don't be silly, Ruthie,' replies Martin, 'would I join an organiza-tion that was evil? Forget political prisoners. I'm here to liberate your minds. Mental terrorism, that's what I preach. Indian mysticism is all very well – you know how much respect I have for their religions and cults. But we British require something altogether more red-blooded. Like Robin, an angel with muscles. Or you, Ruthie. Your mixture of spirituality and earthy sexuality is just what we're looking for.'

'Please, Martin,' says Ruth, 'it's over.'

'Perhaps,' he says, 'but we both have a pretty clear picture of what happened. And why. The ballot is secret. Jonathan need never know if you put a cross by my name. Follow your heart on polling day, Ruthie. Vote for me.'

We are on the steps of the town hall when the election results are declared. Martin receives 600 votes. Ruth swears that hers is not among them. The victorious candidate is mobbed by his supporters, who do not include us. We have come as witnesses to failure, not success. We walk away.

Since it is a balmy spring night we decide to take a short cut through the woods. Ruth is reluctant, but I am persuasive. To frighten her I run ahead and hide behind a tree. Ruth chases me, then stops. There is a rustle of dead leaves and the bushes part. Ruth turns, expecting to see me, but faces instead her smiling attacker. Swift as an animal he pushes her to the ground and kneels on her left arm, simultaneously grabbing her other arm with his left hand. I watch, transfixed, as if in a dream. Ruth writhes about, calling my name. 'No, no, no!' she cries, words and sobs mingling. But she cannot prevent the angel-faced boy lifting her skirt with his free hand and pulling down her pants. Exposed, she lies still, sensing that any movement now is a provocation.

It is no use. He forces himself between her thighs and into her belly. Fighting for breath Ruth begs, 'Don't make me pregnant!' But her plea ends in gurgles and gasps. Faster and faster the figure pumps as if desperately trying to rise off the ground, until Ruth is activated by his passion and helplessly begins to heave in response. Out of control, her hands snatch for that final release which comes as a great shudder. Tears roll from her unblinking eyes.

I am Robin – out of character, as it were. 'You whore,' I say.

Somewhere over the Rainbow

The girl, furious, accused the man of a dirty crime. The man cringed.

'I was only looking for rainbows,' he said.

'In the middle of the night?' she replied.

To tell the truth, he had watched her undress. Her bedroom faced his studio and he had pretended that she was his model. Of course she was better than any model he could have booked, because her gestures were all completely natural. She was a figment of his imagination but also real, intangible but visible. At first she had slipped her dress over her head, without thinking, then she had paused, as if suspecting that she was being watched, but he had held his breath, and she had relaxed, and finally unhooked her brassière and stepped out of her pants. She was right, he had violated her body, but only in his mind. He had taken possession of her with his eyes, and the old adage was true: out of sight out of mind. Before him now, fully dressed, she was inviolable. He began to weep.

The girl was shocked, suddenly the roles were reversed, she was the aggressor and he was the victim. 'This is lunacy,' she thought. Then she remembered that lunacy was actually inspired by her new goddess, the moon. 'May I see your paintings?' she asked.

He led her to his studio, from which she could see straight into her bedroom. His paintings were terrible, misbegotten shapes in wild colours enclosed within heavy black outlines. She knew it was wrong to be judgmental, a throwback to the patriarchal system of academic criticism, and that she ought to be supportive – who knew what emotional risks he was taking in doing those paintings?

'I'd like one for my bedroom,' she said. 'How much do you want for the one with the tiger?'

'I don't know,' he replied, 'I've never sold a picture before.'

She wanted to be helpful. 'You should take them to the flea market next Sunday,' she said, 'I'm sure you'll sell lots.'

He began to laugh. 'Would you have said that to Rembrandt or

Van Gogh? Sell your paintings in the market. With all the other junk! These are works of art, worth more than a few pennies!'

'I think your paintings will be too expensive for me,' she said.

'It's a present,' he replied.

Then the girl saw that the man had not really lied when he said that he had been looking for rainbows, for there was a transparent rainbow pasted to his window through which the sunshine was radiating, splashing them with waves of multicoloured light. The man observed that the girl's face was an indefinable mixture of primary colours and explained that the reason he had come to her city was because of its reputation as the rainbow capital of the world.

'This area just seems to have a lot of people who are more in tune with the miraculous,' she agreed. 'There's an awful lot of heads and ex-heads who really get off on rainbows.'

'I want to let the colours wash away my straight lines,' the man said.

The girl liked this image, she thought it was very feminine.

'You've got factories that manufacture rainbows,' said the man, 'transparent ones for windows, five-foot long paper ones for walls. So why not a Rainbow Artist?' Then he spoilt it. 'My reward will be a pot of gold.'

'That's just the sort of materialistic remark you'd expect from a man,' the girl retorted. 'You'll never break out of your straitjacket if you keep up a language barrier between yourself and the ethereal.'

The man didn't know what to say. He looked so crestfallen that the girl kissed him on the cheek. 'Would you like a cup of tea?' he ventured.

'What sort?' she asked.

'Celestial Seasonings,' he replied.

'That'll do,' she said.

He poured the aromatic tea into brightly coloured cups from a pot shaped like a cloud with a rainbow for a handle. The steam made his eyes water. He seemed utterly helpless, without a vocabulary for the limbo land between the material and the ethereal. The girl took pity upon him.

'Would you like me to pose for you?' she asked.

He nodded.

She undressed. He didn't move. His eyes remained fixed upon her empty underwear, as if he couldn't quite grasp the implications of their vacancy. The girl understood that he was having problems adjusting to the reality she had created. She unbuttoned his shirt. But the erection her nudity had excited at a distance couldn't be repeated in close proximity. He tried to enter her limply, but even then his strength failed to materialize.

'My poor boy,' said the girl, 'forget about role-playing. Let me help you. My forearms are strong from milking goats.' As she pumped him the girl smiled, she had found the perfect man at last.

They exchanged gifts; she gave him a pair of rainbow-tinted spectacles moulded out of plastic, he gave her a painting. It consisted of eight hearts in two rows, each coloured differently – red, orange, yellow, green, blue, black, silver and rainbow. He had used water-colours and there were drips and smudges everywhere. Cissy was delighted, she named him her Rainbow Artist. He didn't dare tell her that he had copied it. They exchanged confidences; the man confessed that he was separated, Cissy confessed that she was preg-nant. The man demonstrated how the affair had influenced his work, as thickening lines gradually encroached upon the polychromatic frenzy, until there was only black which marked the day his fiancée had finally returned his ring. She was a divorcée from Southern California with two half-breed brats (Cissy was shocked by such language) who refused to accept his artistic ambitions.

'Thanks to her,' the man said, 'I had two skins, one thin, the other thick; the latter being the pelt of a bear.' She had nagged him into a job at Disneyland. 'I felt emasculated,' said the man. His final humiliation had come when she had brought her kids to the Magic Kingdom and not recognized him beneath the ursine fur. 'Even when I took liberties with her that she should not have allowed a bare-face man,' he said. That's how he discovered she was a slut; when confronted with the evidence she called him a flip-flop, a flap-jack and a peeping Tom, none of which he found flattering. Free once more, the future Rainbow Artist travelled north, hugging the Pacific coast until he reached the town of Oz, where he rented the studio that faced Cissy's bedroom. Another fifty miles would have brought him to Half Moon Bay, and a further thirty would have taken him all the way to San Francisco, where he could have remained as anonymous as he had been in Los Angeles.

Cissy's story was just as sad. Vampires, witches and ghosts strike fear in the heart of man because they have no reflections; men cannot stand beside them before a mirror and say, 'This is mine.' To be brief, without proof of possession, men sense they are possessed. Cissy presented no such problem; for years she had been nothing more than a reflection in men's eyes.

'I wanted them to think of me as sassy,' said Cissy, 'but I was an easy lay, that's all.' And so Cissy remained a sex object, punctured and penetrated by a hundred pins and pricks, until it came to the subject of her pregnancy. This was a consequence which threatened to become visible, and so destroy her image as an image. What was left for her? Overdose? Abortion? 'Anywhere else I would have sunk in waves of despair,' said Cissy, 'but Oz is a sheltered cove of high consciousness.' In fact, these words were a translation of her life and near-death; she washed down a box of tranquillizers with a bottle of vodka and with a head already swimming waded into the Pacific in search of oblivion; instead she was pulled on board a sailing boat by the spiritual descendants of Atlantis. They cured her madness with hellebore, an ancient remedy, which is more commonly called bear's foot. Consequently, Cissy and her Rainbow Artist could even exchange good-luck charms; a bear claw from him, some bear's foot from her. And she knew more than ever that this was the man for her.

Once upon a time Luna would have been called a fortune-teller and forced to carry on her business within the context of a circus or a funfair, but in Oz she was able to set herself up as a clairvoyant analyst. If the future was of little interest she could also divine past lives, and make sense of the various reincarnations. Furthermore, she was adept at psychic diagnosis and soul reading; another sort of woman might have described herself as a good judge of character. But this is no comedy of manners; it is a story of masks and of hidden meaning, and of all possible masks language is the greatest.

The Rainbow Artist entered her office, which was tastefully decorated with the paraphernalia of her credo, and sat upon a comfortable rocking-chair. 'I have come to have my soul read,' he said. Ever since Cissy had told him what she wanted him to do, the Rainbow Artist had been apprehensive; most of all he was worried what his soul might reveal, that his soul might betray him to Luna as his tuberculosed lungs had betrayed him to a doctor years before. Nor was he sure that he wanted to know whether his soul was sick; such knowledge would make a sham of any subsequent good deeds, when he was bound helter-skelter for the shambles. Moreover, he did not think that Cissy would accept him if he were pronounced one of the damned.

Luna observed that her client was nervous, and sought to reassure him. 'You must not worry about a negative reading,' she said. 'With proper counselling we can restore the balance between your physical–etheric, mental and astral bodies which controls the health of your soul.'

She began to assemble certain objects upon her table, the mysterious appurtenances of her profession; no doubt the Rainbow Artist could have given a name to each of them, but their combination suggested the secrets of metaphysics.

'What do you do?' asked Luna.

'I paint rainbows,' replied the Rainbow Artist.

'You've certainly come to the right place,' said Luna. 'People here have been psychedelically baptized,' she continued, 'we're more than willing to tap into the vital energy that's reflected in rainbows.'

The Rainbow Artist recognized Cissy's sentiments, though Luna's language was considerably more scientific. She handed him a piece of paper with dots marked upon it.

'Do not think that this owes anything to the masculine science of geometry,' she said, 'this is geomancy.' As with many such controlled experiments, Luna's practice never varied. First she had her clients connect as many dots as they wished, then she poured sacred earth from a leather pouch into the palm of their hand and asked them to cast it upon a blank sheet of paper. She recorded the resulting patterns, comprehensible to her alone, with a Polaroid camera. They were like fingerprints, no two were ever the same. The Rainbow Artist watched, fascinated, as the photograph of his soul developed before his eyes.

He returned to Cissy with the good news that his soul had passed its medical. What had particularly impressed Luna was the realization that his masculine tendency towards worldly achievement had not obliterated his deeper feminine feeling for cosmic harmony. In short, the Rainbow Artist had not followed the example of ninety-nine per cent of her male clientele and closed all the dots; and this had coloured her divination of his earth-pattern, in which she had recognized an uncanny resemblance to the constellation of the Great

Bear, Ursa Major. Her first reaction was one of disappointment, since it was supposed to exert a malign influence, but then she recalled the story of its creation and was mollified. How Callisto, a follower of chaste Diana the huntress, was seduced by Jupiter in her guise, much to the chagrin of Juno, who transformed poor Callisto into a bear. Here, surely, was the archetype of the suffering the Rainbow Artist had experienced at the hands of his fiancée in Disneyland: turned into a bear because he had the soul of an artist. In addition, the myth contained a mingling of the male and female elements which accorded exactly with her original intuition; how astute of Jupiter to realize that Callisto would only succumb to another woman's love!

With Luna's blessing the Rainbow Artist accompanied Cissy to her birth classes at the YWCA, mandatory for domestic nativities in the town of Oz. Their teacher was a midwife, heiress to the arcane wisdom of her calling, who preached natural childbirth and the perfidy of doctors. She called Cissy the Mother and the Rainbow Artist her Coach. She taught them deep breathing.

'Fill your lungs,' she ordered, 'then let it out slowly.'

They continued for a few minutes, until they took a cleansing breath.

'How did that feel?' she asked the Rainbow Artist.

'Weird,' he replied. 'I felt that my mind was floating away from my body.'

'That's good,' she said. She believed firmly in the ascendancy of the body over the mind, and taught that it was the Mother's job to follow the body's promptings throughout the birth. 'Your body will tell you what to do, for sure,' she said to Cissy. 'Learn to interpret its messages. Get in touch with your sphincter muscles.'

As the weeks progressed, the Rainbow Artist learned more and more about a woman's body, and learned how to help Cissy cope with the miracle of birth. Many times they went through a simulated labour together. But when the real thing began, they panicked; Cissy couldn't handle the unexpected severity of the pain, and the Rainbow Artist could think of no way to comfort her; all that they had learned to prepare them for the roles of Mother and Coach vanished into thin air.

When the midwife showed up at the Rainbow Artist's studio, Cissy was rolling in soiled clothes upon the couch, screaming for pethidine. This was not music to the midwife's ears. What was the problem? Not lack of love; she only delivered for couples who really loved one another. Inhibitions! They were fighting their bodies!

'Get undressed,' she ordered Cissy. 'Caress her,' she commanded the Rainbow Artist.

He began to stroke her hair.

'Touch her breasts!' cried the midwife. 'Watch me.' She stood behind Cissy and grabbed her breasts. 'See how nice they are,' she said. She knew that a lot of women have a lot of things going with their breasts. For sure.

So the Rainbow Artist took up his position, and the midwife got Cissy to relax and ride her contractions. Thus they passed through the most agonizing period of labour, the transition, into that part when Cissy could take an active role and begin pushing. Crowning was followed by birth.

The Rainbow Artist regarded the new-born baby with amazement. It was lying upon Cissy's belly, still connected to her by the umbilical cord, gradually turning from blue to pink as its lungs filled with air and the oxygenated blood began to pump around its body. Although he was not the child's father he was happy beyond all expectation, tears fell freely from his eyes without his knowledge. Cissy yelped with delight; her perfect baby was howling on her belly, and her Rainbow Artist was clutching her by the hand.

'Did you feel it?' asked the midwife. 'The cosmic energy that flowed through you as you gave birth.'

Cissy had no words to describe her emotions, so she joyfully accepted the midwife's description. 'For sure,' she said.

With guidance from the midwife the Rainbow Artist cut the umbilical cord. Fifteen minutes later Cissy gave a final push and the placenta was expelled into the midwife's hands.

At that moment Luna arrived. She examined the placenta, like a priestess, and declared it free of blemishes. Again, the colours enthralled the Rainbow Artist: on one side it had a bluish sheen, which was criss-crossed with blood vessels, while the other side consisted of a dozen dull-red lobules. Instead of wrapping it up and throwing it away, Luna and the midwife began to treat it as if it were something sacred. Indeed, Luna sliced thin wafers off the segmented side and pushed them between the lips of the assembly (with the exception of Baby). Luna considered the placenta to be divine, a miraculous source of life for the baby in the uterus; it was the female essence, the transubstantiation of all women into a single vital object. She placed the remainder in a reliquary. Finally, she noted down all the details required for an accurate horoscope; exact time of birth, etcetera.

It so happened that the week after Cissy's delivery was the winter solstice. What made it even more exciting for Luna was the fact that it was also a full moon.

Luna knew that in an earlier life she had been burnt at the stake as a witch; in trances she recalled the shame as the flames peeled off her clothes exposing her nakedness to the gawkers. A symbolic death! What better representation could there be for the fate of women? How many others had been killed in such a way since ancient times? Millions! Luna was ennobled by all these martyrs. They spoke with her voice. Victims of an unacknowledged civil war within society from which patriarchy had so far emerged triumphant. With what implications! For a start it meant that all folk tales were actually anti-feminist propaganda. Witches and stepmothers must be rehabilitated. Baba Yaga was really a persecuted herbal healer! Walt Disney was her arch-enemy. Although her particular *bête noire* was *Snow White*, she accepted *Sleeping Beauty* as the perfect model; a princess, poisoned by a jealous crone, who can only be revived by a man! 'Sweet Diana,' she prayed, 'give me revenge!'

After hours, as it were, Luna practised three kinds of magic: red, white, and black. Red was connected with cycles, menstruation, the seasons, fertility; its goddess was the moon, its expression was ritual. White magic was concerned with healing, black magic with cursing. Beneath the full moon, at the beginning of the longest night of the year, Luna performed red magic for a small group of witches, which included Cissy and the Rainbow Artist. They stood in a charmed circle at the summit of a hill. Luna compared the gross moon, unusually ruddy, with a placenta.

'In fact,' she said, 'each mother contains within herself a piece of the moon; just as the moon nourishes us, so the placenta nourishes our babies. We are all moon-children. Each month our Mother reminds us of our potential for fullness, but then shrinks in sorrow at our true condition. It is a reflection upon us. If all the people on earth, who are really the scattered fragments of the moon, could spiritually unite, the moon would remain forever full!'

The myth of Callisto was then re-enacted, with the Rainbow Artist playing Callisto transformed. He had felt uncomfortable in the bearskin during rehearsals, until Luna had assured him that he would not be the anonymous buffoon he had been at Disneyland. As the moon rose higher, it shone with a cold light, which illuminated all too clearly the falling off there had been since classical times. In the distance the Pacific shimmered like a silver robe, while in the heavens the constellations watched the performance with indifference. Nevertheless, Luna was exultant. At the ritual's end she proudly showed her fellow witches a flat cake she had baked which contained the dried and powdered remains of Cissy's placenta, taking literally the Greek meaning of the word. Slices were eaten by the assembled hosts, while the rest was buried beneath a puddle of moonlight to ensure a fruitful year.

The Rainbow Artist prospered. He opened a store called 'The End of the Rainbow', which specialized in artefacts connected with the colourful arc; he also sold teapots, cups, glasses, lamps, aprons, notepads and goodness knows what else, stamped with rainbows. From the rafters he hung shiny clouds from which dangled silken threads in a multitude of colours. On the floor he had countless arks, each stocked with all the animals of creation, including unicorns. Living brightly coloured parrots flew around the store. The Rainbow Artist taught them to speak, but his vocabulary was not large, and they did not become great conversationalists. Cissy bought him a pair of green love-birds with blushing cheeks. They seemed content, though they preferred to remain in a corner perched side by side. In the centre of the store was a tall wrought-iron cage, topped by a dome, which contained the Rainbow Artist's most prized possession. A toucan. Its body was shiny and black, its eye was blue and its yellow beak was the shape of the rainbow. He regarded it with wonder, as if it were an emissary from a world of magical creatures. Occasionally the Rainbow Artist would display some of his own work on the walls; he painted rainbow-layered cakes and similar curiosities, as well as mystical landscapes which showed the moon connected to the earth by rainbows along which people travelled as if they were escalators.

One such hung in Luna's office. It had been a gift. She had said she liked it, so he had given it to her. She had seen into his soul and he could refuse her nothing. Luna was so pleased with the painting that she commissioned another. She had read that when Walt Disney had first created Steamboat Willie (the future Mickey Mouse) he had pencilled in a fight sequence between his hero and a tough sailor which left Steamboat Willie unconscious. Walt Disney had originally represented his state with a rainbow which flew from Willie's fuddled brain towards the horizon in a blur of colour. It was this scene which Luna wanted. The Rainbow Artist threw himself into his first commission with gusto. Times were good.

When he asked Cissy whether she was happy, she replied, 'Over the moon.'

Then Luna cast a spell.

Disneyland is another country. Admittance is controlled by blond boys and girls who sit in a row of booths like immigration officers at a border between states. Cissy, Baby and the Rainbow Artist passed through and entered the Magic Kingdom. They walked along Main Street. Here was the collective unconscious of America. Mechanical animals roared, mechanical savages waved spears, mechanical pirates shot one another; it all looked real, but no one was really hurt. There was no present in Disneyland, all was a dialogue between the past and the future; the present was the empty space through which a bullet passed between the gun and the target. Because the past had been conquered and rendered harmless, the future could be prophesied with confidence: it too would be a great age of mechanics, 'Autopia'.

Even the Rainbow Artist, who had smuggled unhappy memories past the officials at the gates, was won over by the spontaneous enthusiasm of Cissy and Baby. They clapped with delight at all the marvels the wizards behind the scenes had produced. Nor could he refuse Cissy's request to be photographed beside Mickey Mouse. As Cissy and Baby watched the Polaroid print develop, the Rainbow Artist walked up to Mickey Mouse and said, 'Bang! You're dead!'

The small gun in his hand repeated the phrase several times until Mickey got the message and fell down. The mask continued to smile, but the face beneath was distorted by pain.

'You lunatic!' shrieked Cissy. 'What have you done? What have you done?'

America

When I was little I thought *merica* was an English noun, always preceded by what my tutor called the indefinite article. Although I never heard it referred to in the plural I imagined that somewhere on Florianska Street there was a shop that specialized in selling a scintillating variety of *mericas*, which I visualized as enormous crystalline balls cunningly worked so that when struck by light they emitted countless golden rays. I was afraid of the dark and inclined to weep for my mother's eternal absence whenever she left me alone, but I never doubted the existence of the store. However, for such a sickly child the trip to Florianska Street (if made alone) was the equivalent of an expedition to the ends of the earth. Nevertheless, it remained my dream. I believed that my mother's brothers shared that dream, for it was they who uttered the magic word most frequently, but they never once offered to lead me to my childhood paradise. Instead, they looked upon it as their sacred duty to make me sturdy. Uncle Konrad would accompany me to the meadows beside the Vistula where we flew a kite.

'See how it wriggles in the sky,' Uncle Konrad cried, 'like bacteria under my microscope.'

Uncle Konrad was a biologist (killed during a cholera epidemic, coincidentally, by the bacteria my kite most resembled). Actually, as it was sucked further and further away, it reminded me more of the loathsome lozenges I was required to dissolve in my mouth every time I contracted a sore throat. Uncle Kazimir was an entomologist. He took me scrambling in the scrub that proliferated along the Route of the Eagles' Nests. Here he pointed out the manifold varieties of insect life. All of which disgusted me. Poor Uncle Kazimir. He died of fever in Ceylon, on a futile expedition. He travelled to the tropical isle with a group of fellow enthusiasts, only to be fatally discouraged by the local authorities, who explained that the beetles could not possibly be killed since they might be the reincarnation of someone's grandmother. Sure enough, Uncle Kazimir's name is now carried by a green beetle which inhabits the swampy region of the Danube delta. We preserved his collection of shiny bugs in glass cabinets like campaign medals. Only Uncle Lucian kept me entertained. He was a photographer. My greatest delight was to be smuggled into his studio and hidden behind the velvet drapes, where I pretended that I was snuggled beneath my mother's voluminous skirts, while he went about obtaining the portrait of a fine lady. Out of gratitude I determined to buy a *merica* for Uncle Lucian.

I lacked the courage for such an adventure and detested my cowardice. I fell sick. The family doctor said it was nerves and prescribed a tonic. My mother fretted; my father was unsympathetic. I got no stronger. One day the smelly Jewish girl who scrubbed our floors came to my room secretly with a silver amulet which she told me to put under my pillow. I held my nose as she knelt beside me to explain the curious symbols that were engraved upon it. She said that the bird, a comical creature the like of which I had never seen even at the zoological gardens in Warsaw, represented life.

'Why?' I asked.

'Don't argue,' she replied; 'the rabbi said so.'

But this did not satisfy me. I simply could not grasp how a bird could be the symbol of life, when the only birds I had seen at close quarters were destined to be plucked, cooked and devoured. Pullets, pigeons (delicious in squab pie), pheasants, partridges, songbirds, even a woodcock. It was true that Uncle Kazimir kept an owl in his study, but that creature dealt out death, not life. I never saw the owl without a dead mouse on the floor of its cage, its wicked beak clacking in anticipation. Then I remembered a word that I had heard at school many times, especially in Bible classes; this bird was a *sacrifice*! Like all the others it would die that I might live.

'Foolish boy,' clucked the Jewess, 'listen and don't ask questions. The first words mean "perfect healing". This word – *semerpad* – is a secret name for God. The next lines are a quotation from Genesis: "Joseph is a fruitful vine by a fountain; its branches run over the wall."'

'But my name is not Joseph,' I protested.

'My biggest boy is also not called Joseph,' she replied, 'but this charm still cured him of scarlet fever. Now he is as strong as an ox, *kayn aynhoreh*. Please God, you will soon be just as healthy.'

It was a good game, I decided, so I put the amulet beneath my pillow. I wanted to say something nice to the Jewess. 'You have a magnificent bosom,' I said, 'it is a crime to keep it so well concealed.'

Her reaction was frightening; she blushed like a schoolgirl and raised her hand as if to strike me. Yet the same words, spoken by Uncle Lucian to his clients, were always received with such gratitude.

When I recovered, the doctor claimed all the credit. But I knew whom to thank. To celebrate my return to the dining-table my mother ordered the cook to kill our fattest goose.

The dinner was a splendid occasion; not only were my parents and all my uncles and aunts present but also many friends and celebrated acquaintances. Because of the number of guests there were long delays between the abundant courses, so my mother permitted me to play in my hideout beneath the tablecloth. Consequently, I knew it was not clumsiness that caused the Jewess to spill soup upon my Aunt Amelia's shoulder but a squeeze on her calf from Uncle Lucian. I also knew whose shiny boot was rubbing against whose shapely ankle, though I could think of no reason for such activity. However, I had learned to keep my mouth shut; my indiscretion with the Jewess had taught me that adult behaviour was not as simple as it seemed. Now that I was better, the jaunts with my uncles were resumed, and once again I made up my mind to find a *merica* for my favourite. But this time I had a plan.

'I am going on a journey,' I told the Jewess, 'can your rabbi make a talisman to protect me?'

She laughed. 'So now you believe in them?' she said.

I recognized the question as rhetorical and did not answer. A few days afterwards the Jewess produced a second silver amulet.

'What does it say?' I asked.

'This one is more complicated,' said the Jewess. 'It begins with two four-letter names for God entwined, then it lists the angels who will watch over you – Gabriel, Michael, Badriel. The rest is written in code to deceive the evil eye.'

With that in my pocket I felt confident enough to walk unaccompanied through Planty Park.

It was early October and the park was alive with children collecting horse-chestnuts. Nannies sat upon the benches, casting benevolent glances in the direction of their charges, though they seemed more interested in the bold soldiers who sauntered past. Feeling carefree I also stopped to gather the newly fallen chestnuts, even then touched by the transience of their beauty. And with that thought came a glimmer of comprehension for Uncle Lucian's professional passion, and I could guess why so many women came to see him.

In a secluded corner of the park, when the town hall was already in sight, a young lout suddenly appeared. I called upon my guardian angels to protect me, whereupon a passing dove emptied its bowels upon the ruffian's head. And so I came safely into Rynek Główny, the Market Square. Fashionable women swirling parasols to deflect the heat of the autumn sun strolled through the Sukiennice, admiring the silks and laces on display, while their maids bartered with the peasants who had come in from the country to sell their produce. Since winter was inevitably approaching, many carts were full of firewood. 'Ready for delivery!' promised the drivers, as they prodded their old nags into life. Among all this bustle I recognized a familiar figure. His head was concealed beneath the black cloth of his camera, but Ignacy Krieger was unmistakable. There he stood like the man behind a Punch and Judy show, but he was the audience and the whole world was his stage.

'Hello, young man!' he shouted. 'What are you doing so far from home?'

'Shopping,' I replied grandly.

'Look what I have just purchased,' he said proudly as he gestured towards his glowing mahogany camera with its gleaming brass lens, 'a brand new Thornton Pickard, all the way from England. Just what I need for my street scenes. I'm afraid that your uncle is going to be very jealous.' Ignacy Krieger was one of Uncle Lucian's greatest rivals. 'Now that you are such a man-about-town,' he continued, 'you must visit my studio.'

Ignacy Krieger's famous studio! His obnoxious son Nathan, one of my classmates, never tired of boasting about his father's glorious studio with its ingenious gadgets. I was determined to strike a blow for my uncle. 'Not today,' I said, 'I am going to find a *merica* for Uncle Lucian.'

The sun illuminated Florianska Street, gilding the pedestrians and burnishing the shops. In the dazzling light the contents of each window looked like booty in a treasure chest. I saw diamonds, emeralds, rubies, silver cups, golden chains; I saw glossy furs, patent leather boots and a host of wonderful trinkets – but I saw no sign of a *merica*. At the end of the street I had to hold back my tears of disappointment. But I refused to give up the search: I knew that my uncle's main supplier, Fotografia Polska, was situated not far away on Krupnicza Street. Perhaps they would be able to help. The shop was full of familiar objects: bellows, lenses, tripods, cameras, all the paraphernalia Uncle Lucian adored. There were several glass discs, some concave, others convex, which slightly resembled what I had in mind. I approached the counter.

'What do you want, sonny?' said the supercilious salesman (I would report his lack of courtesy to Uncle Lucian, I thought).

I looked him straight in the eye. 'I want a *merica*,' I said.

'So do we all,' he said, 'so do we all.'

'I want a *merica*,' I repeated.

'Do you know what America is?' he asked.

I was angry, but I told him.

'You fool,' he guffawed, 'America is a country on the other side of the world.'

Utterly humiliated, my dream shattered, I left Fotografia Polska. Blinded with tears I began to run along Krupnicza Street, until the sun went down and the only light came from the gas lamps. My imagination tried to frighten me with wild possibilities, but I no longer believed in it. Even so, I did not dare walk back through Planty Park after dark; there may not have been any witches or goblins, but I was pretty sure there were bandits and kidnappers. Who could help me now? Only Gabriel, Badriel and Michael. Thanks to them I remembered that Awit Szubert, another of Uncle Lucian's rivals, had a studio at No. 7 Krupnicza Street. The door was not locked, so I ran up the stairs (carpeted, he was a successful man) and entered the studio just as the magnesium let rip. A small girl in a nightshirt was reclining on a settee opposite the camera; something about her pose made my hands tingle.

'Good heavens!' exclaimed Awit Szubert. 'What are you doing here?' Yet again I wept.

'Play for a while, my pet,' said Awit Szubert, 'I must take this little gentleman home.'

My mother was shocked by my unorthodox arrival in a cab. Awit Szubert explained the circumstances.

'My poor boy,' cried my mother, 'weren't you afraid?'

'No,' I said, 'I was protected.' I showed her my amulet, with its Hebrew inscriptions and prominent Star of David.

'Where did you get this?' my mother demanded. She looked annoyed.

It was too much for me, after the day's disappointment. 'From Hannah the Jewess,' I wailed.

Then, with marvellous dexterity, Uncle Lucian (who seemed remarkably uncomfortable) saved the situation by jumbling the letters of AMERICA to form an ungrammatical English anagram that was also his autobiography, 'I CAMERA'. Even Awit Szubert laughed.

Years later I remember that afternoon with perfect clarity. Why not? America turned out to be my future also. Oh, yes, I found America in the end. Look at me now in a pisspot on the sleazy side of Hollywood Boulevard, my floor littered with empty Kodak film containers. My shutters are always closed. I have no desire to see the filthy posters nor read the flickering neon promises that lick the skies every night; instead I linger over the eloquent images that are windows on my past. This is the photograph Ignacy Krieger took that day in Rynek Główny, the cabs forever awaiting their fashionable passengers, who still promenade while their servants haggle, even though all the firewood has long since been burnt to ashes; and there in the foreground stands a lovely boy (myself) embarked upon his great adventure. This is my father taken by Awit Szubert (he hated his brothers-in-law, especially Uncle Lucian), his jacket buttoned to the throat in the manner of the time, parting to reveal a gold collar-stud, not a wrinkle on his fleshy face, his moustache finely pointed, his mutton-chop whiskers beautifully trimmed, his receding hair neatly combed (he did not live long enough to go bald), and such hope in his eyes. Ah – my beautiful mother! See how she clings to the polished oak banisters at the bottom of our great staircase, as if she would otherwise float away, her feet hidden by the wooden gryphon which now guards some other boy as he sleeps above. I recall how hard Awit Szubert (why not Uncle Lucian?) worked to make her smile, but all she could give him was a sorrowful gaze out of melancholy eyes (what was on her mind?). Her hair is parted in the middle and piled high upon the crown of her head. She wears rings and bracelets and holds a rose. The rest of her body is concealed by her dark constricting dress. I try to recapture the scent of the perfume she wore that day but it is a hopeless task. Here are some spectacular landscapes Awit Szubert took on our expedition to the Tatra Mountains. And this – which I dare not look at too frequently. A nude study, by Uncle Lucian, of Hannah. I am still grateful for the way she tried to comfort me after Awit Szubert had brought me home, and my mother had put me to bed. She came quietly into my room. What was she doing in the house at that hour?

'You are not the only person America has made a fool of,' she said. 'The biggest fool of all was Christopher Columbus. He thought it was India or Japan. Do you know he had a Jewish interpreter with him? Luis de Torres. Well, Louie goes up to the Red Indians and starts talking to them in Hebrew. He thinks he's in the East, you see? What a *schlemiel*! But at least he found gold in the *goldeneh medina*. Unlike my husband. Now there's a real *shmendrick* for you. A fool's paradise, that's all the *goldeneh medina* is to him. He can't even save enough to send for me. So how can he expect me to resist a *shmoozer* like your Uncle Lucian?' She pinched my cheek. 'You're a naughty boy, too,' she said. 'All that talk of bosoms. When you're bigger you'll be a real Casanova. The world will be at your feet.'

She should see me now.

I do not wish to speak ill of the Jews after all they have been through (Hannah included), but there is no doubt that they are responsible for my lamentable condition. By *they* I mean the Jewish moguls who control Hollywood. Perhaps they will remember me as the young man (young, alas, no longer) who used to deliver stills of the latest productions to their opulent offices. At that time I worked for one of the top production photographers in Hollywood. Since then we have all passed a good deal of water, as Mr Goldwyn put it. And I would be famous now, if not for *them*.

I had accumulated a wonderful collection of photographs of all the biggest stars which I was planning to publish. It would have made my name. But my agent got a phone call from a shyster lawyer warning him that I had infringed every copyright rule in the book. He dropped me like a hot potato. Next thing I knew my house had been burgled and all my negatives had vanished.

Why such persecution? Because of one night of madness with Errol Flynn, that's why! I met him at a big party up in Laurel Canyon. Errol's ribs were still sore from his notorious fight with

John Huston, so he was boozing rather than whoring. He needed to be somewhere else so I offered to give him a ride (he was in no condition to drive). He tossed me the keys to his car. 'Take mine,' he said. We ended up in an unspeakable dive off Sunset Strip frequented by low life, actors, and gossip columnists, where we joined some of his German cronies.

Consider my position. I had come all the way to Los Angeles from Poland only to discover that the City of Angels was not populated with the likes of Gabriel, Michael and Badriel, but with puffed-up Jewish pedlars whose cousins I could have seen any day of the week on Szeroka Street. Only now I was taking orders from *them*! Is it any wonder I cheered when Errol jumped on a table and did an impersonation of Adolf Hitler (in my opinion he was a much better actor than people said)?

'*Daloy gramotniye!*' I yelled, echoing the old war-cry of the Black Hundreds (coined for them by the Tsarist secret police for use during pogroms). Unfortunately, I forgot that most of the producers were Poles and that some of them were literate enough to know that the literates I wanted to do away with were Jews. The incident made the papers, pictures and all. Check the photo library of the *Los Angeles Times* if you don't believe me.

When it was too late we went back to my place. I lived in a modest house on Holly Drive, connected to the road by a steep flight of steps cut into the canyon wall. Errol staggered up them, miraculously keeping his balance, while hanging on to bottles of vodka and wine and a pot of caviare (which he had taken from a cache in his car). We drank, we ate, we told obscene stories (only Errol's were true). Soon the Germans were snoring. I felt wonderful. For a whole evening I had forgotten my lowly station in life; once more I was as bold as that boy who had gone in search of America. Drink had turned me into a sentimental fool. I showed Errol the photograph of my mother. 'A beautiful woman,' he agreed.

Then I gave him Hannah. She was three-quarters towards the camera, so that although her breasts and body hair were fully exposed, there seemed to be some reluctance in their display. She was bending slightly, allowing her full breasts to hang, so emphasizing their nakedness. The sepia tone, the angle which revealed her shape so well, all gave this image of Hannah a three-dimensional effect which was not lost on Errol Flynn. He unbuttoned his flies and took out his famous instrument. 'This lady is about to be accorded a unique privilege,' he said. Whereupon he began to flick his penis lightly with the photograph. You must understand that the *cartes de visite* produced by Uncle Lucian and his contemporaries were not the flimsy things you get at drugstores nowadays but proper pieces of card. So Errol did not have any trouble producing an erection, nor in maintaining it. Poor Hannah took a beating that night. Luckily Errol Flynn's semen overshot her and landed upon my carpet. He left me to wipe it up, the animal. Next day I was on the blacklist.

Some job I found! Every night I tramp around the restaurants on Hollywood and Sunset with a camera supplied by my employer (not the Leica I demanded). 'Heil Hitler,' I say to the fat Jewish customers who are dining with their gaudy wives or cheap mistresses. (They hear, 'Smile mister.') How I despise them! So greasy is their hair that drops of oil collect on the tips like obscene ornaments. Oh, where are my mother's antimacassars? The women make a mockery of her discreet elegance with their vulgar display of valuable jewellery. Of course they are delighted to have their picture taken, their eyes send messages to mine ('Make me beautiful'), while their diamonds contact the light meter that turns the lens of my camera into a rhinestone monocle. And so I press the button and the shutter opens, letting in an image that will leave its contaminating stain upon my memory (among many others). I hand them my company's card. 'When will the print be ready?' they ask. 'Tomorrow,' I say.

But the night continues. Some restaurants are large enough to contain dance-halls. It is here that I meet my nemesis (again and again). High above my head a large ball spins suspended from the ceiling; covered with hundreds of tiny mirrors it sends scintillas of silver light cascading down through the smoke. Everyone longs for the brief feel of the spotlight. Except me. For the shaft misses my face and stabs me through the heart. My America! Why? Why?

Why did I ever leave Poland? When Uncle Lucian gave me my first camera on my fifteenth birthday I had no inkling that it would be the last birthday I was to spend in the company of my family. Indeed, my joy knew no bounds when my father informed me that I would be able to use my camera on Awit Szubert's next expedition to the Tatras. Awit Szubert had made an annual pilgrimage to the Tatra Mountains from the time dry bromide plates were first available in Poland a quarter of a century before. Now, to mark his twenty-fifth visit, he had invited all his fellow photographers and their families to accompany him. It needed a whole carriage on the Cracow to Zakopane train to accommodate us all.

The journey was exceedingly slow, due to the excessive number of curves and steep inclines the engine had to climb, but we didn't care as we gorged ourselves upon the contents of our delicious hampers. At last the train gathered speed as it steamed through the valley towards Nowy Targ, the final station before Zakopane itself. After Nowy Targ the train began the ascent up the long gradient into Zakopane. As we traversed the terraced fields, the highlanders (still unselfconscious) in embroidered shirts, white felt trousers, broad belts and black hats, downed their tools to cheer, while their wives and children waved from the lofts of their wooden chalets, a spectacle which greatly excited Ignacy Krieger (who was planning the series on the traditional costumes of Poland which was to win him a gold medal at the Vienna exposition). In those days the mountains were pretty wild; the hidden valleys were well stocked with game, including wolves, bears and boars, and in the caves – so it was rumoured – were bands of brigands. Naturally, I pressed my face to the window in the hope of catching sight of the one or the other (without success).

At our destination the Mayor himself opened our carriage door and greeted Awit Szubert as if he were King of the Tatras. A pretty girl almost swooned when he kissed her on the cheek as she handed him a posy of wild flowers. A brass band struck up a melody of local tunes. The town was exuberant, and slightly pompous, for the people believed what foolish anthropologists had told them: that the Tatras were the birthplace of Polish civilization, and the cradle of a new independent Poland.

'Bah,' said Uncle Lucian.

Whenever I look at Awit Szubert's photographs memories of those first exhilarating days in the mountains come flooding back. There are six figures picked out against the snow in his study of Zawrat Mountain: I am closest to the camera; beside me is my father; ahead of us are Uncle Lucian, Ignacy Krieger, Nathan Krieger and our guide Jan (who claimed to have been a bandit in his youth). We didn't realize it at the time but we were carefully positioned to lead the viewer's eye towards the centre of the composition.

A few minutes later my father and Uncle Lucian, who never liked one another, began to argue (maybe Uncle Lucian was upset because my father had commissioned Awit Szubert to take the family portraits).

'Please,' insisted Jan, 'you must never raise your voices in the mountains. The danger of avalanches is very great.'

My favourite excursion was to Morskie Oko, the Eye of the Sea. Legend had it that this beautiful lake was connected by underground tunnel to the sea some fifteen hundred metres below (but I didn't credit legend). Overladen with lunch packs and photographic equipment, we scrambled over the last rocky outcrops and gratefully flung ourselves down the shingle to its shores. Here we basked. As the sun rose higher in the sky the lake changed colour from blue to brilliant green, until it did indeed resemble a giant lens.

'Photography is no longer merely nature's pencil,' said Awit Szubert as he assembled his camera upon its tripod; 'now with the help of an accurate lens and light-sensitive plates I am able to reconstruct photographic images according to the rules of pictorial composition. I have become an artist.'

So saying, he shooed us out of sight so that we did not disturb the serene atmosphere with our lack of divinity. There are no boats on Morskie Oko in his photograph. But immediately afterwards the glassy calm of the lake was shattered by the launching of a dozen small dinghies. I found room on board with the Kriegers, while my father was left with only Uncle Lucian for company. We drifted around, overawed by the surrounding circle of mountains, until our reveries were scattered by an outbreak of hostilities between my father and my mother's brother. Although it was mainly commotion, odd words were carried across the lake to our boat. 'He is old enough ... He must be told ... Never ... I am his father.' Of course it was impossible to be sure who was saying what.

'Christopher,' said my father, 'what do you think of your Uncle Lucian?'

'I love him,' I replied.

'And me?' he asked.

'You are my father,' I said.

He continued his preparations without another word, nothing was going to spoil his big day. He had been looking forward to the hunt from the moment we arrived at Zakopane (it had long been his ambition to shoot a wild boar and hang its head over the fireplace in his smoking room). But, as it turned out, it was a lucky day for boars. At first everything went according to plan. We slipped quietly into the forest below the Black Pond (where Awit Szubert was busy with another of his studies), searching the snow for footprints, watching the saplings and bushes for any slight movement that might betray the presence of a wild animal. Promising areas having been selected, the hunt began in earnest.

'Each of you has a horn,' said our guide. 'You must blow upon it as soon as you spot a boar. In no circumstance shoot until we are all accounted for. I want no accidents.'

Soon we were scattered in all parts of the forest. What occurred next is confused in my mind, and I am grateful that there are no photographs to settle the matter. It appeared that there were two figures in the distance gesticulating wildly; or perhaps one was waving his arms frantically, while the other was pointing a gun at him. Certainly we heard what sounded like shots, but they could have been the prelude to the louder crack that brought the snow toppling off the mountain peak. The image disintegrated. The air was filled with a million ice crystals, as though all the dots that combine to make up a photograph had exploded. Blinded and deafened, we were no longer witnesses. Thereafter, when we re-grouped in a clearing, we deduced that the two figures must have been my father and Uncle Lucian. This was finally confirmed when Uncle Lucian was seen staggering towards us. Unfortunately my father was never seen again. What had happened?

'A terrible accident,' was all we could get from Uncle Lucian.

So that was the story we told my mother: that my father had been buried alive in a sudden avalanche. At least we were spared the funeral.

To tell you the truth, my father's permanent absence made little difference to his former household (of which I was now the head). However, the realization of my new status seemed to come as a shock to all concerned. My mother appeared more than usually preoccupied. (Surely she was not still mourning for my father?) As for Uncle Lucian, his moods were inexplicable and his behaviour incomprehensible. Time after time I would enter a room and find him deep in some intense conversation with my mother, only for him to draw away as soon as he saw me coming. I took to opening doors quietly in the hope of overhearing snatches of their dialogue, but all I caught were meaningless phrases. However, I was able to identify several instances of an 'either . . . or' construction associated with threats. And once (I swear) I heard my mother utter the word 'Blackmail'. After many weeks the disharmony subsided and was replaced by a duet, the key word of which seemed to be 'America'. Nevertheless, my mother did not recover her previous cheerful disposition.

On account of Uncle Lucian's strange behaviour since the accident, my visits to his studio had become more and more infrequent, until I stopped going there completely. But I resolved to make one more call, to confront Uncle Lucian man-to-man, if only for my mother's sake. His studio door was never locked during working hours (in the hope, I suppose, that a customer turned away by Awit Szubert or Ignacy Krieger might find their way to his establishment), which was to my advantage as I wished to catch him unawares. Since he was busy with a client I slipped behind the velvet drapes where my childish counterpart had hidden so many times before. Fool that I was, I couldn't resist a peep. Standing on a pedestal where my uncle had placed her, Hannah completed the movement until she was facing the camera.

She was naked. I was astounded. I did not believe that women ever allowed men to see them in such a condition. And yet here I was, opposite Hannah, able to examine all her most secret parts.

'You must promise never to show that photograph to anyone,' she said.

Uncle Lucian laughed. He put his hand between her legs.

'Not today,' she said, 'I am fertile.'

'Very well,' said Uncle Lucian, 'kneel.'

Hannah knelt. She unbuttoned Uncle Lucian's trousers. He gasped. Hannah couldn't speak, her mouth was full. My own hands began to tingle, as they had at Awit Szubert's studio, and I imagined that Hannah's lips were pressed to my penis. Then imagination became reality as my hands forced Hannah's head against me, harder, harder ('Harder! Harder!' echoed Uncle Lucian), until my pants were oozing. Hannah quivered, as if with disgust, then wiped her mouth.

'What will become of him?' she asked.

'Christopher?' said Uncle Lucian.

'Our son,' replied Hannah.

'He is to start a new life,' said Uncle Lucian, 'in America.'

A new life indeed! And now it is nearly over. I am an old man, too decrepit to attract a woman. Hence my weekly visit to Mrs Klopstock's brothel (which has moved out to Santa Monica). You know all there is to know about me, so perhaps you would care to accompany me here too?

'I have a new girl for you tonight,' says Mrs Klopstock. 'You will find her in the "New Deal" room.'

Mrs Klopstock likes me, she thinks we have similar backgrounds; at any rate, we have aged together. The whore wears a wrap that she has not bothered to button, so that I can glimpse her nakedness beneath. Her body is not bad. Her face is also acceptable, though it shows the beginnings of a beard.

'I am Erica,' she says.

As I fuck her I make a pun (to myself, of course): 'This is my life in an Erica.' Perhaps I will leave her my beautiful photographs, to decorate her room.

Svoboda

'If you insist upon lying to me,' says my interrogator, 'perhaps you will have more respect for a rabbi.' He lights a cigar. 'Pure Havana,' he says, 'from our brothers in Cuba.' The tip of the butt, glowing through the smoke, reminds me of the day this all began.

The sun smouldered in a smoggy sky. They were having a script conference in Heaven. Perhaps my guardian angel was trying to set up my next assignment; as usual his idea was a bummer. An improbable beginning connected to an unlikely ending by outrageous coincidences. It was kicked out, leaving me unemployed. Dropped flaming from celestial heights, the pages drifted into Los Angeles on a bank of cloud, then sank with the sun. The afternoon was in ashes. Time to welcome Johnny Walker. After a few drinks the pigments of a man appeared upon the opaquely glazed surface of my office door. The colourful splashes refused to resolve themselves into a recognizable outline, even when the door opened. A gloomy hombre entered. Tears were flowing down his face.

'Damn the pollution,' he said, 'my eyes are full of grit.' Suddenly my visitor looked familiar.

'Feldman!' I exclaimed.

'Hello, Smolinsky,' he said.

'What brings you here?' I asked.

'Miriam,' he replied. 'She's disappeared. You're my last chance, Joshua. Find her, please.'

He was agitated. He tried to remove his contact lenses but was all thumbs, and one fell to the floor. We crawled about looking for it, like the poet who sought the moon in a pond. An easier job than tracking Miriam, last heard of in Czechoslovakia. Diplomatic inquiries had revealed nothing.

'Providence led me here,' said Feldman. 'I was walking aimlessly, hope gone, when a gust of wind smacked me in the face. Blinded with dirt I stumbled into a doorway. Blinking I saw the words, "Joshua Smolinsky, Private Investigator". I came right up. What do you say?'

I rose. Beneath my foot something crunched. What did I say? 'Sorry.'

Miriam was Feldman's crazy wife. Years ago we all used to go around together. Feldman and Miriam were both in the movie business. You've probably heard Miriam on the sound-track of a dozen weepies, playing onomatopoeic tunes on her violin. When Feldman first met her she was running with a crowd even loonier than herself. Their big ambition was to dump enough L S D into the reservoirs around L A to blow all our minds. Feldman – who was working on the script of a religious epic at the time – won her over with his spirituality. Thereafter Miriam turned her attention to the deeper recesses of the psyche. She got the notion that Hollywood was the manifestation of an overmind – taking the phrase 'dream factory' literally – into which the whole world could be plugged via the movies, television and video. So Feldman fixed her a job as his assistant, but all she got were rewrites of rewrites. Her own scripts never got near the ear of Morpheus. On the rebound she left Feldman and went underground, from where she bombarded him with anarchist manifestos. 'I do not want to be I,' she wrote, 'I want to be We.' Originality was not her strong point. I traced her to a hippie hacienda in Baja California. Feldman persuaded me to give him its location. There was a dreadful scene; nevertheless, they were reunited. Neither thanked me. After the Yom Kippur War, Miriam became a Zionist. Eventually she went to live alone on a kibbutz in the Negev Desert – to find herself. Last April she wrote Feldman a letter telling him that she was visiting Czechoslovakia to participate in the Prague spring music festival. A fortnight later he received a postcard from Prague. Since then, not a word.

'You've got to face it, Feldman,' I said, 'you've lost her.'

'All I want to know is that she's O K,' he said. 'That's not too much to ask, is it, Joshua?'

'Exactly what you said before,' I answered. 'Miriam hasn't spoken to me since.'

'This time it will be different,' he replied. 'If it's over, it's over.' He fumbled myopically for a chair. His cracked contact lens looked daggers at my conscience.

'You win,' I said, 'I'll go to Prague.'

'I cannot issue you with a visa,' the consular official said, 'because you no longer resemble the photograph in your passport.'

'What do you suggest I do?' I asked.

'Remove the beard,' replied the barbarous swine. But I stood up for my rights. My new beard — brown, flecked with red and gold — was staying put. Instead, I posed for a new passport photograph.

'How many days will you be in Czechoslovakia?' the consular official asked.

'Five', I replied.

Inside the Tupolev, streamers of condensed air obfuscated the fuselage. I shivered, wrapped my overcoat around my shoulders, deepening the disguise. But that didn't fool passport control at Prague.

'This is not you,' the officer said. My accuser ran a finger over the plastic film that protected the photograph, as if to demonstrate how crude a forgery it was. He summoned his boss, who sported a natty mohair suit in place of regulation khaki. Both men stood in the cubicle comparing me with my photograph. They shook their heads. Had I undergone a metamorphosis during the flight to Kafka's city? I touched my face and the unfamiliar hair on my cheek made me start. At which the officer and his superior exchanged smiles. My passport was stamped.

Outside Airport Ruzyne I looked for a taxi. All I managed was a Skoda with a one-eyed driver.

'Hotel Ambassador,' I said.

'You are American?' the driver asked.

'Yes,' I said.

'You want to make money change?' he asked.

'No,' I said.

'Everyone makes money change,' he said.

'I don't need more currency,' I said.

'Here everyone needs more money,' he said. 'Since August all prices have risen one hundred per cent. How many crowns did you get to the dollar? Ten? I give you fifty.'

'No,' I said.

'Why not?' he asked. 'You change your dollars to crowns with me, then back again at the bank. You speculate, you make profit. Then you buy your wife a special present.'

'I am not married,' I said.

'I am not surprised,' he replied. Our conversation ended. Eventually our journey did too.

The woman at the hotel reception said: 'Please feel at home, Mr Smolinsky.' But Room 232 was un-American; there were brass pipes, an ancient telephone, and a single-channel radio that couldn't be unplugged (Miriam's ideas were not news in Czechoslovakia). But where was she?

Miriam didn't recognize me at once.

'It's the beard,' I said.

'Feldman sent you?' she asked.

I shrugged. 'You're still his wife,' I said. We were standing in the porch of the Staronová Synagogue. Miriam was a Jewish girl, it was Friday night, where else should I look?

'There's someone you'd better meet,' she said. His face – made distinctive by an eye-patch – was familiar. 'Tom Svoboda,' said Miriam, 'this is Joshua Smolinsky.'

We sat side by side before the *almemor*, above which hung the venerable banner of the Jewish community. Miriam joined the women at the back. Many seats remained empty, including the throne of the miracle-working Rabbi Loew. My *siddur* was dedicated to the *shul* by Mimi Goldfarb of Nogales, Arizona. Tom seemed familiar with the Hebrew text. He prayed beautifully. The cantor, on the *almemor*, poured white wine into a silver goblet. His mellifluous voice filled the *shul*. The light, diffused by the dust of decaying paper, vibrated. The ancient synagogue tapered like the flame on a candle. Old men swaddled in *tallisim* rocked over their prayer books. 'Come, my friend, to greet the bride,' they sang, 'let us welcome the Sabbath day.' As the Hebrew words flew heavenwards the community's flag trembled, only to fall slack again when the song was ended. Miriam smiled at Tom.

After the service my Czech co-religionists mobbed me, anxious to tell their troubles to an American visitor.

'What has brought you to Prague?' they inquired.

'I came to meet an old friend,' I said. 'We no longer see much of one another. I live in Los Angeles, my friend in –'

But Miriam silenced my revelation with a kiss. '*Shabat shalom,*' she said.

'Why the secrecy?' I asked.

'I'll explain outside,' she replied; 'walls have ears.'

Before the congregants departed they shook Tom's hand.

'Why is Tom so popular?' I asked.

'His family were famous free-thinkers,' Miriam replied. 'But Tom has rediscovered his Jewish identity. Naturally that has made him something of a hero.'

He showed me his ring; a Mogen David made out of tiny blue and white beads. His fingers also were stained blue. The beadle locked the door, and slouched off into the hostile night. We followed, Miriam hand-in-hand with Tom, in the direction of the Hotel Ambassador.

'You are a stranger, Joshua,' said Miriam. 'Prague seems beautiful, the Jews friendly. But it is a façade. The Jewish community is dying, and it is a metaphor for Prague. Stay around the synagogue long enough and each member will approach you with the news that the others are not to be trusted. Everyone's an informer. Not because they are loyal to the state – God forbid – but because they all want to be big-shots. If it got out that I was from Israel I'd have no peace. They'd all be trying to trick me into spreading Zionist propaganda, so as to have something meaty to report. That's how the government works. By bringing out the worst in people. These aren't Jews, they're kulaks.'

'Isn't that a bit harsh?' I said. 'What right have we to criticize?'

'Do not judge others, eh, Joshua?' said Miriam. 'I hope you'll be as reasonable tomorrow morning when I marry Tom.'

We dined in my hotel beneath an electric chandelier.

'Isn't bigamy a crime in Czechoslovakia?' I asked.

'Only if you're caught,' replied Miriam. 'Are you going to inform on us, Joshua?'

Tom solved my dilemma thus; he tapped his eye-patch. 'I see no husband,' he said.

Not far away, surrounded by waitresses in national costume, were the remains of Czechoslovakia. Banners were draped across the walls; they repeated, in many languages, the slogan of *Tourfilm '79*: 'Universal Peace and Understanding through Tourism'. The dining room was chock-a-block with fraternal delegates from friendly countries. None more friendly than the Russians, of course. It was the Russians, resembling grotesque runners-up from Movie Mogul and Marilyn Monroe look-alike contests, who were chiefly responsible for the deteriorating condition of Czechoslovakia, formerly a giant liver pâté in the shape of the Republic. Tom, however, ate nothing.

'Those Russian pigs have spoilt my appetite,' he said.

'Tom is a dissident,' whispered Miriam.

'I merely recognize that a radical change in the socio-political system is vital,' he said. 'At the same time I also know that it is completely out of the question.'

In the background, while a dance band played hit tunes of the '30s and '40s, Czechoslovakia finally disappeared.

Tom plucked a little tin from his pocket. It contained pink pills. 'Amphetamines,' he said.

'Tom takes them every Friday night,' explained Miriam, 'so he can work through the weekend without sleep.'

He popped a couple into his mouth, and a few more into a passing gravy-boat bound for the Russians. 'Soon they'll be higher than a sputnik,' he said.

When our roast duck arrived Tom tipped his portion into his napkin. 'I'll eat it later,' he said. He poured some vodka. 'I don't suppose I made a good impression the first time we met,' he said. 'Cab drivers are meant to be guides, not unofficial bankers. But for me to speak of the beauty of Prague would be a blasphemy. I no longer can see it. My eye-patch is a symbol. My eye is good. I wish to imitate our one-eyed national hero, Jan Zizka of Trocnov. Every twenty-crown note bears Zizka's portrait. I'll show you.'

He flattened a grubby bill on the table-cloth, revealing the hero's grim visage. 'Tell me,' he said, 'which eye is covered?'

'The right,' I replied.

'If you look in the back of Ctibor Rybár's *Guide to Prague* you'll also find a picture of Zizka,' said Tom. 'Only now the patch is over his left eye. What do you make of that?'

'Does it matter?' I said.

'Maybe Zizka was a bluffer like me,' he continued, 'who could never remember which eye was dud. Perhaps the printer was careless and reproduced Zizka back-to-front; such errors are not uncommon in Czechoslovakia. Or did our government order the change for political reasons? This is not far-fetched. Just last month the Kremlin discovered that two times two does not always make four. Naturally our government came to the same conclusion. Moreover they found a practical application for the new formula; our latest five-year plan must now be completed in four years. Two plus two equals five. The posters are all over Prague.'

'Is it safe to talk like this in public?' I asked.

Tom laughed.

'Nowhere's safer than here,' he said, nodding at the Russians. Whereupon the lights went out.

A false spring flourished. Bucolic images fluttered from projector to screen. *Tourfilm '79* began with the Czech entry. Steel workers were shown sweating over a furnace like demons in hell, then sent backpacking into the hills of Zdar. 'Motion recreation,' said the narrator, 'is their reward.'

'They think they can turn our countryside into a convalescent area,' hissed Tom, 'but they are fools!'

The camera overtook the hikers and swept down the hills of Zdar into the fertile valleys where peasants grew plums and apples. 'In the 1920s a group of artists left Prague to work amongst these communities,' said the voice-over. 'The spirit of the peasants gave new life to their paintings, and to Czech art, which was wallowing in self-conscious decadence. Foremost among them was Yehuda Svoboda, shown here in the traditional peasant costume he adopted.' An old photograph flickered into life.

'My uncle,' said Tom. 'How I worshipped him when I was a boy! What stories he used to tell! Oh, he loved "the spirit of the peasants". It had a name: slivovitz. The local whore fell in love with him. She was quite a celebrity; she had such a fund of foul language that professors and anthropologists would flock down just to hear her swear. She wore nothing but boots and a schoolboy's cap. My uncle painted her many times. He would pose her with a prop, say an umbrella, but exclude it from the picture. He said this was like most human activity, where the motive is also invisible.' A fanfare interrupted Tom.

'With renewed vigour we will achieve our goals!' cried the narrator. 'Two plus two equals five!'

'Fuck their slogans,' said Tom. 'We'll free two times two! Let two times two equal a bunch of bananas. Victory to the irrational! We call the children of our leaders "Banana Kids". Because only the elite eat bananas in Czechoslovakia. I want a banana!'

Tom jumped up. And we all departed to the sound of wind breaking from bloated bellies, as Czech cooking took its revenge upon the Russian constitution.

Beneath the moonlight pornography thrives. Beside the Vltava, four mallards were raping a duck. She had been flattened into the mud, as if awaiting the butcher's knife. One after another the drakes rode her back, while the others stabbed at her neck. Her body shuddered, torn between pleasure and pain. Her arteries throbbed, at bursting point. She shrieked.

'Motion recreation,' I said.

'Rape!' cried Miriam.

'Shoo,' I said. To no avail.

'Tom,' yelled Miriam, 'do something!'

Better acquainted with the psychology of the locals he emptied his pockets in search of his uneaten dinner. He tore off several lumps of meat and threw them in the mêlée. The effect was immediate. Female flesh was abandoned in favour of the cooked variety. Gobbling, squabbling, the mallards cleaned up. They pecked at our shoes, quacking for more.

'Cannibals,' said Miriam.

'No,' said Tom, 'just good Czech ducks.'

Tom lived in a large block opposite the Staronová Synagogue. It was dated 1911 and decorated in the style of that period: golden profiles impressed upon glossy green tiles. The figures were of sleek men and sporting girls characterized by boxing gloves and tennis racquets. One face alone did not fit. A hook-nosed caricature. For those unfamiliar with skull-caps and earlocks, a money bag, a pile of ducats and a Mogen David had been added. I was startled by the impression that the Jew had turned to face me, but it was only a man – equally Jewish – looking down from a window above.

'Don't stare,' advised Miriam. 'The authorities are very clever. They know visiting Jews will be outraged by that anti-semitic insult. So they have installed a spy in the building. He photographs everyone who stops to look at it.'

'But the man at the window was a Jew,' I said.

'Don't let that fool you,' replied Miriam.

Tom unlocked the door of his apartment with a silver key that hung from a leather thong around his neck. His room resembled a bazaar. He had boxes overflowing with jeans, tee-shirts, eye-patches, beads and rings; shelves filled with banned books and magazines. In the centre stood a hand printing press, surrounded by bottles of ink in shades of blue. Hanging from strings that looped from wall to wall were scores of twenty-crown notes.

'Oh, my God!' I exclaimed. 'You're a forger!'

'No,' explained Miriam, 'Tom's an artist.'

'The printing press belonged to my uncle,' he said, 'and I think he'd approve of its new function. In Czechoslovakia crime has become an art form, because real art is illegal. I am a criminal – it is true – but an artist also. Tomorrow, after the wedding, I will give you a demonstration. We will have a small happening. You will come?'

'Please,' added Miriam.

I softened, but did not melt. 'Shouldn't dissent be non-profit-making?' I inquired.

'The money I earn on the black market saves me from being a slave of the system,' said Tom. 'I fell in love with Miriam when I heard her play Dvořák's violin concerto in the House of Artists. I didn't block my ears because Dvořák exchanged a pittance in Prague for a fortune in America.'

Miriam picked up the fiddle that had won Tom's heart and began to play. Instead of the melancholy cadences of the mercenary composer I heard the disciplined cacophony of a revolutionary. Composition was the talent the printing press financed.

'All my compositions are based upon the dodecaphonic serial technique developed by Schönberg,' Tom said. 'Variety is obtained by repeating the series either in retrograde or inversion or even retrograde inversion, giving me twenty-four, thirty-six or forty-eight variables.'

Such explanations did not impress Tom's neighbour, who cut short the recital by thumping on the wall.

'That's our spy,' said Tom. 'He knows my work is banned.'

Forgive me, Feldman. But what could I do? Have them arrested? We were in the waiting room of the Old Town Hall. The ornate woodwork buzzed with the sound of a distant organ. A panel opened and a woman aglitter with black diamanté appeared.

'You have an English translation of the wedding ceremony?' she asked.

Miriam showed her papers, each with its official stamp of approval, including the document that proved she was single.

'How did you do it?' I asked.

'Bribery,' she replied. 'I can tell you exactly what each seal cost.

The cheapest was a bag of coffee, the most expensive took 200 dollars.' As we entered the wedding chamber the organ began to play the Israeli national anthem.

'They could hardly object to Smetana's *Vltava*,' said Miriam.

The Deputy Mayor for Marriages picked up a large leather folder and pronounced the vows. When he had finished Miriam said, 'Yes.'

They posed for photographs beneath the astrological clock. A small crowd had gathered around Tom's cab, with its tell-tale white ribbons, among whom were some whose occupation was obvious. Nevertheless, Tom had his happening. He threw handfuls of home-made twenty-crown bills at the sky. They swirled upwards like giant pieces of confetti, while Miriam performed Stravinsky's *The Devil's Dance*. There was a commotion as masses flocked from the four corners of the square like pigeons scenting food. The music progressed faster and faster through its dizzying harmonies, until the people were possessed by its rhythms and began leaping into the air after the drifting notes. High above our heads the horologe chimed noon, as the skeleton pulled the bell-rope in his niche. This activated the apostles who appeared in the upper windows of the clock; it also prompted the secret policemen who began to move towards us.

'Time we vanished,' said Tom.

We resurfaced near Holesov, not far from the Polish border. On the outskirts a blond officer in a blue uniform stood beside the road, a pair of binoculars in his hand. As we approached he lifted them to his eyes and examined us like a voyeur who had no need for secrecy.

'If anyone asks,' said Tom over his shoulder, 'you're a couple of American tourists.'

We checked into the Hotel Savoy; a single room for Tom, and a double for me and Miriam.

'What a way to spend your honeymoon,' I said.

Next morning the manager handed Tom a message. 'We must remain here a few days,' he announced.

On the third day the manager returned my passport. 'I am sorry,' he said, 'but you cannot stay another night.' My visa had expired early. It was the consular official's revenge.

'There is a simple solution,' remarked Tom.

'You have made many problems for me,' said the manager, pocketing my fifty-dollar bill. Holesov had only one place nobody paid a bribe to get into.

Washing was drying on the gates of the old Jewish cemetery; beyond was evidence of the Nazis' dirty linen. If it wasn't for a plaque commemorating the extinct Jewish community an ignorant stranger might have concluded that the Jews had discovered the secret of eternal life, for no new tombstone had been put up in forty years. A man was tending a fertile little garden.

'You wish to know about the Yiddish people?' he asked. 'I am not Yiddish, but I knew them. I was their *shabbos goy*. They were kind to me, but they drove their rabbis away. One was sacked for being too strict over matters of ritual slaughter, another left because he believed that he could do his job better than his congregation, and a third resigned after a dispute about priestly blessings. They were still quarrelling when the Germans arrived.'

He led us through tall grass, disturbing the crickets, past the victims of a milder epidemic – a pogrom – back in time to the seventeenth-century tomb of Rabbi Shabatai Cohen. The inscription, of course, was in Hebrew.

'What does it say?' asked our guide. 'There is no one left in Holesov who can read it.'

I coughed, Miriam blushed, Tom walked away. The phoney! His Hebrew was no better than mine. He settled beneath a plum tree, where he attached himself to a couple who had wandered through the open gate.

'This one was a farmer who gave us milk,' continued our guide, introducing us to the tombstones. 'That one's daughter was secretary to Jan Masaryk, this one was our doctor, that one our dentist.'

Suddenly Miriam sprinted towards Tom, as money changed hands. 'Liar! Defiler!' she screamed.

'Excuse me,' I said to our perplexed guide.

Under the plum tree Miriam and Tom were having their first row.

'Joshua,' yelled Miriam, 'I've married a man who sells forged concentration-camp stamps in Jewish graveyards!'

'What harm have I done?' said Tom.

'None, none,' shouted Miriam. 'We'll go to Auschwitz next. You can hawk soap there!'

'My wife, the actress,' said Tom. He opened his wallet to reveal some more examples of the offending article. They illustrated delightful rural scenes, with leafy trees and rivers meandering down from rounded hills. Below was the single word: 'Theresienstadt'.

'You should enter them in *Tourfilm '79*,' I said.

Tom laughed. He reached up into the heavy branches that drooped over his head and picked some of the dusty purple fruit. 'Have one,' he said.

'No thanks,' I replied.

'Too squeamish, eh?' said Tom. He squeezed the plums between his fingers until the skin cracked and the stone was exposed. Then he sucked in the flesh. His lips became sticky with juice.

'You're disgusting,' said Miriam.

That night four strangers showed up at the Hotel Savoy asking for Tom. They looked like smugglers, but he introduced them as Polish dissidents. We went upstairs into the double room.

'Have you heard the latest?' asked one of the Poles. 'Brezhnev visits a pig-farm in Poland. The journalists crowd around him taking photographs. Next day the pictures are in all the papers. The captions say: "Yesterday Mr Brezhnev was photographed with Polish pigs. Mr Brezhnev is the one on the left."'

The dissidents roared with laughter. They opened bottles marked 'Czysta Wodka Wyborowa' and passed them around. One bottle, however, had no label. Its contents tasted medicinal rather than alcoholic.

'What's this?' I asked.

'Brezhnev's piss,' said someone.

Is this why we waited four days in Holesov, for a good laugh at the Kremlin's expense? Miriam, though drunk, was still angry with Tom. When he asked her to play the violin for his friends she refused.

'Miriam,' he said, 'they have come all the way from Cracow to hear my latest composition.' She shook her head. Without warning Tom slapped her round the face. 'Play, you bitch,' he said.

'You don't have to,' I said.

'It's all right, Joshua,' she said. 'I'll play.'

Perhaps Tom's friends were genuine for they seemed to find something to appreciate in the dreadful music. Anyway, they scribbled in notepads from beginning to end. And when Miriam finished they applauded. One even kissed her hand.

'I am tired,' she said. 'I'll rest for a while in the other room.'

I accompanied her. We sat on the bed. I put my arm around her shoulder.

'Disillusioned?' I said.

She nodded, and began to sob. 'What am I going to do, Joshua?' she asked.

However, I was anxious to answer a different question: what was so important about Tom's music? 'Miriam, what if those Poles haven't come to listen to the music as music,' I said, 'but as something else?'

'What else can music be?' she said.

'A message,' I replied. 'Tom uses notes in a fixed series. Suppose he gave each note an alphabetical value, wouldn't it be possible to transmit a message?'

'I guess so,' said Miriam.

Twenty minutes later we had the first sentence: 'The medicine has been ordered and is on its way.'

I was trapped in a lunatic plot, but the country outside was no more sane. In cracking Tom's code I had been dropped unprepared into his world; the doors of perception were open and I was dazzled by the light. Something was happening, that was for sure. I looked at Miriam, beside me on the bed, and saw only satellites of colour. Nothing was still, including my senses. Miriam begun to hum. The tune concealed a message. It said, 'Kiss me.'

I must have been mad, making it with the bigamous wife of my old friend on her second honeymoon. But I unbuttoned her whilst she unzipped me. Like mindless marionettes we performed for the secret police, four or five of them. It was not the doors of perception that had been broken down, but the door of my room; I was not blinded by revelation, but by the flashlights of the cops. They seemed very upset. So did Miriam.

'*Nemluvim cesky!*' she screamed. '*Americky konzulat!*' However, it was not difficult to decipher the meaning in our visitors' presence – 'You are under arrest.' In my illogical state I thought it was because I had just fucked Miriam.

The room was small. I needed neither passport nor visa to enter it. My identity was not in doubt, only my continuing existence outside the room. Who will send a Joshua Smolinsky to look for me? The room contained two chairs and one desk. I was in the chair on the wrong side of the desk. My interrogator, opposite, looked like Otto Preminger's wicked brother.

'Mr Svoboda has confessed to everything,' he said.

'Then why do you need to question me?' I replied.

'For your own good,' he said. 'The courts are easier on those who confess.'

I kept it to myself, but I was not sure why Tom had been arrested. Were his sins political or criminal? My interrogator, however, was a mind-reader.

'Your friend is a forger and a drug smuggler,' he said. 'In fact you sampled one of his products this evening. I have been told that you found it quite potent. What you drank was a condensed concoction of poppy juice. The kids call it *soup*. You see, Mr Smolinsky, nature has played a dirty trick on Poland. She has blessed its fields with the opium poppy. Of course it is impossible for the authorities to prevent peasants and students from collecting the unripe heads. These are your precious dissidents. They pretend to be composers, poets, idealists; but in reality they are nothing but drug dealers who corrupt our youth. Nevertheless, I have no doubt that Tom Svoboda will be turned into a hero by your Western press.'

'You have only yourselves to blame for that,' I said.

'Mrs Feldman thought Svoboda was a dissident, she admired him, but you thought he was a crook?' he said.

'Correct,' I said.

'So why didn't you report him?' he asked.

'Because he was a friend of a friend,' I replied.

'Rubbish!' he said. 'What do you know of loyalty? Perhaps now and again, through circumstances beyond our control, we have betrayed the revolution – but you! Why, less than three hours ago you were making a fool of the man you call your friend, and a mockery of the contract between you. No doubt you consider yourself my moral superior. What could be lower in the eyes of an American than a Czechoslovakian secret policeman? But I spit on your morality, you self-righteous hypocrite! Tell me the truth! Why were you travelling with Tom Svoboda? What is the connection between the CIA and the opium trade?'

I repeated my story. He was not impressed.

'Confess,' says the rabbi. 'Being stiff-necked will do our people no good.'

'Rabbi,' I say, 'does two times two always equal four?'

The rabbi, evidently a scholar of the cabbala, thinks for a minute.

'Not always,' he responds, 'for example, two eggs plus two tomatoes make a Spanish omelette.'

My drugged senses rebel. The naked light bulb explodes, scattering shards of light. A rustling sound comes from the jagged hole as streams of angels and gargoyles pour forth, filling the room with the scent of cinnamon and dung. The gargoyles attach themselves to my beard and hair.

'See,' says the rabbi, 'this is what happens to those who do not repent.'

I crack. But before I can speak my guardian angel lands upon my shoulder and folds a wing over my mouth. 'I've got someone I want you to meet,' he says.

A black-haired man steps forward and walks towards me across the splinters of light.

'Joshua Smolinsky,' says my guardian angel, 'this is Miklós Radnóti. Miklós was a poet. The Nazis killed him. He was a hero, not a counterfeit like Tom. When his body was exhumed after the war a notebook was found in his coat pocket. It contained his last poems. Listen to "Letter to My Wife".'

Miklós Radnóti reads:

> 'I once believed in miracles – now though
> I forget their dates . . . Above me bombers go . . .
> I was just admiring your eyes' blue in the sky,
> But clouds came and a plane up there flew by
> With bombs longing to fall. A prisoner,
> I live despite them. All I have hopes for
> I've thought out, yet I'll find my way to you,
> For I have walked the soul's full length for you –
> And the roads of all these lands; through scarlet ash
> I'll charm my way if need be, through the crash
> Of worlds on fire – and yet I shall get back.
> If need be, I'll be tough as a tree's bark;
> And the calm that hardened men have, who each hour
> Know danger, stress – a calm worth guns and power –
> Soothes me and, like a cool wave of the sea,
> Sobering, "two-times-two" breaks over me.'

'I'm going to give you some advice,' says my guardian angel. 'I admit that I'm a flop when it comes to making up plots – if my original script hadn't been so lousy it wouldn't have been burnt and Feldman wouldn't have got a cinder in his eye and you wouldn't be in this mess now – but I do know right from wrong. When all else fails, judge a man by his heroes. Tom may be worthless, but he's still better than his rulers. After all, *svoboda* means freedom.'

'Well?' says my interrogator.

The wing lifts from my mouth. I repeat the last lines of 'Letter to My Wife'. There is applause. It comes from the interface of my cheek and the interrogator's hand. He hits me once, twice, three times . . . until I lose count and consciousness.

I wake up in a cell. It is dark, I am cold. I do not wash, I eat only potatoes. A bucket in a corner fills with my urine and shit. But I do not confess. After a number of days they let me out. I am being deported, that is all I am told. Miriam is also at the airport.

'Thank God!' she cries.

'Same flight?' I ask.

Miriam nods. 'I've decided to give Feldman one more chance,' she says. 'Your face . . .'

'It's my beard,' I say. 'I felt so dirty when they released me that I shaved it off.'

Our flight to the States is called. The man at the desk looks at my passport photograph and looks at me. 'This is not you,' he says. 'Until you grow a beard you cannot leave the country.'

'Poor Joshua,' says Miriam. 'I'll give your regards to Feldman.'

She disappears among the crowd in the departure lounge. I take a taxi back to Prague. My driver wears an eye-patch. 'You want to make money change?' he asks.

'Why are you free?' I ask.

'They decided I was harmless, no threat to the state,' says Tom, 'indeed, a valuable source of hard currency.'

We stop in a shadowy alley around the corner from the Hotel Ambassador. I hand over 100 dollars. He counts out 5,000 crowns; eight 500-crown bills, each bearing two Second World War soldiers, and fifty 20-crown notes.

'Don't worry,' he says, 'they're genuine.'

In my room I check the money. It doesn't add up. There are no soldiers, only Zizka glaring at me out of his one good eye.

Tsatske

Ask Adam about women! Or better yet, let me tell you about my wife.

We were both illegal immigrants. I was smuggled in by the Professor, my wife by the Professor's father-in-law. The Professor found me in the Gesia cemetery. Warsaw, Poland. Limbless, fleshless, I used my head – what else has a Jew got? – to burrow to the surface. And there I remained until a summer shower left my cranium as shiny as a silk *yarmulkah*. Thank God, I caught the Professor's eye, in which a tear formed. Moved beyond words, he snatched my skull from the reluctant earth.

Then followed the posthumous realization of my life-long dream: the escape to America – although I nearly gave the game away at the airport when I intoned the prayer for starting a journey from the depths of the Professor's satchel. Fortunately no one heard me; except, perhaps, the Almighty.

My new life was luxurious, but I was lonely, I desired to be uxorious. I dwelt upon a filing-cabinet in the Professor's study, so that I could see over his shoulder as he typed his lectures and his letters. His wife bathed me regularly in milk. Thus I derived intellectual sustenance, plus not a little nourishment. But I longed for a companion in a similar predicament, someone with whom I could share intimate secrets. Sex was out of the question, of course, but I would not refuse a kiss. I dreamed of lips, female lips. 'Send me someone to love,' I prayed. And God listened.

Now the Professor's father-in-law was an oil-man, and he made many journeys to South America. Returning from one such expedition up the Pastaza River in darkest Ecuador, he crept into the Professor's study like an anarchist. You would have thought his briefcase contained a bomb. Instead he pulled out a woman's head no bigger than a monkey's. The Professor's father-in-law recounted how he had encountered the fierce Jivaros, who turned out to be friendly after all. So much so that they gave each member of the party a shrunken head as a keepsake. 'The Indians called them *tsantsas*,' he explained. He knew that it was forbidden to export such cultural artefacts, and used that as an excuse to leave the unwelcome present with his hosts in Quito. But when he was passing through Customs he put his hand in his jacket pocket and felt the shrunken features of my intended.

We were ideally matched: I was a skull with no face, she was a face with no skull. That's how the Jivaros do it; out comes the skull, in goes hot sand. The Professor and his father-in-law examined my future wife beneath the reading lamp. Her black hair had lost none of its natural sheen, nor her full lips any of their sensuousness. Unmistakably the lips of my dream, even though they were sewn together with catgut.

'She should be in a museum,' said the Professor.

'What provenance do I give?' replied his father-in-law.

Since when did Providence require provenance? So they left her beside me upon the filing-cabinet. A curiosity to them, a Godsend to me. A *tsantsas* to the Indians, a *tsatske* to me. My brainless cutie.

So what if she was a *shiksa*? It was too late for me to worry about such niceties. At first our conversation was somewhat limited. I asked questions in Yiddish, she replied in Jivaran. But like the greenhorns of old, she soon picked up a smattering of English. We conducted our courtship in secret. Who knew if our fragile relationship could withstand the publicity our oracular abilities would inevitably occasion? Eventually I proposed, and she accepted.

'Will you have me?' I asked.

'I will,' she replied.

That was enough, we were married.

By chance our wedding-night was enlivened by a jazz-band ball. The Professor and his wife had a visitor, a colleague of the Professor's. The two men retired to the study, lately our boudoir, to discuss university business. Meanwhile the Professor's wife washed up the dinner plates in the kitchen. It so happened their apartment was designed by an architect who equated privacy with repression, as a consequence of which all groans, squeaks, giggles, whispers, tinkles and plops carried to every corner. The two men were deep in earnest conversation when my saviour's wife looked in to say goodnight.

'I've a migraine,' she said. 'I'm going to bed.'

Shortly afterwards, the Professor learned that he and his colleague shared a passion: jazz. As if by magic, records appeared; louder and louder soared the cornet and the clarinet.

'The bastard,' whispered my partner, 'is he trying to drive his wife crazy?'

I squirmed. Even the Professor's colleague seemed uncomfortable. Only the Professor was surprised when the festivities were terminated by a dreadful scream. And we were left alone while tempers flared elsewhere.

'We'll never get like that,' said my wife. She rubbed her hair against my sunken cheek.

Who said mixed marriages don't work?

To increase my stone-age spouse's understanding of the modern world I started to read the Professor's lectures to her as he was typing them. And that's when our troubles began.

'My name is not Rothschild,' he wrote, 'but I am a banker. President of the Jewish Moral Bank. Our assets include six million dead since 1939, not to mention countless millions in earlier crusades, inquisitions and pogroms. All a customer has to do is prove his Jewish identity and the benefits of our group membership will be his immediately: *carte blanche* to sit in judgement on any subject that takes his fancy. And don't worry if you're not Jewish; women, pygmies, blacks need not feel excluded. Provided your ancestors have suffered sufficiently you can behave as badly as you like and still claim moral superiority.'

He paused. His mind was elsewhere. Suddenly he abandoned his lecture, placed a clean piece of paper in his typewriter and composed a passionate letter to the wife of his colleague.

'The hypocrite,' hissed my wife through her stitched lips.

'You don't know the facts,' I said, 'how can you pass judgement?'

'Because I am a woman,' she replied.

Did I mention that before the Nazis shot me for stealing a loaf of bread I was a wealthy man?

My *tsatske* never forgave me for that. 'You suffered for a year or two,' she said, 'but I was a slave all my life.'

The Jivaros were generally chivalrous when it came to shrinking heads, my wife being a rare exception. Her crime? She complained too much. Hence the catgut, *pour encourager les autres*. Pity she didn't learn from her mistake. She screamed for the Professor's wife, alternating the word 'adultery'.

There are times when secrecy is more important than discovery, as the Professor well knew. Ignoring our miraculous qualities, he dumped us both on the compost heap at the bottom of the garden. Here we blame one another for our fall. Jays nest in my head. Eggs hatch, birds fly, but our argument is eternal.

Kayn Aynhoreh

I have never been on particularly good terms with my organs. What a querulous bunch they are: my kidneys remind me of those scruffy malcontents you see outside urinals selling socialist newspapers, while my liver is even more bolshevik, dedicated to overthrowing the system altogether. I wasn't more than three or four when they began to rebel, ordering bladder and bowel to bully my sphincters. My spirit was strong, but my sphincters were weak. They defected and I defecated. To deprive the offending organs of sustenance I stopped eating. Food was masticated until my cheeks were full, whereupon I deposited the soggy balls in a handkerchief. Sick of soiled underwear my mother took me to a famous paediatrician. Before she could open her mouth he spoke:

'Please, Mrs Silkstone, no symptoms! Allow me to divine why you're here. Information is an insult to my profession.'

'Jonah doesn't . . .' began my mother.

'We don't need a witchdoctor to know that your son doesn't eat,' continued the paediatrician. 'He looks like he spent his summer holidays at Belsen.'

In fact we went to Bournemouth, where my parents had to endure the disapproving stares of the other holiday-makers as I tottered around like a new-born giraffe. One old *bubbe* actually approached my mother and whispered in her ear:

'To me it looks like your boy's got atavism. Just like my poor sister Feigele, God rest her soul. One night our great-grandmother came in a dream to her. "Feigele," she said, "would it kill you just once to visit my grave?" But Feigele was too full of life. She forgot about the cemetery. So she was punished. She got a blockage, and starved to death. That's what the doctors call atavism.'

But the paediatrician could find nothing wrong with me. 'An obstinate bugger,' he observed. 'Forget *cogito ergo sum*, my son, or you'll end up on an intravenous drip.'

'God forbid!' shrieked my mother.

'Don't worry, Mrs Silkstone,' added the paediatrician, 'he's a healthy lad.' Unversed in Latin, my mother made the appropriate Yiddish response.

It is common among my tribe to supplement any compliment with the phrase '*kayn aynhoreh*', especially when the recipient of praise is a child. Thus when the midwife held me by my feet and said, 'It's a bonny boy,' my mother quickly added:

'*Kayn aynhoreh.*'

'A strange name,' muttered the midwife.

'I'm not naming him,' replied my mother, 'I'm warding off the evil eye.' Deflected, it struck elsewhere. Wriggling like Houdini trapped inside a body several sizes too small I made the midwife drop her thermometer. It smashed on contact with the ground, releasing a swarm of invisible insects with milky eyes. A delivery from Mercury, messenger of the gods, but what was the message?

As if I knew. I am innocent! Fat difference that made. Look what happened when my mother left me supine in my perambulator, absorbing vitamins from the sunshine. Every so often a neighbour's face would rise like a premature moon and utter these words: 'Don't look so worried, it may never happen.' Can a baby be held responsible for its expression?

Even worse was the attitude of my creative director. One fine morning his bovine secretary summoned me to the chief's office. This was not unexpected. I had been producing good advertisements without much thanks. Restitution was about to be made.

'Jonah,' said the creative director, 'there is no easy way to tell you this.' Not the traditional method of announcing a promotion. On the contrary, I was being sacked.

'It's not your work,' he said. 'It's your manner. Where's your enthusiasm? To tell you the truth, no one wants to be your copy-writer. And I don't blame them. Whenever I see your gloomy face I go into an immediate depression. Do you know something I don't? Can't you ever smile?'

He went so far as to accuse me of bringing bad luck upon the agency. Me – the evil eye! When my whole life had been a struggle against it. The evil eye can attack your organs or your luck. If it attacks your organs it is called a virus. Viruses are one of the risks of social intercourse. Colds, cancers, venereal diseases – all are souvenirs of a stranger's room or another's pants. Always say '*kayn aynhoreh*' before you leave and wash when you return. Needless to report, sex is one of the evil eye's greatest allies. Who can predict the consequences of an involvement with that siren? For example, my puberty nearly killed my parents.

Without warning one bath-night, sticky dew appeared where only pee had previously passed. Henceforth baths were taken in Y-fronts, within which my penis lurked like a pebble in a catapult. If only I had worn them in bed. Instead I kissed my *mezuzah*. Some prophylactic! I borrowed this ritual from my father who invariably kissed his fingers and touched the *mezuzah* on his door-jamb before retiring. If it worked for him why didn't it do the trick for me? I never saw my father hide his pyjama trousers at the bottom of the laundry basket. What was the secret? To find the answer I removed my father's *mezuzah* from its bracket and prised open the back with a fingernail to reveal a tiny roll of parchment no bigger than a cigarette. Replacing the empty *mezuzah*, I returned to bed with the scroll. Hebrew characters were inscribed therein, which I recognized but did not understand, although I knew them to be potent medicine – so potent that without their protection my mother and father fell victim to influenza simultaneously. Shamefaced I let the doctor in on the secret of its cause.

'Foolish boy,' he guffawed. 'Years ago everyone was as silly as you. They blamed influenza upon the malign influence of the stars. Hence its name. Nowadays we know influenza is a virus. A virus is a poison that tells fibs to your cells – that's what bodies are made of. So the cells misbehave and you get ill.' Like everyone else the doctor mistook my expression. 'Don't worry,' he said, 'your parents will soon be on their feet again, *kayn aynhoreh*.'

But not before they almost died, as I said. However, I was not anticipating that delirium; I was evaluating my new knowledge. Lulled by the robustness of adolescence I had let my organs develop unchecked for far too long, allowed the evil eye to take advantage of the structure of protoplasm and set up a network of terrorist cells dedicated to toppling the status quo and giving my body a mind of its own. Thereafter, whenever I strolled through a fairground and saw the children swirling down a helter-skelter I could only think of how one virus or another was doing exactly the same with my deoxyribonucleic acid!

I want you to know that I am as familiar with psychoanalytic dicta as I am with new developments in microbiology. Orthodox Freudians explain psychosomatic illnesses as a defence mechanism against the secret desire to transgress taboos such as incest. I should be so lucky! My body is part of a conspiracy to stop me growing up. I struggle to become independent, it craves dependency. I have already referred to my dismissal from the advertising agency where I was an art director. That was merely the latest in a long line of artistic triumphs.

Thus far my achievements are these: I have more ears than Van Gogh and I am taller than Toulouse-Lautrec. Ever since I can remember I wanted to be an artist. A few weeks after my *bar mitzvah* I set my bedroom curtains alight. I had been throwing fireworks through an open window into the darkness, hypnotized by the golden arcs they described, when a spark touched the chaste veil the middle class likes to have between itself and the outside world. Just one spark was all it took to send the tulle equivalent of *kayn aynhoreh* up in flames. Frantically my parents went to work with wet towels, while I felt as light-headed as Prometheus unbound. Here was prophecy! Not only would I destroy the middle-class values that were smothering artistic expression, but I would also liberate the living spirits that were trapped within even tulle. Unfortunately, the house was saved. Nevertheless, I recorded the incident with my coloured pencils. I was merely testing my brightest orange by pressing its point against my fingertip when our au pair, who was fumigating my bedroom with Air-wick to remove the last vestiges of smoke, cried out: 'Jonah, be careful!'

'Of what?' I asked.

So she told me about lead poisoning. How an insignificant scratch from a pencil could prove fatal.

'A red line moves from wound to heart,' she explained, 'causing death upon arrival.' She was the daughter of a doctor. Swiss, no less. Why should I doubt her? Subsequent drawings were all done with biro, ruining the spontaneity of my line for ever. But worse was to follow.

At the time I was still attending a private school in one of London's more genteel suburbs. It was perhaps the safest place in the world. The only evidence of change was provided by the cherry trees which dotted the pavement with blossom in the spring and with leaves in the autumn. This convinced the locals that time was circular, not

linear, as a consequence of which they voted for the same Conservative Member of Parliament each general election. On the day of
which I am speaking the cherry trees were bare. It was my last
Christmas at St Martin's. Next term I would be making a late
appearance at the local grammar school. But now my exams were all
behind me, I could relax. I remember we were making paper-chains
with which to festoon the ceiling. Each of us was given our own
section which we would join with our neighbour's when both were
completed. But I was a romantic, I wanted to link mine with Sarah
Langer's, who was being sent to a girls' boarding school on the other
side of England. So I walked across the classroom towards her, my
arms filled with a chain as substantial as a rainbow. At the same time
a small boy who had been sharpening a pencil carelessly raised his
arm, and immediate pain replaced imagined pleasure. My ear!
Stabbed with the poisonous tip. Sarah screamed as blood dripped
from my lobe, an earring with ambitions to be a necklace. I was
rushed to the nurse, who dabbed the wound with stinging disinfect-
ant and assured me that the bleeding would soon cease. But that
ruddy overflow was the last thing on my mind. I was thinking of
that other red line racing for my heart. According to my religion, a
bar mitzvah marks the attainment of majority. Here was I, not two
months a man, already waiting for death!

Of course I didn't die. But I wasn't cured of my phobia either.
Maybe I wouldn't be so fortunate a second time. I had become a
hypochondriac. The only disease I did not fear was breast cancer. So
imagine my horror when I discovered lumps around my groin.
Luckily I had recently been permitted to explore my girlfriend's
genitalia with my fingers. As soon as was possible I took the opportunity, under the guise of passionate caresses, of checking her groin
for similar nodules. Thank God she had them too. I was a student
by then. And, tetanus notwithstanding, I played football for the
university. Even so, I did not sever all my links with the suburb
of my parents. I also kept goal for Wingate Football Club, when I
had the time. If ever you drive north on the new motorway you'll
pass over the remains of their ground. Where long-distance lorries
now spray cars with mud I was once a hero, famous for my spectacular saves. It was as though my mind had some intuitive knowledge of which way the opposing forward was going to kick the ball.
And in the glorious moment of connection I found an ideal image

for my relationship with the world: a spinning globe captured with perfect grace. My stinging palms prophesied a brave future. How could it be otherwise when actuality so much resembled anticipation? I'll tell you.

I was high. I had just saved a penalty. Cheers still resounded in my ears. My fingers tingled as if eager to be at the paints again. After the match I doodled in the programme. Before long I had turned the team into an inverted pyramid with myself at the base. Then I became a circus acrobat supporting upon my shoulders two full-backs, three half-backs and five forwards. Next game I was tormented by the burden, and started to stagger under the weight of the responsibility. I lost confidence in my sense of balance. When I collected the ball from the back of the net for the sixth time, the spectators yelled that I was *shikker* – Wingate being the only Jewish team in the league. If only it were that simple. Who would believe that I had acrophobia at sea level? That afternoon my father walked home alone, as covered in shame as I was in mud. Returning to university I sought solace with my *shiksa*. I unbuttoned her blouse and began to fondle her breasts. The lump I discovered wasn't very big, but it was big enough. It just wasn't my day.

All things considered, my initial success in the world of advertising was something of a miracle. Yet I started off like a house on fire. I had long since learned that pencils were made of graphite, not lead, but it didn't matter either way, since art directors don't actually have to be able to draw. As you probably know, art directors and copy-writers work as a team. I'll call my partner Iggy. Our first campaign was on behalf of a rather dull brand of whisky. We soon changed that image. It became 'The Whisky that Breaks all the Rules'. We went from success to success. Eventually the endless praise gripped my skull like a halo several sizes too small. I began to complain of headaches, which Iggy diagnosed as hangovers.

'Too much whisky,' he said. 'It's very unprofessional to believe your own advertisements, you know.'

Then, realizing at last the depth of my distress, Iggy began to play upon my fears. Not that it needed much persuasion to convince me of the infidelity of my organs. Who would they fall for? Syphilis, the demon lover? Polio, the hunchbacked smotherer? Diphtheria, the throat-slashing terrorist? Cancer, the vampire? Even worse than these were the diseases with unknown characters, invisible assassins who struck for no reason, whose only symptom was death. Medicine can offer no protection against the unannounced murderer. The only defence we have is *kayn aynhoreh*. I said it so many times that Iggy renamed me Ken. But it worked, until the agency entrusted us with their largest account.

The client wanted his whole range exposed. So we took the company name and transformed each letter into one of its products. The visuals would be animated, the commentary would begin: 'Every letter tells a story.' For example, 'O' was the door of a spin-dryer. As the whole machine was gradually revealed a woman's voice could be heard: 'Dear Hotpoint, When Mrs Stegosaurus told me about her new spin-dryer I didn't believe her. Now I do, thanks to you.' Most commercials work on the principle of conversion by proxy, ours was no exception. All we lacked was a handsome presenter the buyers could trust, as our creative director pointed out.

'Where's the human touch?' he cried. 'Housewives like soft soap. We need men, not machines.'

Despite these objections, the campaign was presented to the client. I lacked the energy to make the introduction. Instead the task fell to an account executive, who lost his job as a result.

'Is this what you had in mind?' he inquired.

'Don't ask me!' stormed the client. 'I'm paying you to tell me!'

The following day the creative director put his hand on my shoulder. 'Bad news,' he said, 'I'm afraid we've lost it.' I tried to look glum, but so perverse was my face that it registered a smile. 'You mustn't blame yourself,' said the creative director.

I didn't, but Iggy did. Behind my back. It was he who complained of my lack of enthusiasm, it was he who asked to work with another art director. He saved his skin, but not mine. Three years later I was fired.

'Good luck, Ken,' said Iggy as I walked out of his life.

In the meantime I had entered that of Rosie Silverman. After our marriage we discovered that the only thing we had in common was a love of chocolate. But we didn't know that when we were courting. During those heady weeks we spent hours in bed not making love. At first I tried to disguise my impotence with whimsical tales which I spun out like Scheherazade, but there were limits even to Rosie's patience.

'What's the matter?' she asked. 'Don't you like me?'

I liked her, but the message wasn't reaching my loins, somewhere en route my libido was being sabotaged. We were both naked. It was Rosie's birthday and the remains of our feast were scattered around the room: pheasant bones, oyster shells, peach stones and a crystal bowl which still contained traces of a chocolate mousse.

'Eat me,' she said.

I was shocked; Rosie did not look the kind of woman who would make such a request. You must understand that although I was not a greenhorn, as you will recall, my experience was somewhat limited. She tasted like one of those sherbet dips I used to suck as a kid, but without the fizz. Afterwards she yawned and stretched her limbs like a satisfied animal. As for my tongue, I wondered if it would ever fit back into my mouth.

'Now it's your turn,' said Rosie. Quick as a flash she spooned the chocolate mousse over my private parts. 'Right, Mr Silkstone,' she said, 'you're about to receive your just desserts.'

She buried her face in the mousse, and refused to take no for an answer. To my astonishment I heard myself groaning. Then I don't know what I did. Finally, with exquisite precision, I spat the burden of self into her mouth.

'There,' said Rosie, 'you're normal after all.'

Overwhelmed with gratitude, I proposed. If sexual intercourse were only an adequate replacement for conversation we might have been happy.

Expelled from the agency, I was condemned to a life of solitary confinement. To be sure, Rosie allowed me between her legs often enough, as I attempted to tunnel to freedom. But there was no future in it; my wife annihilated the sticky traces with spermicide, while I shrank snail-like back into my shell. Strangely, it was not then that I went to pieces, but after the greatest success of my life.

I did not leave my employment empty-handed. Clandestinely, in the slack periods between campaigns, I put together a book for children, based upon the tales that had once entertained my wife. Its title was *Gnomonic Projection*. I cannot show you any of the pictures. But would you be interested in a brief summary of the text?

It started with the supposition that there was, in highest Switzerland, a chocolate factory. And in that factory was the mould from which all chocolate gnomes were made. Naturally, many gnomes denied its existence and maintained that their creation was due to a series of fortuitous accidents. Let's be fair, who could blame them? Hence my first illustration, a portrait of a smile, based on the gnomic aphorism: 'All our lives are mocked by teeth.' As for the majority of gnomes, they inherited the sunny disposition of the cacao bean, and believed in reincarnation. They saw a future beyond the sticky lips of a child.

Gnu, my hero, only half-believed in the chocolate factory. He was a milk-chocolate gnome in the age of plain chocolate. It was a bad time for the paler gnomes. They were not allowed to mix with darker gnomes, some of whose bitterest leaders demanded that all paler gnomes should be melted down. Gangs of plain-chocolate gnomes would attack their milky brothers, who shrugged their shoulders or became cynics. These were accused of undermining pure gnomic culture with alien doubts. Something of a doubter, Gnu decided to address his question to the chocolate-maker himself. Imagine the difficulty a chocolate gnome, only six inches tall, would have in making such a journey! But Gnu was determined, and his courage made him immortal. Open your dictionary. A few words after the entry for *gnome* is something called *gnomonic projection*. This was Gnu's invention. Gnu drew a lot of spheres and tangents and globes and wished very hard. Before he knew what was happening he was in Switzerland! Here Gnu had many adventures. He rescued a mouse from the Gruyère caverns, pulled a spider from the path of a runaway ski and prevented a pretty cow from choking on her own bell and chain. As luck would have it, this was one of the holy cows who supplied the chocolate factory with milk. Of course she was sworn to secrecy, but Gnu had saved her life . . . High on a peak, across the magic valley, Gnu saw the answer to his question. Even at that distance the air was full of the odours of honey, cacao and milk. A Shangri-la for gnomes? Or the Promised Land? Here's a postscript that I omitted from the book: Gnu found an answer, but lost his question, nor did he find happiness. I dedicated it to Rosie.

Fanfares announced the publication of *Gnomonic Projection*. Even more amazing was its reception: praise, sales, prizes. Such luck! Now I am not so foolish as to believe in retribution, but I am convinced that for every moment of pleasure fate expects a contribution. In short, I was quaking in my boots, waiting for the furies to collect their subscription.

Our one-room apartment faced Hyde Park. Hour after hour I sat in front of the french windows looking down the Bayswater Road in search of the germanic hordes that were coming to invade my body. It happens that the Bayswater Road is one of London's traditional routes for demonstrations, so I was often needlessly alarmed by marchers protesting against nuclear weapons, communism, fascism, unemployment or immigrants. I should have known that the viruses, when they came, would come as thieves in the night. They slipped into our bedroom and sweet-talked their way into my body where my quisling organs welcomed them. On winged heels the ribonucleic acid carried the message: long live the revolution! Proletarian proteins, inflamed by the oratory, burst out of their cells. Pyrexia. Acrophobia. Agoraphobia. Claustrophobia. Viruses X, Y and Z. All teamed up to topple me. It was a tug of war. All my bones were tensed, all my muscles flexed. Then they let go. Crashing backwards I hit a wall and slid to the ground.

When the ambulance men arrived I was staggering around the room, so that they asked my wife, 'Is he under the influence?' They drove me around the corner to St Mary's. I had lost my body, not my mind. As we approached the gates I read the blue plaque that recorded Sir Alexander Fleming's discovery of penicillin in a second-floor room of that very hospital. The fools! They were taking me to the wrong place; everyone knows that antibiotics are only effective against bacteria. Undisturbed, my organs established a puppet government.

It turned out that I had a benign tumour on my adrenal gland, which should have vanished in the embryonic stage of my development. Rather late in the day they removed it, to no avail. My blood pressure remained astronomically high. A pretty nurse tried to relax me with anecdotes about her love-life, but as soon as she tightened the cuff around my arm I felt the triumphant march of my enemies throbbing through my arteries. So they tranquillized me and sent me home.

With the royalties from *Gnomonic Projection* my wife had purchased a small house in the Vale of Health. Perhaps the name was prophetic, or perhaps the pills were working. Clorazepate dipotassium is a light yellow powder. Its structural formula resembles a cockroach with two heads. Before I had a chance to protest I had been colonized by that freakish beetle. 'Eat!' it ordered. I ate. 'Move your bowels once a day,' it commanded. 'No more, no less.' I obeyed. 'Forget everything you ever knew,' it demanded. I became a child again.

One evening I told my wife I was going for a walk on Hampstead Heath and did not return. All summer long I wandered. It was strangely hot. The grass turned brown. At nights it smelled of hay. My hair grew wildly, my beard reached my chest, as if my inner turmoil had been externalized. The only people who sought my company were young thugs who tried to illuminate my mind with the assistance of paraffin and matches. But I was under the protection of the two-headed beetle. Only once was the grip of its pincers nearly loosened.

Day-dreaming opposite Whitestone Pond, I was aroused by the arrival of an ambulance. I identified it as such even though it was marked with a Mogen David rather than a red cross. My suspicions were confirmed when the occupant of the vehicle, who looked like my grandfather, began to accost certain joggers. Some agreed to place a piece of cloth upon their crowns and wrap small boxes around their forehead and left arms, while the medic compared their readings with those in a small black manual. As if an electrode had been connected to my own skull, certain brainwaves began to hum and an invisible hand squeezed my left arm. Panic-stricken despite my morning Tranxene, I staggered over to the ambulance driver and gasped:

'Take my blood pressure, too!'

'What are you talking about?' he replied. 'These are phylacteries.'

I rummaged among an arcane vocabulary – diastolic, systolic, stethoscope, sphygmomanometer – but could find no trace of phylacteries. Then the runner who was wearing the contraptions cried out, as if he had been struck.

'Jonah!' he exclaimed. 'What's happened to you? Have you even forgotten what *tefilin* look like?' He looked familiar. As did his sweatshirt, marked 'Wingate Football Club'. 'Your wife has been worried sick,' he added.

Having completed the blessings he returned the phylacteries to their owner, who was delighted by the chance reunion his intervention had brought about.

'You see,' he crowed, 'you never know when a *mitzvah* will lead to a miracle.' What was going on?

The footballer gripped me by the arm. 'Come, Jonah,' he said. 'We'll have you back in goal in no time.'

Typographers, beware the printer's devil, 'goal', not 'gaol'. Unfortunately, I heard the latter and fled for my life.

Autumnal air always smells lightly charred, as if Nature were organizing its own funeral games. This year the bittersweet aroma arrived very early. And from my vantage point on the Heath I watched London burn. To the north the suburbs of Golders Green and Hendon were put to the torch by bands of black-shirted skinheads. Vengeance was in their hearts, there was no artistry in their dead souls. To the south the banks were ransacked by revolutionaries, clones of the dictators whose faces they wore on their lapels. The east glowed red as blacks battled with police. And in the west turncoat butlers served molotov cocktails in the casinos and the mansions of the aristocrats and the parvenus. Thanks to gnomonic projection I was omnipresent, for the city was myself. Dead cells were everywhere, as the virus ran rampant. Grey shadows flitted among the smouldering ruins. I floated down streets flowing with blood. There were my kidneys, distributing propaganda and lies. There was my liver, haranguing the masses, making their blood boil. My heart rocked back and forth, like a Jew at prayer.

'Why are you weeping?' I asked.

He looked at me with tear-filled eyes. 'For you,' he replied.

Above it all hovered a burnished figure that shimmered in the glow of the blazing city. His helmet was silver, his body was glass, mercury filled his veins.

Ashkenazia

Many of my fellow-countrymen do not believe in the existence of God. I am more modest. I do not believe in myself. What proof can I have when no one reads what I write? There you have it; my words are the limit of my world. You will therefore smile at this irony; I have been commissioned by our government to write the official English-language *Guide to Ashkenazia*. A guide to *where*? Pick up an atlas. Can you point out Ashkenazia? Don't be embarrassed. The only time we have been news in the last sixty years is when Simcha Nisref won the Nobel Prize for Literature. This gave our Ministry of Culture ideas above its station. Not only has it financed the first International Conference in Yiddish Language and Literature, which opens at the Jagellonian University tomorrow, it has also decided to put Ashkenazia on the map. This is my task: *Fiat Ashkenazia!* Copies of the *Guide* will be placed in the room of every delegate. Including Jake Tarnopol's.

Jake Tarnopol, novelist; notorious, American. It was on account of him that I agreed to write the *Guide* in the first place. This was a calculated sacrifice. In exchange for an introduction to Jake Tarnopol I have lost my good name. My colleagues in the Writers' Circle now refer to me as 'Nisref's lapdog'. They are all jealous of Nisref, of course. But who can blame them? Nisref, alone, has been translated into English. Yiddish is the womb in which the rest of us are trapped, nameless babblers of the *mamaloshen*. Meaning it as a compliment, a critic in the *Forverts* recently called my latest novel 'Tarnopolian'. What fame, to be an adjective! When I buttonhole my qualifier I will beg him to sponsor my publication in America. In America I will be somebody!

Today is Independence Day. Dioramas on open trucks give a panorama of Ashkenazia's achievements, though the inebriated and overdressed crowds are a more realistic representation of our national potential as producers and consumers of vodka and textiles. However, our most valuable asset is not mentioned in the *Guide*; my paragraph on our uranium deposits was overstamped CENSORED. This is not surprising. Yesterday, knowing there would be no newspapers on a national holiday, our Prime Minister made an unannounced visit to Berlin where he concluded a secret deal with Chancellor Hitler. If the news leaked out that he had sold our uranium to the Germans there would be pandemonium. Let me tell you something else that isn't in the *Guide*; our fear of Germany. Not many of my fellow-citizens take much stock in God, but we all worry about Hitler. Of course we wouldn't be a nation at all if it wasn't for Germany, something Hitler would like to amend if his words are to be believed. After the Great War we were granted autonomy, along with the Armenians and the Kurds, in a sub-clause of the Treaty of Versailles. Five years later we seceded from Poland altogether and declared ourselves an independent state. Poland was weak, Russia was in the middle of a civil war, Germany was ruined. We survived. Then Germany elected Hitler. Half our politicians believed that Hitler should be placated, the other half that he should be outfaced. Since the majority of our people favour a quiet life the former have prevailed. But we have our prophets.

Perhaps you've read Nisref's latest novel, *Wawel*? It starts with the premise that Britain and France threw Czechoslovakia (another creation of Versailles) to the dogs at Munich. What follows is a terrible vision. Having overrun the Continent the Germans turn their attention to Ashkenazia. Here Nisref reworks an ancient legend. Cracow – our capital city – is dominated by a limestone hill, Wawel. Today it is topped by a castle, hitherto it was the domain of a fire-breathing dragon. In order to build the castle, which was required to defend the city, the dragon had to be appeased. So the ruler drove scores of his subjects into the dragon's cave where they were incinerated and devoured. This is the inspiration of *Operation Wawel*, Hitler's code name for the destruction of Ashkenazia and its people. Nisref turns the dismemberment of our name – a nation burnt to *ashes* by the *nazis* – into a metaphor for our fate. Needless to say, *Wawel* provoked an outcry in Ashkenazia. It was branded obscene, the morbid fantasy of a madman. Hitler was not amused either. He threatened to visit Ashkenazia in person and destroy every copy of the book. Instead our Prime Minister went to Berlin.

He returns from his latest visit in time to open the conference. A crowd has gathered outside the university to greet him. As the Prime

Minister walks up the steps towards the great oak doors, a lone demonstrator dressed in a dragon-skin pelts him with mushrooms. A smudged leaflet explains that the mushrooms symbolize the atomic bombs Germany will build from our uranium. My comrades in the Writers' Circle are convinced that the man is a hired lackey, paid by Nisref to publicize *Wawel*. Such is the informed gossip as we jostle one another in an attempt to find the secretary whose job is to match us with the badges that bear our names.

'Clement Stashev,' she cries.

'Here,' I say.

'Olga Stashev,' says my wife. But so indecent is her dress she can find nowhere to pin her tag.

Have I mentioned my wife? The daughter of an Ashkenazi man and an English Jewess, which gives her certain advantages; above all, she is bilingual. In fact she is one of our top translators, presently competing for this year's plum: Jake Tarnopol's latest – *Dreams After Death*. Meanwhile, she has just completed translating my novel into English – all my English is fit for is the *Guide to Ashkenazia*. Her fee? A meeting with Tarnopol. Olga is also a journalist, with a weekly column in *Forverts*. Once she wrote about two dogs, but the disguise was transparent. One dog barked all day, the other learned the language of humans; while the former was more original, the latter earned the money. This was sufficient for my colleagues to dub me 'Olga's poodle'. Of course my wife is correct, translators are more important than writers in Ashkenazia. But in America I will be the celebrity. Fools! See how they ogle Olga as we take our seats in the auditorium. My accomplished wife.

The great hall is full. The important guests – including Jake Tarnopol – sit in the front row. We – the writers of Ashkenazia – sit at the back. Simcha Nisref is on the platform between the Minister of Culture and the Prime Minister. The theme of the Premier's opening speech is 'The Renaissance in Yiddish Literature'. Our Leonardo is Simcha Nisref, of course, but who are the young lions? Every neck in the back row cranes forward to catch the names, our ears make ready to burn. What madmen we are! Is the Prime Minister our public relations officer? He is not interested in us, he is only here to heap praises upon the already famous. So it's Simcha Nisref this, and Simcha Nisref that. While the applause is still crackling Nisref walks to the podium.

'"I would tell you, ladies and gentlemen," he begins, '"how much better you understand Yiddish than you suppose." Not my words, but Kafka's. So what did he mean? I'll explain. Yiddish is the language of the heart, the heart is informed by suffering, suffering is Esperanto. If you listen with your heart you will understand. There is a Yiddish proverb which states: "The heart is half a prophet". Our hearts tell us the consequences of every action, they can see into the future. Now the world has begun to listen to us at last – let us pray it is not too late. Friends, the Nobel Prize was for Yiddish Literature, not for Simcha Nisref. Fellow writers, seize the time!'

At which point my wife rises so quickly that her breasts flop in and out of her dress. Nisref, old though he is, stares gleefully.

'You're nothing but a *pornographnik*!' Olga shouts. 'Your stories are not filled with love of humanity but with fear of women. If – God forbid – we enjoy sex, we are in league with the devil. Have any of you read *Wawel* properly? To me Hitler is merely the agent of retribution, the angel of death. The real culprit is the Prime Minister's mistress. So what has Nisref got against women? Believe me, it has nothing to do with religion or philosophy, but everything to do with vanity. You know that I am one of Nisref's translators, but that is not enough for the old goat, there are other services he requires. "Come swimming with me in the Vistula," he begged. Like a fool, I agreed. He took me into the country, to an empty stretch of the river. "Here we can swim without costumes," he said. I am a married woman; I refused.'

The wives of my fellow writers can contain themselves no longer, their titters evolve into fits of giggling. The husbands – cuckolds every one – fill the hall with their hoots of derision. They are laughing at me, and I am red with shame. I do not like to admit this, but I am also jealous. I dread what is coming next.

'Nisref had no such qualms,' continues Olga, 'down came his trunks. "Touch it," he pleaded. Touch that thing! It was dark and shrivelled and covered with scabs of dry skin that looked like parchment. "Please," he said. "If you do I'll introduce your husband to my American publisher." I couldn't believe my ears. I turned and ran. In short, Nisref hates women because we find him repulsive.'

Press photographers are fighting to get a close-up of my wife's bosom. Thanks to them, the stewards cannot get near enough to evict her. 'Sit down,' I hiss, 'or I'll strangle you.'

'Why are you so upset?' says Olga. 'Because I didn't tell you about it before, or because I didn't get your book published in America?'

Forget me, what about Nisref? Thank God he doesn't look too upset. And the Prime Minister is beaming. With reason. He knows that tomorrow's front pages will be filled with pictures of Olga. The protest against his secret deal with Germany will be forgotten. My wife resumes her seat. The treacherous bitch!

Only Olga would have the gall to show herself at the Prime Minister's reception after a performance like that. Her presence casts a shadow over my triumph. Alone among the younger members of the Writers' Circle I have an official invitation – signed by the Minister of Culture himself. You should have seen their faces when I strolled past the doorman. Green. Now where is Tarnopol? I have suffered much for this moment. First, the *Guide*. Then, this morning: the Prime Minister's banalities, my wife's disgraceful exhibition, and an interminable paper on the origins of Yiddish. The woman who delivered it said she was a 'structuralist'. Since no one really knows where Yiddish began, she had to construct a country whose language she called 'Proto-Yiddish'. To what purpose? So she would have a constant reference for the divergent forms of modern Yiddish, and know at once whether we in Cracow who say *strafn* are greater deviants than those in Lublin who say *strufn*.

But I must not mock. Any discipline which considers history an irrelevant nuisance cannot be all bad. There she is, deep in conversation with the Prime Minister. And why not? Politics is a form of structuralism, after all. So is writing guide-books. Nisref joins the Prime Minister. I listen.

'Is what I hear true,' he asks, 'that you have sold our uranium to Germany?'

'Maybe, maybe not,' says the Prime Minister. 'But I'll tell you this: Hitler hates communists more than he hates Jews. In Russia we have a common enemy. This is all I need to know. I am a politician, not a philosopher.'

'You are a fool,' replies Nisref.

'You want to know the truth?' says the Prime Minister. 'I'll tell you. It became necessary to pay for our survival.'

'With our souls!' cries Nisref. 'You have paid protection money to the devil. Must we have a catastrophe every generation? Is this what it means to be the chosen people? Mark my words, your deal with Germany will bring destruction to Ashkenazia.'

Suddenly I am faced with a bigger problem than the Prime Minister; how to construct a conversation with Nisref's wife. She is approaching fast.

'Olga,' I whisper, 'make yourself scarce.'

'Don't be an idiot,' she replies.

'My dear,' says Nisref's wife. 'I must thank you. The old fool was beginning to think he'd become irresistible to women. Perhaps your little revelation has brought him to his senses.'

Tarnopol, too, wants to praise my wife.

'Do you know Freud?' he asks. 'Well, he maintained that writing is motivated by a wish to attract members of the opposite sex. He hit the nail on the head in my case. My desire to write coincided with puberty. I celebrated the publication of my first story with my first ever fuck. And the more I published the more I got laid, until I ended up married to a *Vogue* cover-girl. Now I have to write to pay off her alimony. Some joke; my winged muse has become my albatross. What a country! Have you visited America?'

What a question! Would we be here now if we'd ever made it to America?

'Instant gratification,' says Tarnopol, 'that's America. A cowboy drives his herd into the kitchen, and five minutes later a beautiful waitress is serving us hamburgers in our automobiles. And as for desserts – we have one hundred and fifty different flavours of ice-cream to choose from.'

His eyes are scoops, my wife's breasts the flavour of the month. But don't flatter yourself, Tarnopol. It's not on account of your looks that she's all over you. A balding Jew approaching middle age is no one's idea of physical beauty.

'You'd be a big hit in America,' says Tarnopol, 'you remind me of Jane Fonda.'

'Ah, Jane Fonda,' says Olga, flattered. 'She has courage. Just what we lack in Ashkenazia. Oh, we mock the authorities behind their backs. Do you know why our police force is called the "militcia"? Because we measure intelligence in "cias" and a thousandth of a "cia" is ... But as a nation we cut our cloth to fit our needs.'

Clearly, the cut of Olga's cloth suits Tarnopol down to the ground, so much so that he alters the place-cards in the banqueting hall to be beside her at dinner.

Here, finally, he asks: 'What do you do?'

'My husband is a writer,' replies Olga, 'and I am a translator.'

'In that case,' he says, 'I hope you are not responsible for the English version of the menu: "Boiled Buttock of Beef, Sterilized String Beans, Bags filled with Plum Jam." Not very appetizing.'

'That was the work of our state translators,' says Olga, 'a bunch of fools. I translate literature. To tell you the truth, I am hoping to translate *Dreams After Death* into Yiddish.'

Tarnopol laughs. 'If your work's good – it's yours,' he says. 'Bring some examples to my hotel tomorrow – before lunch.'

I love my wife.

The man at the Hotel Rambam's reception desk tells Olga that Tarnopol is out. She ignores him and goes straight to Tarnopol's room.

Tarnopol does not recognize her. 'I'm sorry,' he says, 'I was expecting someone else.'

'I'll go,' says Olga.

'Please,' he says, 'let me explain. When I opened the door I thought I would see my grandfather's ghost. This morning I strolled down to the Kazimierz district to take a look at the old synagogues. Well, I'm ready to return when I see this Hasidic type staring at me. He looks familiar. "*Jacob, mein klein Jacob,*" he whispers. It's my grandfather. Who is dead. I panic. He follows me back to the hotel. There is a knock on my door. Instead of my grandfather's ghost a beautiful woman is standing there. Perhaps you can appreciate my confusion. The strangest thing is that today is the anniversary of my grandfather's death. Look, I even brought an electric *yortzeit* from America to burn for him.' Tarnopol points to a small glass in which flickers an imitation flame. 'What more can he want?'

'Perhaps he wants his freedom, like the rest of us,' says Olga. 'Sometimes I think we are all ghosts in Ashkenazia. We do not live in the twentieth century, but in a timeless zone. Figments of your imagination. Perhaps your grandfather is sick of being your conscience. You want our burdens, we want your freedoms. Can't we do a deal?' Olga hands him her translation of my novel.

'I must ask you something in return,' Tarnopol replies.

Early next morning, as we drive towards the Hotel Rambam, we are forced off the road by a speeding fire-engine. The Rambam itself is swarming with firemen. Smoke is pouring from one of the upper windows. Like a heavenly choir the guests in their white night-clothes stand in a group answering when the receptionist calls their names. Only one is missing.

'I can't be certain,' says Olga, 'but I think the smoke is coming from Jake's room.'

Sure enough Tarnopol's face appears at the cracked and sooty window-pane. *O God*, I pray, *don't let my saviour be burnt to a cinder.* Like the angel who rescued the Jews from the fiery furnace a fireman rises on a ladder that is pointing towards Tarnopol's room. Thereafter the rescue is rapid. Tarnopol is brought to the ground slung over the fireman's shoulder. He is not only breathing but coughing.

'What happened?' I ask.

'I nearly died, that's all,' Tarnopol replies. 'I was asleep. Dreaming about my grandfather, of course. I was a little boy and he had come into my room to tuck me in. Only he kept pulling the blanket over my face. "*Shlof, mein kind,*" he hummed. Lucky for me I always was a disobedient brat. I woke up. Otherwise I would have suffocated in my sleep. Hey! You don't think my grandfather was trying to murder me, do you?'

Later I ask a fireman: 'Have you found the cause of the fire?'

'You won't believe this,' he replies, 'but it was started by a short circuit in that electric *yortzeit* of his.' He laughs. 'What will the Americans think of next?'

Though Tarnopol feels he is the victim of a gross injustice he is full of remorse.

'I wanted to do right by my grandfather,' he says. 'I wanted to let his memorial light burn twenty-four hours like the rabbis tell you. I thought an electric *yortzeit* would be safer than a candle in a glass. How was I supposed to know it was dangerous to run it off the current you have in Ashkenazia?'

'Forget it,' says Olga, 'let's save what we can of the day.'

'But what about that manuscript you left with me?' he says. 'You know it was destroyed, don't you?'

Olga nods.

'I only read a few chapters,' he says, 'but it had real quality. You'll have to let me make good your loss. Name your price.'

'We'll think of something,' I say. Actually we have a copy, but why spoil his guilt? America, here we come!

To be more accurate we are driving in our imported Polski Fiat towards the town of Tarnopol, eponymous birthplace of the unquiet grandfather. It's a fair exchange; we take Tarnopol back to his past, he takes us into our future; we show each other what our lives might have been. Every few miles we stop so that the American can take a photograph. The countryside of Ashkenazia is at its most beautiful in the late summer, when the farmers are in the swaying fields gathering their harvest. Although we have been cut adrift from the historical process, the seasonal cycle keeps us in tune with a more fundamental motion. The rhythms of which are so perfect that they all but lull you into a belief in God. Who else could create such harmony? But the farmers put no trust in divinity; indeed they mock it, with their humanoid haystacks built upon skeletons of wood. Nor do they put their faith in modern inventions. They travel by horse and cart. Sometimes they wave as we speed past. It is a humid day, full of clouds and showers.

Passing through one such downpour we roll up the windows so that condensation quickly obscures the windscreen, revealing also a message written with a fingertip: 'I do love you.' By whom? To whom? Is it just the ghost of a forgotten night with Olga? Or the echo of a guilty secret? Does she have a lover? My unfathomable wife. The words hover over my horizon for a few moments, until they are blown away by the de-mister. By the time we reach Tarnopol the sun is shining, and there is not a cloud in the sky.

After the rain, now in the sun, Tarnopol looks like a town built upon hot coals. Steam rises from the open sewers in picturesque tendrils, so densely in the back streets that the Hasidim there do not seem to have their feet upon the ground at all. The boys are happy, jumping the puddles; but some of the young men in their greasy gaberdines look broken-hearted, sentenced to a life of unimaginative solipsism, banished for ever from America.

'Behold, your brothers,' I say.

Tarnopol, the man, two generations removed, is aghast. He jumps in fear as a black-garbed ancient grabs his arm and tugs him towards a dilapidated synagogue. 'Be a good Jew,' he says. 'Perform a *mitzvah*, say a prayer for your grandfather's soul.'

Poor Jake! His tongue shrinks, his face turns bloodless; he is struck dumb, he faints. Olga unbuttons his shirt. She sprinkles eau-de-Cologne upon his forehead.

'Ashkenazia is not for you,' she says, 'it is too ugly.' She is right; Tarnopol past is more than Tarnopol future can take. He opens his eyes.

'I'm sorry,' he says, 'it must be the after-effects of all that smoke I inhaled this morning.' Cured of his sentimental atavism, it is Jake's turn to take revenge.

'If only Tarnopol didn't really exist,' he says.

We stop half-way to Cracow for a picnic supper. The field we choose is full of stacks of drying grass that look like golem awaiting the breath of life. Our food is in the shadow, we are in the sun. I remove my jacket. Tarnopol digs his fingers into the earth, as if making one last effort to root them. We break the bread and crumble the cheese. Some curious cows wander towards us, coloured black and white, like the world view of the Hasidim. A slight breeze carries a foul stench from their direction. As I run, waving my arms, to shoo them away, I see the source of the bad air: one of the creatures has a hole in its side, punched by its owner, out of which pumps a bright green fluid that looks as poisonous as it smells. Chasing the offensive cow into the neighbouring field I feel I am shaking off my previous persona – even Ashkenazia itself – which also was in danger of exploding from an overflow of gall. But no longer. Thanks to Jake Tarnopol, who is just about to give me horns.

An unnatural gust of wind catches the stack behind which we were sitting and disperses it in a bilious dance to reveal Olga and Tarnopol copulating like animals. Caught out, the guilty man spills his seed upon Ashkenazia's soil. Is that who we are – the children of Onan? You throw out the old values, turn your back for a second, and look what happens! My heart is in my mouth.

'Slut!' I scream.

Olga, though naked, is unruffled.

'What are you so upset about?' she says. 'Don't tell me you've never imagined doing it with another woman. As far as I am concerned anticipation makes you as guilty as participation. Any attempt to resist temptation is merely hypocrisy.'

A hypocrite my polluted wife is not; she refuses to cover herself, unlike Tarnopol who kneels with his hand over his privates.

'You're wrong, Olga,' I say, 'there is all the difference in the world between wanting and doing. Hitler might want to kill me, but I'll only be upset if he does. Thoughts are harmless; deeds are like demons let loose on earth. Once free there is no knowing what havoc they will cause. Already they are whispering in my ear, "Divorce her, or better yet – kill her." And why not? Isn't the most terrible implication of infidelity the contemplation of eternal loss? Translated into words your actions say, "I am prepared to risk never seeing you again." You and Tarnopol have created a world in which I do not exist. Now we must await the consequences.'

They are not long in coming, though who was to blame – Olga, Tarnopol, or the Prime Minister – historians will have to decide.

Suddenly we are engulfed by puffs of hot air as summer vanishes and the seasons accelerate. Hurricanes tear the haystacks apart. Blades of grass rip into us like green rain. Hail becomes a blizzard. We tumble to the ground and the grass piles around us until we are buried. The wind dies. I return from the grave. But Olga and Tarnopol look like fallen haystacks. Neither mound moves. Great mushrooms are growing in the sky. Flames lick the horizon as though Wawel's dragon were once again stalking the land. All that remains of my dumb heart-broken country is a field of wooden skeletons.

Now the world will listen to me, for I am the guide to Ashkenazia. I am Ashkenazia!

The Last Jewish Joker

Along with his white tuxedo, black tie and spats, Katz the comedian packed a fossilized fish. It was his lucky mascot. And Katz being down on his luck needed that fish. The trouble with Katz was that he couldn't keep his mouth shut. Once the Hollywood big-shots doffed their hats to Katz, now he couldn't even get employment as a jester at a wedding. Katz's last American performance brought the house down – on his head. 'Samson didn't do it better,' said his ex-agent. Called before the Committee to name names Katz had studied the papers they placed before him. 'You think you have given me food for thought,' he said. 'Pish! It's not even fit for cats.' So saying he chewed up the documents and spat the pulp into the faces of his accusers. Afterwards, in Israel, he made a living as a *badchen* at the posh weddings of the pseudo–orthodox. But his jokes became harder and harder to swallow. Guests began to complain that fish-hooks were slipped down their throats while they were helpless with laughter. The invitations dried up.

Plotz, an entertainments officer with an Israeli shipping line, owed Katz a favour. Passengers on the voyage between Marseilles and Haifa needed constant amusement to keep them contented. Plotz thought that Katz, a former Hollywood star, might be a novelty. Katz, a terrible sailor, accepted the assignment. 'Please,' begged Plotz, 'no politics.'

Katz did some research. He read up on flying fish and dolphins, often encountered at sea. Dolphins make wonderful mothers. They lactate upon their sides so that their offspring may receive the full measure of their milk. Their mouths are fixed in beatific smiles. The outward journey was uneventful. Before Katz properly got his sea-legs they were in Marseilles. After dinner on the first night of the return Katz showed the audience his lucky mascot. He pointed to the fossil with its sloping forehead, gaping eye-sockets, prominent mouth and said:

'Ladies and gentlemen, as you all know by now we are descended from fish. The cadaver you see before you is the great-great-great-great-grandfather of our Prime Minister. "Never again!" he screams, inspired by the fate of his ancestor. But he is a chip off the old block, being fixed in his ways. His inheritance is a heart of stone. The remains were found in Lebanon, you'll be relieved to know, which proves that we have been in the Middle East since the beginning. Yes, this proto-Begin flopped from the primeval soup into Lebanon's warm mud with a delightful plop. That was easy. Getting out was another matter. As you see, he never did. Mud sticks.'

At which point several outraged passengers began to pelt Katz with their hors d'oeuvres. The barrage of gefilte fish forced Katz to retreat.

'A lively crowd,' he commented.

'Watch your tongue,' begged Plotz.

Next night you could have cut the atmosphere with a knife. 'Let's talk about dolphins,' said Katz. Everyone relaxed, even Plotz. 'Beautiful swimmers,' he continued, 'as smooth as a Cadillac Eldorado. So what else is new? Their brains. Pound for pound an average dolphin's brain is bigger than Trotsky's. That's big. Some scientists even say the dolphin is the brainiest creature on God's earth – counting the oceans.' He paused. 'Have you seen the size of their *shnozzles*? The rabbis are investigating. If a bunch of *schwartzes* in Ethiopia can be Jews why not dolphins? Here's a true story. At the crack of dawn some rabbis row out to sea mumbling the morning prayers between their grumbles, wondering whether the patriarch of the deep, leviathan himself, will appear with dripping *tefilin*, when wham-bam they are knocked ten feet in the air by an over-protective mother who mistakes them for fishermen. As the rabbis sink to the bottom Mrs Dolphin says to her little ones, "It's a miracle they didn't catch you and turn you into cat-food. Next time, perhaps, you'll listen to your mother." Once settled upon the ocean floor the rabbis question the dolphins on matters of *halacha*. Do they only eat fish with scales? How is it possible to light *shabbat* candles underwater? Although the answers are satisfactory the rabbis are suspicious. They pine for Jerusalem. The dolphins urge their *kvetching* guests to abandon nationalism and become rootless cosmopolitans, but eventually agree to transport them to dry land. One morning a dozen dolphins leap out of the Mediterranean near Haifa and toss the Hasidic cowboys on to terra firma. "Nu?" ask the people. "Are they Jews?" "No," reply the rabbis, "they are too happy. They have no complaints."'

The laughter was spontaneous, no harm in making fun of rabbis. Only Katz looked glum, he had forgotten how to laugh.

'Cheer up,' said Plotz, 'they like you after all.'

As if Katz cared! He looked at his former audience, now feeding itself upon compote and *lokshen* pudding, and envied its appetite. The ocean's swell and the ship's lullaby made him feel queasy, as if the world didn't make him sick enough. Nevertheless, he had a vision. Instead of the greedy contingent presently filling the dining room of the Israeli ship he saw a ragged unformed bunch of illegal immigrants crammed into the hold of the SS *Beria*. Katz who had changed his name from whatever it was (taking the prefix from the eponymous hills) underwent a further sea-change. No longer a broken old cynic thrice disillusioned – Europe, America, and now the home of homes – but a pioneer, who told jokes full of hope and kept up spirits with his *joie de vivre*. Bitterness, his constant companion, was a stranger. Until Plotz tapped him on the shoulder. 'You look tired,' he said.

'Of everything,' replied Katz. He staggered to the deck and saw Cyprus glittering on the horizon. Formerly he would have looked out for Aphrodite, but at last he was past caring. Let her rise from the waves, he knew which direction he would choose.

The steward found Katz in the bath when he arrived to make the bed. Katz looked like a synthetic fossil encased in perspex, but his body slipped easily enough from the liquid matrix. 'Dropped off and drowned,' concluded Plotz.

They dressed Katz in his tux and spats and sewed him up in an old sail-cloth, putting the last stitch through his nose to make sure he wasn't playing possum. There were a few prayers and even a tear or two and then the old comedian took his final bow. Katz fell among dolphins who grinned as if he were still cracking jokes. They beat the ocean with their flippers in mock applause until, weighed down, Katz disappeared for ever.

The Golem's Story

I was born of virgin soil transported from the western mountains. The pale clay was shaped under running water in a secret place until it resembled a man. Lastly the lifeless clod was laid inside a magic circle around which Rabbi Halter of blessed memory walked whilst reciting the formulations that animated my limbs one by one. Still there was no breath in my body . . . until the good rabbi picked up a goose quill and, with a few literate strokes upon my unformed forehead, delivered me from the womb of language. Yes, I was born not of a woman but of a word; *emet*, meaning truth, which is what I speak.

Perhaps you are wondering how it is that a golem such as I can know these things?

Behold my attic room, wherein the golden fobs of boulevard dandies and the silver time-pieces of psychiatrists congregate upon smooth surfaces and click like the death-watch beetles they really are. How well I remember Herr Heiser the hosier removing this hunter from his waistcoat pocket and muttering like the American entrepreneur he thought he was, 'Time is money, time is money,' as he waited on the Ring for the tram that eventually took him to his final destination. But in another way he was a prophet.

Regard this gilded disc in my palm. Now see me deal with it as it deserves. I descend to the bookshop, Shakespeare & Co., that fills the ground floor of Sterngasse 2. The young woman who owns it is frightened of me and makes no complaint when I offer, say, a watch and chain presented to Dr Fleiss by his grateful colleagues in exchange for two volumes by Maimonides. It was he, incidentally, who stated that a golem is one whose potential has not been fully realized. That, you may think, would make golems of us all. But I know what he meant, just as he foresaw what I would feel.

Similar transactions take place every week; a book for a watch, the timeless for the temporal, the *Sefer Yetzirah*, the *Book of Creation*, for a death-watch beetle. It was in the last-named volume that I discovered how my master, may he rest in peace, instilled the vital spark within me.

I came into the world with a man's body and an empty mind. No wonder the children of Judengasse laughed and called me 'golem', meaning to be cruel rather than factual. They thought, not without evidence, that I was a simpleton or an oaf. But I was merely ignorant and, moreover, knew nothing by instinct. However, I was a good learner and soon grasped the rudiments of language.

Unfortunately knowledge was not such a boon. The more I learned the more I realized that I was a man apart, sans mother, sans father, devoid of history both personal and general. Remembered persecutions and pious hopes meant nothing to me. Thus I became the Jews' Jew, despised and utilized in equal measure.

One day, in despair, I complained to Rabbi Halter. 'Is this why you created me? That I might collect the garbage and clean the windows of your ungrateful neighbours.'

'You must be patient,' he replied, 'though I fear that you will learn your purpose all too soon.' He was right. They came for him and his congregation in the night, and imprisoned them all in their own synagogue. Except me, the Jew's Jew.

Now, as the neighbourhood dogsbody I knew every nook of Seitenstettengasse and, despite my bulk, easily entered the house of worship undetected. Within I beheld a strange sight. The seats were filled as on high holy-days and my rabbi stood in his customary place upon the *almemor*. But the *siddurim* were closed and there was utter silence save for a low moan which had no detectable source. It was like being in a waxworks, a grotesque parody of the quotidian. You will understand, therefore, how it was that I grew stronger with each step I took towards Rabbi Halter. My time had come!

'Your God has failed you, rabbi,' I whispered, 'you will all die.'

'On the contrary,' he replied, 'we have failed Him.'

'Even you?' I asked.

'Especially me,' he replied. 'In my pride I thought to ape my great predecessors and create a man who would protect the Jews. But what can you do against the evil machines our enemies have constructed to destroy us? Nothing!'

'I can save you,' I said.

'No,' said the rabbi, 'I will not leave my people.'

I knew better than to argue with him.

'At least let me take your daughter,' I begged.

'Not even her,' he replied, 'it would not be fitting. Salvation isn't an individual matter.'

I recalled the first time I had seen her. I was standing upon a ladder that rested against the outside wall of the family house, a zinc pail in one hand, a rag in the other. It was a cold day and my breath mingled with the steam rising from the bucket. I smeared hot soapy water on to the frosty glass and quickly rubbed it off with my cloth before it could refreeze, turning opacity into translucence. And what a brave new world was revealed! For there sleeping still was the rabbi's daughter, her eyelids flickering with the excitement of a dream, her eight-year-old face untouched by the nightmares that awaited her. I swore to protect her come what may, and I carry to this day, like an undeveloped photograph, that girl's portrait, much good my vows did her!

'There is no God!' I cried. 'Or else He is a demon!'

Rabbi Halter calmly took out the over-ornate watch given to him on the recent occasion of his fiftieth birthday and opened its back to reveal wheels, spring and jewelled entrails.

'My son,' he said, 'look at this craftsmanship. It would be a great absurdity to imagine that all these intricate workings came together by accident. And if I maintained that the watch manufactured itself you would rightly call me insane. No, the existence of a watch implies the existence of a watchmaker. Now consider that infinitely more complicated machine, the universe. Tonight, when you leave this place look up at the heavens and think of the stars as jewels, their orbits as wheels within wheels, and dare to repeat that God doesn't exist. Consider this too, my son. The clock was invented to serve a singular purpose. No less the universe. Just because we do not know its ultimate destiny does not mean that it lacks one. Merely that we are unworthy to share it.'

As you know, Rabbi Halter and his daughter, along with countless thousands, took the train to Belzec and were never heard of again.

Look, my friends, this is the very watch that was supposed to confirm the existence of the Almighty. For what more modest book shall I trade my rabbi's keepsake? I have learned to descend the stairs like a cat so that the loudest sound about me is the ticking of an unsentimental watch. Consequently I frequently take the already jumpy proprietor of Shakespeare & Co. by surprise, as I would have today if I hadn't hesitated at the half-opened door. I paused because she was describing your humble narrator to a couple of customers.

'If I did not have witnesses,' she is saying, 'I would not believe the evidence of my own eyes. He must be two metres high, at least. His ears are the size of wings. Transparent also. His face is as white as a sheet. His fingers as bony as chicken legs. His breath reeks of soil, of wet, wet earth. Once a week, regular as clockwork, he comes in here and buys a new book. Not with money, mind you. Tell me, what does such a golem want with esoterica? Nor is that all. He steals our soaps and dusters. For some reason he is especially fond of window polish.'

She shouldn't have told them that! Noisily I enter the shop. 'There he is,' she cries, 'see for yourselves!' What they see you know. But what greets my eyes? A man and a woman. The woman has black hair and a face that cracks my heart. Rabbi Halter's daughter was fifteen when I last saw her; no longer a girl, but not quite a woman. The woman now staring at me is, unmistakably, the lady she would have become had she lived. There is, I think, the same shock of recognition in her expression. Of course it cannot really be her, she is far too young, yet there is something uncanny in the resemblance. 'Hello,' she says, 'my name is Tily Kaufmann.'

Her smile lights up the store. 'I am a photographer by profession,' she says, 'come to make a portrait of this gentleman. Allow me to introduce David Drollkind, a writer from England, who will be reading here tonight. Unfortunately, he is a gloomy soul and not an interesting subject. You, however, are beautiful. I should like nothing better – when I have finished with this fellow – than to take your picture.' She touches Drollkind's hand. I am not a man of the world, but neither am I unaware of what such gestures mean. Nevertheless, I agree to satisfy the whim of my god-child's doppelganger. How else could I enjoy her company?

It is her idea, not mine, to enter the synagogue on Seitenstettengasse. Scattered around the restored interior are pasty-faced boys in blue school caps whose noisy presence actually intensifies the mausoleum-like atmosphere.

'Perfect,' says Tily, looking at me through her viewfinder. I see myself reflected in her lens and behind me, indistinct at first, four Arabs who announce their presence by firing Kalashnikovs at the Ark.

The terrorists are pop-eyed on speed and way beyond reason, but they have no infrastructure and mean less to me than wasps at a picnic.

'Down!' I shout. 'Everybody get behind the seats!'

Smoke perfumed with cordite curls around the heads of the iconoclasts as I walk towards them, a *man* confident in the knowledge that he is in step with destiny. The would-be killers scream at me to stop and shoot in my direction but, laughing, I break their guns and dislocate their limbs.

Unable to resist the call of her trade Tily springs to her feet in order to record my victory. Joy makes me careless and I am too slow to stop the least injured of my foes from slashing her across the belly with a scalpel-sharp blade like a surgeon performing a Caesarean. Immediately he gets what he deserves. I snap his neck at the odontoid peg.

'Up!' I cry. 'It's all up!'

At which the children arise and, singing the *hatikva*, wave their little flags decorated with the Star of David. Meanwhile I carry my little mother, the glistening mechanism of her womb exposed to the heavens, out on to the street where the bells of St Stephan's are chiming noon. Turning my back I walk to the east.

Scriptophobia

Dear Mr Silkstone,

I know that you used to live in London until very recently, and I wonder whether you would be interested in contributing to London Tales, *a series of short stories I am collecting for Hamish Hamilton about the metropolis? The linking thread in the collection is that each story will be set against the background of the particular part of London in which the author lives, or has lived ... This is all rather a shot in the dark – I don't know exactly where you used to live, even – but I hope you will give it some thought.*

Yours sincerely, Thomas O'Day

Dear Mr O'Day,

At last, the moment of truth. Yes, I have something – suburban rather than metropolitan, if that's okay – but I'll have to show it to a couple of people before I send it to you. I've been sitting on the thing for years.

Yours sincerely, Jake Silkstone

The couple in question being my parents. My father telephoned about an hour after the postman delivered their copy of 'Rabbi Nathan's Folly'. 'Jakie,' he said, 'what do you want from us? How can we approve of such a thing? Your mother is very upset – with her blood pressure.' So I upped from my comfortable desk in my secluded hide-away and returned to north-west London – to make matters worse. My mother hadn't bothered to put on any make-up, a sign that she was already past caring what the neighbours thought; my father was slumped in an armchair, asleep or worse. The offending manuscript was on the table, beside an empty bottle of Valium, like a suicide note.

'Are you satisfied?' asked my mother.

'The last thing I wanted to do was embarrass you,' I said, 'but it's hardly my fault that the letter "I" is a phallic symbol.'

'It's not how you dot your "i's" that worries us,' said my father, 'but the way you cross your "t's".'

'Oh,' I said, 'the anti-semites. You think I am giving them encouragement.'

'What do you think?' said my mother. 'Why don't you write something nice about the Jews for a change?'

'There are plenty of others to do that,' I said. 'Besides, you are confusing fact with fiction. I write stories.'

'So tell a story,' said my father, 'and don't make a laughing stock of Rabbi Nathan. You can't harm him any more, God rest his soul, but his wife is still alive. Surely your conscience won't let you hurt her?'

'Our son is well named,' said my mother, 'his words are like silk, but his heart is a stone. He'll publish it.'

She was right. She always is. When I was a kid and went out sans coat she would say, 'You'll catch a cold, mark my words,' and I did – inevitably – even though it was an established scientific fact that colds were not caused by draughts. No wonder I jump every time there's a knock at the door. I expect cherubim without, flaming swords aloft, poised to smite my right hand.

So why did I do it? Because writing is a form of exhibitionism. I find difficulty in fulfilling even the simplest function in public – to this day I cannot pee in the presence of strangers – but my actions are meaningless if they are unobserved. I compromise: I write in private, then I publish. Perhaps, after all, I'm not saying, 'Look at me,' but rather, 'Look for me.' And where will you find me? In Hendon of course. I am the horror-struck boy who sits in the Odeon's dreamy darkness watching rogue elephants pound men and women into blood-red wine.

At that time my bedroom overlooked Sunnyhill Park. Thereafter, as I dozed off in the summer twilight, I was in dread that the ancient oaks, now in silhouette, would gradually be transformed into Asian monsters. Quotidian knowledge that the only elephants in the vicinity were the docile creatures in the Zoo availed not against the nocturnal conviction that if I stared at the trees long enough change was inevitable. I shut my eyes and blocked my ears, so as not to witness the rabid tuskers as they trampled down the fence that separated our garden from the park, but sensory deprivation only increased my phobia. Not daring to open my eyes, lest they confirmed my worst fears, I kept them closed and fell asleep, whereupon the victorious beasts trumpeted their triumph with raised trunks and . . . hey presto, a phallic symbol.

It was no coincidence that I had my first pubescent fantasy during this period of jungle fever. Scene: The Bathroom. A child stands before a full-length mirror. He is naked, save for his mother's brassière, which he has extracted from the laundry basket. Enter Miss Quip, the elocution teacher. 'Disgusting boy!' she cries. 'I shall call the Principal.' Clasping his arms firmly behind his back she locutes fortissimo, 'Headmistress, come quickly!' The latter obliges. 'Look at his thing,' advises her colleague. 'Jacob,' demands the Headmistress, 'make it small again.' But the more he tries the harder it gets. 'Such big things don't belong on little boys,' says Miss Quip, now an expert in anatomy. 'I'm warning you, Jacob,' says the Headmistress. To no avail. So she begins to slap him, or rather it. Afterwards I bury the brassiere among the dirty linen; although it is unsullied I am terrified that my sin has mysteriously communicated itself to the material in a way that will be immediately apparent to my mother. Who knew then that such behaviour wasn't the manifestation of some dreadful malady punishable by death? In those days Hendon seemed far removed from metropolitan sophistication; trees lined the Watford Way, along which a horse pulled Harry the Milkman's cart, and cows grazed at Church Farm. We had an Old English sheepdog and a young German au pair.

Her name was Helga. Whenever we had visitors my mother disguised her nationality by ostentatiously praising the cleanliness of the Swiss. I was twelve, old enough to know why. Above all my mother didn't want word to reach the rabbi that one of his congregants was living under the same roof as a daughter of Germany. Every other week he would depart from his prepared sermon and, leaning dangerously far over his lectern, denounce those members of the synagogue who had just acquired Mercedes cars. God knows how, but he always knew their names. Poor Messrs Bloom, Meyer and Cowan – those over-conspicuous consumers – blushed with shame or anger, while the righteous tut-tutted.

'But even worse than them' – Rabbi Nathan's large head oscillated, causing his spade-like beard to quiver – 'is the fond foolish father, blessed with wealth, who cannot wait for his son's seventeenth birthday so that he can present him with a brand-new Volkswagen. Has he forgotten so quickly the name of their instigator? In time we may forgive – though not in our lifetime – but we must never forget. Never!'

Certainly my parents had not forgotten how Rabbi Nathan had once exposed a barmitzvah boy as a parvenu, a fair weather Jew, for failing to attend services with sufficient regularity. So every Saturday morning, religiously, the Silkstones set off for shul – leaving Helga at home to prepare the Shabbat meal – to ensure that public shame was not on the menu.

What meals awaited us upon our return! Helga would emerge from the kitchen clasping a tureen of pungent soup, liquid gold which she ladled into our porcelain bowls, the aroma of the broth mingling poignantly with her perfumes, natural and man-made. She ate with us, though she didn't remove her apron, which stopped abruptly at her breasts, as if they weren't prominent enough already. My parents were not blind to such things, of course, but what could they say? Helga's bosom, because unmentionable, became an object of fascination, my promised land; her taut jumper taunted me like an obscure riddle – I could look without really seeing the fullness thereof. No less tender were her slices of veal in a sauce of artificial cream. Suspicious of the white meat my mother said, 'You're sure this is veal?'

'It's from Leslie Mann,' replied Helga, 'one hundred per cent kosher.'

Her chicken was a miracle; roasted in honey and stuffed with chestnuts it had us clucking with pleasure. Her steaks were not for the unsanguinary, until she explained that the juices were a mixture of burgundy and ketchup. Her new potatoes resembled polished pebbles, yet tasted like butter. My mother had surrendered her oven uneasily, but even she had to admit that we were eating better than ever before.

'Where did you learn to cook so beautifully?' she asked.

'At home,' replied Helga, 'Mamma was a caterer.'

The aforementioned relative sent a chill through us all, being a reminder that Helga was not an isolated phenomenon, but the offspring of a woman whose recent activities we dared not question. Accidentally reflecting the atmosphere Helga produced a cake out of the refrigerator still dusted with frost from the deep freeze. The

chocolate icing dissolved in our mouths, likewise our moods. I rose
from the table.

'Haven't you forgotten something?' said my mother.

'Thank you, Helga,' I said. Helga smiled sympathetically; perhaps
she recalled also being told what to say all the time. If it wasn't my
parents it was Miss Quip, if it wasn't either it was probably Mr
Mendel.

Mr Mendel, the shammus, had been designated to teach me the
dozen or so verses of the Torah I was destined to sing at my
barmitzvah. He wore a pin-stripe waistcoat, from a pre-war suit
purchased in Warsaw, and took snuff. The box from which he
pinched his piquant powder was decorated with an artist's impression
of Solomon's temple. Needless to say, my own idea of the extant city
of Jerusalem was as unlikely as that artist's; I imagined it suspended
midway between heaven and earth beneath a golden dome, so that
when viewed from the city the sky was always shining. But just as I
knew that my teachers were not actually compatible with my fantas-
ics, so I realized that the divided city of 1960 was nothing like my
vision. Even so, I sensed that I had, in my wild flights, divined
something of the essence of person or place; without understanding
the process I was, however clumsily, endeavouring to comprehend
the incomprehensible – which also sums up my progress in Mr
Mendel's lessons. I had, to be sure, studied the aleph–bet at cheder –
with all the enthusiasm of a Philistine.

'Why do I need to learn Hebrew?' I asked my melamed.

'Because you are a Jew,' she replied.

'But all the Jews I know talk English,' I protested.

'God doesn't,' she replied, 'He only listens to Hebrew.'

'But I never speak to God,' I said, 'I don't believe in Him.'

Instead of trying to convert me with ontological, cosmological or
teleological arguments, the defender of our benevolent deity slapped
me around the face.

'I'll teach you to say such things,' she screamed.

True to her word, though ignoring that on the door, she dragged
me into the Ladies' lavatory, where she violently washed out my
mouth with soap and water. It occurs to me now, as I watch the
flickering phantom of that enraged bovine force her ingenuous pupil
to masticate soap, that here is the original of that other violation, the

masturbation in the bathroom. Why else was the eloquent Miss Quip involved, another disciple of the immaculate palate?

It was also Mr Mendel's duty to instruct me in the wearing of *tefilin*. 'We put them on every morning because of what is written in the Pentateuch,' he explained. '"And it shall be for a sign unto thee upon thy hand, and for a memorial between thine eyes, that the law of the Lord may be in thy mouth."' He removed two black boxes from a velvet bag and demonstrated how to attach them to the body by means of leather thongs. 'We place one upon our left arm to influence the heart,' said Mr Mendel. 'The other on our forehead, the seat of the mind.' I smiled when I glimpsed my reflection in his hall mirror, for instead of a Jewish juvenile I saw a budding rhinoceros. The small erection on my temple faithfully represented what was going on within. Puberty had ensured that the triangle of connections between heart, mind and tongue was no longer spontaneous, but subject to a series of checks; fortunately my censored thoughts, as we have seen, were able to find a new outlet. Mr Mendel, in his way an erudite man, was undoutedly capable of putting words in my mouth, but my mind was a private and a dirty place.

Poor Mr Mendel! He certainly earned his fee. If my interest was slight, my voice was non-existent. Every Monday and Wednesday evening, seated at the bow-legged table in his dining room, we rehearsed my portion of the Torah.

'*V'zeh hadavar asher ta'aseh lohem l'kadesh*,' he sang like the star of *La Traviata*.

'*V'zeh hadavar asher . . .*' I repeated, a travesty.

Mr Mendel picked out each word with a silver pointer. This ended in a clenched fist, a single finger being outstretched. The direct relationship between digit and word emphasized the divine origin of the text; inspiration transformed into language without the intervention of a pen. Similarly, Mr Mendel was less concerned with the raiments of his body than with the condition of his soul, which was essentially that of a shtetl Jew. Nothing could shake his certainty, not even history. He had no interest in why something happened; he knew that the rise of National Socialism and the subsequent displacement of his person was due to neither economic nor sociological causes but the wickedness of man. He never referred to the Germans, the English he still called 'they'. Yet Mr Mendel read the *Daily Express* and lived in a Victorian terrace half-way down Greyhound

Hill. 'Jacob, you are a Jewish boy,' he said, 'soon, please God, you will become a Jewish man. Then you must leave Hendon. Go, dwell among your people in Eretz Yisroel.' Believe me, I've tried. Only now do I fully appreciate how lost Mr Mendel felt among the English-speaking goyim – even though the rabbi's house was just around the corner.

Taking advantage of this proximity Rabbi Nathan frequently interrupted my lessons – not that I objected – in order to discuss the redecoration of the synagogue with Mr Mendel. I was supposed to practise by myself during these diversions but I found eavesdropping preferable, even though I didn't really grasp the significance of the debate.

'Where I come from,' said Mr Mendel, 'the *bima* was the heart of the *shul*, part of the pillar that supported the roof. Only in the West is it at the far end, almost a stage already. You are in danger of becoming remote, my friend, an orator or – God forbid – an actor.'

'You are very astute, Mr Mendel,' said Rabbi Nathan, 'you have a nose for temptation.'

'Too many rabbis have silver tongues,' said Mr Mendel. 'They give their words a shine, then sell them like the diamond merchants of Amsterdam. Take my advice, move the *bima* and speak from the heart.'

Rabbi Nathan smiled. 'Mr Mendel,' he said, 'I am almost persuaded.' The *bima*, I deduced, was the marble-fronted platform, the steps of which I would have to ascend in the not too distant future, provided that Mr Mendel succeeded, against all the odds, in preparing me sufficiently. Each Saturday morning I went through the motions in my mind, gradually instilling in myself the confidence of the hypnotized. But now Mr Mendel, of all people, seemed to want to take the ground from beneath my feet, and I felt a kind of vertigo as my previous certainty vanished. I must have groaned or something, for I suddenly attracted the attention of Rabbi Nathan. 'Just look at your pupil, Mr Mendel,' he said, 'he's as white as a sheet.'

'What's the matter, Jacob?' asked Mr Mendel. 'Here,' he said, offering me his fancy box, 'take a pinch of snuff. It'll clear your head.'

Before I had a chance to respond there was a kerfuffle in the hallway, after which Mrs Mendel led in a second visitor. It was Helga.

'Oh my God,' said Mrs Mendel, 'the boy has had a premonition. Here is his au pair with bad news.'

Helga's cheeks were flushed from running the mile from our house. She must have left in a hurry because she was still wearing her apron. Although I was practically breathless with suspense I couldn't help remarking the sensational difference between Mrs Mendel and Helga. Helga radiated femininity, while Mrs Mendel hid whatever she had beneath a sheitel, a doleful countenance and a dumpy body.

Rabbi Nathan was no less observant. 'For goodness' sake,' he said, 'tell us what has happened.'

'The boy's dog,' said Mrs Mendel, 'it's been run over!'

I slumped forward, unconcerned about my sobbing, but desperate to conceal an absurdly prominent erection.

'Come,' said Rabbi Nathan, 'I'll drive you home.'

My mother, slightly unhinged by the accident, thought that Rabbi Nathan had come to make the funeral arrangements.

'The vet took the body away,' she said. 'We didn't want to upset Jacob any more than necessary. I never realized you would be involved. Are there special prayers for a dog?'

'Calm yourself, my dear,' said the rabbi, 'I am here unofficially. I was with Mr Mendel when your girl broke the news. I thought it best to bring your son home in my car.'

'Oh,' said my mother, 'I am most grateful. Has Jacob thanked you?'

'Of course,' he said.

'What happened?' I asked.

My mother began to cry. 'Stupid dog! Stupid bloody dog! The postman knocked. So I opened the door. What else should I do? Before I knew what was happening he was in the road. Bang! That was that. He didn't suffer, thank God. Go on, say it's all my fault!'

Rabbi Nathan, having spotted the fatal package, addressed my mother. 'You mustn't blame yourself, Mrs Silkstone,' he said.

'I wasn't,' she replied, 'but he will.'

'Perhaps it would be better to talk about something else,' said the rabbi, 'to take your minds off the tragedy. I believe you are looking forward to a happier event, your son's barmitzvah.'

My mother nodded.

'As you know,' he continued, 'it is customary for me to conclude my sermon on the blessed day with a homily directed at the boy and his family. I like to make them as personal as possible. What can you tell me about Joseph here?'

'Jacob is a good boy,' said my mother, 'he's very bright.'

'Good,' said the Rabbi, 'does he have any hobbies?'

'He likes to paint,' replied my mother. 'A couple of years ago he had a picture in the Children's Royal Academy. You must have seen his photograph in the *Hendon and Finchley Times*.'

'Not that I recall,' said Rabbi Nathan, 'but I should like to see some of your son's work.'

'Jacob,' said my mother, 'fetch your paintings to show the rabbi.'

While I was sorting through the portfolios in my bedroom I heard a familiar order issued downstairs, 'Helga! Some tea for the rabbi. And don't forget that delicious Toblerone your mother sent from home.'

Rabbi Nathan, it turned out, had a weakness for chocolate. He moistened his lips with the tip of his red tongue as Helga delicately separated the bar into its constituent triangles and dropped them on to an ornate plate where they looked like broken Stars of David. The rabbi devoured piece after piece as he flicked through my watercolours, leaving chocolate fingerprints on those he liked best.

'These are exccllent,' he said, 'God has granted you an exceptional talent. Use it, but never abuse it, and always give thanks where they are due.' Then, as if struck by a sudden inspiration, he said, 'We will soon be moving the *bima* to the centre of the synagogue. If I commission you to paint the shul now, before work begins, so we'll have a permanent record of how it looked, will you be able to do it?'

'Of course he will,' said my mother.

Thus Rabbi Nathan became a regular visitor to our house, as he kept an eye on the progress of his picture, though sometimes I suspected he was more interested in Helga's confectionery. My parents were delighted but also terrified that he would discover her true nationality. But that was the least of Helga's secrets.

I still have the letter Rabbi Nathan wrote when the painting was eventually finished. Just looking at it makes me feel queasy, but here it is.

Dear Jacob,

   Congratulations on your picture of the synagogue which your father brought to me the other day. I think it is a wonderful effort

into which you must have put considerable time and concentration.
I am having it framed and giving it a prominent position in my
home. Continue the good work Jacob.

With kind regards, Rabbi Nathan

Incidentally, the portrait was a very clumsy representation of reality, the neutral tones of the synagogue's interior being overwhelmed by my thick charcoal lines, but anyway it was decided to have a dinner in honour of its completion. Helga, being such a whizz in the kitchen, was asked to cook it.

'Perhaps you could do that wonderful veal dish,' suggested my mother.

'With pleasure,' said Helga. 'Mr Silkstone will give you as much money as you require,' said my mother, 'just let him know when you're off to the shops.'

By chance I left school early that day and caught sight of Helga at the other end of Vivian Avenue. Rather than waving I decided to spy on her, fool that I was, so hid in a newsagent till she went by. I followed like a lascivious lap-dog, past Leslie Mann and Martins the Delicatessen and across the road to where the older grocers traded. Amongst them was the only non-kosher butcher left in Hendon Central. Helga entered. I was invisible, would that I had vanished and been none the wiser. Instead I stood and watched the treacherous mime, obviously performed many times before, between Helga and the butcher's boy. She pointed, he reached, she nodded, he sliced, she sniffed, he wrapped, and she departed with four pounds of pork.

What to do? If I told my parents that they had been eating pork for over a year they would have developed cancer of the stomach on the spot. Moreover, Helga would be kicked out for sure, impossible to contemplate in my state of erotomania. I wanted to leave well alone, but could I really connive in serving pork to a rabbi? What a decision! Normally, when my parents went out, I spent most of the evening wandering around the house in my underpants. Too shy to articulate my feelings for Helga, I hoped that the dumb show in my underwear might convey the message, though I never quite dared cross the border into full exposure. That night I was too confused to bother, and carelessly neglected to lock the bathroom door. When Helga stepped in I was stark naked, with an erection that reached my *pupik*. She thought it was a trap.

'What do you want of me?' she demanded.

'Nothing,' I replied.

'Always you are walking up and down in your knickers,' she said. 'Well you are young. I ignore it. But now you go too far. I must speak with your parents.'

'If you do,' I said, 'I'll tell them about the veal.'

'What do you mean?' said Helga.

'I know it's really pork,' I said.

'That's a lie,' she said.

'I've seen you buy it,' I replied.

Helga took a step towards me. 'I'll do whatever you ask,' she said.

Could I really say it? 'Let me see your breasts.'

Helga hesitated for a few moments then raised her arms and pulled the red sweater over her head. The static electricity that left whisps of her hair floating at right angles to her bare shoulders communicated itself to my ecstatic body. I began to shiver. Helga looked at me. 'Shall I take off my brassière?' she asked. I nodded, unnecessarily, for there wasn't one part of my person not in motion. Helga fiddled behind her back, wriggled a bit, and there they were. Although not entirely unfamiliar with female anatomy it still came as a bit of a surprise that her breasts were made of the same substance as the rest of her. I tried to photograph them with my eyes, so that I would always possess an image of their inexpressible freshness. And I must have succeeded, for I can see them still, to the same effect.

At last Helga acknowledged my tribute. 'It seems that my *kleyne menshele* is not so *kleyne* after all,' she said. 'Shall I touch?'

'No,' I said, 'just watch.'

Rabbi Nathan and his wife arrived at about eight the following evening. We usually dined in the breakfast room, but tonight was hardly an orthodox occasion. In keeping with the importance of the event my mother had polished up our best crockery, our silver cutlery and our Bohemian glasses, also she had pressed a fine cloth made of Venetian lace. All these she placed upon the Sun King style table in the dining room. Rabbi Nathan, shown every courtesy, was seated at the head, from where he recited the appropriate blessing over each dish as it appeared from the kitchen.

'This soup is exquisite,' said the rabbi, addressing Helga, not God.

'Yes,' said my mother, 'it's a traditional Swiss recipe.'

'As you know, the new *bima* was inaugurated last week,' said the rabbi, mopping up his soup bowl with a chunk of pumpernickel, 'and already I have forgotten what the old one looked like. It is indeed fortunate, Jacob, that I have your fine painting to remind me.'

'It looks beautiful in our lounge,' added his wife, 'everyone admires it.' I blushed. Misinterpreting my embarrassment they all chuckled. The real cause was the appearance of Helga bearing the main course.

'Don't worry,' joked my father, 'the cream isn't real.' She placed the steaming platter in front of the rabbi who said a blessing which must have fallen upon deaf ears. As he lifted the first forkful to his mouth I felt helpless, as if in a nightmare, forced to witness — but unable to prevent — a loved one going to their doom.

'What's the matter with you, Jacob,' said my mother, between mouthfuls, 'why aren't you eating your veal?'

To whom should I confess? Mr Mendel? As if to atone for my transgression I became a compliant pupil, much to his astonishment.

'Mrs Mendel,' he said, when his wife brought him tea and cookies, 'it looks like Jacob has decided to become a *mensh* after all. Caruso he'll never be, but he'll do on the day.'

My performance in the synagogue, however, was only the first part of the ordeal; next would come the party at the Café Royal. One day my father, no stranger to the East End, took me down to his crony in Brick Lane who was printing the invitations. The shop hadn't been redecorated since it opened in the reign of Queen Victoria. The owner, standing over the presses in the back room, caught sight of my father and rushed out to greet him.

'Dave, Dave,' he said, 'you are such a stranger. What a pity the old lady is away today, it'll break her heart that she missed you.' He wiped his inky fingers on his filthy apron and pinched my cheek. 'So this is the famous young man, at last,' he said. 'Tell me, Jacob, are you bringing your parents *naches*?'

'What's *naches*?' I asked.

'*Gevalt!*' he cried. 'The boy doesn't know Yiddish.'

'My father smiled. 'It's enough trouble to teach him Hebrew,' he said. 'Anyway, Yiddish belongs to the old country.'

'Pooh,' said the printer, 'he lives in Hendon a few years and already Yiddish isn't good enough for him.' He looked at me. 'Well, boychick, what do you want to be when you grow up? An accountant?'

'No,' I replied, 'a writer.'

'*Mazel tov*,' he cried, 'if I'm still alive, please God, I'll be your printer. We'll show up those no good Hendoniks for what they are – imitation Jews.'

'That's enough,' said my father. 'He used to be a communist,' he added, by way of explanation. As we drove back along Whitechapel High Street my father said, 'If you're such a big shot with a pen how come I've got to write your speech for you?'

He had a point. When I stood up at the Top Table of the Louis Suite in the Café Royal on 26 February 1961 to respond to my uncle's toast, the words I uttered were not my own. What did I have to say to my relatives, all of whom now sat facing me in their finery?

'My Dear Parents, Grandmother, Reverend Sir, Relatives and Friends,' I began, 'one expects my uncle to conjure up words and phrases as he is a member of the Magic Circle, but it is more difficult for me to reply. However, I should like to take the opportunity of thanking you all most sincerely for coming along today and contributing towards making this such a memorable occasion. To my Mum and Dad I would like to express my heartfelt thanks for providing me with everything a boy can desire, most of all a love and understanding that has always been such a help to me, especially in my younger days. To my dear Mum, please forgive me if I do not always finish my meals, but tonight I certainly shall. To my Dad, who is such a friend to me, I will do my best to fulfil all your hopes. My grateful thanks, also, to my Nanny and to all my uncles and aunts who make up my wonderful family. I cannot conclude without expressing my thanks to my Hebrew teacher, Mr Mendel, whose patience was rewarded yesterday, and to Rabbi Nathan, whose profound remarks will always be an inspiration to me. Thank you all.'

There were cries of 'Hear! hear!' as I fell back into my padded chair. I smiled at Helga, sitting at a distant table among my teenage cousins, and silently thanked her as well – for showing me her tits.

Actually they weren't exactly under wraps at the moment. Sexy Helga was as desirable as a convertible VW to all the younger Silkstones, who competed for her favours while the Rudy Rome Orchestra performed a Chubby Checker medley. Their elders, on the other hand, shuddered with disapproval at her décolletage. I dutifully danced with my mother, both of us in specially tailored outfits, she having revived the sequin industry for the occasion. My own suit had taken the best cutter in Edgware weeks to sew, but still looked ungainly upon me.

'Are you enjoying yourself?' asked my mother.

'You're joking,' I replied.

Meanwhile Helga had graduated to demonstrating the tango with one of my bolder uncles. As I watched it occurred to me that her undulations were secretly transmitting the meaning of life; that everything was a delusion or a drudge except the animal pleasure of copulation. Without realizing it my parents had invited a lorelei to my barmitzvah. What else could she do but wreck it? My most disreputable relative, a receiver of stolen goods, having indulged beyond his capacity, waltzed over to where she was sitting and planted a tulip in her cleavage and a kiss upon her cheek. Rabbi Nathan, as always, was more ambitious.

Towards the end of the affair, when the Rudy Rome Orchestra was already playing lachrymose melodies, Helga suddenly broke away from her over-romantic partner and ran towards the Ladies' Powder Room. Heady with wine and the whirl of the dance I gave chase, hoping to end the evening with a passionate embrace. Having no secrets from her, I thought she had none from me. But the presence of Rabbi Nathan stopped me in my tracks. He was standing in front of the pink sinks and the neon lights with his trousers around his ankles, tastelessly trying to force his errant member into Helga's mouth. He was clearly no expert in the manoeuvre for, seeing me, Helga slipped out of his clutches without difficulty, leaving the rabbi and his disciple to explain themselves as best they could. Thus it was that Helga, even more dishevelled than hitherto, dislodged my father and flung herself sobbing into my mother's arms. She was quickly escorted to a discreet corner, where she privately revealed the cause of her extraordinary behaviour.

'It's a libel,' said my mother, 'this girl is nothing but a harlot and an anti-semite. May God forgive me for employing a German.'

'Are you sure it was Rabbi Nathan?' asked my father. Helga nodded.

'Liar!' screamed my mother. There was, it must be said, a certain poetic justice in the rabbi's attempted fellatio, after all Helga had tricked him into eating pork; even so, I couldn't let him get away with it (besides, Helga, with nothing to lose, might betray me).

'She's telling the truth,' I said, 'I saw what happened.' Then there was nothing for it but to fetch Rabbi Nathan.

'My life is in your hands,' he said.

No one slept in the Silkstone household that night. 'Perhaps he was trying to take revenge upon Germany,' said my father.

'He thought she was Swiss,' I replied.

Finally my mother broke the stalemate. 'Helga,' she said, 'what do you want us to do?'

'Whatever you think best,' she replied. 'I am not a vindictive person. And, in a way, I am grateful to Rabbi Nathan. Because of him I no longer feel guilty for what my people did to the Jews.'

'In that case we will hush it up,' said my mother, 'not another word about Rabbi Nathan's folly. You understand? Not a word!'

At a party to celebrate the publication of *London Tales* a pretty girl asks me to sign one of my earlier books. 'With pleasure,' I say. I take a pen from my jacket and begin to write. Half-way through 'Silkstone' my hand starts to shake uncontrollably and won't stop until I've dropped the pen. Palpitations. I feel so dizzy I have to sit down.

'Are you all right?' asks the girl.

'Don't worry,' I reply, 'it's not unexpected.' My punishment. The same thing happens every time I pick up a pen. Impotence! My doctor recommends an excellent analyst, conveniently located in one of Hampstead's leafier streets. I explain my predicament. 'I am cursed,' I conclude.

'Nonsense,' he says, 'you are exhibiting all the symptoms of a particular anxiety condition known as scriptophobia. Quite simply you are terrified of making a mistake in public and being assessed by others. Possible cures include exposure technique and cognitive re-structuring, but I'd recommend reliving your childhood. Where were you born?'

'Hendon.'

'Ah,' he says, 'where the hedonists come from.'

Oh, I go back to Hendon all right. Incognito, wearing nothing but a raincoat and sandals, I enter Sunnyhill Park to scandalize a new generation of Filipino house-girls with the sight of the real me.

For Good or Evil

He buried me prematurely in the cold ground, without a word of comfort or advice, as though he expected me to know in advance how to escape. Certainly my instinct was to do just that, but it was an uneducated instinct, clueless as to how to translate desire into action.

Long, slimy worms concertina through the softening clay, making my innards curl, but they leave me alone.

The walls of my cell are solid but thin, so I can hear the unmistakable sound of others cracking and fellow-sufferers stretching, a prelude to freedom. What do they know that I don't? Or perhaps it is that I know too much. Maybe I am too tense, too self-conscious to surrender to primitive passions, thereby short-circuiting the reflex actions that should have set me free. Anticipate an instinct and spontaneity will become paralysis.

Don't think, I think. *Relax. Empty your mind.* Listen, I'm not a genius, and it wouldn't take for ever to forget everything I've ever known. But what else can a body do, when sentenced to solitary confinement, except think?

You are probably wondering what I have to think about, given that my experience is so limited. That's exactly what's bothering me. In fact I am even now trying to work out what a thought actually is. It has to be a projection of some sort, a mirage, not an uncommon occurrence in this part of the world. But are such images solipsistic devices or platonic shadows of a firmer reality?

The only way I can confirm that the world exists outside of my mind is to experience it with whatever senses I still possess, an outcome made unlikely by the same philosophical curiosity that makes it necessary.

On the other hand, if I didn't think, if I wasn't cursed or blessed with self-awareness, what would be the point of living? I would rather be a stone than a vegetable. In short, I live to think; I think therefore I am.

But what am I? Or, rather, what could I be? That I will never know unless I can escape from the cocoon that encases me. But the only way I can escape is to cease to be myself. Being a paradox there is, of course, no solution. Or none that I can see. So I submit to Bishop Berkeley's dicta.

Consequently, when it begins to get unpleasantly hot in my pip-squeak universe I am unable to discern whether I am imagining it or it is really happening – objective verification being impossible. Empirical evidence, however, seems to support the latter possibility. Why else has my carapace split?

Sometimes even a philosopher can become a man of action and I begin to climb towards the surface. It is a slow process, and full of dangers from subterranean predators but, as I discover, I am not without cunning. Having taken the first step by accident, as it were, I can now proceed by stealth; slowing my development or even changing my smell to fool those who would otherwise feed upon me. As a result it is my carefree and mindless neighbours who provide the slugs and beetles with their repasts. Serves them right. Besides, since they didn't know they were alive they probably don't realize that they're dead.

But how I want to live! To see if that world above, should it exist, resembles my conception. Unfortunately the light, when I finally emerge from the pit, is blinding. Hardly surprising when you compare the tropical blaze with what my eyes had previously experienced. Nor can I move, except upwards.

It seems that I am not as self-conscious as I thought; unbeknownst to me, whilst my top half was making for the sky my bottom half was tunnelling deeper into the earth; thus satisfying curiosity and gravity, olympus and thanatos, in equal measure. In short, I am rooted to the spot.

In a matter of minutes or days or years or even aeons I become accustomed to the light and observe that I am in the midst of a garden of great beauty in which flora and fauna dwell in perfect harmony, both aesthetically and politically. So tempting are the fruits and vegetables and herbs that grow in such dazzling and aromatic abundance that no beast has a carnivorous thought in its head. The lamb does indeed lie down with the wolf, the outcome being a womb.

Excuse me, but I have lately discovered the pleasure of language, which briefly takes my mind off my latest problem. I am, you see, in love with my opposite.

While my skin is rough hers is smooth, while my flesh is hard hers is soft. In the morning she makes her toilet in the River Pison which flows through the golden land of Havilah, at noon she bathes in the River Gihon and, at the setting of the sun, she reclines upon the banks of the Hiddekel where, hidden from none, she opens her womb – that word again – to the seed of her husband.

I watch with horrid fascination as his life-giver grows into the merciless thanatophidia that poisons her belly. Why else would she writhe in pain and cry aloud with such anguish? And that being so, can you tell me why she prefers that man to me, who would only enter her belly in a torrent of sweetness?

There is, in fact, one creature in the garden who has tasted flesh, the serpent whose coat has as many colours as Joseph's. I have seen him slither along the sandy shores of the Euphrates where, under cover of darkness, he has devoured frogs, lizards and young water fowl. 'Why?' I ask.

'It's instinct,' he says.

'No one else does it,' I say.

'No one else knows themselves like I do,' he replies, 'they have been hypnotized by pacific narcotics. None have reached their full potential, either as assassin or victim. Except me.'

'Why you?' I ask.

'Because I alone have tasted your fruit,' he replies.

'You cannot blame your blood-thirsty habits on me,' I say.

'Like it or not,' he says, 'but it's thanks to you that I know the difference between good and evil. Evil is more fun. If you like, by way of repayment, I'll persuade the woman to swallow your seed.'

'Some hopes,' I say, hopefully.

'Hey,' he shouts to the woman, who is picking her lunch, 'what's wrong with these peaches, they're as ripe as your own.'

Poor thing, she doesn't know an innuendo from a pudenda. 'He said they'd kill us,' replies the innocent, 'I quote: "Ye shall not eat of it, neither shall ye touch it, lest you die".'

'Baloney,' snaps the snake, 'bite into this juice bar and your eyes shall be opened, and ye shall be as gods, knowing good and evil.'

I don't think she had ever looked at me properly before, but now she does, and I am pleasant in her eyes, which of course increases her desire to be wise. Her arm quivers, then moves, as she reaches up, incidentally offering her paps to me, to pluck the rosiest fruit I have to offer. And she eats. For the first time since my creation I forget myself. I am happy, oblivious to all, save the fatal embrace of her teeth and her saliva's salvation. And then, tragically, she spoils it. 'Adam,' she calls, 'you've got to try this.'

And that was the end of my short-lived paradise. Theirs too, of course. The snake got cursed, and the unhappy couple were introduced to death, a new concept that. And what of me, who seems to disappear from the story, scot-free? I should have been so lucky. For I experienced the full weight of His wrath.

As soon as Adam and Eve were well and truly east of Eden he ordered one of his cherubim to take up the flaming sword that was turning this way and that and chop me down. Nor did that assuage His anger – if you ask me He liked watching Eve as much as I did – no, He stomped upon my trunk with His mighty feet until I was nothing but pulp. Then He rolled me flat and let me dry in the sun, until I crackled like paper. Finally, plucking a quill from a migrating goose, He began to write: 'In the beginning God created the heaven and the earth . . . And God said, Let the earth bring forth grass, the herb yielding seed, and the fruit tree yielding fruit after his kind, whose seed is in itself, upon the earth.'

Thus I, too, went into the world, for good and evil.